The Scribe

Aura Weavers, Book 3

LizAnn Carson

Cover photos used under license from:
Deposit Photos

Thank You

To the wonderful, supportive women of my critique group. You set me right and keep me going!

And always, to Michael, who puts up with my flights of fancy and obsessive streak, and has never been less than encouraging.

Prelude

As soon as the head man turned up at the door, thirteen-year-old Quinn Featherstone knew she was in trouble. More trouble.

As the daughter of the village shoemaker, she'd spent much of her young life tanning the hides, shaping wood for clogs, weaving straps while her father produced summer sandals and bad-weather boots. The smells of wood shavings, leather, and oil were ingrained in her bones. In her more cynical moments – and even at her young age she'd become seriously cynical – Quinn wondered if she had been tanned, too, if that accounted for her dark skin.

Whimsical thinking. Such flights of fancy wasted time, when the real, physical world held more than enough mystery. Besides, with several other dark-skinned families in Colgate, hers was hardly unique.

"Georg," her father said formally as he ushered the head man into their small room.

"Frederick."

The men sat. A lump forming deep in her chest, Quinn hovered by the door to the sleeping quarters, trying for invisibility in the evening gloom. Her mother bustled through the room – a born bustler, her mother was, so different from Quinn's uncanny stillness. Soon cups of caff would be placed on the table, and her latest transgression would be unfolded before her increasingly exasperated parents.

"This is about Sana, isn't it?" Word traveled quickly. Quinn didn't detect condemnation in her father's voice, but weariness, as if he lacked the energy to deal with any more of her escapades.

Her mother served the caff. "Thanks, Ophie," Georg said, and poured without waiting to be invited.

A bad sign.

"Come on in, Quinn," her father said, knowing in that way of his exactly where she hid.

"I didn't do anything." She slouched across the room and perched on the chair usually reserved for her older brother Ifram.

"Only rushed off and fetched Tonia and scared Sana half to death," Georg said.

I had to! Surely, this time she wasn't the only one who knew? Surely they couldn't blame her? It wasn't like she'd caused the problem. She'd just tried to fix it.

But they never saw things that way.

"Tell us what happened." Her father's directive was aimed at the head man, not her.

"Seems Sana's baby decided to take a nap and stop kicking her black and blue."

Quinn's mother chuckled; Sana had been complaining for months about the kid's activity, to the amusement of most of the older women in the village.

"Then Quinn here went haring off to Tonia with a wild tale about losing the baby."

Quinn squirmed. Tonia, their village healer, had headed to the threshing floor where most of the young women had gathered, with a firm order that Quinn make herself scarce. She'd been on tenterhooks ever since, waiting for news.

"And?" Quinn's father finally poured caff for her mother and himself, then, as an afterthought, half a mug for her. Quinn clutched the small mug, schooling herself to sip. Gulping it would just bring further disapproval. They said caff was addictive; she didn't care. Some days she lived for caff.

"And nothing. Sana said she was fine, Tonia went away."

Quinn sat up straighter, too horrified to remain quiet. "She didn't fix it? I *told* her. The baby – it's dying. She's got to do something. She's got to—"

"Quinn." Her father's no-nonsense voice froze the words in her throat. "Even if this were true, what could a healer do for a babe in the womb?"

"*Deliver it,*" she screeched. "Birth it. Give it a chance." She looked from her parents to Georg. The knowing swept into her mind

2

like the dry leaves that chased each other down the lanes. "The baby died," she said, deflated.

"Nonsense," her mother said. "Sana's having a normal, healthy pregnancy. You're letting these imaginings get the better of you, sweetie."

"And meddling, again," Georg added. "You've caused unnecessary unhappiness and disruption. This must stop."

He wasn't talking to her anymore. Her parents nodded. No one believed her, and Ifram's little unborn son was dead.

She slumped back in her chair. "I only wanted to help."

"Your help is no help at all, young lady," Georg said. By now he was on his third mug of caff, indicating his agitation. "This must stop," he repeated

"Go to the sleeping room, Quinn." Her father used the voice that brooked no argument.

"Yes, sir." She stood and shuffled away, not daring to linger in the doorway; her parents were wise to that trick. She left behind conversation too quiet to overhear, conversation about her, dissecting her supposed transgressions, the ways she had erred yet again.

Quinn flopped onto her pallet and for the umpteenth time tried to figure it out. She had always known simple things like where to find a lost tool or how to predict the weather. Now that she was officially a woman, the knowings were scarier. Although not the case with Sana's tiny, unborn baby, she did sometimes foresee future events. And hidden thoughts found their way into her mind. Recognition of lies and deceits was the hardest to deal with.

If only maturity came with a guarantee she could keep her mouth shut. In a small settlement like Colgate, she'd quickly acquired a reputation, and lots of people shunned her, others mocked her, and pretty much the whole town considered her an aberration.

She'd spent most of her childhood figuring out that not everyone knew things. When she was little, she'd assumed it was normal. Later, when the other kids started calling names and avoiding her, she still supposed such abilities counted among the mysteries adults kept from children. But her womanhood feast had been months ago, without any great revelations. Now her mother delivered gentle lectures about not blurting whatever crossed her mind, and her father kept watch, worry lines creasing his forehead. The evidence forced Quinn to accept the truth. She *was* a freak. The hated *knowings* drove her out to the far fields, where she could scream in frustration, because no one understood, much less helped make sense of it all.

She curled her long, lanky body on the pallet and wondered if she should cry. She was frustrated enough to. And she mourned the loss of her little nephew, which no one but she even knew about yet.

Instead of crying, she fell asleep, exhausted by conflicting emotions and rampaging fears.

The next day Ifram joined her family at the noon meal in the communal dining hall. He looked worried, fatigue dulling his eyes. A big man, eight years older than she, Ifram had opted for agricultural work. His dark skin shone with perspiration; although harvest time, the sun beat down with the intensity of mid-summer. She'd always adored Ifram, the way he smelled of the outdoors, fields and soil. He'd been her defender once, before those strange *knowings* became the subject of public scorn... and fear. Now he glared at her through narrowed eyes.

"Sana sent me to tell you. The baby's still not moving."

Ifram didn't sit. Her parents looked on, worry etching their faces. As if it were her fault. Quinn studied her trencher, suddenly fearful.

"What did you do, Quinn?" Ifram demanded, arms folded as he loomed. "Did you use your witchcraft against my child?"

"*No.* Of course not. How can you even say that? I haven't got any—"

"Because if anything's gone wrong now, only a couple of weeks to delivery..." Ifram let the threat hang in the air.

Defiant, Quinn forced herself to look up. "Don't be stupid. I only tried to help."

"Don't you call me stupid, little girl." Ifram leaned across the table, jabbing a finger at her. Their parents sat speechless and unmoving, and the rest of the dining hall fell silent, watching the confrontation. "I promise you, if Sana loses our baby, you'll pay."

Quinn sprang to her feet, hands in fists. "What for?" That horrible screech she hated took over her voice, but she couldn't control it. "I tried to *help*, you big jerk. You just leave me alone."

Ever logical, she snatched up the meat pasty from her trencher before bolting from the dining hall.

❖

Later, her mother came into the sleeping room and sat on the edge of the pallet. Quinn turned away.

"Sana's gone into labor. We'll soon find out."

"Find out what?" Quinn muttered into the thin pillow. "What kind of oddity I am? The baby died, Mother. I can't help that. It couldn't... breathe, or whatever. But it's nothing to do with me."

Her mother's hand gently rubbed her knobby shoulder. "Your ability to predict these things scares people, little daughter."

"*Predict?* I didn't predict it. I *know* it. And I don't want to." She'd cried during the day, alone in the sleeping room, but she fought the tears now, trying for indignation instead.

With no success. Strong hands pulled her up, cuddling bony Quinn against her mother's warm softness. "I'm sure you don't. Nevertheless, people fear you, and they're starting to call you a witch."

"I'm *not*."

"Hush." Work-worn fingers stroked the tight curls on her head. "Quinn, promise me something."

She nodded against her mother's bosom, now damp from the tears she hadn't been able to contain.

"No more. No matter what you think you know, say nothing." She set Quinn a little away and looked into her eyes. "No matter what. Do you understand me?"

Quinn nodded again, numb.

"The safety of our family may be at stake."

"They wouldn't—"

"They might. Superstition's a frightful thing, and once it takes hold there's no stopping it. You're grown now. You need to take responsibility for your own actions, and for your family's security."

Quinn looked down; she could no longer handle the intensity underlying her mother's words. "I understand," she muttered.

"That's my girl. We'll eat here tonight, give things a chance to settle after that scene in the hall. Your brother's scared. He didn't mean what he said."

She wondered. Her brother had as much as called her a witch. Witches weren't real, just a folk tale meant to scare little kids, but still... If superstition held the power to cause brother to turn on sister, maybe he did mean it. The refuge of her family suddenly seemed a whole lot less secure, despite her parents' support and love.

The next day Sana birthed her baby. A boy, and early, and dead, the cord around his neck. Ifram avoided her; Sana, when she recovered, made it clear that Quinn was to be excluded from the group of young women who gathered by the threshing floor to socialize.

That night, eggs were lobbed against their front door. She heard the jeering from her pallet. Children, but that's where it started.

Jude, her best friend, called at the shop the next afternoon. "My mom says I can't see you anymore."

"Then don't." Quinn made a point of turning away first. No way was anyone, even Jude, going to witness the hurt that squeezed fresh tears from her eyes.

Through the autumn, Quinn mostly kept to the house, or worked in the cobbler shop, or wandered solitary out in the fields. No one disturbed her; no one sought her out.

Winter in Colgate didn't amount to much. Although leaves fell from the trees and crops had definite sowing and harvesting seasons, they almost never saw snow. Winter meant rain, though. Kept indoors by the weather, Quinn spent the bleak months side by side with her father, fashioning boots, exchanging few words. She had hoped that, with time, the wariness that seemed to follow her like a haunting wherever she went would dissipate, but no such luck. After a few glares and distrustful looks, she'd learned to disappear when anyone came in for a new pair of sandals or boots. Ifram and Sana seldom dropped by, and Quinn ate less and less, given the distrustful atmosphere in the dining hall. Already slender, and with no sign so far of developing the promised womanly curves, she became waif-like, her eyes large in her gaunt face. Her mother took to bringing pastries and treats home from the hall. Quinn dutifully ate these, but remained too thin.

Early in the spring, a Healer came to the village. The Healers visited only rarely and were spooky, in Quinn's opinion. They didn't adhere to her faith in logical explanations. They read people's thoughts, too, or so she'd heard, and cured incurable ailments and used plants and stones and what-have-you in ways that no one else understood. Quinn had avoided them in the past, but now she wondered. Perhaps this Healer could cure her of her 'intuitions', as her mother had started calling them.

Her parents must have had the same thought. The second day of the Healer's visit, Quinn came in from a ramble to find her in the sitting room, at the table with her parents.

"Quinn, come over, please," her father said. "This is Yolande. She wants a look at you."

Quinn slunk into the room and dropped into a chair, cautiously eyeing the green-sashed woman with wild, graying hair.

"May I touch you, child?" Yolande asked.

Quinn looked from mother to father. Receiving a small nod from each of them, she muttered, "Okay."

Yolande stood behind Quinn and moved her hands up and down, around Quinn's head and torso. A tense quiet filled the room, as if her whole family was holding its collective breath. She knew she was. The woman's hands… she felt a strange energy in them, a magnetic pull like the black stones the kids found in the foothills to the east.

The Healer finished whatever she had been doing and returned to her seat. "Yes," she said.

Quinn's father nodded. Her mother closed her eyes for a moment, then fixed a gentle gaze on her and said, "Sweetie, have you ever considered becoming a Weaver?"

It didn't take long to finalize arrangements. The evening before she left with Yolande for the mysterious Motherhouse so far away, where they would understand and fix her, she called at her brother's house. "I wanted to say goodbye," she said, her heart pleading for a sign they cared. "It may be years before I come back."

Ifram and Sana stared, expressionless. After an awkward moment that stretched into an eternity, she backed away and ran home.

The next morning, the populace turned out to bid farewell – to the Healer. Her mother and father hugged her one last time, their eyes wet. From the security of their arms, she looked over the gathering for a friendly face. Finding none, she gave them each a last kiss, donned her pack, and followed Yolande on the road north.

She didn't look back. Not even once.

Chapter 1

Quinn prowled her suite in the Scribes' lodge, wishing she hadn't bothered to get out of bed. The small lodge sat east of the green, and her rooms faced outward, toward the morning sun pouring over the hills and flooding the valley. Part of the massif that loomed over the Motherhouse complex to the north was visible, adding its appearance of either menace or safety, depending on your point of view. The swath of fields and meadows it sheltered was not as lush as it appeared, stony ground more fit for goats than corn.

A familiar, inspiring vista. But not this morning.

She was fed up with being at Arwen's beck and call, for almost a year now, as she held things together and trained for her role as heir apparent to the council head.

Fed up with the way her two closest friends, Willow and Bryar, had both become doe-eyed, mindless idiots over the new loves in their lives.

Life at the Motherhouse had acquired a patina of sameness, making her question her stated preference to work from here and not move around the Midland. She'd be gone this very morning, if she could present herself with a logical reason. That despite the fact that the time working with Arwen had resulted in the most complex and beautiful weave she had ever devised, and quite possibly had saved their civilization.

And where her friends were concerned... well, Willow had been willing to sacrifice everything, and damn near had, to contain the power cell. Bryar had not only risked his life, but forfeited two fingers, surely the most painful loss imaginable for a musician. They deserved their mawkish moment.

Wasn't that the problem with being the rational one? She couldn't even muster a hateful day without compelling herself to hurl out valid justifications.

Grow up. You're exhausted, that's all.

Nevertheless, Quinn was not best amused when a messenger kid came to the door. Arwen again. Her workroom. Immediately. Please – a clear afterthought.

She thanked the child and ignored the message. The power cell that had threatened the very underpinnings of their civilization was contained and safely on its way to where nobody would ever find it. Problems loomed, but nothing that couldn't be dealt with in half an hour.

Other than Kiril, that is. But she'd been barred from work on that particular problem. She knew why – Arwen doubted her objectivity, given the antagonism that flowed between them. Among all the other reasons for irritation this morning, Quinn resented her exclusion from the healing room where he had lain catatonic for days.

She peered out the window of her sitting room. Everything as usual. Circle the massif to the north and strike east into the hills, and you end up... in a land she'd never visited. Bryar and Willow both had spent time in Borgonne. She, the Scribe, had only their stories. She had never seen the country with her own eyes, nor had she been able to probe it in depth... and what was that about? Did the hills block not only travel, but also records stored in the Aura? Or did Borgonnians work such potent magic that they could screen their activities?

Her own Entrée, her ability to access the life-giving powers of the Aura, was among the strongest in her generation, and she couldn't do these things. The Aura itself was stronger on the Borgonnian side of the hills. Did this mean they could manipulate it in ways never contemplated in the Midland?

And if all this was true, the Mages of Borgonne were a force to be feared, and Quinn was grateful that the spells on the hills kept them on their side.

When you got right down to it, what good did her investigations do, anyway? Who really cared about the origin of life on their planet, the snippets of history she wove together like varying weights of linen thread on a loom, culminating in the life they lived today? Big picture, small picture... no picture, for most of the inhabitants of the Midland. They planted and harvested, celebrated their triumphs and festivals, worked through their disasters, and faced another day. History? Not so much. Even Bryar seldom wrote songs about actual historical events, relying on tales that had come down from... somewhere.

Maybe Kiril or Joss would recognize those legends. Because with the similarity in their languages, there had to be a historical connection.

If Kiril lived.

Quinn was seized by a moment of guilt. When had she last enacted a morning ritual? Days, anyway, perhaps as much as a nine-day. She'd never put as much stock in such things as Willow and Bryar did, but still...

She lifted her hands, palms up.

Sustainer of Air, disentangle my thoughts. Grant me clarity and decisiveness.

Thank you for the brilliance of the sun, for friends and commitments...

She fell silent and let her hands drop as the words dried up. It wasn't that she wasn't grateful for the Aura and the Entrée she'd been born with, but she lacked the intuitive poetry to say so. 'Hey, thanks' didn't feel very ritualistic.

Quinn snorted. At least she could still laugh at herself.

Bryar and Tai had left two days before; they'd be at Ezra's compound by now. She wouldn't mind a stay at Ezra's herself. The most powerful Scribe in generations, he had made her journey year, spent primarily under his tutelage, one of the most rewarding of her career.

What did Arwen want? And why now?

Quinn knew better than to give in to her sour mood. She was just so *tired*, though. Tired of the unrelenting challenges and changes of the last year, which had kept her away from her usual historical research and left her feeling lonely and isolated.

She wandered into her even smaller bedroom and flopped on her bed. Perhaps a nap...

The knock came again. No point questioning who was there, or what the message would be. With a huff of exasperation, Quinn rolled upright yet again.

"Sorry, sister," the messenger kid said. "Arwen says you're to come, no matter what you're in the middle of."

Even if I'm mired in a sulk of epic proportions?

Not the boy's fault. She sent him off with a half smile and fished her sandals out from under the table.

Arwen waited in the entry lobby of the lodge. As Quinn came down the stairs, she could sense fire smoldering in the older woman, who rounded on her as soon as she reached the foot of the staircase.

"I don't have time to search all over the Motherhouse for you," she snapped. "You're the one who's so determined to mine the Aura for every secret it can divulge, so *where the deuce have you been?*" She grasped Quinn's arm and shook it. Quinn noted that the older woman was panting lightly, as if the prevailing tension had closed up her chest.

"Sorry. I needed to—"

She didn't sound sorry enough, evidently. Without further explanation, Arwen wheeled toward the door, dragging her along as if she were still a young teen bent on exploring boundaries and had just exploded a stink bomb in the dining hall.

"Hold it." Quinn dug in her heels. The two women stopped at the threshold of the small lodge – small because there had never been more than fifteen Scribes at any one time. "Before we create a spectacle out there for the apprentices, tell me what this is about."

Arwen sighed, and Quinn at last noticed the deep circles under her eyes, the slight slump in her shoulders. "That man. What else?"

That man. Kiril. The Healers were keeping him alive, but nobody had been able to figure out what ailed him.

"And this concerns me?" Her snapped comment gave clear evidence of her resentment at being shut out.

"You know it does," Arwen snapped right back. "Whatever's got hold of him, its origin is the Aura. There's some... magic." The word, familiar enough but never used in regard to the life-giving energy that sustained the Midland, seemed to tangle Arwen's tongue.

Never until recently, as it now transpired that the Aura was far from the beneficent energy they had assumed.

"I didn't want to do this, but we need you involved. We're getting nowhere trying to fathom what it is," Arwen continued. "The Healers lack the skill set, and you're the best currently in residence for this type of exploration. For everyone's sake, stop being difficult."

"Sorry," Quinn mumbled again, feeling as if she were thirteen instead of three times that. Arwen had that effect, when she chose to.

Arwen released her grip, and the two women set off together across the green to the healing rooms.

As they crossed in front of the amphitheater, Quinn strove for unbiased reflection. She and Kiril had been antagonists ever since he tumbled into their world on that little space ship of his. He'd made no attempt to integrate into their society and had seldom been less than abrasive. Worse, he looked at her like a meal to be devoured, which left her uneasy. Not because of the look, but because of the reactions it triggered – mostly negative ones. But not entirely.

Damn.

She'd visited the healing room once before since his collapse the day of the binding that finally rendered the power cell harmless, and like the others had sensed a weird energy in him, but... her mind went to work, seeking the one thing that might prove to be an entry into his current state.

"Where Kiril's concerned, we can guess the origin of his problem, but what's happening to him now... I'm perplexed," she admitted.

"I'm relying on you to dig out the truth. I consider this a crisis, and I'm about to break every rule in our code and ask you to violate his personal privacy. Don't argue," she added, anticipating Quinn's reaction. "Something happened in those hills, and it's been carried into the Midland. This isn't only for Kiril's sake, although my instinct suggests that if we manage to save him, we'll be glad."

"You're thinking of his eyes?" Quinn was only half joking. Blue eyes were so rare that a folk belief suggested those who had them carried a special destiny. Kiril's eyes were shockingly blue.

Arwen made a noise that sounded like a hiss. "No. There's no evidence for the validity of that tale. But I sense trouble in Borgonne as well. A disruption in the patterns to the east. Keeping Borgonne stable is vital to us – the reasons are buried in history, but I believe in the truth of it. We *need* to understand what's going on in the hills, Quinn."

Still fighting off her earlier grumpiness, Quinn grunted.

"This thing with Kiril is a clue. And," Arwen added, as if dangling a scrap of meat before a starving dog, "it's the sort of work you love. Don't deny it. But for this, I need your absolute commitment."

"I'm surprised you'd doubt me." She ran one hand through her short, tight curls; the other formed a fist.

"Normally I wouldn't... I don't. But there's danger here, and so far we haven't been able to isolate it. It's like being threatened by an invisible enemy."

"You specialize in tearing me apart, don't you?" Quinn retorted mildly.

Arwen smiled, nearly a first since the binding, and drew them to a halt. "This last year has been hard for us all. My responsibility is to cultivate in you the confidence and toughness for whatever lies ahead, not tomorrow but next year, and the years after. Something tells me the council will face troubling times. Not the easy road we've walked for generations."

At the door of the healing room, Quinn paused before pushing through the heavy curtain. "I'm uneasy about what we might be unleashing. The Aura's not what we believed it to be. These days, every time I venture into it I feel as if it's alien territory. It makes me nervous."

"I understand." The older woman's eyes were serious, the lines in her face prominent, even in the filtered light of the overcast day. "There come times we are given no choice."

With the accord struck, Quinn pulled aside the curtain and allowed Arwen to precede her into the healing room.

Kiril looked like a skeleton in skin.

His hypnotic blue eyes were open but empty, his body unmoving.

"He's aware," Beatris, an experienced Healer, reported. Usually Beatris could be relied on to inject lightness, if not humor, into a situation, but not today. Besides the tension in the room, attending to the participants in the power cell binding had left lingering fatigue behind her eyes. "There's no fever. In fact, there's no sign at all of illness. He's not comatose or unconscious. Yet you see his condition for yourself."

From a corner by the workbench, Dal nodded agreement. Currently senior among the active Healers, he had attended Kiril since he himself recovered from the energy drain of the binding. Dal looked as bad as Arwen, his finely drawn face reflecting the strain of the past four days.

"Can he hear?" Quinn asked.

"We don't know," Dal said. "Given his personality, he'd not be in favor of being left out of whatever we plan, so I'm not worried about being overheard."

"He rejects our ways," Quinn said. "He'll resist any kind of Healing."

Dal shrugged, evoking a tiny smile from Beatris. "He's learning."

"Quickly enough?" Arwen asked. "Where are his loyalties?" She addressed the immobile man on the cot, although it seemed evident he could not respond to her. "Kiril, are you with us? Are you willing to accept our help?" She received no response, nor had they expected one. Arwen forged on. "Are you seeking death?"

Kiril's right hand twitched, then lay still. He'd heard.

"I say we proceed," Dal said. "It's good to have you here, Quinn. We're hoping that once you figure out what's happening, between us we can devise a remedy."

"Maybe," Beatris muttered.

"Maybe," Arwen confirmed. "But we're out of options. Quinn, do you need time to prepare?"

She did, but every instinct told her they were short of time. Kiril was fading. He might not be alive in another day. "What are you doing now?"

"Treating symptoms," Beatris said. "Sustaining, but not Healing. And our remedies are losing their effectiveness. Whatever it is, it's growing in strength."

"As we might have anticipated, had we known he'd been infected by that beast in the hills in the first place," Dal said. "Even before he collapsed, he was losing weight and becoming weaker by the day. We were so wrapped up in the binding we failed to notice."

Self-recrimination colored his words. Arwen crossed the small room and put a hand on Dal's shoulder. "Don't do this. He didn't seek help. No one is to blame."

Dal met her eyes, wearily. "I suppose not. But this..." He trailed off and said nothing more.

Arwen turned back to the room. "Quinn, are you ready? What do you need?"

As the conversation continued, Quinn had set aside her early pique. She felt sufficiently calm and focused to answer the question with confidence. "Quiet, a glass of water, and a lifeline."

"A full link?" Arwen asked.

"No, I don't think so. This shouldn't be that deep, merely intricate."

Dal crossed the room to her. He had been a figure in her life since he taught her very first class in Healing, many years ago. She admired and trusted him for his skill, his judgment, and his innate sympathy. "You're familiar with Ezra's prophecy?" he asked quietly.

She frowned.

"He said you three would be involved in events to come."

She had forgotten, but remembered now; Willow had relayed Ezra's unsettling words, over half a year ago. "I didn't consider it prophecy, just a... foretelling? One of Ezra's odd ways of seeing things?"

Dal didn't smile. "Willow and Bryar both paid a price—"

"And are prospering now," Arwen interrupted.

"Mostly," Quinn said, remembering Bryar's hand.

"Yes," Dal said, "but both stood on the brink of catastrophic loss. Nothing has happened to you yet. All I'm saying is, don't take chances. If Ezra's right..." His eyes changed focus, seeing far into an invisible horizon.

Quinn hugged the older man. "I'll be careful," she whispered.

"I'm staying," Dal concluded. "I won't get in the way, but I want to be here if you need me. This thing is energetic, but there are medical implications, too. It's likely to require both of us to deal with it."

"Thanks."

Dal turned to Beatris. "Why don't you take a break? With so many in here, we're stepping all over each other's energies. I'll send for you when you're needed."

Beatris touched Kiril's forehead, nodded, and said, "Watch yourself, Dal."

She poured a mug of water from a flask, handed it to Quinn, and left. Quinn assigned positions to Arwen across the cot from her and Dal along the wall furthest from Kiril. "I need space. Since I'm not going deep, don't fill the room with worry. If there's a problem, I'll signal."

Arwen's grim face and silence did nothing to reassure her, but Quinn was counted among the most experienced explorers of the Aura. Whatever plagued Kiril must have its roots in the spells blanketing the hills, and probably in the attack by the beast that savaged his arm. Facing a challenge unlike any other of her career, and with Dal's caution ringing in her mind, she settled on a stool next to Kiril, murmured a quick invocation – *Sustainer of air, guide my exploration* – placed a hand lightly on his chest, and began the process that would culminate in access to Kiril's demon.

Chapter 2

Quinn was faintly aware that Arwen was in Kiril's energetic body, monitoring her, and sent out a call for help as soon as the monster's tentacles first tickled at her awareness. She emerged from the trance shaking and sweaty, clutching Arwen's hand, and more scared than at any other time in years of exploring the Aura.

Dal was next to her in an instant, helping her with the mug of water she'd placed beside the stool. Arwen rested both hands firmly on her shoulders and spoke in a continuous low voice, bringing her back. When she was confident her mind had returned fully to ordinary reality, she started to speak, choked, and gulped at the water. Finally she said, "This is... I hardly know how to describe... It tried to grab me. Take me, too... as if it's conscious."

"Alive. Spawn of the beast that attacked Kiril," Dal said.

"Not just a spell, then," Arwen said.

"It is, but it isn't." Quinn swallowed more water, then held out the empty mug. Dal refilled it and handed it to her, wrapping his own strong hand around her shaking one.

"Kiril's hosting this thing, as if the beast planted a demon inside him that wants to devour him. Or... no, that isn't accurate. As if it *will* devour him if it can't drag him back into the hills. And if he does go... as an educated guess, the hills themselves will destroy him. There's too much I don't understand."

"You understand enough," Arwen said. "We've only grasped the most basic aspects of the spells on the hills, benign actions like turning non-Weavers around and dumping them out where they started. It makes sense that there would be more."

"But this?" Dal said. "I never dreamed the hills held this much menace. Or that the Aura itself could cause harm. It's our lifeblood. Our sustainer."

"My stomach's roiling." Quinn glanced at the still man on the cot, then looked more closely. A tension that hadn't been there before marked his face, pulling his mouth into a taut line. She sensed panic in his eyes. "Something's changed."

"I see it, too," Dal confirmed. "It's time to take action, whatever we decide. Fast."

Arwen had already gone to the door and rung the bell for a runner. When the child appeared, she barked out her orders. "Energy bars and caff, quick as you can. Have them delivered, then go fetch Beatris and Dorcas. Tell them it's urgent."

"Yes, ma'am."

The boy disappeared, and Arwen sagged against the doorframe. "That's what I felt when I helped you get out? An attack on you?"

Quinn nodded, her mouth set in a line matching Kiril's for grimness.

"Come with me." Arwen strode from the room. Quinn and Dal exchanged glances as he assisted her to her feet.

In the Healers' garden, out of Kiril's hearing, Arwen said, "I've called the others for a confab. We need to decide how to handle this, and quickly. I assume it's impossible for the demon spell to escape Kiril's body, and I'm absolutely sure we don't want it to. We can't risk letting this thing go viral. We may have no option but to sacrifice him, and it with him."

"Oh, Diou," Dal muttered. He'd paled under his tan.

"No," Quinn said. "There's too much to learn—"

"And the need to question everything we believe in," Arwen said. "But I felt it, Quinn, and I was only in for an instant. Nobody expected that. If it had been a Healer, or even a less experienced Scribe who ventured deep enough to touch the demon, the consequences could have been catastrophic."

Dal shifted uneasily. "As Healers, we make a commitment. When we take a life, or allow that life to extinguish, it's for the good of the patient, at his wish and to prevent intolerable suffering. Not because he presents a danger to society. But we've never dealt with a challenge like this. Morally, I wonder if Kiril's demon could be considered an epidemic." He frowned and turned from the two women to pace the courtyard. Dal had always been a thoughtful man, interested in the philosophy behind his Healing skills as much as actual Healing.

"If it gets loose, the risk compounds." Quinn followed Arwen's thought to its logical conclusion. "And remember, we have no way of knowing the effect on the demon, should Kiril die."

Beatris hurried up. "They found me in the dining hall. The caff and food are on the way. What's happened?"

Arwen filled her in. Quinn stood silently, still too appalled by what she'd experienced in Kiril to speak up.

"We just did the binding on the power cell," Beatris said. "We have experience now. Can we go in there and find that thing and tie it up?"

That forced a hoarse snort from Quinn. "It's hardly that simple."

Beatris stood a fraction taller, offended. "I was called here. My solution may not be the best, but it is a starting point. You've no right to laugh, Quinn."

The day had galloped out of control. Quinn still clenched the mug of water; she took another swallow. "You're right. I'm sorry, Bea."

"Quinn's just had the stuffing scared out of her," Arwen put in. "She's off base."

"You should have said." Beatris reached into her pocket and extracted a small vial. "Here. Two drops."

As she administered the remedy into Quinn's compliant mouth, Dal rejoined them. "It's a measure of how shaken we all are. I should have seen to that. Dose Arwen and me, too, please, Beatris. And then it might be wise to administer to Kiril. He's frightened."

A runner from the dining hall appeared with a tray. Arwen took it, managing a tight smile in thanks.

Dorcas arrived shortly after Beatris finished dispensing her remedy. She looked older than her years, her weather-beaten face etched with new lines. Quinn's frayed nerves had begun to release; the shock had lessened, leaving her more grounded. Arwen led their small group to a circular seating area at the far side of the Healers' garden, Dal filling Dorcas in as they walked. She placed the tray on the center table and poured caff for them all. *Manna.* Quinn eyed the energy-giving liquid, but she opted first for a seed and honey bar, to settle her stomach.

"Suggestions? A binding has been proposed, as has sacrificing Kiril to rid the community of the threat." Arwen used the voice she adopted for fractious meetings and recalcitrant apprentices, brooking no nonsense.

Dorcas sat, pulling Quinn down beside her. "You okay?" she asked quietly. "You look pale."

Quinn couldn't resist a bark of laughter. Her, pale? There had been dark-skinned Weavers in the past, but at the moment her caff-colored skin was unique at the Motherhouse.

Her arm still around Quinn, Dorcas asked the group, "There's no chance of Healing this?" As a senior Scribe and the person who had controlled the binding of the power cell, she was well positioned to grasp the implications of Arwen's narrative.

"We believe not," Dal said. Quinn heard defeat in his voice. "It's not an illness or injury. It's energetic."

Dorcas nodded. "We can't remove it?"

Quinn shuddered. "Uncertain, with dangers either way."

"And is there a benefit to keeping Kiril alive?"

Beatris bristled. "He's a human being. A man. Of course there is."

"Perhaps," Quinn said more slowly. "There's always the possibility that if Kiril dies, the demon will leave his body and... be on the loose in the Motherhouse?"

Arwen muttered a curse under her breath.

"Anyway," Quinn continued, "we have so much to learn from him, if he ever gives us the opening. If he ever trusts us enough."

"Nothing stops us from talking to Joss instead," Dorcas said.

But Joss was in Hallan Hot Springs with Willow now. Furthermore, the two men's perspectives were radically different. "Kiril was the commander. Arguably, his knowledge differs from Joss's, and may be more valuable."

"But is this necessary information?"

"Yes," Quinn said flatly. "Even apart from the beast in the hills. If what they told us is true, we're soon to be invaded by thousands more from their planet, maybe millions."

The group sat silently in the morning sun, absorbing this.

Dorcas broke the impasse. "How dangerous is it?"

Quinn took her time before answering. "If we get in and out quickly, there *may* be minimal risk. But I'm not sure I believe that. It's as if it has feelers. If it gets a chance to grab one of us, it will. The initial attack was about six nine-days ago. Not even a season, but it's had time to gain strength..."

"Beatris may well be right. Our only viable alternative is to bind this spell." Arwen's eyes reflected her discomfort as she surveyed them. "How long can you keep him alive, Dal?"

"Another day or two, perhaps."

"The longer we wait, the more challenging it becomes," Quinn mused. "But devising a binding takes time, even based on what little we know from Kiril and Bryar."

"Bryar's at Ezra's," Dorcas said. "We can reach him there."

"At some energetic cost. Energy we can't spare." Arwen stood. "I will cajole an early lunch from the dining hall. Then we must set to work. Dal, please assign others to Kiril's care. I want you involved. Dorcas, round up any available Scribes to handle the link to Bryar. Quinn, come with me."

Crossing the green, out of earshot, Arwen said, "I assume that if we attempt this binding, you will lead it."

Surprised, Quinn shook her head. "After what just happened? I'm still shaking."

Arwen's face set into the hard lines that told her they were both out of options. "Don't think I'm extrapolating my own expectations on you. It's imperative you be involved this time, despite the potential cost. When I was monitoring your progress, I touched his energy as well. I preferred not to discuss this in front of the others, but you need to know. Kiril resisted me. He didn't resist you."

"That makes no sense."

"It makes every sense. Anyone with eyes could see he feels something for you, even if it expresses as antipathy. You and Dal are the two he's likely to let in. If he fights us when we try to do the binding, the potential for disaster increases. You'll go in first, not so deeply that you risk exposure to the demon, but enough to reassure Kiril. Make him accept what we're doing."

She couldn't deny the attraction; the decades-long trust between Arwen and her was too strong for that. She just didn't like it. The man was insufferable, arrogant, dismissive, and looked at her as if he wanted to throw her onto any available surface and...

She shut down that line of reflection quickly, but not quickly enough. Arwen smiled. "We'll have your back. How many will we need for this template, do you think? And do we use only Scribes? I'm inclined to involve Healers as well. Dal, for sure. Is Beatris sufficiently recovered from the cell binding?"

Quinn shrugged. "You know she'll insist, now that we've brought her in."

"So she will." Fatigue permeated Arwen's words as she added, "It may be a season before the Motherhouse recovers from this."

The two women discussed the logistics of the upcoming work, keeping it light, until they reached the dining hall, where the others caught up with them. Quinn recognized what Arwen had been doing: talking her down, bringing her focus back.

She was the tough one. But for the first time she questioned her stamina, given the magnitude of the challenge they now faced.

Arwen had grown more determined as time grew short. They needed to understand the spell – or spells, Quinn thought grimly – in the hills. They needed to know more about Terrans before boatloads of them turned up in the Midland. They had no idea what might happen if Kiril, as host to the demon in him, died.

All in all, Kiril was worth saving.

They had allowed themselves a window of two days, an absurdly short timeframe but still too long, to devise the binding and practice. Two days during which a team of Healers kept Kiril alive, barely, utilizing every energetic and physical tool in their extensive arsenal to prevent his further deterioration. It was a rearguard action, fought clumsily since it dealt only with symptoms, not the root cause.

In the end, space determined the participants in the binding. To work within the confines of Kiril's personal aura, they decided on a maximum of three: Dorcas, Dal, and herself as lead explorer in the uncharted terrain that was Kiril. Hunting down his demon. Through linking, they relied on Dal to navigate his anatomy. She and Dorcas would deal with the weave, binding the demon inside him and hopefully saving his life in the process.

They worked with minimal information, scant idea of the boundaries of the thing inhabiting him, and no true concept of its powers.

Quinn's lack of sleep manifested as total absence of peace of mind. She lived on a knife edge of caff, anticipation, and dread. Everything had to go perfectly, without room for error.

Oddly, this binding relied more on life force than had the one for the power cell. She and Dorcas had spent a worrying hour scanning Kiril's inert body, looking for any clue to the best way to subdue and contain the beast inside him. Although they came away empty, they both sensed that life force was inimical to it, and so an effective method to weaken, possibly destroy it.

The afternoon of the second day, Arwen tracked Quinn and Dorcas down in a workroom on the ground floor of the Scribes' lodge, an elaborately marked sheet of paper between them and ink stains on their fingers. The template they had diagrammed was functional, Quinn believed, but it lacked refinement. Both of them worried that it would leave gaps, places where the demon might loose its poison again.

"Time's up," Arwen said. She sank heavily onto a stool with no sign of her usual, erect posture.

"Can't be," Dorcas riposted. "We're going to be working into the night to refine the template."

"What's happened?" Quinn felt a chill cross her skin.

Arwen heaved a heavy sigh. "Kiril's sinking. They doubt he'll last until tomorrow. His legs are spasming, and Beatris says his face is contorted, as if he's in pain but catatonic, so he can't explain."

Dorcas swore. Quinn was silent.

"What I'm saying is..." Arwen spoke as if each word was an effort, each fact more difficult to express than the last. "The best we can hope for now is whatever we've got. If we partially contain the demon, we'll go back in later and tie it off. But if we wait, we'll lose Kiril. With no clue if the demon's a parasite or a scavenger."

At the image, Quinn grimaced, then looked to her fellow Scribe.

"Give us an hour," Dorcas said.

Annoyance crossed Arwen's face. "Why? I've just told you what—"

"Because in the state we're in now, if we go in we'll both mess up. Neither of us is alert enough. Find a runner and get a fast-acting sleep remedy, or whatever the Healers use for instant energy – except caff. We're both high on the stuff." She slapped her hand on their diagram and addressed Quinn. "An hour's nap. Then we nab the beast."

Dorcas hadn't met the beast in person. Quinn wished never to meet it again. But as happened so often lately, there were no alternatives left. She nodded.

Unhappy but resigned, Arwen went off to find either a Healer or a messenger kid to obtain the remedy. Dorcas rolled up their diagram. "I assume you've memorized this? And remember where our energies join?"

"Yes." Quinn's shoulders slumped. "I'm heading for my quarters." Because to be honest, nothing sounded better than to nap for an hour. Or a day, or a year.

Time up and plans laid, Quinn eyed her team as they stood around the cot in the healing room, each of them preparing in their own way for what was to come. Shafts of pale, late afternoon light from clerestory windows penetrated the somber atmosphere, heightening the awareness of the contrast between life and the darkness inhabiting Kiril. Arwen, Beatris, two other Scribes, and a junior Healer sat along the far wall. Their emergency rescue crew.

The work, creating a template, delving into the Aura, was familiar. This application was not. As in the day in the field, their hands were bound together. Quinn stood next to Dorcas on one side,

Dal on the other, their arms reaching across Kiril's torso to form the circle.

Quinn took a breath, nodded to her partners, and closed her eyes. The others linked with her in the Aura, and the work began.

Because they had no idea of the demon's dimensions, she and Dorcas encompassed Kiril with their weave, then gradually shrank it. They followed the anatomical trail forged by Dal, but Quinn had the feeling she was moving through something dark and unexplored, every movement, every tightening of the template presenting a new risk. Only desperation and years of training kept her going. Through the link she felt her comrades' competence, and their fear.

Abruptly Kiril cried out. All three of them flinched but continued, until the template was as tight as they could make it. At her signal they tied off the binding and emerged into ordinary reality again.

Simple.

Except that she had no idea how much time had passed. Dal collapsed forward across Kiril's chest. Dorcas fell to the ground, her hand still clutching Dal's in a form of rigor. Quinn felt... she couldn't even describe it. Helpless, perhaps. Unable to grasp the depth of what they had just accomplished. Arwen reached their side in an instant, releasing their hands, helping Dorcas to stretch out on the floor. Quinn stood staring at nothing, waiting for reality to return. Dal didn't move.

His voice rusty from days of non-use, Kiril said, "What the hell?"

After that, the healing room devolved into chaos. Arwen thrust a pastry into Quinn's hand, then went straight to Dal, helping him to the floor. Beatris distributed the magic drops Healers always kept stowed in their pockets. The other onlookers stepped over them to tend to Kiril, who had begun to shift about on the cot.

With Dal stretched out and under the care of the Healers, Arwen turned Quinn toward the door. "Outside," she said.

An evening mist coated the world and pulled diffuse aromas from the healing plants in the garden. As soon as she'd managed to stumble into the garden, Quinn raised her arms to allow the soft caress of moisture on her skin.

"Success?" Arwen demanded.

"Think so," she said, full sentences being too demanding. Quinn realized she held a pastry and nibbled it. Abricoe, sweet and tangy against her tongue.

"The three of you?"

As her legs stabilized underneath her, Quinn led the way to a bench under the eaves of the Healers' lodge. "Okay, as far as I know."

"And the binding?" Arwen asked.

"We'll check once we've had time to recover. Kiril spoke, didn't he? That's a good sign."

"Very good. I hope someone in there is keeping him under control."

Quinn produced a smile. "Headstrong?"

"You two are a match."

She shuddered. She and Kiril? Not a chance.

Dorcas had managed to walk back to the Scribes' lodge; Dal had been helped to his quarters in the Healers' lodge. Quinn didn't feel that great herself, although she'd be hard pressed to explain exactly where the problem lay. It was more as if her entire body had been subjected to a nasty influenza. A Healer administered to her, support she accepted gratefully.

None of them had emerged with injuries, physical or energetic, beyond the shock of the working itself. Quinn hoped that meant they had escaped infection.

After allowing herself an hour to recuperate, interrupted by Arwen who attempted a debriefing until Quinn finally refused to say any more and walked out, she made her way back to the healing room. Kiril sprawled in a chair, idly watching as Noni, a junior Healer Quinn knew only slightly, remade the bed. She seemed to be at a loss as to what to do with her patient.

"Better?" Quinn asked the young woman, ignoring Kiril.

"I can't find anything wrong, other than weakness. I'm waiting for Daren." Although he no longer actively traveled, as the head of their guild Daren was the ranking Healer at the Motherhouse. She'd rather have Dal there, but knew it to be unlikely. He was at least ten years older than she, and those years made a difference, especially with two crucial bindings within a nine-day.

She turned her attention to Kiril. "How are you?"

"Fine."

"Communicative as always. We just saved your life, you know."

"Good for you. Another feather in your cap." His face didn't reflect quite the indifference his words conveyed, but his tone shut her out as if to make it clear that however deeply she'd penetrated his energy field, she hadn't been welcome.

She stood over him, hands on hips. "For a reason, not because we particularly wanted to. The least you can do is cooperate."

He met her eyes without shying away. "You perhaps have the mistaken belief that I care."

"You'd rather be dead?"

He shrugged and looked away.

Frustrated, she ranted on, ignoring Noni's gentle hand on her arm. "Did you ever consider how bad it could be? Given that thing that possessed you, you might have died in agony. You could have suffered for days, seasons even, before it let you die. While it consumed you. Ate you up from the inside. Is that what you wanted?" her voice climbed as she spoke, until she was virtually shouting in his face.

She got no reaction. He shrugged again, but said nothing.

"He's all yours," Quinn said to Noni. "Fool."

She wheeled and stormed from the room. Conflicted, exhausted but also with energy she needed to burn, she headed for the little lookout over the turbulent river where she'd spent so many hours as a teenager.

She heard the unexpected flute before she saw him, a shadow against the darkening sky.

"Bryar!"

He was on his feet in an instant, arms wide. Quinn threw herself into them and let herself sink against his chest. Bryar. "I'm so glad you're here," she said, her voice muffled by his tunic.

"After the communication at Ezra's? Did you think I'd stay away?"

Finally releasing each other, but still touching, they sat side by side watching the water. "I left as soon as I could. Got here an hour ago. I didn't see any of you in the dining hall."

"Arwen cornered me. All I wanted was sleep."

"Kiril?"

"His usual obnoxious self, but shaken, I think. He won't give. What's he protecting, Bry? What's he afraid of?"

"He never lets on. He saved me, though, when he didn't have to. And he took the fall for Duncan's death."

"Hush." Quinn turned to him and put fingers across his lips.

Bryar seized her fingers and kissed them. "No, you hush. If I can't say this to you, who can I ever say it to? My knife sank into his body. Whether there was another, a final blow... I don't know if I killed him, Quinn. But I can't deny my intent."

"To save your life."

"Yes. By taking someone else's. I live with that. And Kiril... he could have made a decent life for himself in Borgonne, if he'd stayed instead of sticking with me. It's a better fit for him over there."

"Will you go see him?"

"You don't believe I came this far to see you, do you?"

She punched his shoulder, and he laughed. "Maybe I can help. But for as long as we were together, I can't say he ever revealed a clue to his thoughts. He helped me, though. Unnecessary things that made my life more comfortable until we could escape from Borgonne. I'm glad you saved him, Quinn."

"Temporarily. The weave wasn't as tight as we'd wanted. Dorcas and I may need to repeat the whole thing. We rushed. We were out of time, and once we got in, we were afraid his demon, whatever it is, would get us, too."

They sat in silence for a while, the sound of the river filling the spaces.

"We'll be okay," Bryar said. "We have to be."

"Did Tai come?"

He shook his head. "She'll enjoy being without me. Tai's... untamed. She needs her space."

"Not a domestic bone in her body?" Quinn nudged him with an elbow.

"Damn good cook, actually. You should visit."

"I'd love to. I need to get out of here. The last year's taken its toll."

"On everyone."

"And not over yet. The threat of more Terrans turning up – hopefully they'd be more like Joss than Kiril – and Arwen says she's picking up something in Borgonne, so everyone's on edge. I just want it finished, Bry."

"It will be. Don't worry. Relax. You've done the work of multitudes today."

"And the only reward is Kiril. Persuade me that's a good thing."

He grinned. "Not yet. But I'll go see him. Maybe I can convince him to be polite, at least."

Chapter 3

Part of my brain's been cut out.

Two days after their voodoo treatment, Kiril sat on the edge of his cot in the healing room, trying to put words around the sensation that enveloped him like a soft blanket. Daily his head cleared in the wake of a Healing, only to revert to this horrid muzziness after an hour or two. Joss deserved credit. His sergeant had seen the truth behind their hocus-pocus long before he did.

At least his inclination to go to the dining hall for breakfast suggested a return to normality.

This place was an improvement on the obscure dump in Stanstead where their voodoo healing had put him back together after their space pod crashed, but even so, being in the healing room gave him the creeps. Kiril stood in the blessed solitude, fought unsteadiness as he donned trousers, then changed out of his sleep shirt into yet another shapeless tunic and headed outside, his stomach rumbling. He crossed the green, aware of a subtle tug toward the hills to the east, but forged a conscious determination to ignore it, as he'd done in the days before his collapse. After what the hills had inflicted on him, he intended never to go near them again.

He carefully made his way to the dining hall and joined the line. He understood queuing for food. On Terra, mess lines were commonplace.

Kiril wanted, more than he could express even to himself, for things to be normal again. For the pod to be flight-worthy. For communication with Terra. For men under his command, respect he'd earned.

If the events of the recent past had taught him anything, it was that normal existed only in his memories. Adapt, he told himself, or die.

He'd almost died. While at times his waking mind suggested that might be the best thing all around, the experience in the grip of the demon that, according to the Healers, still inhabited him had graphically shown him otherwise. And not even the Weavers, the spooky residents of the Motherhouse, could tell him what his permanent guest was.

Breakfast in hand, he spotted Bryar and Quinn in the area reserved for Weavers – no kids allowed. Company sounded good; he'd seen Bryar a few times, but the healing room got lonely with no books or video games, no fellow squadron members to spar with.

"It's going to be a hot one today," Bryar said by way of greeting, and gestured to an empty chair.

The chair was more welcome than he chose to admit; a fine tremor ran up his legs from the exertion of walking to the dining hall. "Are they going to restrict what I do? I've had enough of that room." He poured syrup over his pan cakes.

"You should listen," Quinn said. "Dal told you yesterday you were free to move to the guest lodge whenever you felt up to it, as long as you turn up for Healings every afternoon."

Kiril frowned. Dal said that?

"You don't remember?" Quinn asked. "Residual memory loss shouldn't be happening. Sustainer, I hope we don't need to—"

Bryar's hand landed on hers. "He's been though a lot. When your mind gets into overload, you forget things. Give it time."

Kiril nodded, grateful for Bryar's intervention. He had grown to respect the man, especially given what he had faced and continued to face. Not at all the pretty boy he'd first believed him to be.

"Still leaving today?" Quinn asked.

Bryar nodded. "I miss Tai. We'd barely arrived at Ezra's when I got the call. Why don't you come?" he said to Kiril, as if a sudden inspiration.

"Not until he's finished his treatments," Quinn said.

"No, but later. Ezra's wise, and his place is... restorative, I guess you'd say. Like coming home. Anyone would be better for a stay there."

"We'll see," Kiril said. Another trek through their forests held little appeal.

Bryar stood, pulled Quinn up, and hugged her. "Lightness of air be yours."

"Flow of water be yours," she whispered.

He reached out to shake Kiril's hand, then crossed to the other side of the dining hall. Looking for his daughter, probably.

Leaving him alone with Quinn. They eyed each other over the table.

"Tell me," he said, "Bringing the cell back – was it worth it? Did you manage to bind it up and dispatch it?"

"Bound and on its way to a safe place. Absolutely worth it."

Dal joined them. "It's good to see you up, Kiril." He seemed pale under his perpetual tan, and the subtle shaking Kiril first noticed in the healing room still affected his hands.

"I'm glad to be out. I want to take a walk this morning, stretch a little."

"Do it, but don't overdo. Build your strength gradually. Caff, anyone?" Dal set his tray on the table. Quinn looked as if she might fall on the caff pot and consume it whole. Dal poured. Love of caff was assumed in this culture, but oh, how he longed for coffee.

He'd never taste it again.

He accepted the mug of caff, but didn't hurry to swallow it down.

"How's your mind? You complained of feeling muddled yesterday." Dal downed his caff and poured another. Quinn was already on her second, Kiril noted. Addict.

"Better." He hoped that Quinn wouldn't mention his forgetting Dal's permission to leave the healing room. He wasn't ready to have his failures spread around.

"A couple more treatments should see you right. But alert us if you experience anything – *anything at all* – out of the ordinary. Thoughts or cravings you aren't usually subject to."

"We almost lost you," Quinn put in. "It had gained more than a toehold. I'm not sure I'd want to risk another binding like that."

He considered commenting that no doubt she longed to lose him, but it didn't seem appropriate with Dal sitting there attacking a stack of pan cakes. It was childish, but he enjoyed poking at Quinn, riling her. He'd spent plenty of time with her in the last two days, helping her build a more accurate picture of the unwelcome demon inside him. Yet her presence continued to be an irritating burr under his waistband.

Her dark eyes watched him, as if waiting for his next move.

His own breakfast finished, he pushed back from the table.

"You know how to get to the village?" Quinn asked. "Take the trail north. There's a branch to the left, just past the last outbuilding. That's where the men go for shaves."

"I'm aware. And I like the beard," he countered. Even if he hated it, she had no business dictating whether he shaved it off. "One of the few benefits I've found to your civilization."

Their eyes locked. Dal might not exist.

"It suits you, but it's scruffy."

When did getting his beard trimmed become a challenge?

"Before you go, call in at the guest lodge," Dal said. "Just alert them that you're back, as a courtesy to housekeeping and laundry."

"And bathe," Quinn put in. Unnecessarily. He'd been subjected to regular, humiliating sponge baths in the healing room.

He acknowledged her shot with a nod, gave a friendlier tip of his head to Dal, and carried his dishes to the hatch.

The room in the guest lodge waited as he'd left it, the day they bound the cell. A walk to the village appealed to him, and Quinn's comment notwithstanding, he sensed he could do with a trim. *A mirror.* Yet another thing he missed in this backward place.

Maybe tomorrow he'd explore the path that paralleled the river. That level of raw power and turbulence didn't exist on Terra, where hydraulic engineers captured all fresh water. They said Bryar swam in the out-of-control torrent flowing by the Motherhouse. Insanity. The river scared him, although, like so much else, he'd never admit it.

Kiril ran into Quinn again the next afternoon. She was sitting on a rock looking out over the river, seemingly doing nothing.

When she saw him approaching, she scrambled up, ready as always to force herself into his peace of mind. "This trail loops around and comes out west of the Motherhouse. It's a nice walk when it isn't mobbed with apprentices. And Dal wants you up and moving." She joined him, giving him no option. "We'll walk slowly, in case it's too much for you."

"I'm doing just fine, thank you," he said, feigning neutrality.

"Don't lie."

All right, he wouldn't. Kiril's old restlessness had reasserted itself with his increasing strength. "How soon can I leave?"

"And go where?"

"Stanstead, for starters. After that, it depends. I need to find a way to earn my living until my people come."

"What makes you so certain they're coming?"

Nothing. But he wasn't going to say that. "Trust me. Joss didn't get it wrong, Terra's in trouble. Anyone with guts and half a brain is going to clamor for a place on one of the ships."

Silence dragged between them. Despite the gentle slope, his legs were tiring under him. Too much, too soon, after the jaunt to the village the day before.

After a while she kicked at a stone in the path and said, "What's it like? Besides the regimentation and men and women kept separate. Everyday life – what do you miss about it?" Her eyes studied him, earnest and for once not taunting. "I want to understand how it's different from here."

"Here," he pointed out, "is uneducated, pastoral, and primitive. There are no books, no videos, no gymnasiums—"

"Gymnasiums?"

"Buildings. For exercise, games, competitions."

"Perhaps they aren't necessary here. Most of the work is physical and cooperative. And we play outdoor games. Futbol, for instance."

He'd seen it, a form of soccer. "But there's no league, competition between cities or corporations. It's all so..."

"Unskilled?"

"At home, members of the athlete caste are respected."

"For what? You're fit. So's Joss. So am I, for that matter, and almost everyone else. Why do you need gymnasiums?"

Time to change the subject. "Then there's the food."

"Joss says the food here's the best he's ever eaten."

"Joss is from the worker caste."

"And you obviously aren't. So perks came with being in your caste – or your rank?"

"Both. The first I was born into. The second I earned."

"Born in one of those laboratories of yours? Do they plan the caste ahead of time?"

Not a question he'd ever asked. "I guess they must, from the genetic material they work with. Or maybe they analyze the genetics post gestation and assign caste based on what work you'll be qualified to take on."

Quinn picked up a stick from the side of the trail and began switching the tree trunks as they passed. Her disapproval radiated from her walk, the way she squinted her eyes, but she kept her voice neutral.

Small mercies, Kiril thought.

"And if the baby's defective in some way?"

"That never happens. Given the population and environmental challenges, we can't afford it."

"So they would have taken one look at Bryar's birthmark and thrown him away."

"Probably."

"Already I hope those people of yours never turn up."

The conversation left him glum. To picture himself through the lens of her questions, life on Terra was hardly worth living. An existence regulated by the corporation.

Magical demons never inhabited your body on Terra.

They reached the southernmost point of the trail and stood looking down on the amphitheater with its backdrop of the Motherhouse complex and the massif. The village perched to the northwest. The valley was considerably bigger and more open than it seemed from the confines of the inhabited areas. Rolling pastureland spread like a green carpet. Figures made small by distance moved around the buildings, while above him a warm breeze caught in the trees that dotted the landscape. Despite the hot day, up here the air was fresh.

What would be the point of going back, supposing he could?

Prestige, status, knowledge of a job well done and recognition for it... So far, the path to any of those here proved elusive. His skills were of dubious value, his leadership potential irrelevant since they had their own leaders, men – and women – born to the culture and conversant with its nuances. "Any suggestions?" he asked with forced casualness. "Where work's concerned, I'm at a loss."

To her credit, she gave his question consideration. "In larger settlements like Stanstead, they need administrators to monitor things. It's a big job, tracking clothing and crops, knives and production and who's sick, who wants to change jobs, who lives where. So that's a possibility, if you're willing to work for someone else while you learn. And they'd certainly want a commitment that you'd stay."

Bean counting. Primitive logistics. He could handle those with his eyes closed. But to spend the rest of his life at it?

"Any other suggestions?"

"One." She walked slightly ahead of him. Not for the first time he admired the straight line of her slender back under the shifting tunic. Today she wore no skirt or trousers, merely the thin piece of linen. He reined in his reactions. This thing about wanting to dominate Quinn was getting to be a nuisance.

"Sorry, I missed that. Mind wandered."

She gave him a look part frustrated, part disgusted, as if she knew what he'd been thinking. "I *said*, in the short term you'd be a valuable resource here. We can't plan without knowing more about the hordes you say will invade us soon. The more you share, the better for everyone."

Well, he asked for it. "I could do that," he said slowly. "I think I... sorry. My head... if we..." He stopped before he made a total fool of himself. Whatever he'd been about to say had evaporated.

Where was he, anyway? He looked around, puzzled.

"Are you okay?" Quinn drew to a stop and studied him, frowning. "You don't look so good."

Disoriented, he abandoned his accustomed sarcasm. "I feel kind of... it's hard to explain."

"Can you make it as far as the healing room?"

He nodded, and hoped he was right.

Quinn took his arm and piloted him along the trail, matching her pace to his.

Like a damn baby.

His head cleared as they walked. He frantically cast around for a way to convince Quinn that nothing at all had happened, or, barring that, not to tell anyone. Especially Dal, who had the power to confine him again. He came up empty. "I guess I'm stuck here for a while, until this stops happening."

"I hope the fuzzy moments clear up. The thing I want least in the world is to start the binding all over again. It's too scary."

"As much for me as for you."

"At least you believe in our Aura now."

"Oh, yes. I'm a believer." He hoped she didn't notice the shudder that ran down his back.

They completed the circuit largely in silence. The sooner he moved on, he reflected, the better. In the meantime, he'd consider how much of Terran life to tell them, and the ways he might facilitate settlement for his people.

"Quinn, give me your opinion of this."

Quinn looked up from the Scribes' workroom table. Arwen had a second of paper in front of her, its front already covered with old notes, and had sketched out a weave. Incomplete, with gaping holes, connections going nowhere, and...

Quinn leaned closer. The weave made no sense. She frowned, confused.

"I know. I found this over Borgonne, but look." Arwen's pen traced a line. "When you combine this with this part over here..." Her pen shifted across the page. "It seems to connect to something, or try to."

Quinn followed the pen and Arwen's description. "This current... look at the intersections. The same signature we've found when we've isolated pieces of the spells on the hills." She looked up. "Someone over there is messing around with the spells. Given what we've learned, Bryar and the attack on Kiril... that can't be good." She returned her attention to the rudimentary diagram.

"It could be very good," Arwen said. "Or very bad. It might unleash unimaginable problems, should he – or she – succeed. It's erratic. You won't find it now, but it was strong half an hour ago. That's why I've concluded that it's not naturally occurring. And not generated by the hills."

"No. A Mage created this." She traced a couple of the lines with a finger, frowning when they led nowhere logical.

"I wonder if he's trying to remove one of the spells, or add another. Whatever, he could end up making a bigger muddle of things than they are now. I don't like this, Quinn."

"How did you find it?"

"Chance." Arwen dropped her pen onto the holder and stretched. "I first noticed traces of the weave a few months ago, but I concluded it was background energy, because of its inconsistency. Then, while I was tracking your progress to meet Willow, or trying to, it showed up more often. The hills block most energetic signals, so I only got glimpses. But because I was spending so much time monitoring anyway, I was able to establish it was always the same imprint."

Quinn slipped off her stool and paced the flagstone floor. Sunlight poured through the two windows, giving the room an almost festive air as the ancient stone walls glowed in the afternoon light. "The hills scramble signals from Borgonne," she began slowly, thinking her way through. "So we can't be sure what they're doing over there. Any idea who?"

Arwen shook her head. "The weave is messy enough for apprentice work, but internally it's much too elaborate, even the fragment we have. Gauvain is closest to the hills. With Duncan out of the picture, only two or three others have the depth of Entrée and training to accomplish this. But the hills wouldn't interest them."

"Gauvain, then."

Arwen sighed. "I wonder what he's up to now."

Chapter 4

Cedric Prudhomme paced the council chambers, irritated as usual by the inability of the others to arrive punctually. As head of the Orlan council, and by default leader of Borgonne itself, since the outlying towns hardly counted in the grand scheme of things, he prided himself on his scrupulous attendance to matters of protocol. Without the underlying structures of ritual and tradition, they risked sliding into anarchy, something he, Cedric Prudhomme, defended against with all his considerable weight.

He jingled his sash and chain of office against his ample middle, watching with barely contained irritation as first one person, then another, drifted in.

Naturally, Ester Sauvage arrived last, striding to her chair in a distinctly unfeminine way and wearing trousers, of all things. Damn woman. Cedric saw no reason women should be represented on council at all, given their illogical, stubborn approach to governance. She'd been an irritating itch on his backside ever since some trivial hamlet an hour outside of Orlan insisted she be elected, at penalty of refusing to submit to Orlan's dominance should she be refused.

Ester had the temerity to smirk at him as she sat.

Now, where the deuce was that blasted Mage?

Cedric surveyed the five men and one regrettable woman seated at the table. Nobody had anything to say; they all respectfully waited for him to call the meeting to order. Outside, the sun beat down, the same sun that had pounded on their heads daily since midwinter.

The spring rains had not come. The seedlings withered in the fields. Not even summer, and the crops hovered on the verge of complete failure.

Reports from outlying hamlets told him that the fruit trees were failing to set. The market gardens closer to Orlan diverted virtually all the water from the sluggish river flowing down from the north, but it provided barely enough. Telling the citizens of Orlan they were entitled to only a mug of water each day was a sure recipe for insurrection. Borgonne could be on the brink of starvation by midsummer if action weren't taken.

Damn Gauvain anyway! He represented the best, simplest hope for solving the drought problem, and he didn't even care enough to show up on time. A power play, Cedric assumed. Normally he enjoyed fencing with Gauvain, but today there was too much at stake for such silly games.

The Mage arrived as the tisane and pastries Cedric's assistant had requisitioned from the central dining hall appeared. The pastries were abricoe, not Cedric's favorite. Gauvain dressed as always in unrelieved black, his raven hair swept back from a disapproving visage. Cedric wished he'd been able to maintain the physique of his twenties; only the other day his wife had commented on what a fine figure of a man Gauvain was.

"Gentlemen, and lady," Gauvain said to the table. To Cedric's disgust, he then approached Ester and raised her hand to his lips before settling in the remaining chair. Pure showman; Cedric hoped he had something more substantial to offer today.

"I'm assuming this concerns the drought," Gauvain continued, helping himself to a pastry as he spoke. "You must know the risks associated with manipulation of weather phenomena. We prefer not to attempt it."

In a bid to regain control, Cedric rapped sharply with the gavel. "The meeting is called to order," he pronounced in his best magisterial voice. "Is there any unfinished business?"

"Oh, just get on with it, Cedric," Gauvain said. "Nobody cares about your unfinished business. You've got a problem. You've requested my presence, so I'm here, but without much patience for power maneuvering. Tell me the scope of the catastrophe."

Ester's plain face wrinkled into a frown. She spoke without waiting for Cedric to recognize her. "I hear from my village occasionally. Even that far east, the spring rains are scant, and the seedlings are struggling. We've maintained minimal food stores from last autumn, but they will run out in early summer. We've always relied on market produce to carry us through to harvest."

Lac, a thin, intense man with a poor complexion, chimed in. "Around Orlan, some of the grain has withstood the shortage of water, but next to none of the vegetables. In a town this size, we face not only starvation but insurrection."

"Just what do the peasants think we can do?" Cedric blustered. "Uneducated idiots. We don't make the weather."

"Mages do." Lac riposted.

All eyes turned to Gauvain, who sat slouched in his chair, his hands templed under his chin, watching them as if they were nothing more than a group of disorderly schoolchildren.

"As I said, we avoid tampering with the weather."

"But a little rain..."

"Just enough to establish the crops..."

"This could mean the survival of Borgonne..."

The voices tumbled over each other, pleading with Gauvain to save them.

"No." The Mage surveyed the table with his eyes, never moving from his insouciant position. "It is too risky. The possibility of causing catastrophic harm to one region while helping another is too great. My colleagues will agree, if consulted. You won't find any help there."

"How much more catastrophic can it get?" Cedric demanded.

"Tornados, scorching heat waves—"

"And you don't want to bother," Cedric added bitterly.

"You are mistaken." Gauvain's cold gaze skewered Cedric where he sat. "The challenge appeals to me immensely. But I at least have acquired the maturity to weigh my enjoyment against the risk to others."

Chastised, the council exchanged glances.

"Then what do we do?" Lac asked.

Ester sat straighter, a new steel in her voice. "I will not see my world perish. If we have no water, we go someplace that does."

Silence filled the chamber. Cedric glared at her, annoyed. The drought was comprehensive; reports coming in from far-flung regions confirmed it. Females! What was she thinking? They didn't have time for pie-in-the-sky remarks with no substance.

"You are aware of the challenges?" Gauvain drawled. "No one even knows if it's possible."

"They say you've done it," Ester shot back. "And they say that poor young woman you kept prisoner in your tower came from there."

What were they talking about? There was little Cedric liked less than not being in the know. This was his council, dammit.

"Perhaps you'd care to clarify for the rest of us?" he asked, his voice silky.

Gauvain straightened. "Your colleague's idea is perfectly clear. Crops are progressing well in the Midland."

The Midland? "But... we can't go there," Cedric sputtered. "It's proscribed."

"Not entirely." Gauvain reached across the table and helped himself to tisane before he continued. "In my younger years, I spent time in the Midland. But it doesn't follow that you could. Any of you."

"Even if we managed to get there, it'd be near impossible to ferry water back," a man at the end of the table said.

Idiots, Cedric shrieked internally. Of course they wouldn't transport water. They would carry grain, seed, fruits and vegetables... the conversation faded as his mind explored the possibility of using Gauvain to cross the hills. The mysterious Midland. No one knew much about it, although it was said to be backward compared to Borgonne. No cities like Orlan, no fine foods or luxurious appointments such as the elite enjoyed here. But they had crops... and their bounty was wasted on yokels. How he could make use of such abundance...

"As for the woman who was my guest last winter, she and I collaborated on an experiment related to the Aura. As it happens, she is skilled in that area. Now, as you undoubtedly have observed, she has returned to her side of the hills."

"Then it's not impossible."

"For those of us with Entrée, no. For you, yes."

"If we traveled with you, though..."

Cedric watched the excitement mount as the dim-witted council realized the potential in finding the way through to the Midland.

"Unlikely," Gauvain said, interrupting the chatter. "The spells protecting the hills are unusual, and comprehensive. Those without Entrée are inflicted with a confusion that leads them back where they started, with no idea how they got there."

They barely heard him. Cedric listened to the babble and once again allowed his mind to drift – into planning this time. Make use of Gauvain. Let him earn his keep, instead of lording it over society from that tower of his. Conduct a party across the hills – which he, Cedric, would naturally lead, using Gauvain as a guide of sorts. Find out how much trouble the peasantry was likely to give them, and arrange to transport the food they needed back to Borgonne. If they brought chart-makers with them, there'd be no possibility of getting lost. He'd return a hero, his wife would cease commenting on his expanding girth, and his hold on power would be cemented.

Yes. Cross the hills with Gauvain. He could buy into that.

Cedric let the conversation swirl while he poured a mug of tisane, then he pounded the gavel and called attention back to himself.

"We will send a negotiating team, which I will lead. I've no doubt Gauvain will do his part, as the drought affects him as much as it does us. When we meet the peas... that is to say, when we open negotiations, I'm confident we can persuade the Midlanders to assist us."

And fall under our governance. An expanded Borgonne, with no further worry about harvests and riots.

"A party of three, besides myself," Gauvain said. "Cedric has appointed himself, and I suggest Ester, as women hold positions of authority in the Midland. One other, of your choosing. The journey takes approximately fourteen days, allowing for expected fitness levels." His gaze fell on Cedric, who, to his own dismay, squirmed. "Make the plans for provisions and notify me. And, as I'm sure you know, it is impossible to take beasts of burden. They cannot scale the trail into the hills. Therefore, we carry our own supplies and hunt. We leave in four day's time, at sunrise."

"It's good of you to agree," Ester said.

Gauvain stood. "Not at all. I admit to a desire to see the Midland again. I shall enjoy the opportunity." With a curt nod, he left the room.

Cedric pointed a finger at Lac, as being the one who had made the most sensible contributions to the meeting. "Notify your families and arrange supplies. Gauvain overlooked the need for porters, so plan on two each to carry provisions for the crossing. Meet with me tomorrow."

With plans in train for their expedition, Cedric stood. Time to go home and report this satisfactory outcome to his wife, including the way he, Cedric Prudhomme, had handled Gauvain with his aristocratic airs. Let her appreciate his stature in the community for once. And admire him for his fortitude, his willingness to undertake the perilous journey into the hills for the sake of Borgonne.

When Gauvain arrived at the weed-choked clearing marking the start of the trail into the hills, the sight that greeted him was more risible than tragic, but nothing worse than he had expected. Remaining next to Leo on the seat of the horse cart, he sent a young boy to find Cedric in the mob.

The man's face appeared flushed as if he'd already expended a day's exertion. "So many well-wishers," he began.

"Well-wishers ought to have remained abed." Gauvain spoke mildly to hide his irritation. "We must leave, and soon, to make good progress. Disentangle this crowd, if you please. And no pretty speeches. The day promises to be hot."

But disentangling the crowd proved to be a challenge to Cedric's limited capabilities. Everyone milled about as if determined to convert their departure into a cause for one of those rustic agricultural festivals the common people insisted on. The sun shone well above Orlan in the distance before Gauvain was able to ascertain the full extent of the disaster that greeted him.

Surveying the crowd around the cart, he put frost in his voice. "I stipulated three, and myself."

Cedric, still riding high on the glory of leading this party into the hills, waved away the comment. "But you weren't serious, or at least not accurate. We require bearers for the provisions, and a cartographer to map our route. I asked Corporal Doonan here to come along as a guard. We have no idea what threats might assault us."

"Making, I believe, a total of fifteen plus myself?"

Beside him, Leo maintained a straight face but clearly enjoyed the ludicrous situation.

Ester stood apart, watching the scene. He sensed irritation; she wasn't a woman who suffered fools or enjoyed outlandish displays. Across the clearing from her, a woman wearing layers of frothy skirts attached herself to Cedric and seemed likely to devour him in kisses. Gauvain turned away in disgust.

"Your opinion?" he asked Leo in an undertone.

"They are foolish. They don't understand the nature of the spell on the hills."

"Or they do, and believe it does not apply to them. What is your advice?"

Leo looked over the disorganized mass of humanity. "I take it as given that Cedric will not be able to carry provisions for twelve days. The others..." He shrugged. "Weaklings, although the woman's wiry appearance suggests a lifetime of manual labor. They may be correct about the need for bearers. The cartographer is extraneous."

"And considering the temperament of the hills, useless. I swear the trail changes each time someone ventures along it. From my earlier crossing, I retained no memory of the place I met Willow last year."

"Which was many years ago," Leo said. "It's possible you have forgotten."

Gauvain's mouth twitched; Leo was the only one of his circle of acquaintances who dared contradict him, now that Willow was gone, and even from him the suggestion came hard. He never forgot anything. Ever.

Leo continued. "The guard – will he be of any use at all?"

"No." Gauvain didn't elaborate, but suspected that any challenge they faced would overwhelm the young man in his fancy uniform who stood uneasily with his mother and a bevy of giggling women at the edge of the crowd. "Better a decent hunter. We shall undoubtedly need to provide our own meat."

"How do you propose to reduce the numbers, sir?"

"The manipulation and control of groups of people is a skill worth acquiring, as you yourself know. It is a subject to which I have given some study."

Leo waited.

"I propose," Gauvain said slowly, "to let them have their way, against my protest. When their plan fails, my ultimate authority is guaranteed. So, three council members, a cartographer, and a guard, with attendant provision bearers. And myself. Sixteen all told."

The old man beside him grinned.

He stood on the cart and clapped his hands. The crowd instantly fell silent.

"Those not participating in the trek through the hills, go. Now."

No one argued. Gauvain had not expected anyone to. There was a brief, last-minute flutter of goodbye hugs, and the wagons cluttering the clearing slowly began to unspool into a line making its way across the dry plain.

Cedric attempted to mount the horse cart with him and Leo. Gauvain brushed him off.

"Gather up your packs and begin the ascent," he announced. "You will have scant time to rest, so be prepared for a challenge. At the top is a boulder offering a fine view. We will reconvene there and discuss how we go forward." By which he meant, he would inform them of the ways they would organize themselves, camp, eat, all practicalities he had reviewed with Leo over the last two days. "Move!" he snapped, as if they were recalcitrant sheep – which they might as well be, he reflected as he watched Cedric and Lac eye their small day packs, no doubt crammed with delicacies to ease the weariness of travel. They hoisted them onto their backs and set foot on the trail, following Ester who had already begun the ascent.

The *steep* ascent. Gauvain gave a half smile of satisfaction. When the hills turned them around and dumped them back in this clearing, it would be all the sweeter for the exertion.

"Take care of things here," he said to Leo. "I expect to return within three or four days. After that, we'll begin planning the serious trek."

"Yes, Master."

Leo gave the lie to his humble words with the twinkle in his eye.

Gauvain swung off the horse cart, donned his own properly provisioned pack, and followed the cartographer into the hills.

By the end of the second day, the entire group battled a sense of being hopelessly lost and a long way from anything familiar. The hills, with their misty valleys and barren, forbidding peaks, oppressed them. Exacerbating the uneasiness, two men had wandered off with no one noticing until they reached a stopping point. Dissension raged, whether to retrace their footsteps and find the missing men or forge onward. Confusion gripped them; how could anyone become separated from the group when there were no cross-trails? The remaining members of the party sank into nonstop grumbling about the rough track, miserable weather, fatigue, sore muscles, and blisters, fueled, Gauvain speculated, by fear. The hills offered them no welcome, no points of reference, and even he felt a chill at times. They would have fared better to bring along a healer than a cartographer. The trail wove constantly, unlike the generally straight thoroughfares of Borgonne, and the poor man struggled to record sufficient notes and graphs to map the way. Based solely on the sun, Gauvain could see that they spent far less time going west than in the other three directions.

He'd been confident of the expedition's fate, however, from the moment they failed to pass any of the landmarks from his excursion to restore Willow's friend. The boulder still guarded the entrance to the hills, but the ravine and the clearing where they had nursed Bryar were gone.

He scoffed privately and remained quiet publicly. He'd warned the fools, after all, and was perfectly capable of tending to his own blisters.

So to him it came as no surprise when they rounded a peak, looked out at the valley to the east, and recognized it as home.

"What the—?"

"By the Creator, I don't believe this."

"We've been on the wrong trail."

To a person, they turned on him. He took a moment to make himself comfortable, leaning against an expanse of rock escarpment, and said, challenging them, "Did you see an intersection? Any place where we could have made a false turn?"

In the lee of the scarp, the path widened into a small meadow. The party as one dropped their packs and themselves onto the grass.

Ester settled cross-legged, her back to the rock, her quick eyes missing nothing. A tiny smile played around her mouth. She also had known where they would end up. Gauvain was sure of it.

"You bastard," Lac growled. "You knew all along, didn't you?"

"That the hills take us where they want us to go? No, I wasn't certain, but I suspected. The spell dictates that only Mages can cross successfully. From the experience of our friends in the Midland, I concluded that one or two others could manage, under the aegis of a Mage."

He waited until the grumbling died down, then added, "I did say three, besides myself. If you're seeking a scapegoat, I suggest you remember who ballooned this party to sixteen."

Eyes turned to Cedric, who was bright red from exertion but managed to darken the shade slightly. "You never said there was a magical limit," he blustered.

"I shouldn't need to. You asked me to undertake this journey. I stated my terms. You dared to defy them. Our best – our only – option now is to continue forward until we reach the trail to the Orlan valley. I will notify Leo of our arrival."

And so the heroes return, defeated by the hills.

Gauvain turned from them, shouldered his pack, and struck out along the track to Borgonne to the tune of groans and fervent expressions of discontent. For himself, he kept his thoughts firmly on getting back to the black tower, his home, and turning mundane tasks over to someone else.

❖

For all Gauvain's insouciance in the face of the failed mission, he wasn't pleased to have wasted three days. The time had been instructional, yes, and had undoubtedly cemented his position as the eventual leader of any attempt on the hills that stood a chance of success. But a waste nonetheless.

He commented on this to Leo as the elderly servant served his meal that evening. Earlier, Leo had filled him in on the doings of the town, including the mysterious appearance of two men from the expedition. "Out of the blue, with no explanation for how they returned to the starting point."

"Not a surprise. Good news, though."

Now, as Leo shuffled the serving dishes, Gauvain said, "The question remains, which of the fools best deserve a chance to broach the hills? Unfortunately, I cannot predict the maximum possible. And I admit that provisioning might be a challenge, unless we number a hunter among us."

"Take the lady Ester, someone skilled at both hunting and diplomacy, and yourself. And Cedric, if you absolutely must." Leo turned to the door.

"A tall order. Sit down and share a glass of wine. I value your counsel."

With no trace of subservience, Leo nodded, poured a second goblet from the bottle on the side table, then sat in the chair that had been Willow's. This was a ritual rarely enacted but not unfamiliar; the two men shared a history that transcended their current roles.

"By choice," Gauvain continued around bites of succulent game bird, "I would take you. But I recognize the impossibility."

"Thirty years ago, I could have been your eyes-and-ears as well as your hunter," Leo responded. "As I have done numerous times in the past. But we both know that's impossible now." He raised his goblet and inhaled the fruity aroma of the red wine. "Good."

Gauvain nodded. "Order another crate, would you? While we can still get this vintage. And in the meantime, tell me... politically, do I dare exclude Cedric? The man's a buffoon, but he is head of Orlan council, and that makes him the most powerful layman in Borgonne."

"And a poor leader," Leo said with acerbity. "He glorifies himself, but has no clue how to set his policies in action or inspire devotion, assuming he gives any consideration at all to the good of Borgonne,"

"True. But?"

"I wonder if he'll be willing to try again, after what he's been through. He looked rough when he came off the trail. And ready to blame anybody but himself for it."

Gauvain laughed. "He did, didn't he? We agree about Ester, though?"

"She is a fine woman. From her appearance, raised with simple values. Hard working, and sees things clearly. Yes, I agree."

The level of the wine in both goblets fell steadily, but when Gauvain suggested a refill with a gesture, Leo declined. "My old head becomes muddled, not like in the days of our adventuring. And I still have work tonight."

"As do I, and thank you for the reminder. So, how best to approach presenting our reconstituted party to the council?"

By the time the goblets were empty, the two men had formulated a plan.

Chapter 5

It soon became apparent to Cedric that a showdown was inevitable. That blasted Gauvain made too many assumptions about his own importance, puffing himself up just because he could compel objects to fly across the room, or so the common people said. All higgledy-puffery, as far as Cedric was concerned, and scarcely an adequate qualification for leading an expedition. His role could be defined by four words: make the hills behave.

Cedric himself knew he commanded the moral high ground, despite having returned to Orlan exhausted, hungry, with aching back and blistered feet. That day, in the face of incredulous, contemptuous stares from the populace, which hadn't expected to see them for three nine-days at a minimum, he had cursed the demands of leadership.

His wife had failed to be suitably sympathetic to his complaints.

So it was with artificial courage, in the form of sampling a marvelous apple brandy he kept tucked in a drawer of his desk in his mayoral chambers, that he faced Gauvain two days after their return.

"Our delegation will consist of three, besides me," Gauvain said. "And one must be a hunter, or we're likely to starve. It's obvious that even the most fit of us cannot carry twelve days' provisions."

"Insufficient to drive home our point," Cedric riposted. The Mage had no political savvy at all. "A show of strength is required. We can't expect these Midlanders to be sympathetic. No doubt they'll seize any opportunity to take advantage of our current situation. Any man would."

"Not necessarily. But the fact remains that there are practical, incontrovertible limits."

"Unless we find another Mage or two."

Cedric felt inordinately proud as he waited for the idea to sink into his rival's mind. Like a revelation, it had appeared in his head the night before. The solution to their problems; he'd barely slept, anticipating the moment he revealed his own superior strategy.

Gauvain, however, took his suggestion in stride. "Naturally, the possibility had occurred to me. With Duncan dead, though, there is no Mage of any power within two or three days' hard travel from Orlan."

"Ah, but my good man, that may not matter. What about those apprentices of yours? And there are probably others in or near here with a touch of this purported Entrée you claim. We simply round them up and use them to form our party."

Gauvain barked a laugh. "You're willing to gamble the success of this expedition on a gaggle of untrained and undisciplined children? After last time? Foolish, Cedric."

"Come on, man. We're at a crisis. There's no time to waste, and it's vital we present an imposing argument to the Midland."

"And how soon do you expect to leave on this next venture? And whom did you wish to participate this time?"

"Myself, of course. Lac has expressed a wish never to set foot in the hills again, but I suppose we must include that uncouth Ester."

"A cartographer is useless," Gauvain said. "I doubt anyone ever traverses the hills on the same path. They take you where they choose, and woe betide you if they don't choose to release you."

Cedric went light-headed at the image and hoped Gauvain couldn't see the blood drain from his face. To cover his momentary lapse, he flew into greater animation. "With more mage types along, we could even expand the size of the party. Truly impress them. Take a burgher or two. Solid businessmen to convince them that trade with us would be beneficial. And perhaps several guards, who might double as hunters..." He let his diatribe fade out as he lapsed into a vision of a glorious invading force, all power and sashes of office, arriving at whatever kind of capital city the backwards Midland provided.

Gauvain laughed. "Nothing like that will matter in the least to these people. There isn't even a central government. And the first place we'll encounter will be their Motherhouse, where they train their Mages – Weavers, they call them. Absolutely no pomp, no overt recognition. The best you can hope for is a rustic meal involving lentils and a chat with someone on their council. Excellent pastries, as I recall."

Somewhat deflated, Cedric said, "So where do we go from here?"

"I will take your idea into consideration and present you with a plan within a day. As you know, the weather imposes its own deadlines." He glanced at the window behind Cedric, where the late spring sun beat down on the barren fields. "We agree on little, but on one point we are in complete accord. We must acquire provisions for Borgonne. However, be sure you understand my terms. No dissention, and no disobedience this time."

Gauvain stood and left the room without further words. Cedric sank back in his chair, fingering his badge of office resting against his ample middle and feeling, overall, pleased. For once, the bastard Mage had listened to him.

"Plan B," Gauvain said to Leo when he returned to the tower. "Not the best, but the idiot had already thought of adding a Mage or two. I will speak to Amalie and Reed. They show the most promise. Then you and I can finalize the participants over dinner this evening."

"As you wish, Master."

The men's eyes met. And they both laughed.

Gauvain informed Amalie and Reed of their new roles at the end of class, and told them to report to his study following lunch. They were sufficiently impressed by the gravity of their assignment, he noted. The girl, especially, had proved to be a refreshing change from the normal run of apprentices into whose heads he attempted to pound some concept of how to manipulate weaves formed from Auric energies. Mostly they ended up as clueless as they started, fit only to be dispatched back to their villages.

Not for the first time, he wondered if there might be a better use for failed Mages. A system similar to the practice in the Midland, training them in healing arts, for instance. Ruminations best saved for another day. Right now, he needed to assure that Amalie and Reed would be solid. Not inclined to play silly games with their powers while they traversed the hills.

Neither had been allowed to enter his study before, and both seemed awed if not cowed by its formality.

"You will not speak with others in the party. You will not indulge in ridiculous antics involving Magelight. Your presence is solely due to the strength of your Entrée, not for any skill you might show in manipulation. You are apprentices still. Are we clear on that?"

"Yes, sir," Reed managed. He seemed to be choking on his breath. Fool boy was frightened.

"Do we get a choice?" Amalie asked. Gauvain noted that she did not address him as 'sir'.

"You do. But this is an unprecedented opportunity. I advise you not to take it lightly. Have you some objection?"

"No, but..." The girl hesitated and turned bright red. "You said you leave in two days. But in four days..." If possible the girl's face grew redder.

"Some earthshaking event happens in four days? I seem to have failed to note it on my calendar."

She heard the sarcasm and looked down at her hands. "It's just that I suffer from cramping. Walking all day..."

Her courses. No wonder he resisted taking girls to be apprentices. The mystery of women and their procreative abilities struck him as far more daunting than anything the Aura revealed to him.

"I'm told there are remedies."

"Yes, but sometimes I can't... they aren't enough."

Sustainer, give him strength.

"This – problem of yours. How long does it last?"

"A day, when it happens. Perhaps with the walking... I just don't know." She visibly marshaled courage, which Gauvain had to admire, and met his eye. "I don't want to be the one to delay your mission."

"No, I daresay you don't."

He extracted a sheet of paper from his desk and scribbled a note. "Take this to Ester Sauvage. She sits on council and will be a member of the delegation. Resolve the matter between you. This is no concern of mine."

"Thank you, sir." Amalie clutched the paper.

"Now, go, both of you. Speak to Leo in the kitchen; he will provide you with a provision list."

The children dismissed, Gauvain resumed his work, attempting to disentangle a particularly intriguing weave he had found in one of his ancient scrolls. He had determined that it related somehow to the spells on the hills, but its ultimate purpose eluded him, even after months of study and experiment. A suitable challenge for a Mage of his talents, he thought as he bent over his diagrams. With the chain of command established, the minutiae of organizing expeditions were best left to others, those with a taste for the mundane.

Quinn looked up, shaking off the remnants of a weave. She'd been deep in the Aura, walking a template as if she were tracking a ground animal. An unfamiliar, desert-like part of their world had come alive around her, silent beyond the sound of wind pushing sand and the rustling of dry grasses; she was glad to return to the normalcy of the Motherhouse. She grounded herself, then attuned her senses eastward. "A disruption," she said after a minute, "and this time they're penetrating the hills. Are you sensing it, too?"

Across from her place at the table in the Scribes' workroom, Arwen sighed. "I feared as much. How many?"

Quinn shook her head. "Definitely more than three. That's the most we've ever tracked. But I have no point of reference."

"Let's go for a walk. I need a break."

"To the river? It should be cooler there."

Outside, the day had progressed from hot to sweltering. Quinn wasn't wild about subjecting herself to the discomfort of the late morning sun; the thick stone walls of the Motherhouse buildings provided a built-in defense against temperature extremes. Numerous people in the course of her life had informed her that she must love the sun, with her dark skin, but they were so wrong. It had never bothered her as a child, but by now, acclimated as she was to the northern Midland, she'd probably die of heat prostration back home in Colgate.

As they exited the Scribes' lodge, she commented, "There's something you haven't told me. You're more concerned than you should be."

"Not really." Arwen squinted in the sudden blinding light and turned them left, toward the path leading to the manic river. "This isn't a benign visit, and theirs isn't the kindest society. I can't predict the outcome."

"At least the man called Duncan is no longer a factor. Surely we can handle Gauvain."

She'd first met Arwen, then tasked with the discipline of apprentices, when she was almost fourteen years old. Now, as senior Scribes and council members, they seemed to be constantly in and out of each other's pockets. She was uniquely positioned to catch telltale signs of unease in the older woman, and something about Arwen's demeanor suggested she wasn't at all confident about handling Gauvain. From Willow's description, he intrigued her. Like her, he devoted his life to researching the Aura, although for different ends.

Quinn looked forward to meeting him.

Chapter 6

Gauvain endured only the expected physical challenges of aching feet, inadequate food, and dirt as they made their way through the hills. His much reduced band of eight included two members of council, one hopelessly out of shape; the two apprentices, who treated the entire voyage as a lark; one guard who doubled as a hunter; and two bearers.

That fool Cedric was determined to install himself as leader of their expedition, the person designated to make their case to the powers that be, and no doubt see his name glorified by singlehandedly resolving the drought problem in Borgonne. This despite his inability to maintain the pace, which seven days' walking had done nothing to improve. No amount of explaining the actual political structure, or lack thereof, in the Midland dissuaded him, nor did the blatant fact that the man would be helpless as a newborn out here in the hills without the others' support.

"Sir?" Amalie showed proper respect, although he frequently doubted her sincerity.

"Yes?"

"His Excellency says to tell you he believes it's time to stop for the midday meal. And Zanthan's blister is no better. He's struggling to keep up."

Gauvain, who had been covering ground and pulling the others along in his wake, reluctantly drew to a halt, suppressing a smile at Amalie's determined use of the absurd moniker Cedric favored. "I think not," he said in answer to her first statement. "It's still at least an hour until noontide."

"The mayor's legs bother him, sir. Shin splints, unless I miss my guess."

The sound that escaped Gauvain was less a sigh than a snort of exasperation. "Have you any remedy that might enable his legs to carry him a few more leagues? I for one am ready to be out of these hills."

Although ethereally beautiful, they felt... off. A wrongness, like magic gone astray, unable to find a master. Just yesterday the bearer Zanthan had reported that he'd been stalked as he assisted with the hunt for their evening sustenance. Nobody saw or heard anything, but Zanthan hadn't been able to shake the feeling of being watched, and not in a friendly way.

If nothing else, Gauvain was more than ready for a hot bath and clean clothes.

"No, sir. This is about conditioning, not medicinals. He refuses to stretch. The blister I can deal with, but it would require a few minutes."

"You recommend that we stop early, I take it?"

The girl shrugged. "I don't want to. But given the situation..."

They both looked back. Their contingent had strung out to the point that the ones lagging could not be seen around the last bend. Only Ester, the apprentices, and the hunter matched his pace. That wasn't good. Failure to keep up could lead to the same result as on their first foray, with members of the party disappearing along trails that didn't exist, and no way to locate them.

They ought to match his pace, or so he argued with himself. The leader shouldn't have to slow down.

Gauvain was out of patience with the whole lot of them. The sooner they reached the Motherhouse, the better.

"Very well. Pass the word. We'll stop as soon as we've forded the stream ahead." He could see what appeared to be a pleasant enough grassy area alongside the water.

Amalie flashed him a grin. "Will do." The girl headed back toward the end of the line.

"And in future, stay with the stragglers," he shouted to her. "We need someone with Entrée to protect them."

"Reed can do it," she shouted back.

Gauvain plodded on, dreading lunch. The worst aspect of this whole venture, in his opinion, was the convivial gatherings at mealtimes.

Three more days. Or maybe five, because they couldn't possibly be traveling as quickly as Willow and her companions had. An interminable five days of plummeting morale, escalating minor health issues, and his nerves frayed to snapping, and they'd be out of the hills. The Motherhouse, for all its cold, imposing stone buildings and isolation, had never sounded so welcome.

Removing his boots to wade across the ford, he wondered if they knew of his party's approach, and just how welcoming they would prove to be.

Once they emerged from the hills, the remainder of the walk involved skirting a massif towering over the valley that was home to the Weavers' Motherhouse. Being to the south of them, the massif, an odd, irregular formation unconnected with any other outcropping, cut out the sun for part of the day. Despite this, the spirits of Gauvain's party buoyed as they neared the end of their journey, leaving the hills behind, and after spending the final two days walking through a lush, green forest without the taint of the spells, his ragged group was in a festive mood when they came to the cross trail that led to their destination.

Years ago, in a wild and poorly planned escapade, he and Duncan had escaped their training to explore this other, unknown land. He wondered how many of the Weavers he'd met then would still be here, and if he'd recognize them – or they him. Willow, when she graced his dining room, obviously knew Arwen and Ezra.

Cedric, who had planted himself at the head of the expedition and refused to budge, however much his pace slowed them, called a halt at the junction. They shucked packs and used some of their water stores to wash faces and hands. Barely sufficient, in Gauvain's estimation, and a waste of time. No doubt he smelled as bad as the rest of them, but they had been on the trail for fourteen days, after all. To his disgust, Cedric fished his sash and badge of office from the bottom of his pack and placed them across his ample girth. Gauvain held out only the faintest hope that he could manage not to make a fool of himself and, by extension, the entire party.

Then they turned left and struck out on the four-hour exertion that carried them to decent food, hot water, and a possible amelioration for their looming food shortage.

From her perch halfway up the western edge of the amphitheater slope, where she was unwinding in the shade of a tree before supper, Quinn watched as an oddly assorted group of people straggled from the trail leading to Ezra's compound and stopped in front of the Centra. Activity on the green slowed as everyone's focus turned to the newcomers. A woman, five men, two teenagers, disheveled and one of them with a limp.

Quinn settled down to enjoy the show.

The limping man, a round popinjay dressed in tattered finery and wearing some kind of emblem on a chain, appeared to lead the group. He looked around as if trying to decide where best to announce their arrival. Then, after a whispered consultation with the man behind him, tall, dark, and aristocratic even in filthy garb, he made for the Centra's door.

That door opened and Arwen stepped out. She wore a long skirt with her tunic, despite the heat, and had donned both her Scribe's sash and the other one, thinner and of a pale blue with a white border, that fitted over it and marked her as head of council.

The popinjay directed his tottering steps toward her, looking for all the world as if he was preparing to welcome them all to his court. Bryar should be here to see this; the scene unfolding below her could fuel his songs for a year.

Arwen ignored the round man completely, her eyes fixed on the tall one behind him.

"Gauvain. You made it."

Their hands joined. Quinn left her place on the slope and headed downhill. This was too good to miss.

"After some travail, yes. How good to see you again, Arwen." Their words floated on the still air. So this was Willow's Gauvain. His voice, in the baritone range, sent a shiver up Quinn's spine. A little too resonant, a little too commanding, even in the neutral exchange taking place below her.

"And you. You've changed little."

He smiled. "If only that were so. Age encroaches on all of us, but you have only improved. You were gangly back then."

"And with terrible manners. You must be exhausted." Her gaze encompassed the group, including the man fingering his chain and shooting irritated looks at Gauvain. He sputtered and strutted, trying to insinuate himself into the conversation. They both ignored him.

"As you might expect, we are tired, filthy, and hungry. I assume you expected us."

"Naturally," Arwen said, not mentioning that they had been uncertain about the size of the delegation or when they would arrive until after they cleared the hills.

So, Quinn thought, the dominance game begins.

More interesting, however, was that Arwen and Gauvain still held hands.

By now most of the council had assembled, watching with varying degrees of amazement, amusement, and curiosity as the newcomers shuffled about, waiting for whatever came next.

Gauvain released Arwen and turned to face his group. "This is Arwen, who heads the Weavers' council." He quickly named his companions.

"Rooms await you in the guest lodge," Arwen said smoothly. "You remember where that is?"

"Of course."

Arwen clapped her hands, and a messenger kid appeared. "Lute here will see to checking you in with the registrar and show you the amenities. Supper will be served in an hour, but I'm sure you will feel more comfortable if you wash first."

Quinn wrinkled her nose. The whole dining hall would feel more comfortable, she wagered.

"You will find fresh tunics in your rooms. These will carry you over until we can clean your own garments for you. After supper, I suggest we meet, however briefly."

The rotund man elbowed Gauvain to the side and planted himself in front of Arwen. "Madam, I am the head of Orlan council and the leader—"

"Happy to meet you." Arwen turned away as one of the teenagers, about the same age as Willow's daughter Romarin, stepped forward.

"Ma'am?" she said. "Is there a Healer available? We've heard about your Healers. There are several injuries. Minor, but could become worse if not seen to."

"Certainly. Your name again?" Arwen looked at the girl with interest.

"Amalie, ma'am."

"Thank you for alerting me, Amalie. I will arrange for a Healer to meet you in the common room at the guest lodge. Perhaps you could inform the registrar of your party's needs?"

"Happy to. Can I watch?" Amalie blurted.

"As long as none of the participants objects." The girl darted away. Arwen nodded, as if confirming something she had sensed. "One of yours?" she asked Gauvain.

"Yes. She's done well on this trek. She's tended to all manner of scrapes and blisters." Gauvain's stance indicated his willingness to take credit for the young woman's accomplishments.

Arwen ended the impromptu meeting, letting her gaze pause on the blustering man in the sash and chain but giving him no particular acknowledgment. "Join me for supper?" she asked Gauvain.

"With pleasure."

With a final nod, Arwen turned to Daren, who represented the Healers' guild on council. They spoke briefly, then the group broke up, the newcomers following Lute to the guest lodge, Daren setting off to deputize a Healer.

Quinn grinned as she joined the remaining councillors trickling into the Centra, assuming Arwen would want to meet with them before the meal. Neatly done. Arwen had, without pulling rank, established herself and Gauvain in command of this encounter and set up a preliminary channel to gain information. She was more than a Scribe; she was a master diplomat as well.

Arwen stood at the table in the conference room, eyeing her council. "Initial opinions?" she asked.

Cynth from Healers, Fergus from Bards, and Quinn were present; Daren would join them as soon as the newcomers were seen to. Cynth was a reserved woman, observing more than participating; as expected, she looked at Fergus, then at Quinn.

Fergus grinned. "You fair skewered them, Arwen," he said. Although learned and capable, Fergus tended to see the humor in situations, a trait frequently needed on council these days. "That strutting little Cedric, he fancies himself their leader. It's obvious Gauvain's the power, but the woman, Ester... I liked the look of her. As for the rest, we'll make them comfortable. They're extras."

"The young people may not be," Arwen said. "The girl especially. There's powerful Entrée there, and with an interest in Healing. Is there any chance Willow will be coming up to the Motherhouse this summer?" she asked Quinn.

"Not as far as I know. She's... nesting?"

"She's in love, and building a relationship with Joss, who has his own adjustments to make." Arwen's voice was momentarily gentle, as if Quinn and Willow were still her students. "But the girl... I believe she has the makings of a Healer, which is training she won't get in Borgonne. They don't distinguish affinities the way we do."

Daren entered the conference room in time to hear the last remarks. "I agree," he said. "She's thirsting for knowledge. The lad, Reed, I'm less sure about. He may well be suited to their teachings. A Mage, interested in power workings."

"Which, for obvious reasons, I prefer not to encourage." Arwen twitched her long skirt and sat. Cynth followed suit, then Fergus; Quinn and Daren remained standing, Quinn fighting the urge to pace. "So. Strategies for this evening?"

"Casual," Fergus said.

"Cedric might think otherwise." Arwen smiled; she had noticed the man's absurdity, for all that her attention had appeared focused on Gauvain.

"Oh, my dear," Fergus said. "You can shut him down, surely. Although you'll have to give him his due tomorrow."

"When we should be much more formal," Quinn put in. "Keep things controlled. Do we expect any problems? Would they dare exert force through the Aura?"

"As a means to dominate? It's only Gauvain and the children," Daren said. "The kids should be excused from any formal talks, as should the other men. We limit participation to Gauvain, Cedric, and Ester. They're the ones with the temporal power."

"Let's suggest the men go to the village," Cynth said. "They may be more comfortable there and find others with their interests."

Quinn grinned. "And the young people will find their own contemporaries. I expect all the apprentices from both sides of the hills are curious."

"And then we learn their true intent for being here." Arwen eyed them all. "I will want all of you present, unless something truly urgent comes up. We will keep tomorrow's initial contact as short as possible, then meet in camera after it. I refuse to be pressured or rushed. Assuming they are here about their drought, the problem won't be solved in a day."

The bell rang in the dining hall. "Shall we dine with them?" Fergus, ever the social one, asked.

"By all means. Let's keep things convivial as long as we can. but listen for undercurrents. There's a political agenda that may threaten us, and the sooner we grasp it, the better."

Chapter 7

Quinn was among the first to arrive in the conference room. She'd always been an early riser, and a combination of curiosity and trepidation kept her morning ritual to a minimum.

Despite Arwen's desire for brevity, this meeting was likely to stretch through the morning. She fervently hoped someone had arranged for caff.

By the power of air, let us play this well. Let the resolution be to the benefit of all.

With everyone assembled, the Weavers' council faced the delegation from Borgonne revealing polite curiosity, but little else, as they waited for Cedric, Ester, and Gauvain to resolve their precedence issues and begin.

In the end, the popinjay won. Gauvain leaned back with a shrug, the sort of gesture and posture Quinn had expected from Willow's descriptions of the man. Cedric looked as if he regretted not being seated in Arwen's chair at the head of the table, but made the best of it by positioning himself at her right hand. He cleared his throat.

Across from Quinn, Ester rolled her eyes.

"You may not be fully aware of the important place Borgonne, and its capital city Orlan, play in our world," Cedric began. "Not only is Orlan a primary economic driver, but our lands, more extensive I'm told than those of the Midland, yield well. We support an active industrial zone..."

Quinn let the list of Borgonne's wonders fade. She knew enough, from Willow's and Kiril's descriptions, to be certain that however prosperous, it was no place for her. Her face schooled to politeness, she turned her inner attention to a weave she'd been working on that might – *might* – take them another few years back into the Aura. There was a flaw in it; she longed for the peace to explore it further.

She snapped alert when Cedric delivered what he clearly considered the punch line of his diatribe. "Now, however, we have a challenge, which is largely outside our control. By sharing the situation with you, we hope to offer a cautionary tale, lest the same thing occur here."

Gauvain sat upright, his mouth drawn taut. Willow had said he didn't deal well with frustration. "By the Sustainer, Cedric. Borgonne faces a catastrophic drought, and probable famine. We need help. Do we really have to say more?"

"Is it that bad?" Arwen asked quietly. "We see that the weather patterns have changed. But we had little grasp of the effect on Borgonne."

"I'm sure, if we brought our considerable resources to bear, it's nothing we couldn't manage," Cedric began.

Gauvain gave a short, hard laugh. "We don't have a clue what to do. We're here for temporary supplies, and in the longer term to explore the possibility of establishing a trade route. That's it, plain and simple."

"Not so simple," Fergus said. "Not given the spells on the hills, which we now know are considerably more vicious than we ever imagined."

"And what have you to trade that we require?" Arwen surveyed them. "Trade, to be successful, implies that each party possesses something the other wants. I am not saying we won't help you on a short-term basis, if the other problems can be solved. A trade route is another matter entirely."

The room was silent. A knock sounded at the door, and a delegation from the dining hall brought in caff, tisanes, and cake. Well timed, Quinn thought. Because this promises to be an interesting discussion indeed.

Later, Quinn paused at the door of the Scribes' lodge. A group of apprentices had gathered nearby. As expected, Amalie and Reed were in the middle of the gathering. Young voices tumbled over one another as everyone clamored to meet the strangers.

But what had stopped her was Amalie's voice, ascending into a shriek. "You're kidding. Willow's your *mother*?"

"Yeah," said a male voice still in the process of breaking. "And not only that, her dad's the one who wounded your evil Mage Duncan before the other guy could kill him - and brought the power cell back."

"Whaddaya mean, killed?" the boy Reed asked. "He died down in the slums. They say it was a prostitute deal gone bad."

"What's a slum?"

"What's a prostitute?"

Reed turned red but didn't answer.

"You've got it wrong. There was a pitched battle, and Bryar fought heroically but suffered a grievous wound." The boy's words had unintentionally fallen into the cadence of an epic; a future Bard, that one. "But then Kiril came to his rescue, and slashed Gauvain, and the two of them took the cell, and—"

"And we don't know the truth of any of it." Quinn recognized the voice of one of the older apprentices, calming things down.

"I went to see Gauvain a few days later," Amalie said. "He *summoned* me for a review, and we met in the drawing room. But I peeked in the study. It was a total shambles."

"And *something* slashed his face," Reed added.

"I'm telling you," the breaking-voiced apprentice said. "A noble battle, a fight to the death, in the study."

"Oh, wow." That was Amalie again. Quinn shifted to get a better view. The two girls, Amalie and Willow's daughter Romarin, stood near the path to the apprentices' classroom building. Amalie was tall, slender, and wide-eyed, unlike Mari, also tall but with Bryar's sturdy constitution.

"You are so totally lucky." Amalie had regained control of her voice but not of her excitement. Quinn fought a chuckle. Here stood a young woman who had just braved the hills, fourteen days of privation, and she'd become a teenager again.

Mari grinned. "Yeah, most of the time. They're pretty neat, for parents. I guess."

The future Bard groaned. "Come on, Mari. One of the finest performers out there for a dad? And a warrior as well? Oh, man," the boy groaned. "Imagine going on a quest, and fighting, and enduring hardships, and—"

"He'd rather not have," Mari said. "He can't play chitarre anymore, and... well, I talked to Tai a little. Dad's not very happy how it all worked out."

"That guy Duncan was, like, slimy," Reed said. "When he lectured our class, he told us all about how important he is – was, I mean – and how he couldn't tell us his secrets. Which means he didn't teach us anything. And he hit on Amalie. I'd say your dad, or whoever killed him, did us a favor."

Amalie shrugged; clearly Duncan was old news. "But your mom's awesome, even before her powers came back. I bet she's the best Healer in the Midland."

Mari pursed her lips, thinking. "She works hard. Wait till you meet Dal, though."

Amalie giggled. "And Gauvain's, like, totally hot for her."

"No joke?" the broken-voiced boy said. "And did they...?"

"Nah. At least I don't think so. She's classy."

Amalie hadn't finished. The group began to break up with the call to classes, but she stuck with Mari. "And you can study to be a Healer, too. We don't get any training like that. I'm totally jealous."

"Come into class with us," Mari, always open-hearted, offered. "Both of you. Beatris probably won't mind. As long as you're here, you may as well learn what you can."

Which wouldn't be much in the realm of Healing, Quinn speculated. Mari's future lay with the Healers' guild, but specialized training was still several years away. Now the apprentices in her age group worked together, learning basics from each of the three disciplines. Still, it was entirely possible that the herbal learning at this level might prove more than Amalie had been exposed to.

The two girls linked arms as they moved toward the classrooms. "I'd love to," Amalie said. "My dad's a village healer. Our house always smells of herbs and stuff."

"You should visit the Healers' workroom."

"And just wait till tomorrow," another voice put in. "It's Solstice, so no classes, and there'll be a party you won't believe..."

The girls disappeared, and Quinn continued to the Centra thinking that the friendship, if such it proved to be, might benefit not only Mari and Amalie but all of them.

Kiril remembered last year's Summer Solstice festivities, when he'd been recovering from his injuries in Stanstead. Here at the Motherhouse, the scene wasn't as loud or frenetic, but participation was just as enthusiastic. Foods of all types invited him from trencher tables set up in front of the Centra. The local village, which existed primarily to provide services to the Motherhouse, had come out in force. Across the green, one of the two Bards in residence declaimed a story involving a sword that would prove who was king. Kiril found it tedious; who cared about such nonsense with so many real-world wonders to study? Take his encounter in the hills and its effects. The thing that attacked him wasn't red and didn't breathe fire, but after that, could he be sure dragons were mythological?

Which offered poor consolation. He hadn't bothered trying to explain that his body was no longer his own, there was always something just a little wrong, despite whatever voodoo Quinn worked inside him.

He shuddered.

The apprentices were enjoying the revelry; occasionally one of them called to him, a friendly acknowledgment. Each time he struggled for an appropriate reaction. He knew they considered him Bryar's savior, but being the object of hero worship made him uneasy. By his calculation, they were even; Bryar's intervention had saved him from the lizard, after all. But more than that, every interaction bound him more tightly to this community, where he didn't belong. He was no Weaver. He could almost feel the manacles closing around him.

He called to mind his mission. Pave the way, make this a welcome place for the Terran settlers. But in reality, what could he do? The vast and varied land stretched from the hills west to a purported sea. He had no power base, no communication network, and no means of knowing where the next Terran ship would set down.

If it came. Increasingly he wondered.

Arwen emerged from the Centra and wandered over to him. She had on a long, red tunic. Festivals like Solstice brought out the more colorful outfits, a relief after the year of off-white and brownish undyed linen and wool. She handed him a pasty and asked, "Are you enjoying yourself?"

"Necessary release? Your people work hard. I guess you deserve a break now and then."

"More than that. The Aura promotes fertility and prosperity, and we weave ourselves into its patterns. This type of celebration honors the land, the cycles of seasons."

"You sound like a lecturer."

She laughed. "I am. Introductory Philosophy of the Aura, and advanced Scribes' Practices."

Arwen, laughing? Kiril mostly saw her as chief inquisitor, with Quinn as her faithful acolyte. Given women this powerful, no wonder Northam Corp, back home on Terra, kept them well away from the men.

Activity across the green caught Arwen's eye. "Oh, bother," she said. Kiril followed her gaze and spotted what looked a lot like the first moves of a sexual encounter between a pair of apprentices. "Too soon for those two. I'd better slow things down. We expect these relationships to be conscious decisions, however little fun that sounds."

She drifted out into the sea of people on the green. Thinking he might track down a beer to go with the pasty, Kiril turned the other direction.

And ran smack into a firm, black-clad shoulder.

Gauvain. Even if he hadn't recognized the man, the scar on his face would have served as a never-to-be-forgotten identifier.

They both stepped back, sizing each other up. In the darkness of the tower, he had been unable to see the man clearly. They were well matched, slim rather than bulky with muscle, and close to the same height. Gauvain was clean shaven, with dark, almost black hair bound at his neck, in contrast to Kiril's short, medium brown hair and small beard. He'd guess Gauvain was at least ten years older, possibly more.

The Bard's tale ended, and a band took over, pounding bass over the amphitheater. Both men moved away from the tables as people flowed around them, seeking food or hurrying to dance.

"I believe we have met," Gauvain said, his expression the same as he might use to address a cockroach. A look tailor-made to dispel any guilt Kiril harbored concerning the still pink scar that cut Gauvain's face from the corner of his left eye to his mouth.

"I recall a confrontation," Kiril said with calibrated disinterest, "and rather a lot of destruction."

"You got your man safely back across the hills, I understand?"

"Yes." He'd been on the verge of taunting Gauvain with the fact of his servant's assistance, but bit his tongue in time. Leo had been invaluable; no point getting him in trouble. "He's not here now. Off with his girlfriend, or so I'm told."

"You are no Mage."

"No."

Gauvain wouldn't have been able to tell, during the battle. The power cell had been unshielded, blocking the man's spooky powers.

"There is something odd about you, however."

Kiril sensed he had gone from being a cockroach to a specimen under a microscope, purely to satisfy Gauvain's curiosity. "Oh, I'm odd, all right. Just ask the others." He gestured in the direction Arwen had disappeared. "What about you, Mage? You're an oddity yourself, from everything I've heard."

"Gauvain, there you are." The pompous little Borgonnian strutted up. "Come on, man. Join Ester and me. Quite a party going on here."

"And I daresay you and Ester will enjoy every minute," Gauvain replied, disdain in his tone. "But kindly spare me your delight." He pointedly turned his back on the shorter man, whom Kiril now saw to be swaying on his feet, thanks no doubt to Midland beer.

Which he really wanted a mug of.

Not too sure what devil seized him, he said to Gauvain, "I was just working my way over to the refreshments. Join me in a beer."

The offer surprised Gauvain as much as it did himself. They turned away together, neither of them paying any further attention to the round little man.

"This was gratuitous, you know," Gauvain said mildly, touching his face, as the two men drifted along the edge of the green toward the beer stall, avoiding the mayhem.

"Yeah. Sorry about that." He had felt vague regret for the slash. Even at the time he'd known Gauvain was unarmed, stunned by the bloodshed in his study, and disabled by the power cell. "Heat of the moment."

And revenge for Bryar.

Gauvain shrugged an elegant shoulder. "The ladies of Orlan call it dashing and offer up all manner of unguents, which of course they would be happy to apply. While I find their fawning tiresome, it is beneficial to maintain a certain mystique."

"You kept Willow there all winter."

Gauvain's eyebrows raised. "Rather, she kept herself. Or the hills did. I could never countenance her crossing them in bad weather."

"Only a fool risks crossing them, period."

Gauvain studied him for a long moment. Kiril made a point of drinking nonchalantly from his mug of beer, as if the man's close stare wasn't in the least unnerving. "That is what I sense in you, a trace of the energy pervading the hills. Would you care to elaborate?"

"No, I wouldn't." Kiril had no intention of discussing his experience with anyone, much less Gauvain, whose presence seemed destined to disrupt the tranquil life of the Motherhouse, like it or not. He'd watched the party's arrival and sensed the underlying tension.

"These festivities do tire me," Gauvain said, turning to stand beside Kiril and gaze at the throng. "I suppose it's necessary for the populace, but why Mages should participate—"

"You're the only Mage here, I believe."

"Weavers, then. A foolish title."

"Seems to me," Kiril drawled, "they use that Aura thing in a whole different way. Maybe you could learn from them."

"Unlikely." Gauvain made a small, dismissive gesture with his hand.

Arrogant bastard.

Arwen interrupted their tête-à-tête, bustling over with a swirl of skirts. "There you are. I trust you're enjoying Solstice?"

Her question wasn't directed to him, so Kiril shut up and watched. Gauvain's face took on an expression he hadn't expected – pleasure at seeing the bossy head of council. He suspected they were old adversaries, ready participants in whatever game they were playing.

"I expect the festivities will preclude anything like a decent night's sleep," Gauvain replied.

"I guess we figure that's your problem. For most people here, sleep's the last thing on their minds. We've canceled classes for the apprentices tomorrow. It's simply not worth it."

"My own apprentices are expected to be abed at a modest hour. They are useless otherwise."

Arwen smiled, as if he had just confirmed an important point. "Exactly. But not tonight. Reed's found a young man he seems completely enchanted with, and Amalie and Mari have formed a friendship bond already."

Gauvain's head jerked back at the mention of his apprentice with another boy, but he made no direct comment. "I suppose it will aid their studies in the long run, if they are given a chance to study other cultures' practices."

"You're just as much a stuffed shirt as always," Arwen replied cheerfully. "The adults, on the other hand, will convene midmorning, if that suits you."

"Perfectly, thank you."

Kiril watched the exchange, enjoying himself. Obviously, some sort of relationship existed between these two, but Gauvain was doing all he could to hide it, or at least to control it. Arwen... well, he'd never seen her so close to laughing. While she might be the iron woman of the Motherhouse, today she'd let her guard down.

He left them bickering and crossed the green to the guest lodge. With the party raging, it would be a good time for a leisurely bath, without interruptions.

Chapter 8

Willow watched as Joss tinkered with yet another modification to the odd machine he'd been building, readjusting a metal spoon she recognized from the Motherhouse dining hall. Controlling the whole mess was a knob whittled from a piece of firewood. "Did I tell you we built crystal radios in school?" he asked her. "I must have been about eight. Good thing, or I wouldn't have known where to start."

Among the oddities in the radio were two of her treasures, a clear pointed crystal the length of her palm, and a seashell that swirled around on itself. Some said you could hear things if you listened at the opening of the shell. Joss used it as an amplifier. He'd scrounged a rare piece of metal wire to connect the pieces. The device took up most of the table. *Good thing it's summer*, she thought. *We can eat outside.*

Joss hunched over the machine, tying one connection, fiddling the dial, tying again.

Later they would go down to Hallan to share in the celebration. She had spent the morning in her garden, staking the tomatoes, harvesting a few early herbs. Their spicy aroma already filled the room. Willow refused to regret being indoors. Joss loved being out in nature even more than she did, and she loved him. He believed this contraption was important enough to sacrifice part of the gorgeous day to it.

But on Summer Solstice?

"Here we go again," he said. As he had done a hundred times that spring, he connected two wires, held the shell up to his ear, and waited, slowly moving a knob She, for her part, watched him.

The winter had transformed Joss. He had matured from the voyager through space who had survived untold hardships, as well as the wounds to his body from the crash landing. Training at the Motherhouse with Arwen, Dal, and Quinn, he had become – been restored to – a man confident of his place in his world. He relished life in Hallan and spent his days in the fields and barns, learning from her and others about care and treatments for the animals.

Willow smiled. According to him, the animals themselves told him as much as any person could. An animal whisperer understood the minds of the beasts he worked with. Even the goats that hung around the cabin adored him.

Joss jerked and sat up straighter. He paused, then watched his hand turning the knob slowly back and forth, although his focus was far away. It was hard to tell in the sharply contrasting light, all dark shadows except where the midsummer sun poured in through the door and window, but she thought he paled.

After a minute he said, "Come over here."

He scooted off his chair to allow her to sit and pressed the shell to her ear. Again he moved the knob. After a brief pause, the shell filled with an odd, indeterminate noise, much like waves on the shore, as she remembered from her childhood when the entire hamlet made the one-day trek to the ocean.

She lowered the shell to the table. "What is it?" she whispered.

"Them."

Joss disconnected his contraption and led them both outside, where they settled on the little hillock across from the cabin, a goat lying contentedly beside him. "That thing's not powerful enough to pick up words. But it's the first time we've heard any disruption. Until now, there's been nothing. I'd hoped it would stay that way."

She watched him, concerned, as he rubbed the goat between her stubby horns. "They're aiming transmissions in our direction, probably trying to contact the pod. They're coming, Willow."

She gazed down the long slope toward Hallan. From this distance, she could barely see the festivities as people milled about the square. Every once in a while the bass vibration of a drum resounded through the valley.

"Makes me wonder why I've bothered." Joss's spare hand, the one he hadn't dedicated to driving the goat into a state of bliss, plucked at the grass. "We're on the verge of a calamity, and I have no way of telling you the scale, what to prepare for. Not much use, is it?"

Willow followed his gaze; he glared at the instrument hidden by the cabin walls. "I'd say it's a help. At least we won't be caught unaware. And it may not even impact us. Suppose they crash, like you did? Or they might settle somewhere else, in Borgonne or... everyone's wondered if there's another land, across the ocean. All my life the rumors have floated around. Maybe they'll end up there."

"You don't know my people." He took her hand in his free one. The goat rested her chin on his thigh; she'd swear the animal almost purred. "If there are lands to explore, they will. If they can conquer them, they'll do it."

"None of this is your fault." She scooted closer and leaned against him. Joss's bulk, his solidity, gave her a blissful sense of being protected, even though he couldn't protect her from this. "You didn't plan it, and you couldn't have stopped it."

He grinned. "What are you doing, pointing out facts?" He abandoned the goat and used both his giant hands to roll her down onto the grass. "I'm the logical one."

"Give it up," she retorted, a smile spreading across her face. "We're both earth clan. And it's Solstice."

"A perfectly logical celestial event."

He loomed above her, the sun catching glints in his dark brown hair, one muscular leg pinning hers. He no longer kept every bit of himself covered, as he had when he'd arrived a year ago. The patterns of life here had taken root. "And the events it spawns are logical, too. Or at least irresistible."

It's challenging to smile and kiss at the same time, she reflected as she guided his mouth down to hers. But she did her best.

Later, after racing him across the lake – he almost won – they walked hand in hand to Hallan. Joss asked, "What do we do now?"

She wanted to joke about teaching him to dance – a lost cause, she already knew – and perhaps soaking in one of Hallan's hot pools, but sensed his thoughts had turned far away from the immediate delights of the day. "We must notify the Motherhouse."

"Go there?"

She nodded. "Something's going on there as well. I'm not strong enough in message transmission to tell what. And I want to see Quinn and Mari. Bryar, too, if he's there."

"You miss them."

"I do." She squeezed his hand. "It's the reality of being a Weaver. We begin training when we're young and it's all a great adventure. And it is, always, but the cost is making friends throughout the Midland you may never meet again. Our teachers identify the ones who have sufficient Entrée to become Weavers but would be miserable with the traveling life. For them, life in a town or hamlet is enough."

"Is it enough for you?"

He'd picked up on her restlessness. She should have expected it.

"Usually. I could strike out west, visit a few hamlets on that route, and be back before winter."

"Or spend more time at the Motherhouse. Have you ever considered teaching there? They say you did a fine job with Romarin."

The whole idea of leaving made her sad, solely because Joss was here. "I think of many things."

"And stay here with me, while the need to travel festers in you." He pulled her closer. "Willow, if you must go, then go. We've survived separation before."

Not yet. She wasn't ready to leave Joss yet. "I suppose the Motherhouse takes priority, whatever else the summer brings."

They'd reached the outskirts of Hallan. Music filled the square, as did strangers in town for the hot springs. A Bard had arrived promising special entertainment, not to mention the extravaganza of meats, fresh vegetables, pastries, and beer awaiting them. The day was perfect, clear and hot. Last Solstice she had been with Bryar, on the banks of the river that flowed by Stanstead. This Solstice felt more real, as if she had come home to her true life.

Because of the man beside her? She smiled.

They plunged into the mix of locals and visitors, ready to celebrate another season.

Chapter 9

What a great way to spend the morning after Solstice.

Quinn knocked on the doorframe of Kiril's quarters in the guest lodge. He hadn't shown up at the healing room for a checkup, and questions were being raised, not least by Arwen.

Most of the complex still slept; the green and dining hall were almost eerily quiet. The air had cooled overnight, leaving behind a heavy dew that sent crystal lights flashing across the amphitheater as the sun struck the grass.

She wasn't there by choice. Someone had to do it, and as usual Arwen chose her.

"Come on in," he called. She pushed open the door and paused on the threshold.

His room was tight and tidy, nothing extraneous or out of place. Kiril stood by his bed, his back to her.

"Going somewhere?"

At her voice, he straightened and turned. He wore no tunic, and his trousers hung low on his hips. Quinn shifted her gaze away.

Forced her gaze away, to be perfectly accurate.

"I like to be prepared. What's up, oh wonder woman?"

"What's up with you? You're supposed to report to the Healers." Quinn leaned against the doorframe, her arms folded.

"So you can work your voodoo on that thing inside me, right? The thing and me, we're getting real cozy."

If putting up with this was the cost of being on council, she might resign. "Dammit, Kiril, just go to the healing room."

"Care to make me?" The words ricocheted between them.

"I could."

"And wouldn't that be fun."

Quinn paused to give the atmosphere time to cool, then said rationally, "Even you can't want the demon loose in the Midland. And oddly, there are one or two people around here who care what happens to you."

"Present company not included." It wasn't clear to Quinn whether he referred to her, to himself, or to both of them. "Let's say I don't take well to being kept tabs on, okay?" He turned back to the clutter of objects beside the pack, a tunic, the thing he called an insignia and the strange box he'd had when he and Joss crash landed. He retrieved a pair of sandals from under the window and added them to the pile.

"If you're so afraid of the healing room," she said, marshaling every bit of sweetness in her, "I can do part of the assessment here. Not all of it, though."

He turned on her. "Did you actually say afraid?"

"Sure sounded like it to me."

Kiril mirrored her stance, arms folded over his chest, defiance in his posture. "You have a nerve."

Exasperated, she crossed the room to stand on the other side of the narrow bed. "You're packing. Where are you going?"

He ignored the question. "If you want me in that healing room of yours, I suggest you send Dal. He's the only one of you spooks I trust."

"Dal's in Stanstead, training their village healer and apothecary. He'll be living there for a year or so."

"Well, damn. That sure puts a cap on the level of civility around here, doesn't it?"

Changing tack, Quinn said, "It's important to know whether we contained that thing or not. It ought to matter to you, because frankly, you don't look all that great. If you plan to take to the roads, shouldn't you make certain you're healthy first?"

Kiril tossed the pack on the floor and flopped on the bed. "Here I am, doctor. Check me over." His grin dared her.

Quinn wasn't one to be intimidated by skinny males with gigantic attitude. "Hold still."

When she placed her hands on his chest, he jumped. He must have expected her to use a Healer's technique, scanning his body without touching. But she wasn't a Healer, and she wasn't sensing for an illness or injury. She was ferreting out any remnants of that *thing* sealed in him, the energetic imprint of whatever attacked him in the hills.

"Is this gonna take long, Doc?" he drawled.

"As long as it takes. Shut up."

He stretched. Muscles tightened under her hands. "Just stroke where the mood moves you."

Shut up! She could live without that idea in her head, especially since he forced her to admit it had a certain appeal... she closed her eyes and tuned him out, years of practice coming to her aid.

When she opened her eyes, it wasn't with good news. "It's larger. For the love of creation, Kiril, go to the healing room. We'll recruit a team to do another binding, and the Healers will help your headache."

His brows went up. Did he think she couldn't detect something as simple as that?

"I'll tell them to expect you today. Are we clear?"

"Yes, ma'am. Anything you say, ma'am."

He rolled onto his side and propped his head on an elbow to watch her leave. Which she did, hastily, fumbling the knob as she pulled the door closed after her.

After she left Kiril's room, Quinn crossed the green to the Healers' lodge. Daren needed to know to expect their recalcitrant patient for an examination before they re-did the binding. Then the two of them walked together to the conference room for an early council meeting before the delegation from Borgonne joined them.

"Let's go through this one more time," Arwen opened. "We're facing a dilemma. They require our assistance, and as far as I know there's no objection to giving it. But even if we could accumulate grain for them, how do we get it across the hills? Any thoughts?"

"We could put out a call, see what the closest towns can provide," Cynth said. "But to feed a whole nation... Arwen, we couldn't collect enough, much less ship it."

"Seed won't help if the drought continues," Fergus added. "And the distance precludes fresh produce."

"Convoys crossing the hills," Daren said. "Perhaps they'd be okay if we recruited those with weaker Entrée to lead them? Do you think there'd be any interest?"

"It's still a manual system that puts the participants at risk for ten days or more in each direction." Quinn shuddered, remembering what her hands had sensed in Kiril only a short while ago. "Do we want to subject our people to that? Or theirs?"

"And the spells?" Arwen asked.

Blank looks around the table. "What about them?" Daren asked.

"How do you feel about them?"

"I don't feel anything," Fergus said slowly. "They're a fact, like the hills themselves."

"But is their existence beneficial to us? Or purely a detriment?"

At that moment the conference room door opened and the Borgonnians filed in. Cedric led them, his ribbons and badges bouncing gently on his overdeveloped middle. Gauvain gestured Ester to enter, then followed, taking them in at a glance.

Arwen, no doubt, had just arrived at the meat of the council's discussion; their early arrival compromised her plans.

Well, they all had the sense to be careful with what they said. Arwen's face smoothed out into a welcome. At a nod from her, Daren, who was closest, pulled the cord to summon a runner. Caff would be on its way soon.

Once the pleasantries had been dispensed with, Cedric opened the meeting. "Naturally we are grateful for your offers of assistance. We can foresee certain problems, however."

"As can we," Arwen interrupted smoothly. Quinn suspected that Orlan council meetings lasted for days and were ninety percent posturing. "So far, we have been unable to find an efficient way to overcome them. The reality is, there is no communication network of any kind across the hills, and little structure here in the Midland."

"Oh, come," Gauvain put in. "Traders move up and down the Midland constantly, between those two provinces of yours."

There was a lull while they sorted out what he meant. "You are referring to the Northlands and Southlands?" Arwen asked. "They aren't provinces, Gauvain. They're autonomous."

"And you have no central government to control them, even if they weren't. But the fact remains that the Midland is the dominant economy. And trade caravans regularly ply your laughable roads."

"You said it yourself. North and south. In terms of east-west movement, there is less. Generally speaking, each region is self-sustaining. We rarely receive agricultural produce from the west." Arwen controlled the discussion easily, but Quinn sensed she was grateful when a light tap on the door signaled the arrival of refreshments.

With everyone supplied with caff and pastries, Gauvain smoothly took command of the Borgonne delegation. "How much help could the communities along the foothills be?"

"What is the population of Borgonne?"

"Approximately four thousand live in Orlan. I expect there are another eight thousand or so in the immediate outlying districts. There are a number of settlements further east, which we do not administer."

"No single settlement in the Midland is so large," Arwen murmured. "My guess is, we could arrange for grain for reseeding, or enough grain for grinding to last a nine-day. Based on the Motherhouse village and informal reports from Stanstead and a few other hamlets, that's as far as we could stretch. After this year's harvest, we'll have more information, but in general the towns grow only what is needed, plus an emergency store. The work is too labor intensive to do more."

"My good woman, this is an emergency," Cedric put in. The man wore pomposity like a badge of office. Quinn was amused and a little relieved that everyone ignored him. Where Borgonne was concerned, the true seat of power had never been in question.

"Would you be willing to begin gathering foodstuffs, while we work out the logistics of transport across the hills?" Gauvain continued.

"We might. Depending on what you have in mind."

"I'm sure you've considered the use of those with lesser Entrée to act as guides. If they were strong, they could serve as bearers as well."

"Yes. However, that plan puts members of our population, and yours, at risk every time they set foot in the hills. Add the quantity required to feed your people... I'm not sure it's feasible, even discounting the threat."

Gauvain's caff mug landed on the table with a thump. "I have a proposal that will remove the risk." He used a dramatic pause to cast his gaze around the room. "We remove the spells from the hills."

A beat of silence greeted his suggestion. "Is that even possible?" Fergus asked.

"It might be. Shall I continue?"

At Arwen's nod, he said, "I have in my possession an old scroll which suggests that removal of the spell – or spells, the literature isn't specific – requires a minimum of three Mages on each side of the hills, working in tandem. I also have developed a partial version of one spell."

"But, as a guess, you have no certainty of how to complete the weave, or how many spells there are, or if the weaves from the Midland are the same as the ones from Borgonne." Arwen leaned back in her chair with a skeptical frown. "We don't even know what the hills look like without the spells, although most believe they are both taller and more extensive. Those not Weavers who ventured into the hills have suggested as much."

"All true. Nor can I speak for the extent of your knowledge about the hills."

"Next to nothing. We have no documents, and only recent history."

"Including the unfortunate calamity that befell your Bard. But that was nothing to do with a spell. Rather, it was the Aura's greater intensity on our side of the hills."

"Yes, but that isn't what I refer to."

"You mean Kiril," Quinn said, then wished she hadn't. Gauvain was slick; he wouldn't be above using Kiril as a pawn, or an experiment, as he had done with Willow.

"The one who gave me this unfortunate souvenir." His hand touched the scar on his face. "I collided with him yesterday. There is something unusual about him. Not a Mage, not a person with Entrée, but some type of power I don't understand."

Quinn met Arwen's eyes across the table. "Go ahead," Arwen said. "Best we all provide as full a picture as possible."

"It's nothing good." Quinn briefly narrated the attack by the lizard and the subsequent binding that had saved Kiril's life but still, based on her reading earlier that morning, threatened to overtake him.

Gauvain listened intently, his concentration focused on Quinn. When she finished he said, "The energy I sensed... I was sure it connected to the hills somehow. I don't suppose they brought back a souvenir of the beast, a piece of its hide, for instance?"

Quinn shuddered. "That energetic thing inside him, it's as if it has tentacles. I had to call for help before it snatched me, the first time I went in. Thank the Sustainer they didn't collect a *souvenir*, as you put it. The mere thought is frightening."

"I see." Gauvain poured a second mug of caff and lapsed into silence.

Arwen spoke. "So the spells on the hills aren't simply of benign confusion. Perhaps you can better understand our reluctance to establish any kind of trade route through them."

"I expect Kiril was attacked because he is not a Mage, and he ventured off the trail."

"That's our hypothesis."

He turned the mug round and round in his elegant hands. "If anything, this reinforces my determination to remove the spells. Suppose such creatures were to get loose and venture into the Midland? If we can obviate the danger, both lands stand to gain from the trade."

"What do you propose?" Arwen asked.

"To find or recreate the missing parts of the spells. To devise their reversal and coordinate their execution."

"As I said, we have no documents from those times."

"But you can probe the hills. And you have the man Kiril."

Arwen ended it. "We will consider this. But I must tell you that my first reaction is not positive. Not only because of the challenges in creating reversal spells. I'm not at all convinced of the value to the Midland, should trade routes open between our lands."

"I propose we discuss this further over lunch, if you would care to join me," Gauvain said. "Undoubtedly we could offer goods of benefit to your... nation."

You gave yourself away, Quinn thought. You almost added the word 'backward'.

"I'll meet you in the dining hall shortly after the bell," Arwen said.

Gauvain stood and executed a nod that just missed being a bow in Arwen's direction, then left the room. Ester and Cedric trailed out behind him. The council lingered, sensing something more.

"I've sent for Ezra," Arwen said. "What happens here in the next few days may well determine the fate of the Midland. I'm worried."

"Will he accept our refusal?" Daren asked. "I sense a larger scheme than relieving the drought. There's a bid for power at work here. They view us as a way to solve a long-term problem, and to enhance the status of Borgonne."

Arwen drummed her fingers on the table. "Vassals?"

"Would they dare?" Quinn asked. The entire tenor of the morning had troubled her. By the end of her stay in Orlan, Willow had come to respect, even enjoy the company of the haughty man who had just departed. But that had been in the context of a clash of individual wills, not a clash of cultures. Obviously, pompous little Cedric itched to annex the Midland, but he lacked both the clout and the capacity to do so. Gauvain, on the other hand, wielded power like a machete. She had no doubt he'd cut them down to achieve his ends.

After the meeting disbanded, Quinn walked with Arwen toward the older woman's workroom. "Are you busy this afternoon?" Arwen asked.

"I want to check the healing room to see if Kiril turned up. Otherwise... what do you need?"

"Our mysterious weave... have you given it any attention recently?"

"With the mess with Kiril, no."

With her hand on the knob, Arwen said, "Try to make time this afternoon. It won't be live because Gauvain may well be with me, so he won't be working on it himself, but I've placed an updated diagram in the cubby. He's been manipulating it from here, and it modifies the picture."

Quinn leaned against the wall. "How? Is he compromising the Midland?"

"I don't believe so. Check the diagram and give me your opinion. It has changed, as if the perspective changes when approached from the west instead of the east. I've picked up a few new strands in the weave, but they seem to extend from Borgonne into the hills rather than touch the Midland. I think this represents a spell that is unique to his land." Arwen hesitated. "There's one current especially I want your opinion on. I won't tell you where, but you'll find it."

Quinn sighed. The heat wave had ended and the day was bright, with a high clear sky and warmth to soothe even the most frazzled nerves. Generally she wasn't much for the outdoors, but today her spirit cried for the balm of sun on her skin. "I'll work on it after lunch."

Arwen pulled her door open. "Meet me in the Scribes' workroom before evening meal."

Quinn set off. She had time before the bell rang for lunch, and she was determined to indulge herself in a short walk at least, breathing in clean air free of the taint of the Borgonnian presence in her home.

Chapter 10

Quinn, working with Dorcas, had spent most of the afternoon studying the rudimentary diagram, trying to comprehend the meanings of the energy currents and divine what was still missing from the weave. The older woman's Entrée wasn't as strong as either Arwen's or Quinn's, but her years of experience more than made up for it. Quinn was glad Dorcas had been brought into the mystery.

Arwen joined them just before the bell for the evening meal.

"This is unreal," Dorcas said. "If we're reading this correctly, the idiot's caused the drought." She rubbed her eyes, then put both hands on her lower back and stretched. The binding on Kiril, following so soon after the work with the power cell, had taken its toll on the older woman, although she had readily agreed to study the incomplete weave Arwen had stowed in the cubby, the secure place where Scribes exchanged information not yet stored in the Aura.

"That's what you wanted me to find?" Quinn asked.

"Exactly. He's sucking energy from the atmosphere into the weave, where it flows... into the hills?"

"That current isn't complete, but it certainly looks that way."

"And who knows to what effect?" Dorcas said. "For all we know, it gave birth to Kiril's beast."

"Let's hope not. I'd hate to see such forms of power loose in our world." Arwen frowned at the diagram and the damning current running from above Borgonne into the hills. "The question becomes what to do with it. Is there any benefit to keeping this from him?"

"Blackmail?" Quinn was too tired to be serious and managed to elicit a chuckle from Dorcas.

Arwen, however, ignored the jibe. "We have little leverage where Borgonne is concerned. They outnumber us, and their civilization inclines them to use force to get their way when political machinations don't work."

"Our reality is that we aren't experienced in these sorts of power games," Dorcas said. "And what's the point? With this information, we can alleviate the drought in Borgonne – or Gauvain can, if he'll only see it."

Arwen shook her head. "I'd be happier if we maintained some control. Something to strike with, should they use aggression against us. We need leverage."

We need caff. Quinn kept the thought to herself and returned her attention to the diagram. "This is unbelievable. The amount of energy he's allowed to flow from Borgonne into this weave... surely he knows?"

Arwen smiled a trifle grimly. "Gauvain has always fancied himself a master among Mages. Unconquerable and incapable of making a wrong move. We may have an advantage, in that we're working from a fragment of the weave. The complexity of the completed template may well mask the effect he's had on their weather."

"Which isn't affecting us here in the Midland," Dorcas mused.

"Likely proving that Midlanders and Borgonnians cast different spells on the hills." Arwen hadn't bothered to sit down; now she leaned over the diagram, noting the subtle markings Quinn and Dorcas had made, pointing the way to the energy drain and the disruption of Borgonne's weather.

"If we tell him, he can correct the problem, perhaps in time for this year's crops," Quinn said.

"If we don't tell him, we'll find half of Borgonne clamoring to cross the hills to seize our grain stores," Dorcas added.

The bell rang in the dining hall.

"We need to give this more thought." Arwen straightened. "And I for one am hungry. Diou only knows what tomorrow will bring."

Quinn rolled up the paper and snugged it back into the cubby. "Agreed. I'm not fit to make a judgment call at the moment."

"Have you seen Kiril today?" Arwen asked.

She actually had to stop and think, their encounter seemed so long ago. "Early this morning. He was packing his stuff, but I didn't get the feeling he has any immediate plans to leave. I ordered him to the healing rooms." At Arwen's raised brows, she added, "Yes. It's growing."

"Check on him again tomorrow, please."

The last thing she wanted to deal with. Arwen was right, though. "Will do."

A quiet meal, then an evening to herself. Tomorrow would come soon enough. For tonight, Quinn intended to take some of the magic drops the Healers dispensed and get a decent night's sleep.

Despite her efforts, Quinn slept restlessly. A thunderstorm rolled through in the night, waking her; after that the mounting concerns wouldn't leave her alone. She considered walking across the green to the healing rooms; someone would be on duty, and Quinn knew the Healers' remedy made from mindsease could turn off the relentless pounding of the thoughts in her brain. But the idea of going out in the aftermath of the downpour didn't appeal. Instead, she rolled out of bed, pulled on a sleepshirt, and brewed a pot of caff. The comforting drink in hand, she settled down to focus and clear her mind.

A minute later there was a tap on her door. It opened and Dorcas stepped in, bringing with her an air of worry.

"I saw your light. Want company?"

"Sure."

She joined Quinn at her table and reached for the caff pot.

"I know why I'm awake," Quinn said. "What's worrying you?"

"Besides the obvious? It's the middle of the night, we've got an arrogant, rogue Mage messing up the weather, and then there's Kiril."

Quinn grinned. "Is that all?"

Dorcas snorted. "Don't I wish. Did you hear the chatter in the common room last evening?"

"No. Please tell me nothing else is going on." The grin faded. Quinn suppressed the groan building up inside her by gulping down her remaining caff and pouring a fresh mug.

"Maybe. There's a new star in the sky."

"What? New stars don't happen." Quinn leaned forward.

"As we all know. But it's been seen the last two nights. Fredrik and Kalia were on the roof before the storm rolled in, watching it. The way it was moving... it doesn't behave like stars, even falling ones."

Quinn forced her tired brain to alertness. "How so?"

"Among other things, once it changed direction. Shot off at a ninety-degree angle. The storm killed the visibility tonight, but last night it appeared three times. Poor Fredrik likes his sleep, and he hasn't had any in two nights now."

"Then what is it?" Quinn's nimble mind had already made a leap, but she wasn't going to raise that possibility yet.

"We don't know. Nothing like this has ever happened before. The firmament is stable, it never changes. Every one of us knows how to track the stars to find our way at night, we learn at our mother's knee. If the stars become unstable... by the Sustainer, Quinn. I'd like to think it's just an anomaly, something that will disappear as abruptly as it appeared. But with everything else that's happening... I'm nervous."

"I hear that a lot around the Motherhouse lately."

"I hardly ever see Arwen. She's looking too tired. I chatted with Gauvain yesterday, if you can call anything to do with that man a chat. He sets my teeth on edge."

"Oddly, Willow grew to like him."

"Willow has about her a disarming innocence that masks a core of steel. She's his match, I'd say. With all his airs, I doubt he knew how to handle her."

Quinn sputtered, causing some of her mouthful of caff to escape. She hastily wiped her chin with the sleeve of the sleepshirt – she hardly ever bothered with the thing anyway, and she could put it in the laundry in the morning. "I wish she were here now. We need that balance."

"Do you hear much from her? Or Bryar?"

"Willow, no. There's minimal contact with Hallan, and Willow's never been good at the mind communication thing. They're fine, she and Joss, but that's all I know. Bryar..." She sighed. "I hear from Tai. He's healing, but he's lost that carefree joy he used to have. Tai says he's very serious now, and... hard somehow."

"That boy always did need to grow up," Dorcas said. She had been among their teachers, back when they were apprentices, and Quinn suspected that, like Arwen, she still assessed them accordingly.

The women sipped their caff in companionable silence for a while.

"Let it out, Quinn. There's something you're not saying."

"Damn it." Quinn thumped the little mug on the table. "It's Kiril. I asked around last night. No one remembers seeing him at the dining hall yesterday. Or seeing him at all, come to that."

"And that matters?"

"Yeah. Because of the flawed binding. He doesn't look good. And he hasn't checked in with the healing room. Stubborn fool," she muttered.

"Personal or professional, Quinn?" Dorcas asked.

Quinn's succumbed to a grin. "Both, I suppose. He frustrates the hell out of me, but I don't want anything bad to happen to him. And I'm afraid it is. You know as well as I do that we couldn't be sure we contained that thing."

Dorcas stood and peered out the window. "Dawn. Good." She went to Quinn's door and pulled the cord to summon a messenger kid. When the girl pounded up the stairs and skidded to a halt at the door, she said, "Go to administration, please, and have them put out a call for the man named Kiril. He lives at the guest lodge, so ask them to check there first. He's to go to the healing rooms, under compulsion if necessary."

"Got it." The child shot off.

"Thanks." Quinn moved to the window. Streaks of pink had appeared around the massif, and color painted the forest behind the Scribes' lodge.

"I'm going back to bed, for all the good it will do me," Dorcas said. "Let me know about Kiril. If we have to go back in —"

"Sustainer, I hope not. Sweet dreams."

Dorcas gave an undignified snort and left Quinn alone with her thoughts.

With no hope of returning to sleep, Quinn completed her morning invocation, figuring it might help her get a grip on the day.

By afternoon, there was still no sign of Kiril.

Chapter 11

Kiril had vanished. Two days after Quinn's visit to his room, his pack still lay on his bed, seemingly intact. But no one had seen him, and he hadn't visited the dining hall since her assessment. Quinn assumed he had bolted, although she admitted to a nagging worry. Why would he abandon his pack?

He knew the way to Stanstead, she assured herself. He'd be fine, and Dal would let them know when he turned up.

With the entire business of trade through the hills suspended until Ezra arrived, she was happy enough to absorb herself in other, neglected work.

Quinn was exploring a preliminary but promising traverse of a template, seeking access to an event just outside the usual boundaries they felt safe to explore, when a pounding at her door jerked her back to awareness. Heart thudding – because being pulled abruptly from the Aura was disorienting – she answered the knock.

"Arwen says come quick, ma'am," the messenger kid said.

Did she ever say to take her time?

The child completed the message. "It's about that man—"

Without questioning her urgency – she, who questioned everything – Quinn shoved her feet into sandals. She set off at a trot for the Centra.

Arwen met her outside the imposing door. She spoke in a rush. "Communication from Tai. They've found traces of Kiril. I want two strong men and a Healer, quickly. I've notified the Healers' lodge and the village."

"I'm going, too. Where?"

"Tai and Ezra are almost here, so I assume near the intersection. Go put on some boots, child. And take food with you. You'll miss your lunch."

"Merde." Quinn wheeled and started back to the Scribes' lodge, shouting over her shoulder, "Don't let them leave without me."

By the time she returned, Helene, a younger Healer taking few nine-days' respite from Traveling, was waiting for her. "If you're ready," she said. "I raided the dining hall. The men from the village will meet us on the trail."

Quinn gave her a brusque nod. Then she reflected that Helene was a gracious woman and deserved better. "Sorry. I'm worried."

"I understand that. You'll fill me in as we walk?"

Quinn forced herself to slow down to a reasonable pace as she and Helene headed north.

They encountered Ezra and Tai half way between the Motherhouse and the intersection. Tai, sensing their urgency, said, "There's an energetic imprint. He's gone toward the hills, but I can't tell how long ago."

Helene stood a little aside with Ezra, who waited silently after giving her a tight hug. Neither of them missed a word.

"He took nothing with him," Quinn said. "Was he alone?"

"I don't know, since we can track only Weavers. The only reason I sensed him was that odd demonic energy about him. Is that what's causing this?"

"Probably. Look, when you meet the villagers, tell them to take the right fork. Helene and I need to go ahead."

"Sure. But, Quinn, Helene... take care."

"I've experienced that energy up close. Trust me, I'll be careful."

With a renewed sense of urgency, Quinn led them toward the path leading to the hills.

Mid-afternoon, sustained by energy bars they used when covering long distances, Helene stopped. "He's just ahead."

Quinn also halted, suddenly afraid of what they might find. "Yes. I feel it." She'd been aware of that strange force that possessed Kiril since midday, but it had strengthened over the last hour until part of her longed to run away.

Helene swallowed and took the lead.

Around the next bend they saw him, perhaps a hundred paces ahead of them, crawling as if he could barely pull himself along. He dragged one leg forward, then the other, matching the uncertain movements of his hands and arms.

The women looked at each other and, of like mind, approached him without calling. Only when she was next to him did Quinn say, "Kiril?"

He froze, then began his methodical movement again. She let him.

She drew Helene a little way back and whispered, "We'd best wait until the men catch up, in case he fights. Besides, we can't support him for any length of time, and he seems determined."

"I agree."

She and Helene stayed behind Kiril, following his labored progress but not interfering.

The two agriculturists appeared around supper time. Although young and strong, neither seemed happy to be there. They were on the trail behind the massif and not actually in the hills, but the rumors had spread to the village serving the Motherhouse. Quinn briefly explained the situation.

"Helene and I agree the best course of action is for her to compel him. He'll require physical support, though. He probably hasn't eaten or drunk in two or three days, so he's weak."

"Okay," one of the men said without noticeable enthusiasm. "But that compelling thing... do we have to be nearby? It sounds creepy."

Helene stepped in. "Go back a ways and wait. When he's subdued, we'll come get you."

Relief apparent in their faces, both men turned and rushed along the trail, disappearing around the bend.

"Over to you," Quinn said. Compelling was a Healer's technique, used when a patient was unable to accept the support he needed, and only if he presented a danger to himself or others.

Helene swallowed, then hurried ahead, catching up with Kiril easily. As she kept pace with him, her hands moved, creating the weave to compel his mind to return with them.

She snapped her fingers and breathed out. "Done," she called to Quinn.

For a moment it appeared all was well. Kiril stopped moving forward and looked puzzled. Then he reared up on his knees, his body spasmed violently, and he fell to the ground. The spasms continued to wrack him; Quinn suspected he wasn't breathing. His eyes seemed to bulge from their sockets, and he made sounds as if strangling.

"What the hell did you do?" she shouted.

"Nothing. A standard compelling... wait." Helene turned her attention from Kiril, whose body had gone into rigor, to Quinn. "What was driving him toward the hills?"

Quinn grasped the thought instantly. "Sweet Diou. Get the compulsion off him. Fast."

She stopped breathing as well, not realizing it until Helene completed the reversal spell, which took an eternity, and Kiril collapsed, limp. As Quinn gasped for air, Helene turned Kiril onto his back and began rhythmically working his chest until a shuddering breath rose from him and he coughed.

Helene sat beside him on the ground, shaking, her breathing ragged. "I've never dealt with anything like this. Never. Nothing in our training prepared me."

"We learned something. But not... by all that lives, I hope never to witness anything like that again."

Helene remained seated, her hands smoothing Kiril's energies. "He's chilled and damp. The sooner we get him to the Motherhouse, the better. Will he fight us?"

"Did you bring a remedy to relax him or put him to sleep?"

"Relax, yes. I don't want to risk his sleeping now."

While Helene tended to Kiril, Quinn walked on shaky legs along the trail to the two men waiting for them. "We'll have to carry him back. He's very weak."

"We can do that. May not be comfortable for him."

"So be it. It's vital to return to the Motherhouse as soon as possible."

"Yes'm. He's not... he hasn't got a haint, has he?"

Yes, Kiril's problem could be tidily summed up as a haint. But that wasn't information she wanted loose in the world. "He's ill, and he's delusional, that's all."

The two men approached Kiril cautiously, gaining confidence when they saw Helene, unafraid, kneeling beside him, her hands working over him. Between them they picked Kiril up, and one of them hoisted him over a shoulder.

Kiril would never forgive this. She hoped Helene's remedy assured he would never know about it.

Grimly, they set out for the Motherhouse, sharing the remaining provisions Helene had brought as they walked.

Rather the worse for wear.

Quinn, having been pulled aside by Arwen for much-needed sustenance, not to mention a debriefing, arrived at the healing room at nightfall. Kiril looked as bad as when they'd done the binding on the demon possessing him, but in a different way. His light brown hair was greasy and dusty, the hollows in his cheeks had deepened, and one hand twitched convulsively. He was awake, with a haunted look in those strange blue eyes, as if he had seen the image of the demon sapping his life force and it had terrified him past rational thought. A strap across his waist bound him to the cot.

She gripped his convulsing hand, holding it still. The strength in his hand and arm surprised her.

The trip back had been a nightmare. Kiril had been conscious and uncomfortable, and prepared to fight to return to the hills. Helene's sedating remedy kept him from any ability to act on his frustration, but the agriculturists were forced to swap their bundle regularly; controlling the thrashing man tasked even their considerable strength.

Like her, Helene had turned their patient over to Beatris and gone to wash, eat, and debrief. Quinn had seen her with Daren in the otherwise deserted dining hall.

They all gathered now: Quinn and Arwen, Dorcas, Helene, Beatris, Daren. Six Weavers and one frail man. And none of them with any clear idea of what to do next.

"Tell us about the demon, Quinn," Daren said.

She glanced at Kiril, but Daren shrugged. "He knows about it. He might as well comprehend the magnitude of the problem."

She nodded. "When I scanned him a couple of days ago, it had grown, but not by much. This is unexpected." Although she had already told the story, as had Helene, she briefly recounted the compelling and its effects.

"So we have every reason to believe this thing put some kind of compulsion spell on Kiril," Arwen concluded. "Surely we can break it."

"Except we haven't been able to so far."

"Current treatment?" Arwen asked.

"Palliative," Beatris said. "The best we can do."

The curtain at the door twitched, and Gauvain stepped through.

A shocked silence filled the room before Arwen said, "Is there something you need? A Healer, perhaps?"

His lips pressed in a thin line as he studied the man on the cot. "Information. However much you tried to isolate us from the events here, word leaks out. The hills caused this, am I correct? It's imperative that I understand what happened."

Quinn's eyes met Arwen; the two women exchanged brief nods.

"Very well. I—"

"I object," Daren said. "This man's motives are suspect. I for one don't trust him."

"And you fear he will attempt to use Kiril as a weapon?" Arwen's voice was firm. "I don't. If there's the least suggestion of greater traffic through the hills, everyone needs to understand what we're up against. I do not believe Gauvain would unleash horrors on either of our lands. And he may help us save Kiril."

The deal, Quinn thought. Gauvain could stay, but the next time she ventured into Kiril's energy, it would be with him. Good. Along with Arwen and herself, he wielded the most power in the room. Only Ezra and Tai rivaled him, and for various reasons, neither of them would be put to the risk of binding Kiril's demon.

Gauvain nodded curtly, accepting the bargain, and stepped to Kiril's cot. He sank onto a stool and began a scan. Quinn monitored the energy; his technique was unfamiliar, not like the Healers or the Scribes used.

While he worked, Arwen gathered up the others. "I want two Healers here. It doesn't look like we can avoid going back into his energy field. Quinn, Dorcas. Do you agree?"

Beatris nodded. "This isn't Healer work."

Gauvain jumped, pulling his hands away from Kiril. He rose and joined them. "There's no time to waste. The demon has already breached the binding and threatens to puncture through the man's auric field. We act now. Tell me the procedure you used before," he demanded.

Quinn explained the binding matrix, starting at the edges of Kiril's energy and gradually tightening it until they sensed it was as secure as they could make it.

Gauvain nodded. "Show me the weave."

Quinn drew him from the small room to the empty one next door, gesturing for Dorcas to join them. "Like this." Her hands moved.

When they emerged some time later, the room had emptied. Arwen sat beside Kiril; the Healers had left.

"We're agreed," Gauvain said. "Water first, then we go in."

Someone had placed a pitcher and mugs on the worktable. Recognizing the rightness of his command, Quinn ignored the dictatorial tone and joined the others in downing mugs of water, then did a quick series of exercises designed to loosen her perennially tight neck and shoulder muscles. "I'm ready."

"As am I," Dorcas said quietly. Dorcas was a rock. Quinn knew she'd rather be leading apprentice classes and enjoying the treats in the dining hall, but she never complained. Quinn privately suspected that she'd been brought onto council, and was now training to step into Arwen's role, only because Dorcas had declined.

She got control of her wandering mind and directed it at the problem. From now on her sole focus had to be linking, power consolidation, and reinforcing the weave.

Sustainer, help us.

They settled around Kiril. She sensed Gauvain pulling back when she offered her hand, but he took it. She'd explained their linking technique, which appeared to be new to him, but he offered no resistance when their minds sought each other and began the meld.

Years of training. This is why.

Late in the night they emerged from the link. They had moved more slowly this time, dividing the work, taking better care to tie off the currents and tighten the binding. It wasn't as scary as the first time, because the demon was mostly contained, having breached the original template in only one place. However, Dorcas looked gray in the half light of the Aura globes. Even Gauvain, usually immaculate, had a ragged air and deep grooves either side of his mouth. Quinn's hands were shaking as she gave Dorcas a quick squeeze.

Kiril was asleep. The tension that had marked his face was gone, replaced by much-needed rest. Better, but there was still a lingering... what? Quinn shook out her hands.

Dorcas nodded to Arwen, who pushed aside the curtain and gestured. Beatris came in and brushed them away as she began a Healers' scan. After a few minutes, she nodded. "He'll be fine, at least for a while. But..."

Again the doubt. Quinn sagged against the side wall. She'd been up early, then made the trek to find Kiril, and now the binding... a day and night without respite. She looked again at the man asleep on the cot. "Can you unfasten the strap?" she asked. "He isn't going anywhere."

Beatris undid the latches holding the leather strap in place. "Most peaceful I've ever seen him. Now for the three of you."

Of course Beatris had one of their little vials with her. She willingly allowed the drops to flow onto her tongue and watched with amusement when Gauvain reared back, fought against his initial resistance, and obediently opened his mouth. The expression on his face when the nearly immediate effects of the remedy reached his system almost made the night worth it; she could see the change as he relaxed.

"Now, unless you have any more concerns, get out of here," Beatris commanded. "He's in my care, and you need sleep."

Shooed from the healing room, Quinn could think of nothing she'd like more. Dawn approached, and she was unlikely to accomplish any practical work today anyway. She gave herself permission, fully intending to sink into unconsciousness as soon as her head rested on her pillow.

But her body rebelled; she woke in time to have breakfast before the dining hall closed. By chance, she met Gauvain in the line. It was evident he had slept no better than she. Quinn felt ungrounded and longed for her morning caff.

As she carried her tray from the serving tables, Beatris gestured for them to join her. "It's not over."

Quinn sat woodenly, her brain resisting. "What now?"

Gauvain slid into the chair across from her.

"I called in a couple other Healers," Beatris continued. "We worked over him most of the night... oh, don't worry. He was up at first light, bathed, and right now he's eating everything in sight. The demon's bound, as near as we can tell. But the infection it created is still there. Lessened, we believe, but..." Beatris drew to a stop and heaved a deep breath. Gauvain put down the mug he had just filled with caff and stared at her. "This is new in our experience," she continued. "When we do a compelling – and it's a tool we avoid using whenever possible – but when we do use one, it's a fairly loose weave. It's serious, but gentle. This compelling on Kiril is more amorphous, with little underlying structure."

"Maybe that's why at times, when I was in his energy, if felt like swimming in mud," Quinn mused. "But then I didn't know what to expect."

Beatris nodded. "Usually an auric field is clear, or with well defined thickenings. Not a generalized toxic emanation, which is what leads me to call it a disease. We can't find a way to reduce or contain it, much less remove it."

Quinn and Gauvain both greeted this news with silence. Quinn spooned up a bite of egg, looked at it, and put it down again.

"So," she said, "he'll live with it all his life."

"However long that may be," Beatris replied.

Quinn shivered, despite the warmth.

"But it's to do with the hills, we know that. We Healers agree that the best thing he can do for himself is leave. The further west he goes, the less power will feed the compulsion. Or so we speculate. A guess, really, but all we have."

"Have you told him this?"

"Not yet. Today, though, before we discharge him. If he hasn't already taken himself off."

Beatris picked up her dishes and left. Quinn looked at Gauvain. "Do you still think it's a good idea to open a trade route through the hills?"

For once, the man had no reply.

Chapter 12

Quinn had been assisting Dorcas with a lesson to the fourth-year apprentices that afternoon, so she arrived late and out of breath at the hastily called meeting in the Centra. Ezra, Arwen, and Daren sat around the table.

"My dear." Ezra didn't stand but held out a hand to her.

The Old Man had arrived the day before. She sank into the chair next to his, accepted the hand, and brushed it against her cheek. "I'm so glad you're here."

Quinn had a long and deep relationship with Ezra. First as an apprentice, when they all went in awe of the gray-haired Scribe who wielded power such as they couldn't even imagine back then... and occasionally sat in judgment of their peccadillos. He'd always been fair, which only increased his mystique. Later, she had spent most of her journey year at his compound, refining and learning to control her burgeoning powers. Those were the times she valued most, when she grew to love and value Ezra, his wife Rebecca, and their way of life. So much of what she was now – and Quinn knew, although it was never said outright, that she ranked among the three or four most powerful living Scribes – she owed to him. Because of his patient tutelage, she might one day head either the Scribes' lodge, a role currently held by Dorcas, or the Weavers' council. Quinn didn't seek power for its own sake, but she recognized her abilities and used them.

She released Ezra's hand with a smile. "Sorry to be late. Where are we?"

"Politics," Daren said.

"A necessary evil, I fear," Ezra said. "I met Gauvain earlier. He is a determined man, and for all that he chooses not to acknowledge it, a politically driven one. The drought should concern us, and providing relief as we can is our duty. But he wants more."

Arwen nodded. "I've talked with Gauvain regularly over the last couple of days. Because of his insistence that we open the hills to trade, I'm losing perspective. The more he pushes for attempting to lift the spells, the more I resist. Hence this meeting."

"I know next to nothing about their civilization," Daren said. "But what little I've heard, I don't like."

"It's a system based on acquisition," Ezra said. "The more you possess, the greater your perceived value. There is poverty, and there is great wealth, if we measure wealth in terms of quantity. As you can tell by their clothing, they have gone far beyond our basics."

Indeed they had, Quinn thought. Even the apprentices sported colorful clothes in fabrics unknown in the Midland. Amalie wore a ring in a golden color on her hand, and Reed strutted about in finely tooled boots. She understood the draw toward beautiful things, but to base a society on them?

"You think they would try to impose their culture on us?" she asked.

"Yes," Arwen said flatly.

"Perhaps not intentionally, not at first," Ezra said. "But inevitably it would come, as their luxuries found their way into the Midland. We need to ask ourselves if that might be for the better. We have things they don't, no poverty for instance. But we also are stagnant. With our current resources, our scope for expansion is limited, and if the population grows much larger, we won't be able to support ourselves. An alliance with Borgonne could change that."

"At what cost?" Arwen snapped. "Everything we value?"

"That is what it falls on us to decide," Ezra said calmly.

"Sorry," Arwen said. "The magnitude must be getting to me. Plus Gauvain's constant presence."

"There's tons of unpopulated land west of here," Daren muttered. He had come from the vast central plains.

"Yes," Ezra agreed. "But our hamlets live with a fine balance. Have we the ability to open that land without causing immediate hardship? I think not. Every hamlet I know of operates at the limit of its resources."

How much change could the Midland tolerate? What was the best for their culture? The four of them talked until the conversation circled around on itself. "We'll meet this evening," Arwen said. "Find Fergus and Cynth and fill them in. We vote tonight and inform Gauvain's party of our decision tomorrow morning." Arwen stood and left the room, muttering about the plans to accumulate foodstuffs for transport to Borgonne.

Daren sank back in his chair, clearly exhausted. "So within the course of one mealtime, I have to decide. Sweet Sustainer."

"Remember, the gut is a stronger repository of information than the brain," Ezra said as he slowly rose to his feet. "Trust yourself. Quinn, my dear, would you mind escorting me to the guest lodge? I need rest before dinner."

Was there anything she wouldn't do for the Old Man? "My honor."

"We met in council last night," Arwen said. "I will thank you to hear me out before you speak."

Around the table, all eyes fixed on her. The evening before, Arwen had insisted that they vote in secret. After she announced the result, they had stayed late discussing implications and additions. Cynth was red-eyed from lack of sleep, and Quinn felt as if her head was stuffed with unspun linen, scratchy and muddled.

"We agree to assist Borgonne in any way possible for a single traverse of the hills."

Cedric sputtered, "Only once? Madame, that you could willingly ignore the benefits of increased trade—"

Ester interrupted him. "Our people will go hungry."

"I asked that you wait until I've finished." Arwen's voice overrode the others and brooked no further interruption. "We are prepared to send as much grain as possible back with you. If you check the barns, you'll see it's already begun to arrive. I've put out a call asking for healthy people with some Entrée, and for strong agriculturists to help with transport. I took the liberty of promising a warm welcome in Orlan. From this direction, we could consider the use of donkeys, although we can't predict their reaction to the hills, and I gather the access is too steep for them to leave on the other side."

Cedric squirmed. "Once isn't enough. For Creation's sake, woman—"

"That is our offer." Ezra's raspy voice cut off Cedric's protest.

"It's a fair offer. I suggest you consider it." Arwen reached for her caff mug and sipped. "For the rest, however, we will not to tamper with the spells on the hills."

"Short-sighted, as I might have expected," Gauvain muttered. Then he cleared his throat and leaned forward, moving his gaze from one to another to encompass the council members surrounding him. "Removing the spells will benefit both our lands. You are wrong."

"We believe the risk outweighs the potential. Remember that nobody knows what the hills really are," Arwen said, her voice neutral. "Based on anecdotal evidence, they are both steeper and more extensive than we perceive. And that's only one example. You have no idea of the problems you may unleash."

"Do not question my competence." Gauvain spoke with determination and barely suppressed fury. "I have several powerful Mages at my disposal. If you continue to be intractable, I will relocate them to the Midland."

Arwen merely placed her hands in her lap. "You yourself raised the possibility that it requires energy workers from each side to manipulate the spells. Our skills are different from yours, so your Mages may well prove ineffective."

"Unlikely. While they learn your ways, they will conduct research."

"When we have been unable to find any trace of these weaves, after centuries? And the hills themselves will know their origins, I suspect."

He ignored her. "I leave you to your fate. But understand this. The spells will be removed, whether you cooperate or not. The whims of a bunch of ignorant peasants will not cost me my vision."

Quinn started to stand; Ezra's hand on her arm stopped her. A vein pulsed in Daren's temple, and Fergus's face had reddened. Cynth stiffened; Quinn suspected clenched fists under the table.

Arwen alone showed no reaction. "Hardly that, Gauvain. You needn't be provocative." She rested against her chair back and folded her arms.

He stood, glowering. "Is that all?"

"Have you prepared a team to consider logistics for transport? This might be a good time to recall your bearers from the village. I'm sure you will want to return home with food."

He smiled, an almost intimidating expression on his austere face. "You have made a mistake, Arwen. I took you for an intelligent woman. In this, I was in error." He circled the table and opened the conference room door. "This is not resolved. Do not think it is."

Cedric and Ester trailed Gauvain out. Ester paused to whisper in Cynth's ear and to acknowledge the others with a small nod. She at least saw the wisdom of working with what they had been offered.

Not until after the door closed behind them did Arwen allow herself to sag in her chair. "I should have told him about the weather," she said wearily.

"I disagree," Ezra said. "As angry as he is, he merely would have accused you of being irrational – or incompetent. It must be done, however."

Ezra's face still bore the fatigue of the journey from his compound. Quinn worried and reminded herself not to fuss. The old man was precious to her, a parent when she had needed one, an unparalleled mentor.

"What's this about?" Daren demanded. "Scribes' secrets?"

"Hardly. Not now." Quinn filled them in, watching their faces change from shock, to amazement, to puzzlement or fury.

"The bastard." Fergus got to his feet and paced the room. "For the sake of his own pride, he'd do this to his people?"

"I doubt it," Arwen said. "Even Gauvain isn't that insensitive. More likely he isn't aware of this particular current. In our partial reconstruction of his weave, it's buried under several layers. In his fuller version, he might never find it."

"So the energy's sucked from the atmosphere over Borgonne and fed into the hills," Cynth mused. "What's the effect there?"

Quinn spoke. "For all we know, he gave birth to the monster that attacked Kiril."

"He is a frightened man. Both for his land and because he senses that his expanded power base may be slipping from his fingers." Ezra leaned forward. "But something troubles me even more than his bringing the drought onto Borgonne. Much more." Silence fell as the Old Man met each of their gazes in turn, commanding their full attention. "He spoke of his weavecrafting in front of Ester and Cedric."

Quinn frowned. Then she caught his meaning.

After a pause fraught with negative possibility, Fergus unleashed an oath. "He's that confident."

"Boasting," Ezra said. "His words weren't only for us. He was letting the others see his power while holding out the lure of expanding their territory. I don't doubt he will send his Mages here. Whether they find anything, or could use it if they did... We possess a partial picture of a single weave, and so far we have learned only that it functions from Borgonne, and Gauvain has misinterpreted it. One thing is now clear, however, although I hate to contemplate it. Whatever Gauvain's actions when he learns the true cause of the drought, we have to assume he will continue with his plan to open the hills."

Again he let a pregnant silence fill the room. When he finally spoke, his gravelly voice was subdued. "The risks inherent in exploring the deep Aura are a serious deterrent, so the true nature of the hills and the history behind the spells remain a mystery." He paused. "But now we need that information, urgently. Not to remove the spells. To prevent Borgonne from doing so."

Quinn was too tired to feel more than numb. They all turned in her direction. Ezra and the council knew as well as she that there was only one way to learn more about the spells. And there was only one Weaver with the relative youth, skill, and dumb courage to attempt it.

Chapter 13

Joss and Willow couldn't leave immediately for the Motherhouse. A summer influenza had hit Hallan, and Willow worked day and night. On top of that, a problem had sprung up with the sheep in one of the high pastures; Joss trekked a day with a guide to get there, not looking forward to the coming encounter. *Sheep.* He was half convinced they purposely kept their thoughts from him, just to be contrary. Perhaps the flock's unexplained agitation would be enough to shake their minds awake so he could read them.

Perhaps. But not likely.

They arrived in time for a campfire supper, and the shepherd filled him in. "I'm suspecting a wild dog, but I haven't seen any sign of one."

The sheep had bedded down around them, contrarily showing no sign of agitation at all. "I'll check on them tomorrow," Joss said. "Seem happy enough to me."

"These are the best times," the shepherd agreed. "But here's an oddity. We see strange things, out here alone."

"Hmm?" Joss wasn't paying attention; the long hike and satisfying stew had left him drowsy, and he missed Willow.

"There's something new in the sky. Like a star going across the horizon. Several times a night, for the last nine-day or so. Whaddaya think about that?"

Joss sat up, suddenly alert. "Probably just a comet."

"Yeah, I've heard of them comet things. Never seen one, though."

"Several times a night, you say?"

"Yup."

They were circling. Looking for the best place to land.

Joss shrugged. "Lots of stuff in the night sky." The planet had no moon, but they must get meteors or asteroids occasionally. "That's not what's fussing the sheep, I assume?"

"Nah. They sleep all night. Fat and lazy, that's my flock." He said it with pride. These sheep would be slaughtered for meat, come winter; the extra fat meant richer fare. "As I said, a dog most likely."

For Joss, the conversation meant a greater urgency to get back to Willow. The sooner they could leave for the Motherhouse, the better.

Darkness came late this time of year. Rather than stay awake to get a glimpse of the object in the sky, Joss rolled himself in his bedroll and stared at the dying fire, willing himself to sleep. The next few days promised to be busy.

Three days later, having traced the sheep's agitation to a herb growing along the valley bottom that acted like a stimulant to the animals, Joss assisted Willow with her pack, donned his own, and made a last visual sweep of the cabin he'd shared with her since she'd returned from Borgonne, only five nine-days or so ago – he consciously forced himself to think in their timeframes. He'd left the Motherhouse shortly after she did, sensing that for both of them, Hallan held the answers; now it felt as if he'd been here, with Willow, for a lifetime. And he'd never in his life been more content.

Joss would willingly have foregone this two-day trek to the Motherhouse. But she was right; they had to know.

The lack of timely communication still bothered him. How was Kiril now? Where was Bryar? He had no idea how Ezra and Rebecca fared, or Quinn or Tai or the dozens of people he'd met at the Motherhouse. Each village became its own microcosm, cut off from the rest of the Midland except by the occasional arrival of a Weaver.

And the life of a Weaver inevitably took you far away from those you cared for. It wasn't like back on Terra, where video feeds provided instant contact. Willow must have hundreds of friends, even lovers, although his mind shied away from that idea. Coming to terms with her relationship with Bryar gave him enough trouble. All over the Midland, everywhere she'd ventured in twenty years of traveling, she'd left people behind. Many she'd never see again. It wasn't an easy way of life.

A layer of high cloud made the early part of their walk more pleasant. His hands and arms – and no doubt his face, but he had no way to see himself – were brown now, and his torso had begun to lose the pasty whiteness of life fully clothed. The freedom to wear nothing more than linen trousers and sandals had taken him this full year, since the crash, to appreciate. Yes, there were definite advantages to the way of life in the Midland.

Once they crested the hill and Hallan disappeared behind them, they both increased their pace. They'd spend one night on the trail and be at the Motherhouse in time for supper tomorrow. While he enjoyed the simple meals they prepared, supplemented by the occasional venture to Hallan's dining hall, he looked forward to the greater selection, not to mention competency, of the Motherhouse kitchen.

Willow had been mainly silent the last two days. This wasn't unusual. He let her be, but made sure she knew he was there if she needed him. They'd both endured things in the last year no ordinary human should experience; they both needed time. He found his in the fields, with the animals. His odd way of knowing the minds of the cows, goats, and donkeys felt less foreign now. And he was getting better at screening out the human component, which only Arwen, Ezra, and now Willow, knew about. That had been the best part of his winter of training at the Motherhouse, learning how to protect himself from others' emotions.

Half way to their waysite, she drew him to a halt. "This is one of my favorite views. Look over there."

They'd entered a valley. Far off to his right, to the east, the hills unfolded in shadowed blues. Closer, lower red hills rose above a sluggish river cutting through a field of tall, pointed flowers. "Lupines," she said, correctly discerning his unspoken question. "This is one of my special places. We all find them, the lands we love above all others."

A peaceful quiet filled the valley, just a small breeze ruffling the lupines. Everything condensed to a local, simple level. The beauty of the day, the perfection of the scene, Willow's cornsilk hair tossing gently in the breeze. Damn, she was making a poet out of him.

"You're right. It's perfect." He drew her off the trail and found a place to sit.

She resisted him. "What are you doing? It's not lunch time yet. We have another hour at least."

"No, we don't. We'll go longer this afternoon. Stay here awhile."

Weavers walked to schedules. They were taught how to walk in school, both the mechanics and the strategies for covering distance efficiently. He'd swear it had never occurred to her to simply pause at this spot, soak in the beauty of it.

"Thank you," she said.

As she leaned against him, her face turned toward the amazing hills, he pinched his lips together in a grim line, his mind turning yet again to the ship from Terra, on its way to disrupt his land, his people. You bastards, he thought. You won't destroy this. I won't let you.

Chapter 14

Five days after their hocus-pocus, Kiril couldn't remember ever feeling better. His strength was returning, food tasted good again... He wandered all over the Motherhouse complex, out into the fields and along the river, just to enjoy the strength returning to his muscles.

He'd heard, and understood, the Healers' warning, that the sickness drawing him toward the hills couldn't be cured. With no philosophical reason not to move west, he looked forward to getting a fresh start, but he was in no hurry.

Rain had rolled in at midday. He'd returned from a walk, wet through and eager for a warm bath and dry clothes, but at the sound of voices in the corridor of the guest lodge he drew on his survival skills and drifted back into his room, pulling the door partially closed.

The Old Man, Ezra, spoke with that child-woman Bryar had taken up with. Neither sounded happy.

"It's madness." Tai stopped and planted her hands on her hips.

Ezra seemed, if possible, even older than when Kiril had encountered him in the dining hall – social central – the day before. "For her, yes. For us, for our way of life, no. We've been over this, Tai." His hoarse voice sounded resigned.

"Someone should stop her."

Ezra's gravelly voice was gentle. "Like we've ever stopped you?"

Tai paused. "There's another way. There must be."

"Have you met Gauvain?"

"I see him around. Supervising." Kiril heard the disgust in her voice.

"For him, the grain is a beginning only. His quest for power, and not only as a means to safeguard his homeland, is beyond any I've encountered. He's not a bad man, but he's in the grip of desire and circumstances. Because of that, he will do what he threatens. We need the tools to stop him."

"But the templates become unstable that far back. I doubt we could trust what we learn, even if we do this."

"We have to try. Quinn's willing, and we'll provide the strongest possible link, every Scribe and senior Healer."

The two of them drifted down the hall, Ezra leaning on the young woman – who had the beginnings of a crease between her eyebrows. First Bryar, now Quinn. Poor kid.

Kiril closed his door and waited until the corridor grew quiet. He didn't really know Tai. When they had returned from Borgonne, she'd stayed close to Bryar and seemed to be useful to him. Rumor had it that she was a powerful Scribe, as powerful as Quinn or possibly more so. Hard to believe of the near-androgynous, childlike sprite.

But the message interested him more than the participants did. What was Quinn doing? And what made it so dangerous?

Questions for another day. And they'd just tell him it didn't concern him. Damn, but he was tired of being shut out of the decision-making.

He grabbed a fresh tunic and took his surly mood off to the bathing room.

The next morning, Kiril went in search of Arwen. He'd rather talk to Dal, but Dal lived in Stanstead. He'd accepted that it was time he made his own way in this world, and he needed, of all things, career advice.

But Arwen was nowhere to be found. Nor were Ezra or Tai, or any of the Scribes. Or Beatris or Daren. The apprentices were in classes; a few notes and a declaiming voice trickled from the Bards' lodge – practicing, Kiril speculated. But otherwise the Motherhouse appeared deserted. The low-hanging clouds did nothing to assuage his sense that something was happening. Something wrong.

He found no one in the Centra other than a class of senior apprentices, who appeared to be working without supervision. The dining hall held only the delegation from Borgonne, hunched over caff and looking as puzzled as he was.

Kiril grabbed a pastry to silence the protest in his stomach – he was always hungry these days – and crossed the green to the Scribes' lodge. He still hadn't figured out exactly what Scribes did beyond messing around with the Aura. He'd gleaned that their work could be dangerous, although he didn't understand how or why. By now, though, he didn't doubt; he'd seen enough evidence of the power of the Aura to respect it.

The porter at the entrance tried to stop him; when he refused to be stopped, she seemed to be at a loss. He stood still in the lobby for a moment, then followed his instincts to a closed door. The girl trailed him and put a hand on his arm. "Please," she whispered.

Kiril shook his head at her. A newly minted Weaver, he supposed, and unsure of herself still. He patted her hand and reached for the knob.

She tugged at his sleeve, pleading. "Please, you mustn't disrupt—"

"Shh," he said, and quietly opened the door.

A workroom, he speculated, with light from windows high up in the wall. Was it because of the inhabitants that light seemed dim and eerie? They were all there, the senior Weavers, surrounding a pallet where Quinn lay – or her body did. The quality of her stillness made him wonder if she had died. It was like those Healers' trances, only deeper, more profound.

Not Quinn.

A slight breeze entered the room with him, ruffling the hair of those sitting closest to the door, but no one so much as twitched.

What the hell kind of ritual had he stumbled into? Kiril fought a need to break it up, to snatch Quinn and take her somewhere normal, hurl lightning bolts at her warders. But he'd bet this involved the Aura, and by now he knew better. They were in control, or so he hoped.

The little porter nudged him from outside the door; he waved her away and watched, caught up in the otherworldly atmosphere of the room.

Kiril had no idea how long he stood there. He felt as if he, too, had drifted into a trance, hypnotized by the scene before him.

A godawful scream rent the air, shaking him awake.

Another, inhuman. And another.

Quinn.

She lurched upright on the pallet, her eyes still closed, her mouth twisted in horror. And still she screamed. Panic-stricken, her hands scrabbled at the air as if seeking purchase.

And still no one moved.

The hell with that. Kiril shoved his way through the gathered Weavers and stood next to the pallet. "Hold me," he said, and caught her flailing hands.

She did. She still screamed, into his chest, but her fingers clutched his tunic as if he were her sole lifeline. He put one hand on her head, touching for the first time the springy curls. The other rested on her back, gently, sensing she would panic even more if she were bound.

And still no one moved.

After a couple of minutes, some of the tension dispersed and Arwen appeared at his elbow, livid. "Get out of here," she hissed.

"No." He ignored her and kept his attention on the hysterical woman in his arms. The screams gradually diminished in volume and frequency, replaced by uncontrolled sobbing.

Around him the room stirred. Kiril heard mumbling but didn't trouble himself to listen. Beatris appeared on the other side of the pallet and began some of that arm-waving thing they did. After a minute she turned away, drawing Arwen with her; their voices whispered behind him.

Time hung suspended, irrelevant. At last Quinn stilled, then sagged in his arms. He eased her down on the pallet, smoothing her arms straight, giving her hands a squeeze.

Arwen hadn't finished with him. Her hand clenched his biceps like a vise. "Come with me," she snarled.

This time he obeyed her. Outside the room she spun and spat, "Do you have any idea what you've done?"

"Comforted a frightened woman?" he asked. Arwen's intimidation tactics wouldn't work, not today.

"She wasn't all the way back, you fool. She needed to work out of the template herself. Did you really believe she was helpless? What do you take us for?"

"You let her fight her way back from whatever hell you sent her to, on her own and terrified. Based on that, I take you for monsters. I suspect she's 'back', as you put it, now, isn't she?"

Arwen conceded, but reluctantly. "If you'd pulled your little stunt an instant sooner, she might never have come back at all. You nearly cost her her life, or her sanity."

"Is that what happens when you go wandering in that Aura of yours and get lost? Maybe you're the fools." He was angry, genuinely curious... and not the least guilty.

"I want you back in the guest lodge, and packing to leave. I don't want to see you around the Motherhouse again, except in the dining hall. We'll compel you if you don't obey me."

He smiled, but it was thin. "That's been tried." That day on the trail; he didn't remember it, but he'd been told. "You can't compel me, can you? Not without killing me. I don't think you want to do that."

She got in his face; he felt spittle on his cheek. "You mock us, and you don't even understand what it is you despise so much. Get out of here." She spaced the words so that each one became an individual threat.

Prudently, he stepped back. "Yes, ma'am. With pleasure. Take care of her."

He wheeled and strode out of the Scribes' lodge, leaving Arwen and the wide-eyed porter behind him.

Arwen stayed in her room with her; Quinn was aware of the older woman's presence as she slept, or tried to sleep. The memories refused to let her go.

They tried to ask what she had seen. She shut them out. She couldn't tell it.

Worse, she'd failed. She'd found only the faintest trace of one spell on the hills, and the certainty that there were not one or two, but many. At least she knew Gauvain stood no chance of disentangling them.

Beatris came and went, dosing her from their magical vials, checking her for fever or other signs of illness. It helped, knowing they were there. But she couldn't free herself from the nightmare.

In the morning, they brought food. She sat at her table and ate, tasting nothing, declining caff. The ritual repeated at the midday meal. In between, Beatris forced her to the bathing room, washed her, and dressed her in a tunic that wasn't saturated with her own sweat.

Arwen dragged her out to walk around the green. Back near the storehouses, the delegation from Borgonne was preparing to leave. Even with her mind so wounded, the sheer volume of supplies they planned to transport impressed her.

"We secured the loan of three donkeys," Arwen told her. "Seven people with low Entrée and twenty bearers – it seems every agriculturist within a five day walk of here is determined to prove his mettle by crossing the hills."

Quinn didn't answer, but she took it in.

"The girl, Amalie, has petitioned to remain with us. I've given my consent, but I'm waiting to hear from Gauvain. I don't know how he'd feel about losing one of his apprentices."

"Probably just fine," Quinn muttered. "Being she's a girl."

The first words she'd spoken since... then. Arwen gave a thin smile.

The walk tired her. She turned her steps back toward the Scribes' lodge, Arwen keeping pace.

And there, crossing the green...

"*Willow!*"

Willow spun around. "*Quinn!*" she shouted back.

With strength she didn't think she had, Quinn set off at a lope, almost collapsing in her friend's arms.

Willow walked with Joss by the river, keeping herself tucked securely under his strong arm. Their news about the imminent arrival of more Terrans hadn't caused the consternation she'd expected; the Scribes had already spotted a new object in the sky, one that didn't obey the rules of star movement, and speculation had led them to the same conclusion.

After her reunion with Quinn on the green, Arwen had hustled them both into her workroom, where Quinn stumbled through an abbreviated version of her journey into history that was more disturbing than the imminent arrival of the Terrans. The sight of her restrained friend breaking down, unable to force her emotions back under control, made Willow feel sick. Quinn never let go of her hand as she told of treachery, destruction of homes and businesses, whole towns... and killing, even babies, cruelly, in front of their parents, and then the parents too.... Her people, the people of the Midland, had fled across the hills, and then began creating the spells. In those days, before the Mages of that time built the barriers separating them, the power of the Aura was as strong in the Midland as in Borgonne. They sacrificed power for security. And all because back then, over three hundred years ago, they hadn't been able to agree on a system of governance.

One good thing came from Quinn's venture so deep into the Aura. They now knew it would be virtually impossible to remove the multiple spells that bound the hills and forever separated the Midland from Borgonne.

The story haunted her. That someone might inflict such torture on Mari...

Off to her right, the river tumbled on its way south. Never placid, it provided a familiar rhythm to the day. She stopped and turned to Joss. She hadn't been able to speak the words yet, but he knew how upset she was. A shudder coursed through her, but his big hands were ready with comfort. She'd be all right... but who held Quinn?

She hadn't even located Mari yet. Tonight, she promised herself. And perhaps see Amalie again, since the girls had become best friends. Willow was pleased and amazed, not only that Amalie had dared the crossing but with her determination to stay behind when the others struck out for home.

The hills. She hoped never to venture into the hills again. They loomed in her imagination, as if their malevolence only came into focus in retrospect.

By mutual understanding – and that had become a way of life, the way they understood each other's desires – they walked on.

Willow consciously soaked up the energies of the path, the plants, the surging river, finding her grounding again.

"You could have stayed," she said. Joss had left before Quinn told her story.

"Not with all that jagged energy. I couldn't screen her out. You'd have had two basket cases to deal with," he added with a trace of his dry humor. "I ran into Kiril. He doesn't look great, but he says he's better than he was. I'll eat with him tonight, get the full story."

"Sad times."

"Not altogether."

No, not altogether. The Motherhouse stood as both home and bastion. However much had happened, nothing posed an immediate threat. She could Heal again, travel again. Mari was strong and capable. And there was Joss...

Yes, she thought, there was Joss, the miracle she'd never expected. Now that he'd transformed her life, she had no intention of ever letting it go.

Words weren't necessary. They continued their walk in silence, arms around each other, content.

Chapter 15

The next afternoon, the meeting Quinn had dreaded finally occurred. Around the table were Arwen and Ezra, Daren, Dorcas, and, unexpectedly, Gauvain. Willow sat beside her, solemn.

"From what little I've gleaned so far," Arwen said. "Quinn's experience reinforces our decision not to open the trail through the hills. Gauvain needs the complete picture as much as we do, so I included him today."

Earlier, Quinn had walked into the woods, taking the track around the Motherhouse and its environs while she considered the words she'd use to convey the horror of their early history. The reality was, mere words couldn't hope to be adequate. If she let herself fully remember that time...

She gave herself a shake to cast off the visceral experience of the memories. Willow glanced at her, brows raised.

All eyes focused on her. She took a breath, exhaled, breathed again.

"First, to be very clear, it will be impossible to remove the spells. There are multiples, layers of them, woven from each side without coordination. I got first-hand experience, trying to navigate around their templates, so this isn't conjecture. Over the years they've become entangled, strengthening them and possibly giving rise to anomalies like the monster that attacked Kiril."

Her voice hiccupped slightly when she said his name. Willow noticed; she doubted anyone else did.

"So even with your old document, I doubt you'll be able to disentangle the weaves of the Borgonnian spells," she said, addressing Gauvain. "The Midland ones are lost beyond recovery."

"I see," Gauvain said in a low voice, more as if he were talking to himself.

"Any other questions about the spells?" Quinn asked.

"Is it possible to ameliorate them? Lessen the risk?" Dorcas leaned forward. "For instance, could we find a specific thread that produced Kiril's lizard?"

"I doubt it. The templates are so intertwined, they're like a maze with no exit. I haven't seen anything that points directly to the lizard. Have you?" she asked Gauvain.

He shook his head.

"So if we choose to provide continuing relief to Borgonne, we need another way to convey emergency supplies," Arwen concluded. "This will be a political decision and not one for this meeting. Can you continue?" she asked Quinn.

Kind words, Quinn thought. A request, not a command.

"Bear with me," she said. Once again she breathed, as much as her lungs would hold, then slowly released it. Willow pushed her mug of water closer; nodding a thank-you, Quinn took it and drank.

"It was bad," she began. "It all fell apart. Our ancestors established settlements in what we now call Borgonne, but some kind of crisis struck. I'm not sure what, but I don't think it was drought. Pestilence, possibly. Anyway, they ran low on food. Arguments about shortages blew up into a full-scale revolution. I couldn't sort out the political positions or who wanted what, I just saw father against daughter, neighbor against neighbor."

She stopped, swallowed, began again. "Desperate parents watching their children starve. The brutality... whole families massacred, assaults in the night against unarmed and unprepared people. Guerrilla attacks, and no mercy. I witnessed... a bloodbath. Cruelty I can't even imagine."

As she spoke, her voice became robotic. "Ultimately, a band gathered at the foot of the hills and struck out. No spells guarded the hills then, and they were... different. As we have suspected, the spells make them seem smaller, lower, more benign. These were mountains, harsh and without trails. But the people went, carrying what they could. Other parties followed."

Quinn stopped. No one broke the silence.

"The violence died down. They survived and built civilizations. I was running by then, looking for a safe way out, so I only saw the next years in flashes. Understand," she added, "my deepest penetration took me to the Borgonnian side of the hills. What I learned about the Midland came later, after a hundred years or more."

No one spoke or so much as moved. She held their full attention.

"They'd discovered the Aura before the troubles and presumably knew something of manipulating it. The people in the Midland soon realized that spells had been placed on the mountains to prevent anyone else from crossing. They added layers of their own. By unspoken consent, both sides blocked further communication.

"Our system of Weavers, and Borgonne's of Mages, evolved gradually over the next hundred years. And occasional word did leak through. It wouldn't surprise me, Gauvain, to hear you weren't the first to brave the hills." She nodded to him; he grudgingly returned the gesture. "Gradually we learned that those with Entrée could cross, yet we didn't. We allowed the myth of impermeability to stay." She fell silent.

"Our ancestors didn't want us to mix," Arwen concluded. "With good reason? It's impossible to say now. Our systems of governance, our general philosophies of life, even our ways of working with the Aura are radically different. Quinn's report reinforces what we already knew, so our decision stands. We will not assist in any endeavor to open the hills, other than this one trip for emergency relief during your drought."

"None of this changes my determination to create a safe passage," Gauvain said flatly.

"You will not be successful," Dorcas said. "You cannot be, not with half the protections based in the Midland. Even your Mages, if you sent them, would have no place to start. The spells are lost, Gauvain."

He acknowledged the comment with a magisterial nod of his head.

And then it was over. Quinn found herself whisked away, Willow in tow, as Arwen propelled them both to her workroom.

"I wish you could see yourself," Arwen said as they settled around the workbench. "You're a wreck."

"Yeah. I feel like one."

"This is enough, Quinn. I need you whole and functioning. In the last season or two, you've gone beyond duty, and now it's time to stop. Go home."

"Home?" Quinn's head jerked up. "What do you mean?"

"I mean home. Mother and father. Old haunts. The trek to get there will rebuild your health, and time away from here will give you perspective. I hate to lose you right now, but... realistically, I already have. We'll be fine here. So go. Tomorrow."

Arwen rose from the stool at her workbench where she had installed herself.

"Arwen?"

The older woman paused, her hand reaching for the door. She didn't turn around.

"Care to tell me what happened?"

Arwen turned slowly and faced Quinn. "As you were coming out of the Aura, you mean."

"Yes. Was it Daren? I was grateful for the comfort once I got far enough to be out of danger. But it broke precedent."

"No, not Daren," Arwen said shortly. "It was Kiril."

She opened the door and left the room.

Kiril?

"Sustainer." Quinn slumped, as if she had taken one blow too many. "How did he get involved?"

"I've heard rumors," Willow said. "He heard you screaming and barged in. Arwen tore a piece off him later."

Kiril. Her mind couldn't accept it. She remembered the hands, so gentle. And the strength of his chest as she clawed toward safety. But no one ever, *ever*, interrupted a Weaver coming back from walking a template.

Abruptly light-headed, Quinn closed her eyes. "She's right. I need to get away. My world's galloping out of control."

"It's a great idea," Willow said. Her hand brushed Quinn's forehead, returning her to the here and now. "You can't go on like this, so leave. At least you have a home to go back to," she added with an unexpected hint of bitterness.

"Not tomorrow, though. I couldn't be ready by tomorrow."

"The next day then."

Quinn squeezed her friend's hand. "Come with me."

Willow shook her head. "I've got my place. And you need to do this on your own. Go, Quinn. For yourself."

She didn't answer as she slid from her stool and moved to the door. "Walk?"

"Sure."

They left in silence, each absorbed in her own thoughts.

Kiril caught sight of Quinn the next morning as she crossed the green toward the west, heading for some unknown destination. For once she lacked her usual determined manner. He'd been resting on the amphitheater slope, soaking up the sun over a mug of caff. Without thinking he rose and, mentally plotting a trajectory, set out to intercept her. Rescuing her from that bunch of over-zealous Weavers had at once thrilled him and knocked him off balance; he needed to yell at someone. Overhead, the sky threatened a lingering rain, which suited his mood perfectly.

She saw him coming and ignored him.

He caught up with her on the edge of the Motherhouse complex, near the open forest that marked the beginning of the track to Stanstead. Grabbing her arm, he jerked her to a halt. "What in the blazes possessed you to do something that foolish?" he hissed.

She yanked free from his grasp; he seized her again.

"Let me go." The threat in her voice was palpable.

Instead, he shook her. "Not until you tell me you won't risk yourself that way again."

She rounded on him, as much as she could with his hand holding her captive. "What business is it of yours? You don't even belong here."

"I don't belong anywhere else. Get used to it."

"The trail's right there. How about taking it? Just get the hell out of here. You're no Weaver, and you have no idea what I was doing. Or why." She twisted her arm free; this time he let her.

As usual, she'd triggered his ire, beyond his previously unacknowledged fear for her. "You think I'm so blind to what's going on? You risk being invaded, and instead of talking to people with training and experience, you delve into history and damn near get yourself killed."

Quinn spoke through clenched teeth. "You've hardly given us any reason to trust you."

"Oh, I see. Saving your precious Bryar wasn't enough? Ask him his opinion, why don't you?"

Both their voices had risen; they were shouting in each other's faces now.

"You know nothing about the Aura. *Nothing* about the peril facing us."

"Dammit, I'm the one carrying around the remnant of that thing in the hills. Not you. Not Bryar or Arwen or anyone else. Me. Remember me?"

Her voice fell and dripped with ice. "Despite my best efforts, I find you hard to forget."

"Then say you won't make such a damn fool decision again. Stay out of the Aura, Quinn."

"Stay out of my business."

She tried to turn from him; he yanked her back. "Call it enlightened self-interest. After all, you're the one who keeps this demon in me under control. Or maybe I just want you around until the day I take you. Because make no mistake, that day's coming."

Where had that come from? He hadn't known he'd say any such thing. Hadn't even contemplated it.

Rage flooded her face. "Bastard."

He caught her wrist before her hand made contact. Based on the jolt along his arm muscles, he would have worn the mark for days. "And when it happens," he said with a tight smile, "it's going to be a pleasure to tame you."

Furious, she spat, "I saved your life."

"Did I ever ask you to?"

He yanked her closer. They stood there, eye to eye, each of them seething.

Then his mouth was on hers and her teeth scraped his lip, their tongues fought as hard as their words, he felt her hands clawing into his back, and he had a death lock on her as if he wanted to pull her into him, make them one being...

Simultaneously they came to their senses and stood panting, staring at each other.

"Don't you ever, *ever*, try that again." Her fury lay barely beneath the surface of her words.

"Try?" Kiril did his best to keep his voice light, edging on sarcastic. "Why darlin', you were right in there with me. And not objecting, unless you're a damn fine actor."

She wheeled and stormed off in the direction of the Scribes' lodge.

Seems like she forgot all about where she was going. For some reason, that pleased him.

Kiril picked up the forgotten caff mug and returned to his place on the slope above the green, disconcerted by their encounter, and more sure than ever of his intention to control and tame the magnificent, dark-skinned woman.

Chapter 16

All lay in readiness. Gauvain made a final survey of the provisions arrayed in a storage shed behind the Centra and found nothing to fault. Although insufficient to stave off crop failure, much less starvation later in the summer, what they carried back to Borgonne showed good intent and served as a test of sorts for the trading protocol he intended to implement.

Using his apprentices to defend against the spells of the hills had worked satisfactorily on the trip to the Midland. This time their party would consist of over thirty, plus donkeys. Nine had some form of Entrée; he would make a point of keeping their group tightly together, lest their Auric ties stretch too thin for protection.

Gauvain had been over this numerous times, in his own planning and with the team from the Motherhouse. He was as confident as he could be of a successful outcome, but...

He hated the hills and dreaded tomorrow's departure. Despite the comparatively primitive life and accommodation at the Motherhouse, he'd enjoyed his time here.

Arwen met him as he pulled the door to on the storage shed. "Will you walk with me?" she said. "I'd like a private word with you before you go."

"Certainly." He offered an arm, which, somewhat to his surprise, Arwen accepted. She led them toward the start of the path that followed the circumference of the large valley comprising the Motherhouse environs.

They'd always had the ability to work in accord, he reflected. As if they were of one mind.

"We've had little time to talk," he said.

"My life is busy." Arwen gave him a half smile. "And I doubt the past is worth revisiting."

"For lessons learned, perhaps. I feel the weight of age these days."

Her lips blossomed into the first true smile he'd seen. "You're scarcely an old man, Gauvain."

"I will be, by the time I get my rabble across the hills."

"True," Arwen mused. "I've witnessed the effects on our people, and they are younger than you and I."

"There's more at stake than merely trade." The trail had begun to climb; he felt the pull in his calves. Arwen, he noted, moved smoothly, as if she paced the perimeter on a daily basis.

"What are you thinking of?" She dropped his arm and shoved her hands into the pockets of her tunic. This morning she wore no skirt or trousers, probably in deference to the heat. The Midland habit of running around half clad still left him nonplussed.

"The man Kiril. Who can predict the extent of the menace he represents, or what other threats may occur? Or from what direction? I've heard murmurs about a strange object in the sky, for instance."

"The new object quite possibly relates to Kiril and Joss," Arwen said bluntly. "Both predicted that their home planet will send settlers here. That poses a threat to your way of life as much as ours."

Gauvain was silent. He'd heard that rumor, too; confidentiality was a rare commodity at the Motherhouse. Even the apprentices kept in touch with events going on around them. The openness had worried him during his stay here, because there had to be secrets. Everyone held them. He couldn't fathom how they managed otherwise.

They walked in silence until they reached the highest point above the giant bowl of pastureland. From here the Motherhouse looked like a miniature model, and the village, which of necessity he had visited several times for a shave, was just visible in the distance. The heat created a haze that gave the whole scene a misty, surreal appearance, heightened by the towering massif to the north.

Arwen settled on a bench placed to take advantage of the lookout. Gauvain sat beside her. From her pocket she extracted a sheet of the rough paper they used in the Midland, unfolded it, and smoothed it on her knee. "I want you to look at this," she said.

Mysteries. Arwen had never played all her cards up front... speaking of secrets. But he'd be happy to help her interpret the crude weave diagramed on the page. Although it was surprising that a Mage – a Scribe – of her power required his assistance.

He took the paper from her and studied it. Parts of it looked familiar...

Arwen sat unmoving as he deconstructed the lines in front of him. The diagram appeared to be a partial rendering of the mysterious weave he'd been studying and manipulating for a year now.

He looked up. "Is this mine?"

"Not exactly," Arwen said neutrally. "I think it's one of the spells on the hills. You've been working with it, though. Changing it."

"Testing it," he corrected, and frowned at the annotations in an unfamiliar hand. "I told you I have access to some of the weaves. You're aware this is only a fragment?"

"Yes."

He turned his attention back to the diagram. Arwen wanted him to see something... what? As he allowed his eyes to go into soft focus, the energetic currents leapt into a new pattern, one he hadn't uncovered before. The weave so simplified showed multiple connections between Borgonne and the hills. That didn't surprise him; But one current... the implications...

No. He rejected her conclusion. The diagram was incomplete. She had to be wrong.

Arwen shifted on the bench and traced a work-roughened finger along connecting currents that gradually traversed the weave. "This."

Sustainer help him.

"You're accusing me of creating the crisis in Borgonne."

"Not accusing." Her voice, like the hand she placed on his arm, was gentle. "But suggesting that when you arrive home, you explore this pathway. I believe your experiments drew energies from Borgonne, probably feeding them into the hills. If so, you may hold the power to reverse the drought. In any event, you must try."

Gauvain stared out over the peaceful valley. Sheep dotted the pastures, white balls against the green. Tiny people worked in the few cultivated fields.

He didn't believe it. He'd never make such an amateurish mistake.

At least Arwen had allowed him his dignity. No one need know.

The Scribes at the Motherhouse knew.

An unaccustomed emotion washed over him. How would he face them? Once he was safely home, he'd work day and night, correct his assumptions about the weave, before any of the other active Mages in Borgonne found out...

The humiliation was physically painful, twisting his gut and sending arrow-like jabs through his brain.

"You're among the most powerful people alive, Mage or Weaver," Arwen said. "If what I see here is accurate, I challenge you to turn it around. I trust you to do so. I'll leave you now."

He couldn't look up. Couldn't face her.

Arwen's hand squeezed his shoulder as she stood. "One other thing I wanted you to know. While I don't dwell on the past, I don't forget, either."

He didn't watch her walk away. Instead, he kept his gaze on the bowl of the Motherhouse, symbolic of a land so different from his own.

They left with little fanfare, a far cry from the first precipitous departure from Borgonne. Most recruits came from villages at a distance from the Motherhouse, so there were few relatives present. Although Gauvain was well aware that many of their bearers had volunteered in search of adventure, the inhabitants of the Motherhouse considered the trek a necessity, not a cause for excitement.

High cloud blanketed the sky, for which he was grateful. He sensed no rain in the foreseeable future, and the cloud reduced the heat load.

He had maintained both silence and distance over the preceding two days, but no one, either from his delegation or from the Motherhouse, mentioned the fateful weave.

Amalie approached him. She held herself erect, with a maturity he had not detected in her before. "Please assure my family I am happy and well cared for. And that I will return after I complete my training."

Cast into the role of paterfamilias, Gauvain assumed his gravest expression. "Are you absolutely sure you're not letting yourself be seduced by the casual companionship you've found here? The training will be less complete than I can offer you."

"But different." Amalie wore her new self-assurance like a shield. "We work hard, and the ways they use templates and herbs is different. When I return to Borgonne, I will be a Healer."

"But not a Mage."

Amalie grinned, the first hint that a teenaged girl still lurked behind the assured young woman confronting him. "This suits me better."

"Very well. I will deliver your message."

Cedric appeared at his elbow, blustering. "You cannot expect that peasant to lead the way." The *peasant* he objected to was one of their most ideal recruits, a muscular young man with strong Entrée who had chosen agricultural life over that of a Weaver.

"I can and I do."

"I absolutely insist—"

"That you lead? No." Gauvain turned away from Cedric in contempt.

Arwen approached. "All is ready, and you should go before the day advances any further."

He surveyed his party one final time... posturing Cedric, Ester looking on with a sardonic smile, the bearers displaying a mix of excitement and trepidation. He shook his head and gestured to the leader to set off.

Chapter 17

As long as he avoided the high, half-fingered notes, Bryar was satisfied with his performance. Not the quality he once expected of himself, but the people in the towns and hamlets throughout the Midland wouldn't notice the difference.

He lowered the flute. Tai nodded, beaming her full-bore smile. He'd hated watching her walk off with Ezra to answer the Motherhouse summons, but found that a few days alone, with only Rebecca for company, benefitted him. He felt calmer, centered.

Which didn't mean he wasn't thrilled when they came home again.

This rehearsal was for the benefit of the river, the fish, and the small animals that inhabited the forests around Ezra's compound. Tomorrow they'd try it out on Ezra and Rebecca. Privately, Bryar dreaded fumbling notes, as he hadn't done since well before his journey year, but he'd never find a more sympathetic audience. And once they took to the roads again, he had to get used to others listening.

The day was sweltering. He wore only a light pair of trousers, she a short linen tunic. Beads of sweat ran down his back.

"Once more through 'Tommy Thompson' and we're done," she said.

He groaned but acquiesced. Tai played a decent chitarre, but she'd never been a performer. She was more nervous than he was about their impending debut as a duo. As she picked up the instrument, he swallowed his jealousy and prepared to sing and recite the centuries-old lay, Tai providing reliable harmony on the choruses.

One day, he promised himself. *Left-handed if need be.* The notes she floated up into the sky were his life's meaning and purpose. His to do.

But he'd ceded them to her for now. Bryar launched his voice to mingle with her chords, creating the familiar story as he'd always done.

Almost.

Their al fresco performance over, they packed up the instruments. Bryar grabbed Tai to his side for a quick hug. "Home?" Rebecca had been in the kitchen when they left, which boded well for their immediate future.

"Maybe not quite yet." Tai had mischief in her eyes as she rested the chitarre case against a tree. Her hands found his chest, explored down... to the ties at his waist. In a flash she undid them. Then she stripped off her tunic and ran for the river.

By the time he'd kicked his feet free of the trousers, she had plunged in. He followed with a flying dive. By now he knew where to find her.

Sure enough, she waited for him in the little pool under the draping trees, where they liked to pretend no one could find them. The moment he surfaced, she twined herself around him. Tai understood his bond with his element and was unique among his many lovers in her willingness to mate in the water. There in the shallows, as he rolled her on top of him, he could believe, if only for the minutes of what proved to be an explosive lovemaking, that life retained the simple beauty he'd once believed in.

A considerable time later, they found Ezra in his chair on the porch, looking pleased. "I was beginning to wonder if you'd already left," he said in a mock grumble. "Tai, go fetch an old man a mug of cider, will you? Today is a day of celebration."

"Why?" Bryar settled in his usual place on the top porch step while Tai gathered the instruments and disappeared into the house. "What's happened?"

Ezra grinned. "First, you return looking satisfied. That bodes well for traveling again, much though we'll hate to lose you. Second, I've received word that the power cell has reached its final resting place. No one will find it again."

"Good." Very good. He'd sacrificed two of his fingers, not to mention his innocence and peace of mind, to secure the cell. It had been worth it.

"You're regaining your musical skills, Bryar. And the rest will come."

"Huh."

His grunt spoke more to the constant reassurance he'd been subjected to ever since it happened than to his disbelief in Ezra's words. He knew the effect of the catastrophic events in Orlan was fading, occupying less of his mind each day. But he'd lost more than fingers, and he missed the carefree man he'd been.

"That man needed to go," Ezra said, as usual reading his thoughts. Bryar never bothered to screen his mind around this tight family, Ezra and Rebecca and Tai. Even more than Willow and Quinn, he let them in.

Tai came out with cider from last year's apples. "Relax. We're gonna be great," she said, handing him a mug, then settling beside him and aiming an elbow at his ribs.

"I assume you're not going to tell us where the cell is," Bryar said, blatantly changing the topic. He'd deal with his insecurities by himself from now on... as long as Tai was close by.

"Of course not. In fact, I don't know myself, other than a general area. It's been on a journey, with even the couriers none the wiser."

Tai nodded. "Good. We plan to leave in three or four days' time, Granddad. Sound right to you?"

As Tai chatted with her grandfather, Bryar leaned against the newel post and listened. His wild one, willingly tamed for him. Usually they were inseparable. But he sensed when she needed her freedom, and then he'd watch her go, disappearing into the wilderness for days at a time while he worried. Days later she'd come back, once again willing to be his chitarrist, his helpmate, his lover and mainstay. Life without her was unthinkable, and so far she seemed fine with that.

On the road again. Traveling from hamlet to hamlet, regaining strength in his performance, perhaps he'd find traces of the man he'd once been and integrate them with the cynical, tired man he'd become.

Chapter 18

In the meeting room attached to the bridge of the Eurocorp Adventurer, Harry Belfontaine, Major in the Eurocorp Expeditionary Force and default commander of the ship, studied the readouts before him. He was tired. They'd been orbiting HP-155NC, sector 2, for a couple of weeks now, getting their bearings, and he had a pretty good idea of what the missing exploration pod from Northam Corp had found – assuming they had landed and any of them survived. Who expected an inhabited planet?

His senior staff trickled into the room, gathering around the conference table. Ben Albright, first officer. Constance Devereaux, medic. Georges Toit, security. He ticked them off in his head, these men and women he'd been cocooned with for close to two earth years. Elspeth Gandsdottir, who would assume command once they'd landed, sat quietly at the far end of the table. She said little in these meetings, but missed nothing. Nicole Heidelberg, second officer, wasn't there yet – as usual. No amount of lecture, carrot-and-stick, or punishment made a difference; the woman was constitutionally unable to be on time.

Which was why he usually scheduled these meetings fifteen minutes before he planned to start.

Hans Merkel, Jane Peters, and Henrik Strauss gathered at one end of the table, comparing notes. They represented the three 'communities' on the ship, each its own administrative unit while still accountable to the whole. Establishing these communities had been a stroke of inspiration, providing a communication chain and keeping things under control during the inevitable disputes. Two years in a spaceship hadn't been easy on anybody.

Finally Nicole rushed in, her hair already flying out of her regulation bun. Harry stepped to the head of the table and rapped with his knuckles.

The silence was immediate. This was it. D-Day, destination day.

He cut straight to the chase. "You've seen the reports. Breathable air, water, what appears to be viable cropland. Plenty of empty space. And the complicating factor, the people. Our estimates suggest a total population of no more than forty thousand. Room enough for us, but no way to determine whether the natives will prove to be friendly."

Nods around the table. This had been in their briefing notes the previous night, not to mention on their view screens for weeks.

"The decisions now are, first, where to make our initial contact, and second, the nature of the landing. You know we're low on fuel. Once we set down, we aren't going anywhere, other than with the land explorers, as long as their solar cells hold up. So we have to decide what ecosystem suits us best and how much interaction we want to have with the locals. Ultimately, contact is inevitable, but we don't necessarily need to instigate it so soon. We'll have enough on our hands."

"The southern landmass is a safer bet," Georges said. "In the north they're already half way through their growing season. It's warmer, and we have to consider food."

"And there are no settlements in the south," Jane added.

"True, but there's also the soil," Ben put in. "It's rockier and supports less vegetation now. We've detected seismic activity throughout the planet, but stronger in the south. The weather is more severe."

"Which doesn't solve the problem of having time to produce a crop," Georges countered.

"The agricultural experts think they've defeated the mold," Nicole said, referring to the small farm on the lowest level of the ship. They grew a limited selection of quickly maturing and easy-to-store vegetables; Harry thought longingly of tomatoes, so plentiful in Eurocorp. The reduced harvest due to the mold made it imperative to find other food sources. "So our own production should increase."

"The locals might help," Jane, always a peacemaker, suggested.

"Or they might eat us," Georges countered.

"Could we send a pod to the surface?" Henrik asked.

Several voices said no at the same time. "We can't afford the power," Harry explained. "The pods use the ship's power supply to charge up." He rapped again, breaking up side conversations. "Ben, can we risk orbiting lower, get a better feel for their lives?"

Ben squirmed. "Same argument as with the pod. We'd burn fuel we can't spare."

"But it might tell us if we'll face bloodthirsty warriors or peaceful farmers."

The debate rambled on. The people around the table knew each other too well not to already know everyone's positions on most matters. It all came down to one of three choices. Learn more about the population at the cost of fuel needed to maneuver the ship, settle on the much smaller southern landmass at the risk of more hostile conditions, or choose a less densely settled region of the northern continent and hope the natives proved friendly. None of the options was ideal.

Finally, Jane said, "Quite apart from the practical considerations, I don't mind pulling my weight but I don't want to live in a hostile environment. I want someplace where there'll be mild winters and enough wheat to make bread. Sunshine. It's been a long trip, Harry. We're all losing perspective."

Harry nodded. They'd coexisted remarkably well overall, but he could feel the edges fraying.

"If the natives are hostile, we could take them," Georges said.

"Provided we have power to charge our weapons," Hans said.

"Once we've landed, we'll unfurl the solar panels," Henrik said.

"I agree with Jane." Constance, a woman in her middle years, lean as they all were but with a softness about her, generally was quiet in these meetings, and so far had not contributed to the discussion. Now she spoke with urgency. "That weird flu-like thing a year ago severely depleted our medical supplies. We need these people. We need to replenish our medicines – assuming they've developed a local pharmacopeia."

"They must have," Harry said. "We've seen their settlements. Proper towns, some of them. This isn't a hard-scrabble hunter-gatherer society."

"Arguably, there are two cultures." Nicole had a degree in anthropology. "Either side of that mountain range. They're not the same, I'd lay any money on it."

"So, one more question. Which side of the mountains suits our needs better? The east seems more sophisticated, at least in terms of that large town, but it hasn't rained since we started monitoring. The west is more likely to yield decent crops." Harry had seen the differences too, in the nature of the settlements, but he'd hoped to avoid having it escalate to an issue. He sighed, quietly to himself.

"I suggest we run a factor analysis," Ben said. "Input all the parameters and everything we know about possible landing sites and let the computer tell us the optimum place."

"Is this really a matter for logical analysis? It seems more personal somehow." Peacemaker or no, Jane wasn't a fan of the machines that kept them alive.

Harry had learned months ago not to allow these meetings go on too long. "Run your analysis, Ben," he said. "Then we'll think again. But we have time constraints, don't forget. Let's make a decision and land. I'm sick of this boat."

A few corroborating groans greeted his comment. His team returned to their duties, leaving just Ben and himself, along with the navigator and petty officers, on the bridge.

"Opinion?" he asked Ben.

"We'll touch down on that plain we identified a week ago. We'll plant late season vegetables and winter wheat, make cautious contact with the natives, find fodder for the animals, and start to build. You and I have known this for days."

Harry grinned. "Are you going to run that analysis, or just report the results?"

"Oh, I'll run it. In my copious spare time."

Harry punched Ben on the shoulder and returned to his duties. One way or another, he expected to set his ship on the surface in a week, maybe two. But no longer.

Chapter 19

As well that Arwen sent her packing, Quinn reflected as she put one foot ahead of the other and wished the day would end. The journey into the depths of the Aura had left her useless for anything else. Her mind barely functioned, she jumped at the slightest noise, and her sleep... when did she sleep? The memories still haunted her. Perhaps they always would.

The walk had been therapeutic, just as Arwen predicted. She'd had time to clear her mind, gain perspective on the terrible scenes she had witnessed, and consider the problem of Borgonne and trade through the hills.

And Kiril. That kiss, when it felt as if they were trying to consume each other. And his words: *Did I ever ask you to?* Hadn't he wanted to be cleansed of that malevolent energy that poisoned him? Or did he simply hate to be indebted? Her journey through the templates had triggered the whole encounter – his unexpected comfort, however foolhardy, then his near fury at her for doing it in the first place. She didn't understand any of it, or her own reaction to him.

She'd never even thanked him for being there to hold her when she emerged a traumatized mess.

She should have thanked him.

The trek to Colgate took fifteen days, but she had taken the track through Hallan, accompanying Willow and Joss, and spent two nights there before striking out on the trail west to intersect with the main north-south road out of Stanstead. Quinn seldom left the Motherhouse, with or without Scribes' business to see to, and the ventures into the hills to meet Bryar, then Willow, had been more than sufficient to alert her that she still didn't much enjoy it. At least nothing reminded her of the nightmare.

She arrived on the outskirts of Colgate dusty, footsore, and hot. As luck, if you could call it that, would have it, the first person she encountered was her brother Ifram. He saw her coming and stopped on the track, holding a rope tied to... what? The animal stood well above her brother's height, and he wasn't a short man.

Animal or no, meeting Ifram with no parents or neighbors as buffers, and she considerably the worse for wear, wouldn't be her first choice. It did remind her, however, how close she was to home, so before closing the distance between them she made sure her brown Scribe's sash lay smooth and prominent across her tunic.

"Sister," he said formally as she approached.

"Is it safe?" she asked. "What is it?"

"Usually, and a horse. The parents will be glad to see you."

But not Ifram, apparently. The issue of whether she had caused the death of his first child might never be laid to rest between them. The old anger flashed at the injustice of it, even if the event did lead to her entering the Motherhouse.

Over twenty-five years now. Ifram's sons were grown, his daughter had partnered and was herself a mother.

"You've changed little," she said to smooth over the awkwardness.

"Can't say the same. Do they abuse you in that place? You look ancient."

Thanks to you, too. "I just walked fourteen days from Hallan." She clamped her mouth shut, cursing herself. Ifram probably had never heard of Hallan. He'd never left Colgate.

After a minute of irritated silence, she asked, "Mom and Dad are okay?"

"Tolerable. They're not so young anymore."

Another unspoken criticism. He'd been more than happy to see her go, but resented her absence when their parents began to need more care.

Well, nothing to be done about that. Even her mother and father, whose love she had never doubted, had been relieved when she left with the Healer. The sash proved her identity now – and hopefully put paid once and for all to the rumors that she practiced evil magic.

The land had grown more humid and hotter the further south she traveled. Gullies lined the overgrown track to drain water, and the trees bore long fronds of white moss. Brother and sister walked in silence for a while, the horse following along behind Ifram. Quinn glanced back at it frequently. Donkeys were common, as were cows, and a few farming communities had oxen, but nothing like this magnificent brown beast. Ifram paid the horse no particular attention.

He would be in his mid-forties now. His hair, so like hers with tight curls close to his head, held a sprinkling of gray. He looked leaner, but then the Featherstones had always tended to lankiness.

She hadn't walked this track for ten years or more. Gradually it began to feel familiar, this tree, that side trail leading to her old friend Jude's childhood home.

As Ifram showed no inclination to talk, she joined him in silence.

At the edge of the town proper, he gave her a terse nod and turned off to go to the stables with the horse. Quinn went forward alone, crossing the square to the cobbler shop, seeing no faces she recognized.

Colgate looked tired, and sad. Little was outwardly different. A couple of buildings had vanished; only one had been replaced. Many needed a fresh coat of whitewash. There had been rain the night before – it rained frequently. But Colgate, despite being washed by the downpour, seemed dingy. Was this truth or merely her own perspective? Accustomed as she was to the austere beauty of the stone buildings in the Motherhouse complex, the dilapidated houses and shops challenged her memories.

She tapped on the door of the cobbler shop and went in. Her father glanced up, saw her, and bounded from his bench. He had her wrapped in his arms in an instant.

"Baby," he whispered. She'd swear he was close to tears.

"Hi, Dad." She was getting soft. First, that outpouring of emotion after the disastrous walk through the templates, now this. She pinched her lips together but suspected her father felt the shudder that accompanied her determined effort not to cry.

He smelled the way he always had, of leather and wood shavings. Or maybe the scent rose from the shop; her father and his work were inseparable.

"Look at you."

"Look at you." Wrinkles etched his brown face now, and his hair was gray. But apart from those markers of age, no, he hadn't changed. He was still her dad.

"I'm closing the shop. We need to find your mother."

"You can't just close. What if somebody needs a sandal repaired?"

He shrugged. "Doesn't happen too often these days. Times have changed." After pulling the shop door closed behind them, he threw an arm around her shoulders and led her toward their house.

It was evening before she began to get a clear picture of life in Colgate. Things had deteriorated since her girlhood, now made idyllic in her mind.

"We're too far off the trade routes," her father said. "Once, the caravans passed through here from the Southlands, but increasingly they take the newer road to the west. Not many Weavers come through anymore. Do you know why?"

"I don't, although we are stretched to the limit right now. Not many people choose this way of life. It can be lonely... and you have to enjoy walking a lot," she added with a chuckle.

"You used to ramble all over the place," her mother said. "We never knew where you'd turn up or if you'd make it home for supper. I expect you've had incredible adventures."

"A few, but in fact, I rarely leave the Motherhouse." She fingered the sash she still wore across her chest. "Scribes are a rare breed. Some of us do travel, recording the history of our people. But others, like me, do our work right where we are." She explained a little about templates and exploring information stored in the Aura.

"Makes me uneasy, thinking of you doing such things," her mother said. "Even the Healers work in ways no one can explain. Not that we see a Healer very often nowadays."

"If the caravans don't come any longer, the town must be suffering." The tired square with its plain, worn buildings came into her mind.

"We're fine, daughter. Don't you fret about us," her father said. "Folks always need sandals. Your brother and his boys have steady agricultural work. Petula, well, we do worry a bit there. She became a mother young, and no aim in life."

Petula, her brother's child, her niece. She'd been six when Quinn last visited, an engaging child but one far too aware of her charms.

"Dad, tell me about that horse of Ifram's."

Her parents exchanged glances.

"Tell her, Frederick," her mother said.

"Not sure I can. Not after pledging not to speak of it. She's not a mother here."

"Nor will she ever be, but she's a woman grown, a Weaver and our daughter. Tell her." Her mother got up and began preparing a snack tray and a tisane. She had never been able to sit still for long.

Puzzled, Quinn watched the debate between her parents. What was the great mystery?

Her dad nodded, then grinned as if about to reveal a juicy secret. "He's a beauty, isn't he? Not much use yet, he needs more gentling before he'll take the plow, but it'll come. Ifram's boy Raymond actually rides on him. Took some doing to convince that horse that being sat on was a good thing."

"So he's useful, or will be. But where did you get him? The Southlands?"

Her dad's grin got wider. "Some of the lads brought him back when he was a colt. There's a massive plain the other side of the hills, and horses abound there. They've never seen—"

"Wait." What was her father talking about? "Are you saying the boys in the village cross the hills?"

"Sure." He leaned back in his chair and feigned nonchalance. "They've been doing it forever. I did it as a youngster."

Flabbergasted, Quinn said, "No one ever told me."

"It's like some kind of secret society," her mother said, fond exasperation in her voice. "Boys and their games. They all pledge not to tell us women. Anyway, they certainly didn't want you tagging along with them. You drove your brother crazy."

"But... the hills... that's impossible."

The hills this far south were much less intimidating, Quinn knew, although she'd never learned how wide they were or how many days it took to get to the other side. And she'd never had reason to suspect the spells were less potent here than further north.

"We all know about banes on the hills," her father confirmed, "but they amount to nothing here, just the occasional queasiness. As long as you have a good breakfast, you'll be okay. So why destroy the boys' fun? No one from up north cares if we go back and forth. Leave in the morning, you get there soon after midday."

A half day. To cross the hills. Into Borgonne. Home of these magnificent horses.

"You can't be serious."

"Yep." Her father reached over and helped himself to goat cheese and sliced abricoes. When he'd swallowed he said, "We hope it'll work to our advantage, if we can catch enough horses to make a trade of them. Revitalize the town. Nobody else even knows they're there, near as we can tell. There's a faint track heading north-south, I suppose it goes to the southern sea. But never any sign of people, in all these years."

"Eat something, dear," her mother said.

Good idea. She mechanically mated cheese and cracker, poured a mug of tisane.

"So far we haven't met with much luck capturing them, though. We have two here in Colgate, both taken as foals. The other's female, so breeding's an option, but we need more stock for a decent genetic mix."

"And you're letting the boys... I know people who almost died crossing the hills."

"Northern ways," her mother said dismissively. "It's a good trail. Once Ifram was old enough, your father told me about it. No harm done, just the things boys get up to."

Quinn sank back in her chair, chewing and thinking. The town was right; horses could prove to be the key to economic revitalization, once the problem of catching them was solved. And if this could be a way for goods to flow between the Midland and Borgonne... if they could secure the pass... if they could enhance the spells to assure ownership of the route, or assign Weavers to work here, or...

Her thoughts spun out of control. She needed time and quiet to sort them out. A fact that told her very clearly how tired she actually was.

"I want to know more, a lot more. But right now, would you mind terribly if I retire? It's been a long day."

They both walked with her to the little Weavers' accommodation on the square; on her previous visit they'd agreed that she'd be more comfortable there than on the pallet in the sleeping room she had shared with her parents. It wasn't much, but it was a clean, private place for her to wash and sleep, and put together the new pieces of the puzzle.

The next morning, Quinn got a dose of reality. As she crossed the square from the Weavers accommodation to the cobbler shop, a group of men and women, tight-lipped and on a mission, accosted her.

"So you've come back."

"I've been back a few times since I left," Quinn replied, wondering if the speaker, a woman probably near her own age but looking years older, was someone she should know.

"And for what nefarious purpose?" another person, a man, shouted, getting in her face. "Checking us out, making your evil plans, eh?"

"Yeah, what disasters should we expect this time?"

"Eaten any babies recently, Quinn?"

Quinn listened, fingering her Scribes sash, grateful she'd donned it that morning. She almost hadn't; this was her home town, after all; her visit was social, not part of her responsibilities.

With a voice as calm as she could make it, she asked, "I came to see my parents and brother. I'm a Weaver, the same as the Bards and Healers who come through."

"Fat lot that means," a woman grumbled.

"My job is to record our history," Quinn said. "I'm not..."

147

"Yer a witch," the woman spat. "And now you've put that *thing* in the sky to spy on us."

So that's what triggered the uproar. The new object had been spotted here; no agrarian village in the Midland could have missed it. Still, Quinn reeled at the implications. "You can't be serious."

"Just be aware, you ain't welcome here. And we're watching every move you make, girlie. Don't think you can put one over on us."

The group had grown into a small crowd. Through it a woman pushed to the front and turned to face the others. "People, this is Quinn. We know her. We know her parents and brother. Kala, you stop your fear mongering right now."

"And you'd best consider your loyalties, Jude," a woman shouted. "Or you'll be called to account next."

Jude stood her ground, hands on hips, staring them down. Muttering, the crowd on the square gradually dispersed. Jude turned to Quinn and held out her hands. "You're back."

"I am." Quinn took the hands and let Jude pull her into a hug. "What brought that on? Weavers aren't exactly unfamiliar."

Jude shrugged. "Couple of hotheads, mostly those whose crops don't prosper. Never willing to consider it might be their own lazy ways. They're looking for a scapegoat. Don't take it personally."

"It's hard not to." Quinn watched as the last straggler left the square. "People are worried about the new light in the sky right across the Midland. We aren't positive what it is, either. But it's nothing to do with us."

Yet.

"Figured as much. Are your folks waiting for you? Do you have time for a caff?"

"Sure. I'm not on any particular schedule."

Jude towed her toward the dining hall. "I've missed you. We'd planned to raise our children together, grow old together, remember? It's been ten years at least. Tell me about your babies."

"There aren't any."

Jude's eyebrows shot up. "None? You poor thing. I've got five now. Two left, though, striking west. There's not much opportunity here."

"The horses are new."

At the dining hall they got mugs of caff, the inky strong stuff from the Southland, and toasted slices of barley bread. "Ah, the horses," Jude said.

Quinn studied her old friend, with her faded blonde hair and leathery complexion. "Ifram said he plans to breed them. Market them."

Jude's smile died. More than before, she looked beaten down, a woman with little to look forward to. "There's been a lot of big talk, but nothing much happens. The ones we have, we let them graze and trust that's all they need to eat. We're only just figuring out how to ride them. Breeding, training... so many questions, and no one to ask."

"Same as a donkey, perhaps?"

"We sure hope so."

The pall hanging over their conversation made Quinn nervous. This wasn't what she expected. Ten years ago, Colgate had seemed unchanged from her girlhood. Now, it was as if the shifting trade route had sucked the heart from the village.

"Suppose..." She stopped herself. It was a crazy idea. But...

"Never mind all that," Jude said, as eager as she to shake off the gloom. "What's it like being a Weaver? Are they good to you? Do you get to see lots of places?"

Another change, or changed perspective. Her friend seemed almost childlike in her lack of sophistication. It was easy to forget how seldom traffic passed through Colgate, how little the people of the town knew about events outside their own boundaries. Had she really grown so far away as to forget this?

And yet they were the same two women who had played together as girls.

She smiled across the table and launched into a narrative, making her life both more exciting, and much less weird, than the reality. Jude leaned toward her, rapt, as she reduced the life of a Scribe to a series of adventures and escapades.

❖

Later, she put her idea to her parents. They'd always been good listeners, thoughtful, willing to speak their opinions.

Her father summed up her somewhat disjointed proposal. "You want to cross the hills and bring back a person who understands horses."

"Yes. And possibly explore the options for a trade route – but keep that to yourselves. It may not work out, and the Motherhouse may not approve it. The hills are forbidden for a reason."

"Do you know anything about these people, lovie?" Her mother looked concerned as she turned the idea over in her mind, for once staying put rather than hustling about.

"Don't take this wrong, Quinn," her father said, "but you're a woman. You wouldn't be safe."

"I'm a Weaver, Dad. No one's going to hurt me."

Her mother and father exchanged a well-remembered look, one that questioned how to handle their wayward daughter with the spooky talents. It seemed that no matter her years or experience, in the company of these two people she'd always be that little girl.

Her father chewed a bite of his lentil stew, then asked, "Are you willing to take this to council?"

"Yes, of course. But whatever they say, I may cross anyway. I'm curious."

"Quinn..." The warning tone, the one that presaged punishment, once.

"Yes, Dad?"

Her father shook his head. "Nothing. We worry, that's all."

"I know." She reached across and covered her father's rough hand with her own. "I'm grateful. But I've been on my own for quite a while now. You'll see. It'll be fine."

Would it? Was she insane? Free from the Motherhouse for a two nine-days and already she intended to cross the hills, build a herd of horses, save Borgonne from famine, and resurrect her small town by making it a trading hub. No problem. All she had to do was get the Motherhouse, the Colgate council, and Borgonne to agree to it.

Okay, probably madness. But in her mind she had started planning her discourse to council, as soon as her father could arrange it.

As she walked out to the fields that afternoon, wanting to see more of the horses, she found herself wishing Kiril could be there with her. A thought easily suppressed. Scribes were nothing if not good at mind control.

She'd spoken to council and, as a minimum, had them curious. She'd spent time with her parents, tried to be comfortable around Ifram and Sala, and watched the horses every chance she got.

When it was time, she headed for the hills.

It had been the sort of day a Scribe lived for, entering new territory, learning new ways. Quinn sat on a hillock and watched a herd of horses in the distance, galloping across the dry plain. There was no sign of human habitation, no villages or crops. The two twelve-year-olds who served as her guides romped and played a game of their own devising, probably creating enough noise that the horses would stay well distant, had they shown any interest in approaching.

The idea of catching and taming these beasts seemed a far-away dream.

She'd sat there for half the afternoon, taking in the scene and thinking through her ideas. The Colgate council's enthusiasm had declined markedly when she refused to use her Entrée to subdue and capture the animals. Apprentices had ethics pounded into them, the ways they must never utilize their powers. The lessons hadn't extended to wild animals, though, so to some extent she was making up the rules as she went. She'd spent enough time with the other horse, the female, to know these were intelligent, sensitive beasts, and she could no more see subduing them with a template than she could do the same to a person. She thought of Kiril, caught between the Healers' compulsion and whatever drove him toward the hills, and shuddered.

But with unclear danger arising out of Borgonne, she wondered if it might come to that. She took Gauvain's words seriously, although he'd been much more restrained after he learned of the true cause of the drought. While she didn't doubt the Midland spells would block a serious assault, even a minor confrontation between Mages and Weavers could mean catastrophe in terms of their security and the ways they used their powers. She remembered Arwen's threat to sacrifice Kiril.

Before she risked the hills, she'd wrapped herself in a close cousin to the template Ezra had woven for Bryar, and without her own Entrée protecting her, the remnants of the spells on the hills had made her a little ill. One of the boys had been nauseous but managed to hold onto his breakfast; the other was unaffected.

Sitting overlooking the plain, she'd cautiously released the protective template bit by bit until she reached a point that felt like the level of Auric connection she was used to. In the days to come, as she searched for a horse expert, she would experiment, never releasing the weave too abruptly, but allowing the Aura's intensity to infiltrate bit by bit as she acclimated to it.

She turned her attention to the horses. How could they lure these magnificent animals to the Midland? Would an animal willingly cross the hills? The two in Colgate had, as foals. She'd departed from the Motherhouse too soon to hear how Gauvain fared with his donkeys.

Did the southern Midland provide the environment horses needed to thrive? These plains were much drier, but was that the effect of the drought? They knew so little.

The boys left her mid-afternoon, under strict orders to return to Colgate by suppertime. A distance from her lookout, they pointed out a rough track running north.

Had she really looked forward to this?

The track was no more than an animal trail. Did others use it? How soon would she encounter them? And how would they greet her? Despite what she told her parents, Quinn wasn't at all confident of her reception.

She walked as far as possible before full night fell, a night unlike in the Midland, because the hills cut out the sun so much earlier. Questions assailed her. Did she stand any chance at all of finding someone who could tell her about the habits of horses? Or was her venture into the alien world of southern Borgonne pointless?

She wished Kiril were with her.

No. she didn't wish that at all. She didn't need an extra level of exasperation to add to her nervousness, alone on the trail with night falling.

Although sparse, the forest cover in the foothills was sufficient that she was able to gather firewood. She sat by her fire, eating a piece of waybread, dried meat, and a handful of abricoes, feeling lonely and uneasy and questioning the wisdom of being there at all.

Chapter 20

Leo arranged for Gauvain to be escorted to the council chambers. A delegation of guards met them at the kitchen door of the tower and surrounded him as they working their way through back streets. Orlan's main roads were impassable and dangerous. Gauvain heard the shouts and chants, hundreds of voices, the occasional dull *thunk* as a rock hit a boarded-up window.

The mob had already invaded the food storage warehouses. Finding next to nothing, they took their vengeance on inanimate objects and authority figures. Leo reported that Cedric had been hanged in effigy in the Orlan town square.

He shuddered, pulled his cloak further over his head despite the summer heat, and stayed well within the phalanx of guards. He could use his powers to protect his person, of course, but he sensed – and Leo confirmed – that such a move would only further enrage the crowd.

Food. The seed from the Midland had taken root, and rain had fallen with the promise of more, based on the banking clouds to the east. There was hope of a minimal harvest, but that was still half a season away.

Gauvain had reversed the modifications he'd made to the template. No one need ever know. When the first drops fell on Borgonne, he experienced the same deep relief as the farmers.

He entered the council chambers, dim with the shutters closed, lit only by candles down the middle of the table, and immediately added a handful of Mage globes. He surveyed the others. Ester especially appeared shaken. He noted a stain on her bodice, as if someone had thrown mud or worse at her.

Peasants and fools. Didn't they realize the council were just as hungry?

His gaze caught on Cedric. No sign of deprivation there. Gauvain wondered what food stores he'd been able to lay by. Not much chance of hoarding perishable foodstuffs, but perhaps his cook was a master of preservation techniques.

No matter. Cedric rapped the meeting to order. For once the man didn't waste time on pomposities, but drove straight to the point. "We must open the hills. Invade. Get food for our population."

No one contradicted him.

"How do you propose to do that?" Gauvain asked coolly.

"You. Your power got us safely through those cursed hills before. All we need is to find enough people with Mage propensities – you said yourself there are lots, even if they aren't strong. There's no longer any question, Gauvain. You see what's happening."

He did. The entire social order around Orlan was collapsing. From Ester's tight face, he surmised it was no better in outlying hamlets. At least the idiots on council weren't suggesting he remove the spells. His explorations since Arwen's revelations had confirmed the difficulty in his mind, and there would be no support from the Midland.

"We still cannot predict how many people one person with Entrée can protect," he said. "It's a risk."

Cedric continued as if he hadn't spoken. "Round up all the magical people you can find. We'll gather agriculturists and laborers, the stronger the better. Hunters, too, and as many donkeys as the farms can spare. You'll accompany them."

"You presume a lot, Cedric."

The man's small eyes became hard slits. "You'd never let anyone else assume command, and we both know it. Stop posturing."

Gauvain half stood, offended, then realized the futility of such a gesture and sank into his chair again. Ester met his gaze, sympathetic but without any alternatives to offer.

Outside the noise swelled. Objects battered the shutters. The council as a whole grew more tense, mouths pinched, expressions wary.

Cedric, for all his obnoxiousness, was right. They were out of choices. "How to announce the plan, where to rally, when to leave," Gauvain reeled off. "Do you have answers?"

"We'll post and proclaim around Orlan and in the outlying villages. There's a field lying fallow west of town that will do as a rallying place. Leave in three days."

This time he did stand. "Are you insane? Three days? We couldn't get notice past Orlan, much less coordinate people and supplies. And what about those donkeys? They can't climb the trail."

Cedric for once was unflappable. "Obviously, we'll be sending more than one party. Leave a Mage or two behind, and they'll work on the donkey issue while you're away. Once the Midland is subdued, there'll be trade caravans crossing the hills every few days."

Subdued? They'd proven their generosity, and with settlements sprawled across the landscape and next to no overarching governance, subduing seemed irrelevant, if not impossible.

"Let me explain how this will unfold," Gauvain said. "Once we're in the Midland, I will work with Arwen to put out another call for provisions." Cedric would not be allowed to dictate the terms of such a venture. "There's no value in our tromping all over the land. It'd be a waste of energy, and we'll need our people available to return home."

"Humph. As long as they understand. We *will* collect those supplies."

Gauvain thought it through while the meeting devolved into chaos around him. In short order, he could round up perhaps fifteen people with some level of Entrée. At a rough guess, that meant another sixty to cross the hills, yielding a party of seventy-five to feed and assure safe passage. The hunters would be challenged... and consider the fate of the alien man, Kiril. Gauvain disliked participating in a poorly planned act of desperation, but it was going to happen, whether he liked it or not. Cedric undoubtedly maintained tentacles into the network of healers, sages, and fortune tellers with undeniable powers who for whatever reason never received Mage training. Better Gauvain maintain control.

And with him in the lead, he could prevent the worst of the aggression he was sure Cedric would promote. He would not permit a move to take over the Midland. Any attempt would cause havoc and threaten the harvest. Gauvain knew he was believed to be a hard man, but he had an aversion to senseless suffering. Even the man Kiril's machinations to effect his and the musician's escape from Borgonne – surprisingly, with Leo's help – had been unnecessary, although he saw no point in revealing that.

"Seven days," he said abruptly. "Notify the town and release any remaining stores. We can't organize in the midst of riots. Coordinate the supply list with me."

Ester nodded. Cedric opened his mouth, but sensibly made no protest.

Seven days it was. And then he'd be forced to lead yet another ragtag group through the cursed hills.

As he strode to the door, the building swayed under his feet. Earthquakes were common, and this didn't feel like a big one; Gauvain ignored it and gave the door an emphatic shove on his way from the room.

Quinn had been on the road for ten days, and by her estimation should reach Orlan, the town she'd heard so much about, in another four. Having come so far, it made sense to re-cross the hills along the northern route. She'd be home that much faster. And oh, was she ready to be back in her suite at the Motherhouse.

The plains had gradually given way to open woodland, which made walking more challenging as the path became riddled with roots. The land was poor; where she encountered settlements, they were no more than hovels grouped around a pounded dirt clearing.

She'd learned nothing about the care of horses. When she'd asked, she met either blank stares or a half-hearted desire to own such a beast, to ease the labor of farming.

She could have shared a small hut the night before, but it would have been unfair to the family already living there, not to mention being cramped and smelly. Although no great fan of sleeping rough, she was a Weaver, after all. She had the skills to camp.

The further north she went, the more she saw signs of the early season drought. The few people she met were quiet, almost surly;

while they didn't chase her away, she found no welcome, either. She sensed it was from reluctance to share their food and water, even in exchange for the coin her father had pressed on her, Borgonnian money obtained as a novelty from one of the few caravans that still passed through Colgate. Coin didn't feed empty bellies, and resentment greeted her with every encounter. Not directed at herself, particularly, but at the Aura, at fate, at the council in Orlan whose influence stretched well past the town boundaries.

It was a sunny afternoon, hot but pleasant enough as the shadows of the hills crept across the landscape, when she felt the first shuddering underfoot.

Earthquake.

Common this close to the hills. Numerous templates protected the Motherhouse buildings, and other communities took whatever precautions they could. Loss of life wasn't usual, but happened.

Some said when the land was angry, the Aura doled out punishment.

A sharper shake sent her staggering.

She'd been walking through a struggling forest. Half the trees were dead, or nearly so, and despite rain a few days before, the ground released puffs of dust with each step. With almost no understory, the first hard rain would wash away the topsoil.

Not her problem right now. The earth heaved, knocking her feet out from under her. The movement came in waves, resisting her efforts to rise.

She'd just regained her feet and was trying to muster strength in her legs to move when, silently, one of the dead giants of the forest toppled toward her.

It was too wide to avoid, even if there had been time. She felt a glancing blow across her back, knocking her to the ground again, then it crashed over her.

The quake rolled on for an eternity before the land settled. A bird sent out a single, questioning note. Quinn tried to move and couldn't. Her legs were pinned by a massive branch of the tree.

Alive, she thought. And she still had her pack.

When she twisted to remove it from her back, her right leg muscles convulsed in agony. The ankle was trapped by a branch, with another spearing into the flesh of her foot.

She needed the pack to retrieve her knife, start to claw and hack herself free.

She hadn't seen a soul or passed a settlement all day. Help wasn't coming.

But the pain...

Quinn considered tears a waste of energy. But... oh, Sustainer.

Since she couldn't prevent it, she gave herself permission to sob, because she'd never experienced anything like this. The muscle-destroying earthquake, turning her to jelly, then the tree, seeing it fall toward her and helpless to avoid it, and now, trapped, and the shafts of pain shooting up from her ankle...

Get the pack.

Slowly, unable to stop the tears muddying her face, she partially rose and held her torso rigid, using only her hands and arms to gentle the pack from her shoulders.

Much later, nearing sunset, she fished in her pack for a piece of waybread. She'd done what she could, hacking at the branch, digging in the soil underneath the tree, anything to release her foot. So far, without success. Tomorrow, though.

Free it, and then what?

It wasn't as if she could walk.

The rudimentary lessons she'd received in Healing, in her first years of training, seemed a lifetime ago now. There was a template to help relieve pain, if she could remember the weave...

Then she heard the voices. Loud, quarreling, and coming her way.

She gulped down another sob and shouted. The voices stopped, and she sensed people were running.

"Merciful Diou." A woman. Someone started to clamber into the tree's branches; a voice called him back. "Disturb it, might hurt her more."

"Bring the saw, Liam. Fast like."

"Hang on, Dearie. We'll get you outta there." The woman's voice again.

"By the hills, look at her skin. She's tainted."

At the end of her strength, Quinn passed out.

She woke to a roof of thatch and a single lantern casting a yellow light on bare furnishings. An elderly woman, all bones, sat on a stool nearby, crooning to herself.

"Hello?" Her voice came out thin as a whisper.

The crooning stopped. Quinn missed it immediately.

"An' you're wakin'," the woman replied without emotion. "They'll be wantin' to know who ye be, and why ye got yerself caught in yon woods." She rose from her stool and hovered over Quinn's cot. "Strangers be a rare occurrence, and not much welcomed."

Quinn nodded. Even that minimal movement set off a shock wave of pain from her ankle and foot.

"I'm for gettin' the menfolk." The woman, having completed her perusal, turned and left. Through the door Quinn saw darkness, and concluded she lay in a one-room building, likely a shed, and it was night.

Gingerly, moving very slowly, she rose to her elbows, but lacked the strength to lift the light sheet that covered her. She shivered as she lowered herself back down.

She woke from an inferno of heat and nightmares. Two hard-looking people peered at her, a man and a woman. Middle aged, toughened by life, and not happy to see her.

"Looks like you're right," the man said, addressing his companion. "Fever's broke. Now what do we do with her?"

"She musta been goin' somewhere," the woman said. "We feed her a broth, then get her story."

Her story. What could she tell that would make sense to them?

Almost ancillary to her situation, she realized the fever had indeed broken. Her foot, to halfway up her calf, felt raw and sore, but somewhat better than it had been. Given the stiffness in her muscles, she must have lain there more than overnight.

Her preliminary effort to sit up proved useless.

The woman left. The man called after her, "Not too much broth. Ain't wastin' water on 'er."

Water. The drought. Trade, horses. Orlan.

"You ain't like folks here," the man observed. "Got the devil's skin on ya."

Devil's skin? Quinn's color had almost never been a point of discussion. In the Midland, dark skin was uncommon, but not rare. She'd forgotten about it.

"Water," she croaked.

"A sip." The man hefted her up, oblivious to her injury. "Don't spill. There's none to waste." He jammed a cup at her mouth.

She ignored her unease at its cleanliness and took two sips, then felt it settle uncertainly in her stomach and turned her head away.

He let her fall back onto the cot. "Now, 'spect you're able to give us some answers. Where's your 'usband?"

Even the small amount of water had awakened Quinn's senses. The heat in the room, the flimsiness of the cover over her sweat-chilled body. The man's hard eyes, giving nothing.

A husband. She needed a story, fast.

"Ailing. South of here. I seek a herbalist, one with healing." There were herbal healers in Orlan; that much she knew from Bryar.

"Damn fool, letting you take off on your own."

Probably true.

"He doesn't know. He's in a bad way."

"Humph."

The woman came in, balancing a small mug. "This be made from bone of cow. Got marrow in it. It'll build you up right enough."

She set the mug down on a chest. Ignoring the effect on her foot and ankle, the two of them hauled her up to a sitting position. The foot screamed; only with difficulty did she bite back her cry, but tears flooded her eyes.

The woman perched on the cot by her, limiting her movement. "You'll drink this, then we'll figure out how to get rid of ya."

She thrust the mug in Quinn's hand. Shaky, she wrapped her other hand over the first one and raised the mug – cleaner than the water vessel – to her mouth.

Oh, sweet Sustainer, but it tasted good.

After downing half the broth, she asked, "How long have I been here?"

"Three days. Gotta move you along now. Not enough food or water to keep you any longer." The man stated a simple fact, leaning on the door with a look of determination, as if she might bolt but for his vigilance.

"That and your color. You're nothing natural, that's for sure," the woman added.

"Where I come from, my skin color is common."

"And where might that be?"

"Well south of here."

"Where you headed?"

"Orlan." Quinn returned her attention to the mug.

"She cain't walk."

"Send Liam with the donkey cart. Ain't but a couple of days."

Her pack lay just out of reach, against the far wall. "I can pay," she said tentatively, unsure of the customs in this foreign land but confident that some payment would be demanded.

The man's harsh laugh filled the room. "What good do you think your coin be here? No, I reckon I'll just keep this." He pulled her knife from under his tunic. "Nice tool. Not sure why a woman's runnin' around the countryside with a man's implement. It'll make a pretty recompense."

Quinn's heart sank, but she had no recourse. The man had her knife.

The woman laughed, a harsh, unpleasant sound, but one tinged with a hint of compassion. Or perhaps Quinn, desperate for reassurance, imagined it. "Maybe her footwear, too?" she said.

"Why not? No use to you," the man told her, "Just tell us where to drop you in Orlan. Yer people there can take care of ya."

The next morning, barefoot, her foot and ankle bound by linen strips that at least were clean, she found herself unceremoniously loaded into a donkey cart by the taciturn Liam. They'd added some kind of poultice to the wrapping that lessened the pain somewhat. Her pack was suspiciously lighter than it had been; she wondered what else they had taken.

But they had saved her life. And overnight she'd worked out where in Orlan she needed to go. She held out little hope for Gauvain, but Willow had spoken warmly of his servant, Leo. She'd find help at the black tower.

Gauvain and Leo stood near one of the many entrances to the square, watching the rabble. There were no market stalls; instead, hopeful pilgrims filled the space, those either too poor or too hungry to stay at home. No doubt some dreamed of glory, penetrating the mysterious hills; if so, Gauvain wished them luck. He'd willingly never set foot in the cursed landscape again. Although his earlier crossing had yielded no negative result, he'd felt the hills' ominous threat every moment of the journey.

Those with any trace of Entrée had been herded into the northeast corner of the square. Gauvain had tested each of them, a tedious process that filled a day, but necessary for their safety. Cedric's people vetted the rest. He only hoped the combined force would prove sufficient for safety. The thought of the alien, Kiril, stuck in his memory.

His remaining apprentices counted among the group. As expected, they were in high spirits, ready for adventure. Reed suffered no negative consequences from his previous traverse and had spent much of the afternoon broadcasting his exploits. With half of his motley collection of semi-mages under the age of twenty-five, Gauvain anticipated a challenging trek.

"I've prepared dried mutton, as you like," Leo said, keeping his voice low although it was hardly necessary, given the noise and confusion on the square. "And honey-sweetened travel bars. I trust you'll find them agreeable."

"Thanks." Gauvain turned to Leo, drawing him away from the crowd. "You've said little. Is this scheme as mad as I think it is? Might we be better off to experiment with weather manipulation, or simply allow the population to die back?" He included the question about weather for form's sake; even Leo knew nothing of his bungled experiments.

Leo read him well. "You would want no part in those options. But this doesn't feel right to you, either."

"No. But I see no alternative. I can hardly let that fool Cedric lead these people into destruction. Or worse, return with infection such as happened to that man in the Midland."

"No. But take care. This won't be an easy group to control. They aren't used to military discipline."

Gauvain shook his head, looking over the excited crowd. "Even to convince them of the danger of leaving the trail... I shall miss you, old friend."

Leo chuckled. "Almost as much as you'll miss my cooking and your feather bed. All will be well when you return."

"At the first sign of trouble—"

"I'll defend the tower. It's virtually impenetrable anyway, and I have better sense than to breach its wards."

Gauvain clapped a hand on the other man's shoulder. "Let's enjoy one civilized meal. We *must* leave here at daybreak, but the Sustainer knows if Cedric grasps that."

Leo gave a short nod and turned, weaving his way toward the tower through excited pilgrims, relatives, and hangers-on.

Quinn had experienced no ill effect from the greater power of the Aura, perhaps because she had eased into it during her walk from the south. That didn't save her from physical peril, however. She clutched the sides of the cart to keep from being thrown, watching activity that felt unnatural to her. Too many people, too much agitation. Liam contended with increasing crowds as they drew closer to Orlan. Within the town proper, he had to resort to side alleys and detours to reach the tower at all.

He'd been less than thrilled when she told him her destination. The tower was famous, that much was clear, and not in a positive way. Dark magicks took place there, he'd informed her, and the Mage who lived there was the devil incarnate – she made a note to investigate the history of this devil concept. Despite her protest that she sought only an elderly servant, Liam deemed Quinn either depraved or sadly misled.

So when they got to the small square in front of the tower, which was mercifully quiet after the crowds in the center of town, Liam dumped her, the sticks she used as crutches, and her pack without so much as a fare-thee-well and took off.

"Thanks to you, too," she muttered to his departing back. Then she hobbled to the door.

She had just lifted the fancy knocker when an elderly, hunched man carrying a bag approached her from the other side of the square. "Can I help you?"

She turned. "I hope so. Are you Leo, by any chance?"

"I am, Miss. And you are?"

"My name is Quinn. I'm a friend of Willow's. She told me about you."

"Ah." He straightened a bit. Although probably never tall, he'd once been a good-looking man. Even now he had the air of a man accustomed to discipline, seasoned in the ways of the world, confident if no longer strong.

They assessed each other, the maimed woman and the old man. She saw a decision made; he nodded. "If you'll wait, I will enter through the kitchen and unlock the door."

"I could go with you—"

"No." He gestured at her foot. "Wait."

Leo scuttled around the tower, and soon after she heard the bar lifted to allow her in. He led her through the building to the back, giving her scant time to study the interior of this strange place Willow had lived in.

And Bryar and Kiril fought in.

The kitchen proved to be a comfortable, plain room. Leo sat her at the table and arranged a stool for her to rest her foot. He then put on a kettle and began sorting through the goods in the bag. "Meat is easy to acquire as the folk are forced to kill off their stock. It tends to gristle and stringiness, but we do the best we can. The vegetables…" He shrugged. "There isn't water enough to grow them properly. You must see a healer, and soon. I fear your injury will prove to be beyond my skills."

He placed herbs in a mug, added water from the kettle, and set it before her. "Mindsease, with mint. Relax, my dear. You are safe here."

Leo scuttled off. Quinn arranged her injured foot on the stool, leaned back, and cradled the hot mug. If only they'd permit her to linger for a few days... but no. She knew Gauvain. She knew better than to count on anything.

The healer came, unwrapped her foot, prodded, frowned a lot and hurt even more. He clucked as he applied fresh bandages. "Change the poultice regularly, keep your weight off the foot. You'll not walk right again, I fear. Bones broken and poorly set. Unfortunate, but that's all I can do."

A new voice spoke. "Give her something for the pain, then. She has a trek ahead of her."

The healer's hands tensed on the bandages. Quinn twisted quickly in her chair and gasped as her foot wrenched against his hand. Gauvain stood in the door to the tower proper.

"That would be a mistake," the healer said.

"But unavoidable."

He watched as the healer doled out portions of willow, baneherb, and heal-all. "This will help. But the fact is, she'll never sustain more than a short walk."

"Yes, yes. Leo, see the man is compensated."

When Leo and the healer had stepped from the room, Gauvain sat next to her. "Quinn," he said formally, an acknowledgment.

"Gauvain." She fought to keep her voice steady. The pain of the examination, combined with the healer's prognosis, had shaken her.

"While I'm sure there is a fascinating tale about how you came to arrive at my door, at the moment it is irrelevant. I intend you to accompany us across the hills."

Was this the cause of all the excitement? "You're returning to the Midland? Why?"

"For food," he snapped. "Why else? Leo," he added as his servant returned, "show her to her room and clean her up. I assume dinner will be late?"

"Yes." Leo didn't offer excuses. Willow had told her he was more than a servant, although she'd never penetrated their true relationship.

Gauvain strode off. Leo turned to her. "I doubt your ability to handle the stairs, so you may use my quarters tonight. Unfortunately, I cannot provide you a full tub of water, but enough to remove the soil of travel."

"Anything would be a relief."

He disappeared through a door to her right. After a few minutes, he returned, offering her an arm. "I cannot imagine Gauvain's intent, thinking you can handle a trek. The ascent into the hills alone must be beyond your current capabilities. Perhaps he's experimenting with levitation?" Leo asked with a hint of mischief in his voice. "But never mind that now. Come."

Leo's room was small and plain, but he'd placed a deep basin in it, full of water that... she tested it with a hand. Hot.

Oh, sweet Sustainer.

"There's a fresh tunic on the bed. Take your time, my dear. With all the furor over this expedition, I've barely made a start at dinner. Remember not to get your bandages wet."

With that he bowed himself out. Quinn was left alone with water, soap, the prospect of clean clothes... and growing anxiety. Were all those people they passed planning to cross the hills? And she, with her maimed foot?

If only she could wake up in her bed at the Scribes' lodge to find it all a dream...

She sighed, peeled off her soiled tunic, and began to wash her bruised, stiff body.

Later, over an excellent dinner of chops and braised vegetables, Quinn sipped from her goblet of fruity red wine and asked, "Why are you so determined that I accompany you? From what I hear, there's little chance I can manage the initial climb."

Gauvain lifted his goblet and studied her over its rim. She'd washed top to toe and now wore the unadorned yellow tunic, which she knew from Willow's account would not meet his expectations. That didn't bother her, but nonetheless she kept her bare feet tucked under the table. Leo, who had joined them, watched the silent exchange.

Gauvain sipped the wine and set the goblet down. "First, explain your presence. I sensed a different energy from the south, but I admit my surprise at finding you here."

She had tailored her story. "I was visiting family. It's a poor land on our side, and unsettled on yours, but there is a way to cross the hills far to the south. I am a Scribe. I was curious." She told them of the earthquake and her rescue.

Gauvain subjected her to another long stare before deciding to accept the little she had revealed. "I have assessed you, Quinn Featherstone – yes, I know your second name. Unusual in the Midland, I believe. You are a strong Mage, rivaling even Ezra. Call it fanciful if you will, but I have a premonition that your strength may be needed in this mission. Which I would prevent if I could, but Cedric is determined, and he's rallied enough Aura-sensitive people to his side that he'd go, whether I like it or not. After what happened to the man Kiril, can you ask why I intend to drag you across the hills?"

Quinn again debated mentioning her idea of transporting horses to the Midland. From there, they could be used for the traverse, if the need continued, much as the last expedition had made use of donkeys. But she held back, reluctant to risk sacrificing a strategic advantage.

Since entering the tower she'd kept her mind shielded. She didn't intend to let that shield relax now. She was well aware of Gauvain's powers.

He placed his fork on his plate, took a last swallow of wine, and stood. "We leave day after tomorrow. You have everything you need?"

"Actually, no. I have no footwear, and my knife was taken as payment for care of me and transport to Orlan. I have coin."

"I'll see to it, Miss Quinn," Leo said. "Coin will not be necessary."

She smiled. Willow loved this old man; she could see why. "Thank you."

The meal ended with Gauvain's abrupt departure. Quinn seized her crutches and slowly followed Leo to the kitchen, wondering what tomorrow might bring.

Chapter 21

The Motherhouse was in disarray, although you had to live there to recognize it. The visit from Borgonne, and now the object in the sky... senior Weavers spent inordinate amounts of time huddled together, planning, Kiril assumed, for whatever might come next.

He kept himself as invisible as possible, listening. Arwen wanted him gone, had ordered him gone, and he could hardly blame her. Besides putting himself at perceived risk due to proximity to the hills, his ongoing presence disrupted the smooth running of her little empire. But at the moment he had nowhere else he was in a hurry to be, and the Motherhouse was the best place to stay current with the news.

Especially given the possibility – the likelihood, based on Joss's radio reception – that the new light in the sky came from Terra. He didn't intend to find himself stuck in some remote outpost when it landed.

It was a lonely existence. The Weavers were polite, even inviting him to join them for meals, but he sensed the distance they put between himself and them. They had their own lives and occupations and no free time to devote to his amusement. The older students talked to him occasionally, curious about life on the mysterious Terra, the nature of the cosmos – questions that never arose in their usual course of studies.

But living amid these people with their voodoo powers, even the kids, creeped him out. Increasingly he found himself in the village, and eventually in the little room they called the biblio where the archivist cranked out records of births and deaths, the occasional handfasting, the state of the crops each year.

Not scintillating information, but it represented books of a sort, pen and ink, an opportunity to learn the handwriting of these outliers from Terra.

So he sat with the archivist when he got the chance, and at other times studied the ledgers. He stole a quill pen and made himself ink from black berries that grew in abundance along the roadside. He amused himself by practicing, using bark as paper. If the coming ship offered no hope for return home, at least he might acquire a profession.

Stranded in an alien culture, without either the comforts or the rank he'd enjoyed before, facing the prospect of life in a hamlet, with that demon fighting to break free inside him...

Despite the heat, Kiril shivered as he walked back to the Motherhouse in the late afternoon. He wondered about their assessment, that the farther from the hills he took himself, the better. Probably true.

He was early for supper, so he claimed a bathing room in the guest lodge and treated himself to a soak, thinking of the river that flowed by Stanstead. Might that be far enough away? Stanstead was one of only two or three settlements that large – he snorted a laugh – but he couldn't imagine spending a lifetime in any place smaller.

Relieved to be free of the dirt and sweat of his walk from the village, he made his way to the dining hall. As he passed a table where Arwen and three other Scribes sat, he heard one word that never failed to seize his interest.

Quinn.

As unobtrusively as he could, he got his meal – a stew involving meat today, a pleasant change from the usual fare of lentils, beans, and mushrooms – and eavesdropped.

But Quinn's name wasn't mentioned again. Instead he picked up a deep uneasiness. A large party had entered the hills. No one could divine their intent, but everyone was aware of the potential threat.

He knew it too, he mused as he chewed the tough meat, even without overhearing their quiet conversation. It was as if an invisible cord connected him to the hills, alerting him when the energy there went awry...

Stop right there. He was starting to sound like the Weavers. As if he believed in their hocus-pocus stuff.

Realization hit him, and he blinked. Denial had become a habit. It had taken him over a year of near daily proofs, but he no longer doubted their powers.

Kiril left the dining hall disturbed, his mind uneasy. An urge to defend the hills, to take action, swept over him, but how?

Their problem, he told himself.

Nevertheless, the next morning he started assembling a travel pack. Food, water, a knife, a basic medicine kit. All easily obtained; they pre-packaged necessities, making it easy for Weavers to prepare.

He dithered another day, but the pull of the hills had become a compulsion. Whatever was happening there, he had no choice but to be part of it.

He hated the hills. Dreaded returning to them.

At first light, keeping his own counsel, he left.

Chapter 22

"So that's where we are." Harry Belfontaine, commander of the Eurocorp Adventurer, summed up the situation. He wiped his hands on his khaki slacks as he sat. Once he'd worn a uniform with medals and scrambled egg on the visor of his cap, but that had been sacrificed to a passel of kids for some game over a year ago and had long since vanished into the children's playroom.

Around him, just over four hundred people, men, women, and children, watched him intently in the small, cramped auditorium deep in the bowels of their ship. "It's crunch time. We go to the woods or the plains, but once we choose, we can't change our minds. We won't have fuel enough to re-launch."

They'd been in orbit for over a month. Everyone was antsy, now that they were so close they could see their future home. Everyone ached for land beneath their feet again, longed to begin the work of settlement.

Meet the new neighbors? There was plenty of curiosity, but that worried Harry the most.

Hands waved. He nodded to a man in the front. "How much riskier is the forest landing? Are you gonna get us all killed?"

Harry grinned, although the point was valid. "I sure hope not, Tim. We've located two clearings large enough for the ship, but not so close to habitation as to cause panic. The controls haven't failed us yet, but because of the narrow space, it is riskier. We can't deny that."

A young family rose to their feet. The man spoke. "How long before our food's exhausted?"

Harry nodded to Ben Albright, the first officer. Ben stood slowly. He'd had aching joints recently, a problem shared by many of the adults on board.

"Food's not an issue now that Henrik's got the mold situation under control. The limiting factor is, we'd be so low on fuel in a month that landing could be dicey. The risk increases with every day we delay." Their departure had been rushed, to say the least. It had come down to leaving with a reduced fuel load or not leaving at all – and probably facing prison or firing squads.

"Then why're we still up here?" an angry female voice from the back demanded. "Why you haven't put us down yet?"

It took a few seconds for Harry to decode the thick accent. "Because this is how long it's taken to confirm suitability, test air and make educated guesses about soil. Don't expect miracles, Hannah."

"Humph." The woman's snort as she sat evinced a few chuckles. Hannah wasn't known for patience.

Another woman stood near the middle of the auditorium. "Harry, are you going to tell us what you recommend?"

He glanced at the row of men and women occupying the tables to either side of him. "Truth is, we're evenly divided. Forest is riskier getting down, but the timber would be valuable when we start building. Plains are easier for landing, but not much wood. Water's available in both locations. Both have seasons. Both areas are settled and farmed, but plains are more isolated. What more do you want to know?"

"So what it comes down to is, do we want to eat veggies or porridge all winter." The male voice off to Harry's right got a few laughs, but at heart everyone recognized this was no joking matter. This was the rest of their lives. And their children's. The success or failure of their unauthorized mission.

Harry waited for his grin to fade before he said, "Are we ready to put it to a vote? Any objections?"

The first man, Tom, stood again. "You're asking a lot on the basis of a one-hour meeting. Any chance we can think on it and vote tomorrow?"

Waves of assenting murmurs filled the room.

Harry looked right and left along the tables. Receiving the unspoken agreement from his senior crew, he nodded. "Oh eight hundred hours sharp. Be here, folks. The sooner this is resolved, the greater our chances of success. And the more time we have to get a crop in while it's still summer."

The meeting broke up. Every one of the persons on board had been in attendance, even the two babes in arms. Following the decision tomorrow morning, in a matter of days they'd be on solid ground again.

Equally important, to Harry's way of thinking, was that once they'd landed, he could transfer command to their designated settlement leader, Elspeth Gandsdottir, who had been both an anthropologist and a skilled hostage negotiator back on Terra. She in turn would rely on Henrik Strauss, one of their team leaders and their agricultural expert, who had spent most of his free time over the last two years boning up on survival and homesteading techniques. Harry had argued against using so much of their precious computer storage for the Eurocorp library, but now he was grateful he'd been overruled, and not only for improving Henrik's knowledge. The small video library had grown old, and more and more of his settlers were acquiring a taste for reading.

Not your settlers.

No, but he'd developed a proprietary feeling for this ship and its inhabitants. Something that wouldn't stand him in good stead after the transfer of power. It was time for him to pass the baton, having safely, and with a minimum of strife, shepherded his oddly matched crewmates to a new land.

Heaven help us, he muttered, acknowledging the challenges in their immediate future. Then he joined Ben and Constance, their medic, as they made their way to the mess.

Chapter 23

For two days Kiril had followed the trail around the north side of the massif like a man on a mission, although when he forced his mind to logical thought, he couldn't say exactly what that mission was. He knew something was happening in the hills, and he knew it had to be resisted. Why he thought he alone could make a difference made little sense to him. But he couldn't ignore the compulsion to move forward toward the hills.

He stopped at night, briefly, for food and a nap. His night vision was improving, though; there seemed little point in sleep. He drove on.

As he entered the hills, he made an interesting discovery. He could run more fluidly, with greater speed, on all fours, hands and feet. He'd never tried it before. How stupid of humanity, not to realize this superior form of locomotion was right in front of them.

His skin itched. He ignored it. He was – had been – a commander – or something – sometime, a long time ago...

His pack became a nuisance. He dropped it on the trail and loped along, toward the threat, as conscious thought drained from his mind.

Another two days, Quinn calculated. Then they'd be out of the hills and back to normal reality.

The crude crutches chafed her underarms raw. Her foot never stopped throbbing. Periodically, a hunter or a farmer gave her a piggyback to help her along; they wanted this expedition to be over as much as she did, because the hills were, frankly, creepy. And she slowed down their progress. Usually she stumbled into the evening camp after the others had eaten, accompanied by whoever had held back to walk with her and be sure she got there.

Gauvain was a damn fool for dragging her along. She took every opportunity to tell him so. The climb up from the plains to the beginning of the hill trail should have been enough warning. She'd done it on hands and knees, with an occasional strong shoulder under her rump to shove her up and over some obstacle or other. It had taken all day and cost a perfectly good tunic, now ripped beyond reasonable repair by the stones and roots. Leo had tucked another in her pack, which she was saving for when they finally broke free of the cursed hills and set foot on Midland soil again.

Home.

What had possessed her to leave? The Motherhouse had always been enough for her. Her work, her friends...

And now an uncertain threat posed by Gauvain and his troop.

Quinn sprawled by the last of several fires strung out along the middle of the path, itself no wider than she was tall. Early on they'd lost a man when he wandered farther from the trail than Gauvain deemed safe, based on the combined energy field of the Aura-sensitive among them. Nobody knew if he'd died or found himself back in Borgonne. But after that, everyone stayed near the track; the hunters hauled Gauvain's young apprentices along with them like good-luck charms when they went further afield in search of game.

Not that the hunting had been spectacular. Quinn's stomach growled, but the stew pot over the nearest fire held little by way of meat or vegetables. Their stores were low to the point of critical.

Two more days to the Midland, two past that to the Motherhouse.

Or more, allowing for their slower pace.

Quinn estimated they were half way to equinox. The days were growing shorter, but there was still light as she shifted, trying to find a more comfortable position for her foot. A mist had risen from the valley below their trail; it felt chilly on her skin and contributed to the unease that had plagued her for hours.

The ongoing pain made her snappy; she wanted only her allotted spoons of the thin broth, enough boiled water to brew herself a tisane from the healing herbs she'd been given in Orlan, and, hopefully, sleep.

As she accepted her mug of soup from an agriculturist – farmer, she corrected herself, one of several places she'd noted where their languages had diverged – Gauvain worked his way back along the trail to her fire. He sat next to her, folding his long legs in front of him. He had lost some of his airs and care for finery in the course of the last days, but he still grimaced as he lowered himself to the ground.

"Something's wrong," he said without preliminary.

"What?"

"I don't know. Focus, woman. I need your help."

She'd been on the alert constantly, seeking out any anomaly that might prove a threat. No more than an hour ago, finding nothing, she'd allowed her travel-weary mind to turn instead to food and sleep. She sighed, cleared her mind, and scanned their immediate area. Her stomach jerked. "You're right. We're not alone."

"What is it?" he demanded. "How do we defend ourselves?"

"People, or one person, but... not? I've never—"

Screams rang out from the front of the line.

Everything disintegrated in an instant. Gauvain pulled her to the side of the trail just as panic-stricken farmers and hunters, healers and adventure seekers, stampeded back the way they had come. Quinn watched, her heart blocking her throat, as a young woman who had been sitting near their fire was knocked flying.

From farther up the trail, the screams continued, but from fewer throats. There couldn't be many left ahead of them. Gauvain hauled her to her feet, snatched her crutches from where they had fallen, then shoved her forward.

He didn't say anything. He didn't need to. They alone wielded the power to stop whatever was going on at the front of the line.

They elbowed their way through the terrified people who, so short a time ago, had been relaxing by the fires, chatting, anticipating the pleasure of getting to the Motherhouse.

The trail snaked around the mountainside. Gauvain turned a corner and abruptly stopped. Quinn dragged herself forward to stand beside him.

They found a scene of carnage. Several people lay sprawled in the dirt; dark patches of what must be blood spread on the path. Blocking their way was—

Quinn stared at it, stunned.

It was the size of a man and scaled like a lizard, light brown, with shorter front legs, a whipping tail, and a gigantic head. It stood over one of its victims while the few still in the vicinity scrambled to run away.

Gauvain held out an arm, blocking her from going any farther. "Can we stop it?" he said. No need to whisper; the screams behind them, while farther away, had by no means ended.

"I don't know."

A man was dragging himself along the ground, blind with panic, straight toward the first of the fires. The beast chose that moment to drive forward with its hind legs, faster than Quinn would have thought possible. Before she could shout a warning, it crushed the man in its enormous jaws.

He went limp. Blood, so much blood. The beast dropped him and looked around as if for another prey. As it did, its eyes locked on hers.

Blue. Sweet Diou, the thing had blue eyes. Quinn shivered.

Then the beast turned away, its long neck swaying as it sought its next victim. It spotted a woman, partly hidden behind a tree overhanging the trail, her face a mask of terror.

Quinn's wits came back to her as the pieces fell into place. Just before the beast lunged at the woman, she screamed.

"Kiril! Stop!"

Everything froze.

The beast moved its head, as if surveying the scene of carnage. Then, to Quinn's amazement, it turned and loped off, following the trail to the Midland.

Quinn's legs gave out. She dropped to her knees. Gauvain sank down beside her.

"We need to help them," she said.

"I know."

"I can't. Not yet."

"No."

She leaned against him. He took her hand. She had no idea how long they sat there. Eventually, a couple of the farmers approached them from the direction of Borgonne.

"It's gone?" one of the men asked.

Mute, she nodded.

The woman, a sturdy, practical farmer named Laura, crept from the tree to where she and Gauvain huddled beside the trail.

Five of them left. Two with Entrée and three farmers. And... Quinn swallowed. Perhaps life still flowed in those sprawled on the ground?

"How do we deal with this?" Gauvain said. He sounded unlike himself, weak and uncertain.

Laura stood and wobbled to the nearest fire. With shaking hands, she managed to pour broth into mugs she gathered from the path, where they had been scattered in the stampede. Wordlessly she passed them around.

Quinn didn't argue about the lack of hygiene. The paltry nourishment grounded her and gave her renewed strength.

They still had daylight, but not for long. They needed to see to the wounded... or dead. With Gauvain's help, she got to her feet.

Four of them. And no, none of them alive. The beast had been thorough. In the maw of those enormous jaws, they'd stood no chance. They were broken and... Sustainer help her... chewed. Behind her, one of the farmers retched.

Among the dead was Cedric, the pompous little mayor. Quinn hadn't liked him, but pinched her lips together against the onset of tears.

"We can't bury them," Gauvain said quietly. "There's too much undergrowth to dig through, and we need to leave."

The three farmers stayed close together, waiting to be told what to do.

Quinn swallowed, hard. "Let's move them off the trail. They died in the hills. Let the hills reclaim them."

"Like an offering?"

She half smiled at the notion. From what she'd seen, superstition ran rife in Borgonne, more so than in the Midland. "No, not exactly. More like reclaiming its own. When we're in the hills, we belong to the hills. Don't you feel that?"

It was the first time she'd put it into words, but it made sense.

Gauvain nodded and crossed to the huddled farmers. He spoke briefly. They stood and spread out, kicking dirt over the fires.

He returned to her and said, "We move them, then we get out of here. None of us can handle being in this spot tonight."

"It's nearly dark."

"You and I can create Magelight."

Light globes. They were not bright against the darkness of night, more suited for interior work, but they would do. And she wanted to be here no more than did the others.

Although she couldn't help with the actual removal, she straightened limbs, closed eyes and mouths, soothed expressions of terror. Three men and a woman. The tears overtook her with the first body she attended; by the fourth she was sobbing quietly, in honor of those sacrificed to the hills.

Once they finished, they gathered up abandoned packs, raided them for food – for they had no hunter with them – then left the packs on the trail in case some of their panicked colleagues returned.

They made their way through the gathering dark. No one spoke, and she sent up a silent request that Kiril, whatever he had become, would leave them in peace.

Two days later, days of pain, hunger, shock, and fear, they came upon the shredded remains of a tunic. Quinn and Gauvain exchanged glances. They were equals in power, and he'd assisted in the last binding; they both knew what they might find further along the trail.

Shortly thereafter they emerged from the hills. There was no abrupt change in the landscape, but her senses told her they'd arrived in the Midland. Quinn felt able to breathe again, freed from the grip the spells exerted on her mind.

Everyone noticed the subtle shift; she saw the others relax. The sun shone. It was already a hot, clear day, and would be hotter. After days of damp chill, she gloried in the warmth baking her skin.

They heard Kiril a short time later. He'd moved out of sight of the trail and lay naked, curled in on himself in a nest of beaten down grasses, making a high, monotonous sound through a raw throat and chapped lips. His eyes were open, panicky and unseeing. Grief, she thought, and sank onto her knees next to him, placing a hand on his shoulder. He didn't acknowledge her presence in any way.

"A blanket. Quickly." To counteract shock, and his fear of being unclothed.

Gauvain dropped his pack and opened it, at the same time shouting for the farmers, who had carried on ahead, to wait.

No longer a threat.

Quinn had no Healing skills, but knew more than anyone alive about the demon that infested Kiril's body. Based on his catatonia, she suspected he had been curled in a fetal position for the two days since the attack.

The mindless keening continued. A spasm seized him, then released; otherwise he remained rigid. She soothed his cowlick from his forehead... how often had she imagined doing just that? Using her hands to play with his light brown hair, touch his face, his skin...

Never going to happen. Right now, she needed to restore him to humanity, get him to the Motherhouse. She prayed Gauvain would be willing to help. Frankly, she was a little surprised Gauvain hadn't sunk a knife into him instead of looking for a covering.

By the Sustainer, Kiril, what have you brought on us?

Gauvain tossed a bedroll over Kiril's shivering body. He didn't respond. The farmers backtracked and circled them, puzzled. Quinn met Gauvain's eyes; neither of them explained.

Her own pain forgotten, she sat still a minute, girding herself to face the next, inevitable challenge. Though she dreaded it, they needed to go into Kiril's energy again. Find out how much of him was left, how much the beast had consumed. And redo the binding. "Can you help me?" she asked.

Gauvain caught her meaning instantly. "Yes. But not on an empty stomach."

Quinn accepted the practicality of the words. It was nearing noon, so they joined the others in chewing their way through dry waybread and gristly dried meat, moving down the trail to escape

Kiril's hoarse keening. Then, the skimpy meal done, they sent the farmers ahead to a ford Quinn remembered. Let them relax in the river and enjoy the afternoon.

She and Gauvain would work in private.

Work they did. She hadn't been fully aware of her own weakness, and within the template they wove around Kiril's energetic body she realized Gauvain was in no better shape. At least – and to her surprise – the demon had shrunk and appeared to wield no more energy than Kiril himself did. It took until late afternoon, but when they finished their patient slept, finally released into a semblance of peace.

"We stay here?"

Gauvain nodded.

"Go to the ford. I'll wait with him."

"I'll bring water back for you."

She turned her attention to the man beside her.

Kiril wakened at dusk. Silently she washed him and helped him into her spare tunic. He allowed it, his face blank; for his sake, she hoped he remembered nothing of the events in the hills. But somehow she doubted he'd be granted that mercy.

She fed him some broth, then he fell into an uneasy slumber.

By morning Kiril had improved physically, although he could hardly stand. After attempting breakfast – he turned away from food – they worked out a form of marching order, with the farmers and Gauvain assisting Kiril and her.

Kiril neither spoke nor resisted. Quinn suspected his mind had gone into overload and shut down. She didn't know, and lacked the skill to find out. The Motherhouse would provide the answers.

As they moved forward, she sent a message to Arwen, alerting her. Within a day, by her estimation, a party from home would meet them.

Home. Healing for her foot. Help for Kiril. All she'd learned about the hills to the south, the possibility of a trade route.

Home. Sleep.

She couldn't think of sleep, not now. She still faced two days or more of hobbling along the narrow, rough track.

Chapter 24

The day before, the ship had settled in its resting place with a sigh of relief, Harry thought in a rare burst of fancy. Through their aerial surveys, they'd pinpointed a site as near to flat and horizontal as they could hope for, because it was certain the Eurocorp Adventurer wouldn't be taking to the air again.

They'd put down in the plains, near a river. The land sloped gently up to the west, toward distant mountains. Forest, which stretched to the north and east, encroached on the plains a kilometer or so from their landing site and followed the river; there would be no shortage of wood for heat and construction. A hamlet, perhaps thirty buildings, sat two kilometers away on the edge of the plain, surrounded by planted fields and pastures.

He surveyed the small bridge that had been his virtual home for two years. Ben had the helm; he was talking to someone over the comm. Their navigator, Colin Smythe, sat staring blankly at his controls; Harry got his attention and gestured him over.

"You have a mapping team ready?"

"Sure."

"Then get out of here. There's nothing that needs to be done until we disembark."

Colin gave him a lopsided grin. "Hard to believe it's over."

"Tell me about it."

Colin ambled off. A shipboard romance, his wife was due to give birth in a few weeks; Harry hoped it would go well for their first land-based delivery.

He glanced at the chronometer above the windows of the bridge, now set to reflect the day length of their new home. Time for his meeting. After so long on Terran timescales, his mind struggled to make the translation.

Elspeth stood to shake his hand when he entered. She wore the same cautiously relieved expression he saw everywhere, but especially among those who had carried the prime responsibility for shepherding the Adventurer across uncharted space to this speck of a planet. Smaller than earth, with less land mass, but in other ways surprisingly similar. The day was a bit shorter, as was the year, but not so much that their Circadian rhythms were hopelessly out of whack. They shared a sense of a near-hopeless task completed, a new set of challenges waiting in the wings. After they'd touched down and confirmed that all was well, there'd been a celebration, but it had been somewhat muted, as if everybody was in shock.

Too much to deal with. If his own mind, trained in what to expect from space exploration, was reeling, how could the others feel differently?

Back to today's business. "Elspeth," he said, gripping her hand. From the north of Euro Corporation, Elspeth Gandsdottir was a determined, solidly built woman in her fifties with the blond hair – now showing accents of gray – and blue eyes typical of her region. "How're you doing?"

"Exhilarated, but exhausted."

He grinned. "With good cause." He pulled up a chair beside hers, and the two of them turned to their tablets. "Where do you want to start?"

"Disembarkation protocols and contact with natives."

"After that I'd like to review the current state of the ship. We'll be living aboard for quite a while, possibly until next summer."

"True," she said, "but some are already clamoring to get out. Air continues to test positively, better than on board in fact. Slightly more oxygen rich than we're used to."

"Time to check our filters." Harry made a note. "Moving on, can we manage sending out a scouting party within the week?"

"I'll let you know once we have the report from the probes."

And so they began to work down the lists they'd spent the last year compiling, the ones that represented the period of their shared command before he handed responsibility over to her. Putting names and timeframes to tasks, marking off those completed and how they led to new, unplanned-for challenges.

How about a nice retirement party for the outgoing commander?

He laughed, causing Elspeth to raise her fair eyebrows at him. "Inappropriate thought related to not doing this job anymore. How soon do you think the handover will be complete?"

"Could be a year, if we continue to live on board. Why?"

"Because I've got an urge to go walkabout. Set off on foot and see what's here."

Elspeth caught his light mood. "You know what's here, Harry. You've been watching it for six weeks now."

"Come with me. Let's leave the pilgrims behind and just go, why don't we?"

"Nice dream. Have we sent out the soil probe yet?"

Harry sighed and returned to business. "Soil and water, last night. Samples are in the lab, hence the lockdown in that part of the ship."

"Who knew it would be so complicated?"

"Harry." The disembodied voice came through the speaker.

"What's up, Ben?" No code had been sounded, so it wasn't critical, merely worth interrupting his meeting for.

"Locals. At the edge of the forest, distance five hundred meters. They're just standing there, watching. Ten or so. Armed, if you can call it that. Staffs, what look like bows."

"You see any arrows?"

"Maybe in slings on their backs."

He snapped back to business in a hurry. "Threat assessment?"

"Low. Dressed in bags, but they seem healthy enough. I've got them on the video if you want a look."

"Transfer the feed here, please."

A few seconds later, the image appeared on the screen behind them; Elspeth and he both swiveled around.

The group of perfectly ordinary humans kept their distance, talking among themselves. Harry concurred with the comment about bags, but they were clean and not undernourished.

"I doubt they're sophisticated enough to present a threat, other than possibly disease. I'd say they're curious more than scared. No weapons to worry us." Ben clicked through his points.

"We may not be the first ship to land here, if the exploration pod made it," Elspeth said.

"There's next to no sign of a road network," Harry mused. "If they didn't touch down near here, these people probably aren't even aware of them."

Ben zoomed the picture in. There was at least one child in the group, hiding behind the adults. "My take on it is, we watch and wait. Plan not to disembark until they're not around."

Don't want to be eaten. The running joke about cannibalism had pervaded the ship ever since they'd detected signs of cognizant life.

"Put out a neutral bulletin," Harry said. "Tell everyone about first sighting, but no one is leaving the ship until we have more information. We do this by the book."

"Will do. Shall I leave up the feed?"

"Sure. Might as well keep an eye on them."

Ben's voice disappeared. Harry and Elspeth moved to the other side of the table, so they could check the onlookers occasionally while they dealt with their interminable lists.

"The Terrans are here," Arwen told her council.

"Pretty much just when we don't need them," Fergus said. "Not with Quinn injured."

"Their landing site's far to the west. We've had word from Gwen. Most of you wouldn't know her. She's a Healer who found a place for herself and stayed. She hasn't been back to the Motherhouse in thirty years. The message was garbled – I so wish all Weavers could send decent messages. But the gist was clear enough. Massive, silver, sitting on the plain half a day from Cann."

"Where's that?" Daren asked.

"Southwestern plains near where the forests begin," Arwen said. "Fairly isolated, so with luck we won't have to worry about these newcomers. There could be lots of them, though."

"Seems to me," Dorcas said, "our immediate concern is what's going on in the hills. I've never experienced anything like that energy surge. And how is Quinn involved?"

"She's out of the hills now," Arwen said, "so we'll have answers soon. Gauvain's with her, and I think a few others. The rest of the party... There are traces of energy to the east, so some might be returning to Borgonne, which in itself makes no sense. But I'm more concerned with what happened to Quinn."

There was a tap on the door, and a woman from the kitchen entered. After she'd placed a tray of caff and mugs on the table, she said, "Tomas from the village rounded up a donkey cart, and supplies are ready. They'll be settin' out shortly."

"Thank you." After the woman left, Arwen turned to Daren. "You've seconded a Healer?"

"I have. Noni. I caught her just before she set out for Stanstead."

"Then we've done all we can. Any word on Kiril?"

"No," Dorcas grumbled. "The damn man's vanished off the face of the planet."

"So we're doing nothing about these Terrans?" Fergus asked.

Arwen sighed. "To be honest, I suspect our bigger challenge will be how the rest of the planet reacts."

Chapter 25

"Are you out of your mind?" Arwen was in full rant. Quinn was almost too tired to care.

The donkey cart got them home that afternoon, and they'd tucked her into a healing room to give Daren an opportunity to frown at her foot. A Healer she scarcely knew, a woman in her forties named Meade, danced attendance. Quinn just wanted to be left alone. To sleep until the foot healed and she was free to return to her usual duties.

When she didn't reply, Arwen continued her assault. "To take off into an unfamiliar land where your sash might not be respected, on your own. The miracle is, the mess you made of your foot didn't give you blood poisoning."

Meade slipped from the room.

"Go away, Arwen."

The uncharacteristic rudeness made the older woman draw back. In a milder tone, she said, "When I told you to go home, I didn't mean for you to take up residence. We needed you here. We've got Terrans in the southwest plains, the threat from Borgonne... hell, one of our apprentices is pregnant. I didn't need the extra worry."

"I'm here now."

Arwen sighed, letting Quinn hear her exasperation. "Daren's not optimistic about the foot. How do you expect to get around? Hmm?"

"By horse." With that provocative phrase, Quinn rolled over and turned her back on her mentor, friend, and boss.

"My office. As soon as Daren clears you to walk."

Quinn didn't answer.

She heard quiet voices near the doorway. After a while they all went away.

The next morning, ignoring Daren's dictates, she claimed her hated crutches and hobbled to Kiril's healing room. He lay under a wool coverlet, awake but unresponsive. He'd been bathed; she wondered if they had been able to feed him. The most he'd managed on the trail was an occasional sip of broth.

"You're exasperating." Daren came up behind her, gave her a quick hug, then took her elbow and steered her out of the room.

In a consultation room across the hall, they sat and Daren said bluntly, "Your foot's bad, Quinn. And you're not helping things by walking on it."

"How bad?"

"Breaking the bones and resetting might work. Or could make it worse. There's tendon and nerve damage besides the bones."

"There must be some kind of manipulation—"

Daren laughed without humor. "You of all people should know we're not miracle workers. Even when it first happened, it would have been difficult to restore you to full functionality. Now, after all this time…" He shook his head. "Noni and I did an assessment, and Meade's promised to check this morning. But the prognosis isn't positive. After a mangling like that, it's pure good fortune you haven't lost it."

"Would I be better off? Perhaps get an artificial foot?" Brave words; she was scaring herself.

"Time will tell, but I doubt it. Best I hope for is that you won't need those." He gestured at the crutches, propped on the table beside her. "But give us a chance, Quinn. Wandering around makes it worse. If you really have to go somewhere, I'll arrange transport for you. We have wheeled chairs, or we can ask one of the agriculturists to carry you."

She finally smiled, at the image. "I'm not a small woman, Daren."

"They're not weak men. Do you want time with Kiril, or were you just checking on him?"

"Can we get Dorcas? I need to assess the binding. Given the circumstances, I don't have much confidence in it. She knows what I'm looking for."

"Gauvain as well?"

"Where is he?"

"Guest lodge, last I heard. I daresay he's met with Arwen already."

Quinn sighed and leaned forward on the table, propping her chin on a hand. "They're here about food. They wouldn't tell me what they planned. I was along to provide a safety shield to get through the hills. But I think the idea was to somehow claim the Midland. Take us over. Kiril took care of that. Ask Gauvain, he'll know."

"And I think this is going to be a very interesting debrief." Daren gave her a smile, quickly extinguished. "But I'll tell Arwen she's to conduct it in your healing room. You're not traipsing all over the Motherhouse, understand?"

"Let me look in on Kiril, then I'll be a good girl and go back to my bed."

"The rooms are all bound with Healing templates. This really is the best place for you."

"I know, Daren. Sorry to cause hassle."

This time his smile was genuine. "Take my arm, infuriating woman."

Together they made their way across the hall.

Kiril hadn't moved. Daren shifted a stool to his bedside. She sat and took Kiril's hand. Daren backed away, but waited outside the room.

"You saved the Midland," she told Kiril's inert form conversationally. "Somehow, you knew we were under threat. That thing... I suppose you couldn't control it, or not completely. But you sent them packing. They won't try to invade us again."

No reaction.

"When Dorcas gets here, we'll see what we need to do to keep you safe from it."

Kiril's head shifted slightly, as if he wanted to turn toward her but hadn't the energy. He murmured; Quinn strained to hear.

I killed them.

Was that what he said? Was his current, near catatonic state the result of guilt, not a bodily reaction to the beastly energy inside him?

Quinn squeezed his hand. "You saved us. I'll be back. Rest, let the templates heal you."

Daren helped her to her feet, and she hobbled away to deal with her own healing.

Quinn knew before she reached the conference room after breakfast, two days later, that this meeting wasn't likely to unfold positively. There was something in the air... an emptiness, as if everyone at the Motherhouse was avoiding her. A ridiculous notion; the conversation at breakfast with Dorcas and Dal, back from Stanstead for a few days, had been perfectly normal. But her senses spoke of currents beneath the surface of their chat over hot cereal.

"I'm not late, am I?" It was unusual for her to be the last to arrive. Daren met her eyes with a look of – pity? The others concentrated on their tisanes.

"Right on time, as usual," Arwen said.

"I see." She propped the crutches – more comfortable ones Noni had given her to replace the crude sticks that had carried her across the hills – and took an empty chair beside Fergus.

The full council had assembled, Arwen, Fergus, Cynth, Daren, and now herself. Why did she feel like an outsider? Had they met before her arrival?

Was this meeting about her?

Somewhat to her surprise, Dal slipped in as she sat; he circled the table to the chair next to Daren.

Two Healers with Kiril as a patient, and no ability to Heal him.

"Tell us what happened, Quinn," Arwen said. "Take as much time as you need."

She hadn't yet mentioned the possibility of a southern trade route. She wasn't sure why, but conceded that the whole business of Kiril and the attack by the monster took priority at the moment. Quinn looked at Arwen, puzzled. "I've already told you. And I conclude that you've told the others. What's the point in rehashing it?"

She reached to the middle of the table and poured herself a mug of tisane – mint, not her favorite – before she gave them the bare facts.

As she finished, Cynth nodded, her lips tight. Fergus looked troubled, Daren... sad?

"Each time I hear the story, I hope I'll learn something different. Some ameliorating fact that will change the conclusion." Arwen said.

Cold dread worked its way up Quinn's spine. Surely, surely they wouldn't...

"Four people killed, and under our auspices. We cannot risk his presence any longer. We've given him every chance, Healing, binding with our weaves. Nothing has sufficed."

"You wouldn't..."

Arwen's voice was quiet and unbearably kind. "It will be merciful. He's barely aware of his environment now, and Daren says he's dealing with self-loathing. Let him go, Quinn. It's best."

Cynth spoke. "He presents too much of a threat. We can't allow him to wander the Midland, never knowing when he might..." She broke off with a shudder.

"But he won't," Quinn blurted. "It only happened because of the hills. From where we found the tunic... the hills changed him. Once he's on his feet again, you can help with his mind, help him come to terms...." Her eyes went to Dal and Daren, the Healers.

Dal's position was plain on his face; the decision wasn't his; he supported it but hated it. Daren shook his head. "We can't save him, Quinn. Not with that thing inside him."

Quinn felt the panic of disbelief, but faced Arwen, the only other Scribe present. "We have to try harder. It's bound now, so we can go in and..." Her mind grasped for reasons, for next steps. "And learn, find a better way to bind it. We don't *know* this beast. We need to study it. In case it happens again."

Arwen shook her head. "Exactly *because* the demon's freshly bound, it can't escape. This is the best time to destroy its host."

Destroy. Quinn looked around the table. The decision had been made before she arrived; her speech only confirmed their convictions.

For a moment, she wondered why she was fighting for an obnoxious man who played no discernable role in their culture, when even she had to admit the threat he represented.

She stood. "You cannot do this."

"Sit down, Quinn." Arwen's voice carried its usual command, but with an underlay of weariness. "We don't want this any more than you do. But four people are dead, including one whose loss will have political ramifications in Borgonne, and it's obvious we can't control whatever it is that lives inside Kiril. For the good of the Midland, we have no choice."

Quinn scanned the table, meeting their eyes, one by one. Then she seized the crutches, turned, and did her best to stalk from the room.

At the building's heavy door, she collided with Bryar.

He put out his big hands to steady her. "Whoa, girl. What's happened?"

"Where did you come from?" she blurted. "Is Tai with you?"

"Over at the guest lodge, getting our stuff settled. We wanted to call in here before we strike out."

The day had dawned sunny, but low nimbus cloud was rolling in, keeping the temperature pleasant and promising rain. Of one mind, they turned toward the green. Bryar eyed the crutches and her bandaged foot, but said nothing. The news of her injury and the slaughter would have been communicated to Ezra's compound by now, so she didn't waste breath explaining. At their favorite spot, halfway up the slope in a space where the land leveled out, they settled onto the grass.

"I can't make up my mind if you're raging or about to cry or what," Bryar said. "Your energy's scrambled. Calm down and tell me what's going on. How's the foot?"

"Improving. They say it'll never be right." She played in the grass, tearing off blades and lining them up on her thigh. A senseless activity, but buying her time to sort out what had just happened. She looked square at Bryar. "Everyone's spooked by Kiril's beast. The deaths – there are safety and political ramifications. They're going to execute him."

"Like hell." Bryar half rose, sank down again. Horror filled his eyes, replaced quickly by fury. "Give me the details, Quinn. They can't... no one's been put to death in my lifetime. They can't do this."

Quinn wasn't surprised by Bryar's adamant assertion. Kiril had saved his life. One way or another, it was their turn to save Kiril.

"He's unresponsive in the healing rooms now, so he'd probably never know. That's what they said. And to be honest, I'm not sure he wants to live."

Bryar's face was pale, and his agitation came through in his voice. "Would you, if you'd killed four people that way? He needs time and Healing. I won't let this happen."

"But how? By the time they told me, the rest of council had made up their minds."

Bryar was silent. Below them, Tai crossed the green from the guest lodge, spotted them and waved, then disappeared into the dining hall.

A small smile appeared on Bryar's face. "She'll be up here with some kind of treat soon."

"You chose well. She's perfect for you."

"Who would have thought, huh?" The smile grew larger. Then vanished. "I have to see Kiril," he said.

"He won't recognize you."

"For any medical reason?"

She shook her head. "I don't think so. He just lies there, staring into space. He's so thin now. Not eating."

"Someone needs to kick his ass. Would you be able to react normally if you'd done what he did? If you were facing life with this beast thing inside?"

"Good point."

Gauvain came out of the guest lodge and headed toward them.

"More trouble?" Bryar asked.

"I hope not. Dragging me across the hills was insanity, but he did help me get back." She glanced at her foot.

"A story I want to hear."

Gauvain stood over them, slightly downslope, which lessened his ability to intimidate. "I wouldn't mind getting the full details myself. Such as what you were doing in Borgonne in the first place."

He turned his focus on Bryar. "I believe you to be the man who stole the power cell from me. I conclude my restoration of you in the hills proved... beneficial?"

Subtle, Quinn though, suggesting that Bryar had been ungrateful to take the power cell. Based on her observation, she wondered if his political instincts didn't outweigh even his Auric abilities.

Bryar stood. Although not a tall man, with the advantage of the slope he and Gauvain were eye to eye. "I am in your debt. The cell has been secured."

"Which Ezra orchestrated, no doubt. Seems we both paid a price." Gauvain fingered the scar that cut his face, brow to jaw, as he stared pointedly at Bryar's left hand, the missing fingers.

Tai emerged from the dining hall. Quinn watched her coming up the slope, her hands full of pastries, then said, "If you'll excuse us?"

Both men reached out a hand. She took Bryar's and nodded a thanks to Gauvain. "I'm not so great on hills."

"You're not going to fall." Bryar held her arm, the crutches in his other hand, as they made their way down the slope, sweeping up Tai on the way. At the door to the guest lodge, Quinn turned to Gauvain. "This doesn't concern you, but thanks for the help."

He brushed off her dismissal. "You are discussing Kiril, so it concerns me. I am intrigued, and would value an opportunity to study him further."

After a pause, Quinn said, "You may not get that opportunity. But this is a reunion, not a strategy session."

"Very well. As it happens, I have business to discuss with Arwen."

"She's either in the conference room or her workroom."

With a nod of the head that managed to imply that he had dismissed them, rather than the other way around, Gauvain turned and strode toward the Centra.

Tai and Bryar had a suite on the ground floor. Quinn accepted a hug from Tai, then sank into a chair. "Five minutes on my feet and I'm exhausted. On my *foot*, I should say."

For half an hour they shared news and consumed Tai's stockpile of pastries. Quinn still chose not to mention the possible trade route; the question of Kiril's fate loomed too large.

"I don't know what to do," she concluded. "Kiril doesn't deserve to die, even apart from the mystery of the energy inhabiting him."

Bryar placed a calming hand on her arm, as always reading her accurately. "It's reasonable to conclude that the hills caused the emergence of that – thing – and triggered the attack. Was he defending the Midland? Or with so many people attempting to cross, perhaps he was defending the hills."

Quinn nodded. "That's my opinion. Based on where we found his tunic, he didn't transform until he was in the hills."

Tai had been silent through Quinn's narrative. Now she spoke up. "Then it's simple. The problem's the hills, not Kiril."

"Yes," Quinn said. "It's as if the hills own you when you're in them. There's been speculation around the Motherhouse almost from the beginning, because they exert a draw on him, one he can fight off only so long."

"Until it takes him over," Bryar said.

"So logically, the farther from the hills he is, the healthier he should be," Quinn concluded. "Assuming, of course, that the energy can be kept bound. And I'm not at all sure about that."

"Do you see another option?" Bryar's voice was hard.

Quinn swallowed and shook her head.

Bryar's and Tai's eyes met and locked. Quinn watched an unspoken message pass between them.

"I guess we'll forego our little vacation here," Tai said with a hint of humor.

"But first," Bryar said, "we need to rouse Kiril. Get him mobile enough that we can take him to Stanstead."

"You'd do this?" Quinn, who lately found herself uncharacteristically emotional, felt her eyes filling.

"I owe him. And he's my friend, sort of." Bryar stood, as if the issue was settled. "I'm going to the healing rooms."

"And I guess I'm repacking." Tai grinned.

"Good luck. I can't see council wasting time. We need to get him out of here." Quinn's heart thumped in her chest. She was about to defy council, possibly put the Midland at risk, and involve her closest friends in a scheme that might well not work, because how were they to move Kiril in his near-catatonic state?

"I'll do my best. I won't return here," he said to Tai. "Once we're clear of the healing rooms, we'll take the back trail around the complex. One of you raid the kitchen for provisions and meet me along the Stanstead trail."

"Should we try for a donkey cart?" Quinn asked.

"Check in the village."

"I can't." She gestured at the foot.

"I'll go," Tai said. "It'll only take a minute to pack. You deal with the kitchen."

Bryar entered the healing room quietly, avoiding the workroom where a young Healer he knew only by sight puttered, humming to herself. Kiril lay as Quinn had described, his eyes open, staring at nothing Bryar could see. He looked dreadful, far too thin under the light cover, motionless.

Bryar stepped up to the bed and dealt a sharp slap to his face.

Kiril jerked upright before collapsing against his pillow. "What...?" he whispered.

"We don't have time for you to wallow in your issues. Get up. We're leaving." Bryar rummaged in the supply closet, emerging with a tunic and sandals. He glanced at Kiril. "Now."

"I can't," Kiril mumbled.

In two strides Bryar was back at the bedside. He jerked Kiril upright and tossed the tunic over his head. "Help me, damn you. Your life's at stake. You wanted to learn more about our land? Well, now's your chance." He dragged Kiril's legs off the bed, then knelt to fasten on the sandals. "You feeling that beast energy?"

Kiril looked bewildered. His voice was barely there. "No. Except it never..."

Bryar hauled the other man to his feet, supporting him as he swayed. "Get this clear. We're out of here. First we have to circle around behind the storage sheds without being seen. You'll have to walk – and you going to, whether you like it or not. Let's move."

With Kiril staggering beside him, Bryar checked the corridor, then moved them slowly toward a back entrance. So far, so good. Kiril was compliant, if not physically capable of much. Slowly, too slowly for Bryar's peace of mind, they made their way to the perimeter trail.

Quinn encountered Gauvain on her way to the kitchen's back door. It was almost as if he had sought her out. A sort of understanding had evolved between them after the attack, based on a recognition of matched abilities and a need to work together if they were to make it safely to the Midland, so his appearance on the back trail wasn't a total surprise or entirely unwelcome.

"What are you doing with him?" he demanded as he drew her to a halt near the back wall of the kitchens.

"With...?

He'd mastered looks of irritated exasperation. "Let's not play games, Quinn. You and your friends were discussing Kiril. From your expressions, I'm capable of making assumptions."

After a moment's hesitation she said, "Drop your shields."

They all maintained relaxed shields to a greater or lesser degree, as a matter of self preservation. Otherwise the energies around the Motherhouse would form a constant bombardment, eventually making you lose touch with who you were as a being separate from the others. They taught shielding early, to the second-year apprentices, because it was, in a real sense, a survival skill. Quinn reluctantly relaxed her hold on her own shield and felt for his energy.

He didn't like it, but he complied, if only for a few seconds. Long enough, however, for her to read his intent.

"They're taking him to Stanstead. From there they can go in a number of directions, but ultimately west, as far from the hills as possible. Assuming they avoid detection."

"And the urgency? He's not a well man."

"If he stays here, he'll be a dead man."

Gauvain grimaced. "A foolish decision, but I suppose it was to be expected. I fear this removes any hope of my studying this demon of his. I have no wish to explore any more of the Midland."

"Nor should Kiril be considered a specimen." Although Quinn had hoped for exactly the same thing, she resented Gauvain's assumption that he was no more than a curiosity.

"I will help. Leave council to me."

Quinn shifted, resting against the wall to ease her weight-bearing leg. "Why would you do this?"

He smiled and flicked a speck of dirt from his black shirt. "Specimen, remember? And I owe you for stopping the assault. You and I would have been next. Everyone dies, but I have no wish to perish in the hills."

The chances of making Gauvain squirm under scrutiny were nil, but she stared at him anyway, looking for... what? A sign of humanity? But this was Gauvain. She'd crossed from Borgonne with him; by now she should know better. She heaved herself from the wall and settled the hated crutches under her arms. "Thanks," she said, and swung herself toward the kitchen door.

Chapter 26

Joss sighed with relief and stretched, breathing in the fresh summer air. When the call came to get to the barns, he'd been out in the meadows, checking the health of the flocks of sheep. The cow had been in distress, her calf stuck and unable to be born. Cow and calf both wanted this over with, but with a little leg in the way...

They'd managed it, but it had involved hours of messy work. Joss emerged bruised, drenched with sweat, exhausted, and up to his shoulders in – well, whatever you called the fluids inside a cow – not to mention shit and straw from the floor of her stall.

The cow was relieved. The calf was hungry. Joss left them to their bonding, washed off the worst in the barrel set outside the barn for that purpose, and trudged toward home. He'd finish cleaning up in the lake.

Home.

Willow might be there, or might be off on a herb gathering expedition or a Healing. He sensed in her a restlessness, an itch to get back on the road. If she decided to go, he'd go with her, although he'd be sad to leave Hallan. But before that, he had something on his mind, something he needed to run by her.

The heat of the evening gave rise to the aromas of summer, of scythed grass and flowers. Yes, he thought, home. Through the spring, they had learned to be together over stews and the warmth of the cookfire, both of them going about their work during the day, braving the spring storms. And then the birthing of lambs, watching the land he'd come to love as it burst into life, helping with the tilling and planting. It had been a time for him to consolidate his power, learn its ways and how to manipulate it. The exhaustion of maintaining a screen around himself, the sheer joy of relaxing that screen when he was alone with Willow. Reading her feelings, letting her read his.

On one such evening, when they were lounging on the hillock in the late afternoon warmth, exchanging news of the day, he'd sensed distress from one of the not-quite-feral, not-quite-tamed goats that frequented the environs of their cabin. He'd spent half the night seeking her where she'd gone to ground. Willow had handled the birth, delivering her of a fine kid. Where she'd found a sire was anyone's guess; the only goats around Willow's little cottage were female.

Sire.

The word had never entered his consciousness before his life with Willow. Now it was seldom absent.

Willow wasn't in the cottage, although a pot of lentils simmered on a low cookfire. Joss grabbed a thin rag that passed for a towel and headed down the trail. He swam with more assurance now, so he struck out for the warmer water in the middle of the lake, fed by one of Hallan's numerous hot springs. He had plans to pump the water up to the cabin, one day.

Before long he spotted Willow on the bank; she peeled out of her tunic and skirt and dove in. She still out-swam him, but on the other hand, he could watch the smooth arrow of her body carving through the water all evening.

They met and kissed, Joss rather frantically treading water, hoping not to pull her under. Then they both stroked toward the little beach. There he pulled off the wet but considerably cleaner tunic, and they climbed the hill to the cabin.

And then dry clothes, supper, and time to talk. Share their days, their moods, themselves.

God, he hoped she'd be receptive to what he had to say. He wasn't sure. Because while he'd learned a lot, he didn't know the magnitude of what he'd be asking. Women were still a mystery to him.

Once they were well into their lentils and corn cakes, he cleared his throat, prayed for a steady voice, and said, "Something I've been meaning to talk to you about."

Willow swallowed and smiled. "So talk."

Talking to her was easy... relatively easy. But speaking aloud anything that mattered to him was another matter entirely. On Terra, you sacrificed personal desires to the corporation. Not to do so meant brutal punishment. While conversation with this lovely, gentle woman who shared his life seemed, on the surface of it, simple and logical, in practice... well, it wasn't.

He started again. "I've been thinking..."

"I gathered that. Go on, Joss."

Nothing much scared Willow, but at least she tried to understand his hang-ups.

Swallow. Breathe.

"The way I see it, this is my home now."

"This planet, or Hallan, or here with me?"

"All three. I wouldn't go back if I could."

"Are you sure? They're here, out on the plains. Even if you can't go back, you could live with other Terrans."

He gave his head a firm shake. "I live here."

The line appeared between her brows. "Are you telling me you don't want me to travel? Because that's been my life, Joss. Even if I wanted to, I couldn't stop completely."

He looked at the stubborn set of her mouth and smiled. "Like I'd try to stop you? All I ask is that you let me go with you."

She nodded. "Traveling together is... well, it's good. Because you're sharing your lives. Bryar and I—"

"I know," he interrupted. He didn't need the specter of Bryar in this conversation. "I want more than that."

Jesus. Was it possible to be more ridiculous?

But Willow, as usual, saw through him. "Take a breath, then tell me what this is about." Her free hand, the one without a spoon in it, stroked his forearm. "I'm listening."

And doing things to him that made him squirm. Would he ever be comfortable with the simple sexuality she exuded and shared with him?

Hell, yes. He wasn't on Terra anymore.

"Okay, here goes." Another breath. "It's occurred to me that when I'm gone, I'll be gone without a trace. Nothing left."

"Hardly that. You'll be remembered by so many people. The giant who fell from the sky." Her gentle, tolerant smile turned to a quick grin. "More lentils?"

"Not yet."

"Joss..."

Here it was. The crux. And after his sloppy delivery, it all hinged on her reaction. "Willow, I want to leave more than a memory."

The room was silent; her hand lay still. Even the evening chorus of birds outside seemed muted. He watched her, willing himself not to close off. Because damn, he'd never felt so vulnerable.

Then her smile returned. "You want a child."

Beyond words, Joss nodded.

"Childbirth gets riskier once a woman approaches forty. Not unheard-of by any means, but more challenging, both for mother and for baby."

His spirits collapsed. "I was afraid of that."

"Joss, listen." She squeezed; her touch had been so light, and so expected, that he'd almost forgotten her hand still rested on his arm. "I said more challenging. I didn't say no."

He looked up, swallowed. "So... you'll think about it?"

Willow rose, scraping her chair back against the rough floorboards. She circled the table and stood behind him, her arms draped over his shoulders, palms on his chest, bending down to rest her head on his. Time froze while he sat, afraid to move so much as an eyelid, in the fading light trickling through the window.

Then she straightened, dropped a kiss on the top of his head, and stepped away. "I've thought."

Which meant no. Surely no woman made so momentous a decision in the space of a handful of minutes. His spirits sagged, and he found himself biting his lip, fighting against disappointment.

Willow crossed the cabin to the shelf where she stored containers of herbs. She chose two and put a pinch of each into the small bowls she used for preparing her concoctions. She brought both dishes to the table.

"This one's banebark." She touched one dish with her hand. "It prevents conception. Every woman in the Midland, probably on the planet, knows it."

She picked up the dish, pushed aside the leather curtain that covered the door, and tossed the herb out.

Back at the table, she fingered the other herb. "Motherwort. Can you guess?"

Joss stood.

Willow set the dish on the table. "I'd like nothing better than to make a child with you. And raise him to be as fine a man as you are."

Damn. He'd teared up. That hadn't happened since he was seven years old and someone soaked his shoes in the urinal.

Her hand brushed his cheek, then trickled down his front. "Let's start now."

He'd let her lead him anywhere, do anything she wanted with him. He nodded, wordless, and gripped her tightly against him as they made their way to their sleeping room.

Chapter 27

"They probably don't know we're here."

Ben glared at Jane. "Of course they do. God, woman, it's obvious."

"Of *course* I meant that there are people inside the ship. People like them. Use your brains, Ben."

The tension between Ben and Jane had been escalating for weeks. Harry said nothing. Jane, elected leader of community two, generally was a peacemaker, but not where Ben was concerned.

Getting under each other's hides. Wonder what that's all about?

He knew what it was about. For any number of practical reasons, he'd been celibate himself since they left Terra, and due to circumstance, for some time before that. Ben and Jane, along with their medic the only singles among his senior crew, weren't any more immune than he was. It did make these early morning meetings interesting.

Almost over.

"Willie, any negative indications?"

Wilhelmina Schott, their team lead for science and exploration, shook her head. Harry privately speculated that if there were any negatives regarding their landing place, Willie would single-handedly storm out there and remove them. A large, powerful woman with a personality to match, she was also inclined to be taciturn. Harry was grateful. The potential devastation that Willie on a verbal rampage could leave in her tracks wasn't something he wanted to contemplate.

"Nope. Everything looks good. Hard to imagine a better environment, in fact."

"Georges, anything new from the locals?"

Georges Toit, head of security, shook his head. "They watch from the edge of the forest, but there's been no move to come closer other than to tend their crops. No weapons beyond what we've already seen. Changing personnel, with no particular pattern. At first I thought it was different watches, but now I believe they just drift over to stare at us when they aren't doing anything else. Kids, even."

"No obvious leader?"

"There's one woman wearing a green sash over her gunny sack, but she doesn't seem to command any authority."

"All right," Harry said. "Sounds like we're good to go. Deployment team?"

Elspeth spoke up. "After we've made first contact, we'll have more freedom to explore. If they're friendly, great, and if they're not, we make it clear who's running the show. As planned, we'll take a small party, including at least one or two senior crew, preferably in uniform. Well armed, and with emergency ingress protocols in place. Ship on full alert. Here's the final roster." She brought up a file which displayed on the large wall screens as well as their individual tablets.

Harry's brows rose. "You don't want me to go?"

"Sorry, Harry. They should see me as the leader, right from the outset. And we need one of us on the ship, just in case."

In case it goes belly-up. Harry got that.

"Anything else, folks? Equipment lists ready? Survival packs? Are you taking breathing filters, Elspeth?"

"Not necessary. We've sampled the atmosphere every which way. It's clean."

"What's your ETD?"

Elspeth grinned. "The kids usually turn up late afternoon."

"Safest? Friendliest?"

"Least likely to attack. So, today, sixteen hundred hours."

"Taking any of our kids with you?"

"Are you joking? I'm prepared to be friendly, but not *that* friendly."

Yes, he'd been joking. The sixty or so children on board were their shared inheritance, all the adults contributing to their raising.

"Assemble your team here half an hour before. May as well do the pep talk."

"Not to mention reconfirming everything we've been drilling into them for a week. The last thing I want to deal with is some overexcited idiot firing on these people."

"Everyone, be here," Harry said to the table. "We'll do a grand send-off."

"And a run-through of the hand signs."

The signs had been developed back on Terra, as being the most likely way to communicate with a culture that didn't speak any of the handful of standard Terran languages.

With a round of assents, the meeting disbanded.

The big day. The fate of their embryonic settlement on the line.

And then he could turn over the reins and settle into a deserved retirement.

Harry left the room with fingers crossed that the afternoon would go well.

Harry watched on the screen as Elspeth led her small band out of the ship, the first time any of them had experienced land in two years. The hatch was a full story and a half from the ground; she moved slowly down the fold-out stairs, clutching the handrail. They had opened the air vents to the outside, so they'd been living in the planet's atmosphere since lunch, but still, it had to be an emotional moment.

The next five minutes would determine their fate, Harry reckoned.

The usual small band of natives waited and watched from the edge of the forest, perhaps four soccer fields' distance away. They had changed their stance, sending the children into the woods, nocking arrows into the bows.

Elspeth ignored the implied threat. She stepped down and after moving aside to make way for the next person, she knelt, her head bowed, caressing the rough grass and dirt. Symbolic or part of the show? Harry suspected he'd be tempted to do the same.

Then she straightened and stood, and began a slow walk toward the settlers, her hands slightly out from her sides, visible and empty. The rest of their party stayed back, a few meters from the ship. Among them, Harry detected more delight at being on solid ground than trepidation at first contact with the settlers. They looked around, stretched, talked among themselves. Elspeth had chosen them for their cool, non-impulsive natures. He was fully aware that they were armed; no point in being stupid. But with any luck, no one would be firing anytime soon.

There was discussion among the natives. Several of them left, plunging back into the trees. After a minute or two, a man and woman, both clutching staffs, began to walk toward Elspeth. Behind them several bowmen watched every move.

They met roughly half way. Elspeth smiled. She had clipped a microphone to the jacket of her uniform; Harry heard her say, her voice artificially calm, "Hello." She held out both hands low in front of her, palms exposed, the agreed-to sign expressing non-aggression.

Would they recognize the greeting as peaceful? Would they respond in kind?

The man stepped forward and said, "Welcome to the Midland." He extended a hand.

In the control room, Harry straightened. Elspeth said nothing and glanced back at the ship, her mouth slightly open. The words were familiar, but the accent was strange, with echoes of old French from the times before Eurocorp standardized their language. Of all the possible outcomes, they'd never remotely considered the idea that these people would speak a Terran dialect.

Elspeth returned her attention to the man and reached out to accept his hand. He gave her a firm shake, then stepped back. "You speak..." She had been caught flat-footed. *Come on, girl,* Harry coached silently from the command controls. *Use your words.*

He'd been hanging out with the kids too much, obviously.

The couple from the inhabitants' group smiled, as if they were in on a good joke. "We speak as we've always spoken," the woman said. "A Weaver brought word from the east about a pod of visitors from the sky – I suppose that's what you call that thing, a pod? Are you hungry? We've sent for food."

Others? Pod? Had the exploration pod reached this planet after all? Harry found himself leaning forward, clinging to every word.

"No, I don't think we're..." Elspeth's voice wobbled; she cleared her throat and spoke more firmly. "We have food, but thank you for the offer. How is this possible?" She once again glanced back at the ship. "We didn't expect anyone to be here. And we certainly didn't expect to understand you."

Ask about the pod, Elspeth.

More natives joined the group at the edge of the forest. "We're back," someone shouted. "We brought Gwen."

"I'm Maddie, and this is Jurgen. We've been chosen to meet you." This time the woman stepped forward, offering her hand. Elspeth accepted it.

"Thank you." She was regaining her poise. "I am Elspeth Gandsdottir, Major in the Eurocorp Expeditionary Force and the leader of our settlement team. This is a ship, not a pod."

"That name's a mouthful," Jurgen said. "What do they call you when you're home?"

Elspeth managed a grin, perhaps realizing at the same time Harry did how ridiculous their Terran ranks and titles sounded here. The two natives returned the smile, and the woman turned to gesture to the bowmen. "Elspeth's fine."

Across the field, the bows were lowered but not released.

"Afore we make you welcome, we need to be sure of your intent. You'll not do harm to our village." Jurgen spoke calmly, but it was clear he meant every word.

Maddie chimed in. "The Weavers would help us if need be, should you prove to be a threat."

Who the hell were the Weavers? The men from the exploration pod?

Elspeth spoke calmly and with assurance. Years of anthropological practice stood her in good stead, Harry thought. The coup of a lifetime. Too bad there was no way to write it up in a scientific journal. "We need a place to live. To build a settlement, plant a crop if it isn't already too late this year. We have children aboard who deserve a stable home. Our intentions are peaceful, and we would welcome your help. This is new to us, but we're grateful to feel land underfoot. We've been on the ship for almost two years now."

Elspeth took a deep breath. Harry was pretty sure it wasn't calculated, unlike the rest of her speech. It was more a simple reaction to breathing pure air, with feet planted on the ground.

Maddie and Jurgen glanced at each other. Maddie turned and trotted back to the group. Jurgen gestured off to the south, beyond the ship. "Best place for another town's half a day's walk that away. Near the river, so's you'll have water. Good location for a mill."

"We'll go have a look. Could you spare someone to be a guide?"

Jurgen chuckled but shook his head. "Oh, no, not yet. We aren't that confident of your intent, though you seem nice enough. But you walk south, you can't miss it."

"Half a day, you say? We'd want to move the ship there. It would be noisy, and dangerous if any of your people were close by."

Jurgen shrugged. "As soon not have it in our lower pasture."

Maddie returned, carrying a bag made from the same material as the loose-fitting garments they wore. "We don't know you yet, and we're suspicious, see? But in general, when a newcomer turns up, we offer 'em food and drink. This here's fresh bread and some of the new abricoes. How many be you?" She held out the bag.

Elspeth accepted it "Four hundred thirty-three."

The number shocked her interrogators; their faces froze, and they both took an involuntary step back. "That's more than..."

"More than in the whole of the plains, I'd say." Maddie finished Jurgen's thought. "How we'll ever—"

She broke off, wheeled, and made for the gathering on the edge of the forest.

Jurgen nodded to Elspeth and followed.

Elspeth waited until they had rejoined their group before she gave them a wave. The entire party of natives waved back. Then she turned and crossed the field to the ship. As they re-boarded, she asked, "Anthony, you pick up anything?"

"No, ma'am. Not a thing." A specialist in psychological profiling, Anthony had been tasked with monitoring the inhabitants' speech and body language. "I doubt they're that good actors."

"So your threat assessment is—"

"Low. They're skeptical, that's to be expected. But they aren't out to kill us. They just don't want us to kill them."

"Nevertheless, we'll run this food through the lab before we touch it."

Chapter 28

"Where is he?"

"I don't know."

Arwen's look would have melted a lesser woman into a puddle. Quinn refused to melt, despite mild guilt, fatigue, and the nagging pain, gradually changing to a background ache, in her foot.

She hadn't stayed with Bryar's little troop for long. Once they cleared the immediate environs of the Motherhouse, she had turned back, mentally preparing herself not only for the painful hobble to the healing rooms – and the expected disapproval from whatever Healer was on duty – but also for Arwen's undoubted tongue-lashing. She'd never so flagrantly defied council before, and she admitted to herself that the thought sent butterflies swirling in her stomach.

Gauvain had done his part, to her considerable surprise. He'd kept council tied in knots of negotiation around future trade, and even had the temerity to demand compensation for the loss of their party, ignoring that most of the group had fled and hopefully were well on their way to a reunion with their families back in Borgonne. Quinn had seen him that evening and given him a surreptitious hug, which seemed to embarrass him, but he accepted her whispered thanks graciously enough.

Since Bryar had left the curtain lowered over the door to Kiril's healing room, a signal for privacy, Kiril's absence wasn't reported until after lunch. No one put together his disappearance and Bryar's brief stopover until that evening, and only then when the kitchen and guest lodge staff were questioned.

They'd take the donkey cart in the direction of Stanstead. The cart was a gamble; although it meant they'd move more slowly than at a Weaver's pace, Kiril couldn't walk across the green, much less undertake a four-day trek. After Stanstead, Quinn neither knew, nor wanted to know, where they were going, but somewhere far to the west, perhaps to the western sea.

At least as far as the ship full of his compatriots on the plains.

Arwen's hard voice intruded into her memory of yesterday. "North, west or south?"

Quinn just stared at her.

Arwen changed her tone, softening it until Quinn could almost believe she sincerely wanted the best for Kiril. "Don't do this. If he goes rogue again, it will rebound on Weavers everywhere. We've spent centuries building our reputation in the Midland. People trust us and respect what we do. This one man – *one man* – can undo that. Destroy all we've built." She couldn't hold onto the gentle tone; as she spoke her voice rose in anger.

"And you," Daren put in, more quietly. "If that thing in him is unleashed again, how will you feel? How many deaths are you willing to have laid at your door?"

She looked at him, remembering the last time they had loved. His face showed his concern, and his innate compassion.

Cynth's turn. "We're not downplaying the attraction. It can't be an easy decis–"

"*What?*" Her nerves stretched to near breaking, Quinn barked the word. "You think I'd put some stupid chemistry above the good of the Midland? I don't even *like* the man."

Arwen's voice was almost pleading. "Then why, for the love of all that sustains us, why have you done this?"

Quinn swallowed and lifted her chin. "Because it was the right thing to do. The hills triggered the demon in him. We couldn't... see him destroyed... when it may well be neutralized by distance. Kiril didn't kill those men, Arwen."

"And you want to study him." Cynth's voice was a slap.

"No. I mean, yes, of course I'm curious to understand. It might help us disentangle the spells on the hills, if we ever need to. But right now I just want my foot to heal. And..."

"What is it?" Arwen asked. "What more?"

Arwen came into focus. She looked tired and haggard. Her tenure as head of council had extended for years, and the last one hadn't been easy. Kiril and Joss, their power cell, the sudden traffic through the hills, Kiril's energetic contamination, and now a whole shipload of people from Terra, that mysterious planet so far away. Their stable ground was shifting under their feet. Quinn's actions hadn't helped, but...

No. What she'd done was right.

"I want to study the Terrans."

"I need you here." Arwen's voice was uninflected, echoing the weariness in her face.

No one spoke.

After the silence had spun itself so finely it might shatter, Arwen said, "You're not bound here. I understand the lure. But, Quinn, if you go, expect to be called back. With the problems we're facing—"

"Problems from the Terrans as well," Daren put in. "If Quinn could find a way to neutralize the rumors..."

"Unrest everywhere," Fergus confirmed. "Ever since that light appeared in the sky. My guild's sticking to popular routes, where they'll be recognized. A Healer, I'm not sure who, but there was a rumor he was assaulted, somewhere in the northwest."

"Always a hotbed," Cynth said.

"Nonetheless."

"I fail to see what good Quinn could do simply by going there," Arwen said. "And now with that man loose in the Midland—"

"He's with Bryar," Quinn said, then silently kicked herself. Even that much hadn't been certain.

"So I assumed. And Bryar will keep him safe? He's just—"

"Just what, Arwen?" Fergus demanded. "Have you looked at him recently? Bryar's no easygoing boy anymore. He's a warrior who's fought and probably killed, defending his land against Gauvain and the power cell. I worry that's he's grown too hard," he concluded in a mutter.

Quinn shook her head. "Not with Tai around. She's taken charge of his humanity."

The tension broke; Fergus let loose a laugh. "So she has."

Arwen rapped on the table. "Discussion of Bryar's mental state can be deferred. Now, what are we going to do about Kiril?"

"Leave him alone and listen for reports," Fergus said.

"Not good enough. Acting after the fact."

"I've drawn this up." Quinn extracted a small paper packet from the pocket of her tunic. "It's the binding weave." She tossed it into the middle of the table. "I simplified somewhat, so any Weaver should be able to work it."

Fergus opened the packet and glanced at the weave. "Not Bards. We rarely deal in anything this complex." He passed it to Daren, who studied the weave briefly, nodded, and handed the paper to Arwen. She and Cynth together traced the currents.

"How do you propose to distribute this?" Arwen asked without looking up.

"The simplest is for Kiril to keep it. He knows what's at stake as well as we do."

Arwen didn't like it, but she bowed to the inevitable. "If they were sensible, they'd be going to Ezra's, but I'd gamble they're on the road west. Dal's leaving after the midday meal. Give it to him. He'll catch up with them before Stanstead."

Quinn took the paper, folded it, and tucked it in her pocket. She met the eyes of each of her colleagues in turn. "I'm not minimizing this. I'll help in every way I can. Now... I'm sorry to drag this out, but there's one more thing."

"It's nearing midday, Quinn," Arwen said, annoyed. "What is it now?"

The drama of Kiril had overtaken her other news, but it was time. "The matter of the drought. We can't dismiss that."

"We can until after lunch."

Quinn sensed the fractiousness in the room, but this needed to be aired. "I have information that might be helpful. We all agree we need tools to deal with Gauvain."

Arwen sank back into her seat. "Very well," she said. "What is it?"

"I went home, like you ordered," she began. "The hills are lower, but I didn't know the spells woven through them are much weaker. It turns out the boys and young men of Colgate have been crossing the hills for generations."

"What?" Daren's voice was sharp with incredulity.

"Some of them experience a little nausea, but otherwise they go back and forth whenever they please. On the Borgonnian side, it's unsettled, but there is a rough north-south track. The rangeland supports a large herd of horses. They've managed to capture a couple and bring them to Colgate."

"You're kidding." This taxed even Fergus's Bard's imagination.

Quinn shook her head. "I'm not. I've been there. And I have an idea. We establish a trade route, at first exchanging food for horses. It would be safer and would revitalize that part of the Midland."

"Sheer folly," Cynth muttered. "How are you going to keep Borgonne from taking it over?"

"Both sides have leverage. We can't meddle with the existing spells, but we could add layers of our own. And we've settled closer to the southern hills than they have. It's a four-day walk before you find any sign of habitation."

"The benefit to them is less than to us."

"They're the ones facing starvation," Quinn said flatly. "If they can brave the hills, they can get food convoys that far south."

The discussion degenerated into multiple side conversations. Arwen rapped the table, calling them back. "We won't reject the idea outright, but obviously we won't resolve anything right now. Good news is it's raining in Borgonne, so the drought's broken, although they still face shortages." She rose. "We will continue this discussion later. I may ask permission to tap your mind, Quinn, to pull out a complete picture of the hills down there. In the meantime, I for one am hungry."

"Bryar! Dammit, wait up!"

The hail was expected, but not welcome. Someone was bound to come after them, Bryar figured. It being Dal was at least better than some other options. Besides, Dal could check Kiril, who wasn't weathering their forced march well. Grudgingly, Bryar drew the donkey to a halt and readjusted the wide-brimmed hat that afforded his face protection from the sun.

Tai had disappeared into the surrounding fields, promising to return with supper. If she were here, he'd be happier.

Dal's long legs brought him to the cart in short order. "You've made good time," he said, his chest heaving as he caught his breath.

"Kiril's going with us. If you're here to take him back, you're not welcome." Bryar had unconsciously assumed a stance Joss taught him, ready for attack, even though he knew Dal was among the least inclined to violence. Embarrassed, he relaxed his position and gave a half smile. "Hi, Dal. On your way to Stanstead?"

"Sooner than I'd planned, thanks to you and Quinn. No, don't worry about it," he added, waving off whatever Bryar had been about to say. "I have a home there, and they need me, with a village healer and an apothecary to train."

Both men turned to resume their walk, Bryar leading the donkey. Another day to reach Stanstead.

"How's your patient?" Dal cocked his head back toward Kiril, who rode in the back of the cart and so far had given no sign he was aware of the addition to their party.

"No better. Getting him out of the Motherhouse taxed what little strength he had. Although..." Bryar dropped his voice. "I actually think it's only partly strength. It's—"

"Guilt?" They walked well ahead of the cart, out of earshot. "That's what Daren and I detected. If so, it's the best thing that could happen. It'll force him to deal with it. If he was immune, we'd be in a worse mess than we are now."

"Quinn's okay?"

"Fine. Arwen has her tied up with the whole food business for Borgonne. She's itching to go west, though, to see what Terra's sent us, wherever it is. But with that foot, she won't be traveling any time soon."

Bryar snorted out a laugh. "As long as Arwen hasn't murdered her, I suppose that's good."

Dal grimaced. "Arwen was spitting mad, as you can imagine. But the reality is, the council recommends actions but can't dictate, so they had no authority over Kiril's fate other than moral persuasion. There wasn't anything she could do."

"Interesting, isn't it?" Bryar kicked his sandal at a clod in the track, then reached down and picked up a thin branch lying along the trail. Broken meadowland stretched to either side of them, soon to give way to the forest surrounding Stanstead's agricultural land. He looked forward to getting out of the sun baking down on his fair skin.

Idly he switched at the vegetation growing between the wheel tracks. Willow would recognize the plants, and probably Mari, too. Bryar had planned to spend time with her during their stop at the Motherhouse.

She'd be kept too busy to spare him more than an occasional thought, he suspected. Nonetheless, while he wanted her to understand the urgency of freeing Kiril from his fate, he hoped his daughter missed him. He certainly missed her. Willow too, come to that.

Tai appeared ahead of them on the track, waving and carrying their supper as she promised. She didn't enjoy hunting, but honored the animals that sacrificed so they could eat. "Dal!" she shouted. "Yay! Walk with us the rest of the way."

"I plan to."

Bryar listened bemused as she chattered. Tai knew everyone, and in her time as an apprentice had impressed her teachers even more than he, Willow, and Quinn had. Dal and Tai shared a history he played no part in.

Jealous? No, not of Dal. But it would take most of a lifetime to accept he couldn't claim Tai and shut out all others.

After a couple more hours in the sun, Bryar drew them to a stop for a mid-afternoon break in the shade of the forest. "You should check your patient," he told Dal, keeping his voice muted. "He doesn't look too great."

"I agree. Ignore us... assuming my weight won't overtax your donkey."

"It shouldn't. We borrowed him from the village. He's used to loads."

Dal left him sitting on a moss-covered stone with Tai, munching on waybread with abricoe preserves, and swung himself into the cart. As far as Bryar could see, Kiril made no acknowledgment. Dal settled on the rough boards and began his assessment, using his hands to trace and smooth Kiril's energy. After a while, Bryar faintly heard the two men conversing in quiet voices.

"Let's go," Tai said. "If we make the next waysite before nightfall, there'll be fresh water. I'd love a chance to wash."

"You can wash me, too, if you like." Bryar said in her ear.

Tai gave him a shove, almost knocking him backwards off the rock. Then she ran, shrieking when he caught her around the waist. Another benefit of all the training he'd done with Joss; he was strong, and fast.

Their tussle didn't last long. With distance to cover and a sick man in tow, he gathered up the lead rope and the donkey shuffled forward, setting the pace for the journey through the cool of the woods to the waysite.

Behind them, with soft voice and gentle hands, Dal continued his ministrations, restoring Kiril to life.

Chapter 29

Quinn glared at her door, wishing ten kinds of plagues on whoever was pounding on it. It had been raining for two days, and her foot throbbed. If it was going to be like this every time it rained... well, she was ready to set out for the drier climate of the southwest plains, just to escape the ache.

And check out the Terrans. Reports trickled into the Motherhouse: their ship, as big as a village, had landed in a field, where the green-skinned people on board had promptly slaughtered all the villagers, or taken them hostage, or as slaves, or had destroyed their crops, eaten their babies... Quinn sighed. The bulk of what they heard was garbage, but she worried that false news created a risk of destabilizing their peaceful land. Green people? Really?

With no volition on her part, her thoughts flashed to Kiril, now gone for over two nine-days. He certainly wasn't green.

She hauled herself from her desk and hobbled to the door.

The messenger kid had to catch his fist to keep from hitting her, he'd been pounding so diligently. "Sorry, Sister. Visitor for you," he blurted.

"Who?"

"Dunno. But he's got these giant animals. And he *rode* one." The kid's eyes were popping; words tripped in his mouth as he spilled his news.

"Take a breath, Aaron. A horse?"

"Like in the Bards' tales? Honest?"

Quinn smiled; the boy's excitement was a pleasant contrast to the gray afternoon. "We'll see. Thanks, I'll be right down."

Aaron gone, heading for the stairs at breakneck speed in his eagerness to get back to the strange man and even stranger beasts, Quinn smoothed her tunic, rolled her shoulders to remove the kinks brought on by hunching over an elaborate glyph she'd been studying, reluctantly crammed her feet into sandals – the right one specially made to avoid pressure from the deformation caused by her injury – and followed the boy.

As she half ran, half limped across the green, she spotted Arwen on the porch of the dining hall talking to a tall man with his back to her. A man she'd known all her life.

"Ifram!" she called when she was still thirty paces or more away. The rain and mist ate her voice, but enough got through that he turned. Based on his expression, he wasn't best pleased to see her.

Arwen opened the door as Quinn arrived on the porch. If she noticed the cool greeting between the siblings, she didn't comment. Ifram appeared to have fallen under the same spell as Quinn and every other current or former apprentice when facing the council chair; he followed her meekly into the dining hall.

Over cakes and caff, the reason for this completely unprecedented visit came out. "Mom and Dad heard tell of your foot. They insisted I bring Butter. To help you get around."

"Butter?" Quinn repeated. He didn't inquire about the foot or its prognosis. She'd begun to doubt he'd ever forgive her for the loss of his first child, despite the evidence. He didn't trust Weavers and probably subscribed to the green-Terran rumors.

Ifram slurped his caff, partly masking an expression of mild exasperation. "You remember Butter. Gentlest horse in the stable. Damned waste, bringing her up to you, if you ask me, but our parents are right distressed with you getting hurt."

Quinn had long finished her first mug of caff; she poured another before she spoke. "So, let me get this straight. You came all the way to the Motherhouse to bring me a horse? Because the folks are worried I'm crippled? How did they hear about the accident, anyway?"

"Some Healer passed through a couple of nine-days ago. I told 'em you'd manage just fine, you always do, but..." Ifram gave a helpless shrug. "You know them. They get an idea in their heads, and that's what'll happen. Told me to teach you to ride her."

"Ride?" Quinn felt her stomach take residence somewhere near her knees. "You think I'm going to get up on one of those... Ifram, they're *huge*."

"Used to be you were fearless."

Quinn snorted.

"Tell me more about the horse," Arwen demanded. "Will she be suitable for agricultural work? Until Quinn decides to travel, she's unlikely to need the transport."

Ifram nodded. "Butter's a sweetie, the first we caught. Trained to cart and plow. Dad's been working the leather to make saddles, like for the little kids on donkeys, when he has free time from sandals and boots."

"How long are you staying, If?" Quinn asked. She'd never dreamed of seeing anyone from her family at the Motherhouse. She found she liked it and was impatient to show Ifram around.

His mouth twitched at the childhood nickname. "Hope to head home tomorrow, if you can spare a place to sleep tonight. I'll show you the basics of riding her this afternoon."

In the rain. She flexed the toes of her right foot, wishing the ache would go away.

"Quinn will arrange a room in the guest lodge," Arwen said. "How many horses are in Colgate now?"

"Six, ma'am. It's been a busy summer. We hope to start trading for 'em soon. They're rare in the Midland."

"Unheard of, more like," Quinn muttered.

"And you're bringing them across the hills?" Arwen said. "I'm very curious about that. There's no difficulty crossing into Borgonne?"

"Can't say we even knew that land had a name, until Quinn here turned up. No, ma'am, going back and forth's no problem. It's catching 'em that's tasked us. Easiest to cut out foals. Hundreds of horses live on that plain, but they run in packs. When they stampede, you don't want to be underfoot."

"But the hills." Arwen was insistent. "Quinn said occasional nausea. No one ever gets confused or lost?"

The cross-examination puzzled Ifram; he frowned. "No. We just go and come back. It's a lark. The village lads have been doing it forever. The horses only came recently." He launched into an account of the faltering economy caused by the new north-south road to the west of them.

"Here's a funny thing, though," he concluded. "We most never see anyone over that side of the hills. But we sent a party, two men and three lads, a few nine-days ago, and they ran into another group, a man and his children, boy and girl. Said they came after horses, same as us. So they got to talking, and the dad and kids didn't believe anyone could cross the hills, and the upshot was the family agreed to come visit Colgate. But... well, they were going along just fine, and then ours looked back and the others were gone."

Arwen sat up straighter, her eyes intent on Ifram. Quinn waited, barely breathing.

"Now, they worried, and they retraced their steps, hoping to find 'em. There they were, sitting on this rise near the path into the hills. Puzzled, like they weren't sure how they got there. They'd just been going along after our lot, and before they knew it they found themselves right where they started. Dunno what to make of that." Ifram shook his head.

"I do," Quinn muttered under her breath. "Come with me, brother," she said, rising. "Are the horses at the stables in the village?"

"Said they'd be fed and cared for there. Is that right?" He stood, suspicion in his eyes.

"Yes, assuming their needs are similar to donkeys. We take care of our livestock."

"Well, then." Ifram nodded to Arwen, who remained seated. "Nice to meet you, ma'am."

"And you. Perhaps I'll see you at dinner."

"Yes'm."

Quinn limped to the door, her brother on her heels. She grinned to herself. They had a solution. To Borgonne, to Colgate's poverty. The trade route suddenly became feasible. Under their control.

Poor Gauvain, she thought irreverently as she led her brother to the guest lodge.

❖

"There are a couple of possible scenarios," Arwen said later to the convened council in the conference room, "depending on whether our ancestors were trying to keep people out or in. One way or another, though, we can cross to Borgonne, but they can't come to the Midland without the protection of a Weaver or Mage. And since the spells are lost in time, no one is in a position to reinstate or remove the confusion spell. At this point, knowing the spells are multiple and entangled, a person would have to be mad to overlay them. So we control the southern route into Borgonne."

"We can establish a depot in Colgate and get them to do the same on the other side," Quinn said. "It will mean we lose access to horses, though."

"Encourage your brother to bring across as many as they can this summer," Arwen told Quinn. "But we've lived without horses for hundreds of years, so while I agree it would be nice to have them, and it's a potential revenue stream for Colgate, if they have to make do with breeding their existing stock, they'll survive."

"Can you think of a way to test this?" That was Daren, ever cautious.

Arwen shook her head. "The spells seem to know who comes from where. Maybe it's based on point of origin."

"Then we take it on trust that Borgonne won't be able to use the southern route to send their people in to overrun us?" Cynth asked

"Do you trust the spells on the hills?" Deadly serious, Arwen deferred to Quinn. "Are they stable and consistent? You've experienced them."

She'd given this a great deal of thought, so she had her answer ready. "The spells are different. There's something vaguely malevolent about the northern hills, but I didn't get any such feeling in the south. Also, I've been in the northern hills three times, and not once did I see a familiar landmark." She shivered. "The boys who took me across told me they knew the route well. There are trail markers.

"So at the moment, the only risk I can see is that their Mages presumably could lead parties across the southern hills. But no full-fledged Mage is going to occupy his time that way. And after the attack on the large party in the north, they wouldn't risk a large group with only non-Mages with some Entrée for protection."

"And you trust your brother?"

Her mouth quirked. "Usually we don't get along, but he didn't make that tale up. Ifram has next to no imagination."

Daren spoke slowly, considering his words. "When Ezra was last here, he drew a distinction between stability and stagnation. I've been thinking about this. From what I hear, he may well be right. We need some kind of infusion into our culture. Whether it's horses or some other exchange, I don't know. But we've stopped growing, and I distrust that."

His words met silence.

"Bryar and I talked about this some," Fergus said. "Ezra believes it's inevitable. Our way of life is going. Now we have unprecedented reports of violence, these crazy rumors about the Terrans... If we're facing change, it would be better to have some control of it. To keep it fair for everyone."

"To pave the way to newfound prosperity," Cynth mused. "Can you imagine winter if everyone had glass windows?"

Quinn's mind went to the darkness of buildings throughout the Midland with their shutters and oiled hides blocking out winter's storms.

Arwen let the silence hang for a minute, then said, "Are we agreed?"

A round of nods answered her, although no one seemed too happy. The implications, Quinn thought. This is bigger than we've ever had to deal with, bigger even than the first party of Borgonnians last spring.

Arwen slapped the table. "Then we have a solution. And I can't wait to tell Gauvain."

Quinn next encountered Gauvain that night in the dining hall, where he shared a table, if not a relaxing meal, with Arwen. Not for the first time she wondered about the history between those two. Something was going on between them, something more than his sudden appearance at the Motherhouse as the last remnant of what could only be described as a force of Borgonnians risking the hills to raid the Midland.

The meat in tonight's mutton stew was mostly tender, the stew itself tantalizing in its blend of flavors. Rather like the two she sat with. She'd be more comfortable at another table, given the vibes between them, but Ifram was in the village and Arwen had not so subtly signaled for her to join them. This was business, and she was the witness.

Sustainer help them all if Arwen ever discovered Gauvain's role in Kiril's escape.

Arwen had finished half her stew before she slapped her spoon onto the table and said, "What are you doing here? The truth, this time."

Gauvain rested his spoon in his bowl with practiced elegance, looking for all the world like a man whose servant botched pouring the wine. "Dining, my dear," he said. "Obviously."

Quinn and Arwen exchanged glances. Years of practice told Quinn that they were both thinking about the other trade route, through the southern hills, although she also suspected a longing on Arwen's part to get her hands on the black-clad man across from her, whether to wring his neck or for some other purpose she wasn't sure.

Arwen turned her level stare to Gauvain and waited. Quinn suppressed a grin to see him struggle not to squirm.

"We required both a contingent with Auric sensibilities and strong bearers to carry foodstuffs back across the hills," he said. "As was made plain from our last venture into your land."

"I'm pleased to hear you acknowledge it as ours." Arwen cut straight to the chase. "Because you had more in mind than asking for our aid. You certainly didn't need Cedric to pack food."

"No." Gauvain stopped, a flash of remorse crossing his face. "He was a fool, but he didn't deserve to die. I regret that. I gather the man Kiril is now missing. Another regret, that I had no opportunity to study him further."

"He's not a specimen," Arwen snapped. Kiril was still a sore point.

Quinn ate her stew and waited, letting Arwen lead the conversation.

"The rest of your people – did they make it home?" Arwen asked. "Does the confusion spell work that far from the origin?"

He raised a practiced eyebrow. "You surprise me. You haven't been tracking them?"

"Oh, stop playing games." Arwen's frustration – not solely with Gauvain, Quinn thought, but with the whole state of affairs embroiling the Motherhouse – showed in her tone. "We know one or two did, but most lacked sufficient Entrée to allow us to track at such a distance. I've wondered if the others are wandering around in the hills – or even if they're still alive. This isn't a usual or straightforward situation."

"No, it isn't. I fear I have nothing more to report, however. Two of my apprentices have arrived at the tower, one of them Reed, but the third..."

Quinn speculated that admitting he didn't know was as difficult for him as the potential loss of one of his apprentices.

"Understand this." Arwen's voice assured she retained command of the conversation; Gauvain appeared to be holding onto his composure by the thinnest thread. "We will aid Borgonne in any way we can. But we will *not* allow the Midland to come to harm. I respect your power, Gauvain. But Ezra and I, and at least two others, are your equals. It's glaringly obvious that you are the only Mage available to risk the crossing. You've neglected to train apprentices, probably for fear of being rivaled. And now we wield more combined power than you. Because I respect you, I will give you fair warning. Do not try to subjugate us. In fact, I think it would be in your best interests if you prepared to go home, you and your remaining band. Emptyhanded, because there is no other option."

Arwen had scored; Gauvain's face took on the hard mask Quinn remembered from times during their crossing of the hills when his right to dictate events was challenged. "Be careful, Arwen," he said. "You might push me too far."

Arwen picked up her spoon and finished another bite of the stew. When she answered, her tone was nonchalant. "I have no wish to push you. I want you to understand your position here, and ours. We stand ready to assist, within our means. But that is where it ends."

Rising, Gauvain scraped his chair over the rough flagstone surface of the dining hall. "I will consider this." With that, he turned his back on them and started to walk away.

"Gauvain."

From where she sat, she could see the way he flashed annoyance before schooling himself to his usual smooth demeanor.

"There is one more thing," Arwen said. "Please sit down." When he didn't move, she glanced around the emptying hall and said, "It would be better."

Gauvain glared at Quinn. He might resent her presence, but he returned to the table.

Arwen leaned forward, as if to further assure confidentiality. "The matter we discussed when you were here last. Has it been attended to?"

Quinn saw him swallow. Quinn remembered his help in spiriting Kiril away and felt something approaching sympathy.

"It has," he said stiffly.

"We noticed rain in Borgonne over the last couple of nine-days, so I accept your assurance. Thank you."

Quinn held her breath; from Arwen's intonation, she almost expected her to add a standard schoolroom dismissal: *You may go now.* Instead, she said, "Meet me in my workroom tomorrow morning. We have one last item to discuss. I believe it to be one that will intrigue you."

Gauvain was still for a moment, as if wondering whether to push for details then and there. Instead, he rose and left them, leaving his bowl for them to take to the hatch. Bad manners, but perhaps justified.

"Poor man. He had no rebuttal," Quinn whispered.

"Let's hope he has the self-control not to cause trouble before he leaves."

The women finished their dinner in silence. A strange, wistful look settled on Arwen's face, gone in a flash. Once again Quinn wondered what had transpired in the past between her and Gauvain.

❖

The next morning, only Quinn and Daren attended Arwen's presentation to Gauvain. With them arrayed on stools around her work table, she gave a brief history, then said, "As it now seems our people have been crossing into Borgonne for generations, we're prepared to exploit this ability. So that's the state of things. With your cooperation, we can institute trade between Borgonne and the Midland."

Daren added. "It's a fair offer."

"With you controlling the route." Gauvain's mood had been sour from the moment he entered the workroom. Not looking forward to the trip home, Quinn speculated.

"Naturally," Arwen said. "You can't tell me you didn't come here with a plan to subdue us in some way. We never would have tolerated that, Gauvain, as surely you realize. But we are prepared to develop the trade route. Which could be useful, should the need arise again." Arwen's voice was like honey.

Gauvain's mood, in contrast, grew even more vinegary.

"We all stand to benefit." Quinn thought of Colgate, the need throughout that quarter of the Midland for an infusion of prosperity, and of the magnificent, mild animal awaiting her at the stables in the village. "You have much to offer, as do we."

"But it won't work if there's any hint of aggression or hostility," Arwen added. "And in the meantime, I suggest you go home. Tell your people. Ready a storage depot in the south. If you give us a timeframe, we can arrange to meet at the end of the trail through the hills. I'm told it's uninhabited, so you may need to establish a settlement."

"And a road," Quinn added.

"There's a lot to do," Daren said. "And with patchy communication."

Gauvain stood, his eyes revealing nothing. "Our preparations to return home are almost complete. I trust you have no objection to my meeting with Amalie? I must be sure she is content remaining here, as she may not get another chance to cross the hills."

"Amalie's training is progressing well," Arwen said. "She bids fair to be an excellent Healer. If she so chooses, she'll be able to cross on her own in a few years. She's strong in Entrée."

"Humph." Gauvain strode to the door and pushed it open. "Expect our departure two days hence."

"Coordinate with the kitchen, the Healers' workrooms, and the storerooms for supplies. Let me know if there are any glitches." Arwen exited the room on Gauvain's heels. Quinn almost giggled at the feeling that Arwen was driving Gauvain ahead of her... not true, of course, but that was the visual impression.

"And that's that," Daren said. "How are you, Quinn? Foot better?" His hand covered hers.

She shrugged as she stood, allowing him to help her up. "Probably as good as it'll ever be. I'm fine. You heard about Butter? She's changed everything. She means freedom, speed—"

He laughed. "And for you, a way to get to the Terran's ship." He hugged her tight, then waved her through the door. "You're transparent sometimes, you know. Meet me tonight?"

"I'd like that."

Loving Daren might be grounding. Right now, Quinn's excitement threatened to swamp her. She'd live the life of a Scribe. A true Weaver. She'd go to the Terran settlement. Add their knowledge to the store in the Aura. She'd never expected to want to leave the Motherhouse; perhaps there had never been a strong enough lure.

But first she would learn to ride Butter confidently and care for her. Ifram, who had stayed over an extra day, was waiting for her.

Almost involuntarily, as she stepped from the Centra, she looked off to her right, where the trail to Stanstead began. She'd see Dal on her way west; she wondered who else. Willow and Joss were far to the south, Bryar and Tai could be anywhere by now. And Kiril? Would he have stayed with Bryar or struck out on his own?

And did she care?

Maybe. But now, little mattered beyond hobbling to the village and learning how to ride her new horse.

Chapter 30

Almost two nine-days later, events finally lined up for Quinn to leave the Motherhouse. Gauvain and his small party had long since left; Amalie had had the temerity to kiss his cheek as a parting gesture, causing him to blush, a sight Quinn would treasure for moments when she needed cheering up. Ifram was gone as well, but she'd practiced riding Butter under the watchful eye of several of the agriculturists from the village.

Arwen said little about her impending departure. Quinn sensed she was less than happy, but no one had the right to hold a Weaver back when the time came to strike out. That time, for Quinn, was long overdue.

Instead of going through Stanstead, she now planned to take the track south to Hallan, where she could visit Willow and Joss. Perhaps she'd even soak her aching foot in the hot springs, just to test if the rumors of miracle cures were true. From Hallan she could swing west and pick up the trunk road that connected Stanstead to the south. From there she would have several options to go west. The Motherhouse received sporadic and fragmentary reports from Gwen, who possessed only minimal ability to use the Aura for transmission of messages, so Quinn knew the ship had touched down somewhere near the edge of the savannah. So far, the Terrans' integration proceeded smoothly, or so Gwen implied.

All that knowledge... Quinn almost trembled with the thrill of exploring new research avenues, stronger than when she'd crossed into Borgonne, in fact the strongest in her adult life. Standing in the stable, currying Butter, she shivered with excitement.

Arwen met her after the evening meal, and the two of them took the path to the river. "I felt what you're feeling, once," she said. "A long time ago. Somehow, I got enmeshed in the administration of the Motherhouse and the apprentice program. I never went as far as I wanted to, or learned the things I itched to know."

"Trying to make me feel guilty?" Quinn swung at a nearby shrub with the smoothed branch she used as a cane. "Because it's working. If you want your turn, go ahead. I have plenty of time to travel."

Arwen shook her head. In the fading light of early autumn, Quinn saw the lines now permanently etched on her face, the slight stoop in her posture. Her friend and mentor was showing the effects of the last year, of having to shepherd the Midland through challenges no one ever dreamed of.

"Well spoken, but of course I'm not going to do that. I might leave council in Daren's hands and spend some time in Stanstead, but that's as much as I'm willing to undertake now. I've dealt enough with Terrans."

Quinn laughed. "Joss hasn't been a problem, anyway."

"No, but his situation still required management. He's doing well. Willow gives him stability."

"Works both ways, I think."

Quinn fell silent. Bryar also had found that special form of steadiness, and he had needed it more than either Joss or Willow. She gave her head a small shake; she'd never have predicted that Tai would be a rock for anyone.

"Perhaps I'll go north first," she said. "I haven't seen Ezra in a while."

"He'd like that. They're getting old, he and Rebecca."

And if she were gone for any length of time, she might never see him again. She loved the elderly couple as second parents, and Ezra as the mentor who had brought her powers to their fullest potential.

"I'll miss you," she blurted, surprising herself.

Arwen grinned. "Now don't go getting maudlin on me. Leave in the morning, find these Terrans, and learn what you can from them. You'll benefit more than the value of the information you'll provide us."

"You're right. I've been in a rut. If you call adventuring into Borgonne a rut."

"I'm just glad you're finally spreading your wings."

Damn. Quinn blinked back tears. She was the logical one, right? Not given to emotion. Naturally, Arwen caught it. But she said nothing.

"You'll return one day?"

"Most Weavers do."

"None of us can predict the future, but I believe we will need you."

In silence, they continued their circle of the valley, but Quinn thought they understood each other very well.

Chapter 31

A week and a half after Elspeth's first encounter with the natives, Harry finally left the ship. He didn't cross the plain to the perpetual gathering of their neighbors, still maintaining vigil, but he'd walked around the Adventurer, checking her condition and considering whether using their remaining fuel to shift her a few kilometers away, to avoid encroaching on the nearby settlement, was wise.

He'd been able to track the exploration parties organized by Wilhelmina Schott, their science and exploration officer, from the bridge, watching through their camera lenses as they crossed the field, dipped into the woods – out of sight of the Adventurer for the first time – then following the turgid river downstream, viewing the site the natives identified as most suitable for them to settle. The broad, level plain adjacent to the riparian forest might have been made for the Adventurer. South and west of them the hills rose in ever-higher layers; to the east, across the river, the land rolled as far as they could see in mixed meadow and forest. Although not particularly high, not like the mountains bisecting Eurocorp, sharp peaks pierced the sky to the west. Crossing that range would require skills he lacked, he thought as he showered and prepared for his watch.

The exploration team had taken the opportunity to roughhouse in the river before returning to the ship... and who could blame them? On Terra that could never happen – he made a mental note to add swimming lessons to Elspeth's list. Back home, they guarded every bit of spare water like something sacred. Which he supposed it was, in terms of its value. Clean water was one of the shortages that had started the troubles.

He wondered if any place livable still existed on Terra. The destruction of the shields by rabid mobs had been the final straw that triggered their precipitous, unauthorized departure.

Ah well, irrelevant now. Around the mess hall they were calling the planet Newfoundland, after an old province in Northam. It fit; he'd be fine if the name stuck.

"Harry, you there?"

Ben, his 2IC, on the comm link. "In my quarters. Just about to head to the bridge. Meet you there?"

"In ten? I've got the report and some news."

"On my way. Page Elspeth."

"Will do."

Harry didn't worry about Willie's report; he knew what the exploration teams had found. The only question was the advisability of expending their almost non-existent fuel supply to move the ship. The promise of news intrigued him, though. Had Gretchen Schmidt had her baby? Some unexpected maintenance issue? Teenagers into mischief again?

He and Elspeth arrived at the same time and together joined Ben in the small executive meeting room attached to the bridge.

"No surprises in Willie's report, which I've sent to you," Ben said without preliminary. "So I vote we move. We're here for keeps. No point delaying getting settled."

"If we wait, there might be a better site a hundred kilometers from here," Elspeth said mildly.

"Might. But how much improvement can we expect? We've got water, fertile soil, and amenable neighbors. We've done every environmental test known to humankind. It's time to stop frittering away our summer and put down roots. Let the kids off the Adventurer. Hell, half of them don't remember what solid ground feels like."

"Moving on," Harry said, interrupting a debate better held when the entire senior staff was present, "what other news?"

"Ah." One thing about Ben, he didn't ride his opinions to death. "Don't know what to make of this. A bulletin from Constance. She and Richard Calhoun, a guy in Hans's community, both report unexpected symptoms each time they leave the ship. Sharp, piercing headache, nausea. In Constance's case, it happens almost immediately. For Richard it's slower onset and mild enough he can tolerate it, but it's driven Constance back on board. As soon as they're inside, the symptoms diminish, and eventually go away. Here." He queued the bulletin on their tablets.

"Is this common knowledge?" Elspeth asked.

"Not secret, too many people have seen it happen. But how far it's spread, I can't say."

Harry scanned the brief bulletin. "Page Constance, please. She's the medic around here. I want to talk to her directly."

Ben shook his head. "She went out there yesterday. Said she hoped it'd get better if she stuck it out. She's out of commission today."

"Can we visit?"

Ben nodded. "I checked. She's expecting us."

Constance, when she opened the door to her quarters, looked like hell, her eyes sunken, tension in her body futilely trying to mask pain. "Mistake," she said as she gestured them in. Then she collapsed on her bunk. "I can't think straight, my head's splitting, I can't keep food down."

"Has it improved from yesterday?" Ben asked. Knowing Ben, he'd be keeping a graph of Constance's progress, or lack thereof.

She nodded weakly. "But not much. I'm at a loss what to try next. I've used painkillers and electrolytes and heat and cold and dark and sleep..." Her face, Harry noted, was deathly pale; he nudged a metal basin closer to her bunk with his foot.

"With your permission," she said, "I'd like to talk to the woman they call a healer, the one with the green sash. Maybe it's endemic."

"Bring her on board, you mean?"

"I can't go to her."

While relations had progressed exceptionally smoothly, none of the villagers had been invited into the Adventurer. Nor had they been welcome to visit the locals' village. Wary caution prevailed on both sides.

He, Ben, and Elspeth formed an awkward audience beside the bunk, passing glances back and forth. He knew his senior crew well; no words were needed.

"Let's do it," Elspeth said at last. "I'll get in touch with her."

Because Terran methods weren't working. Harry nodded.

And so, a day later, the elderly woman named Gwen cautiously mounted the steps leading to the outer hatch and set foot in the Adventurer. She submitted to being scanned for anything that might infect their internal environment, then Harry led her to Constance's quarters.

The women spent upwards of two hours together, at one point sending for tea and cookies but otherwise incommunicado. It was nearing suppertime when Constance paged Harry.

With Elspeth in tow, he found her sitting in bed, a little more color in her face. Gwen rose as he entered. "I can give you the simple explanation," she said in her unusual accent. She spoke slowly; they had all learned to allow time to decode speech. "It's caused by sensitivity to the Aura."

"The...?"

"Aura," Constance repeated. "It's right up there with all the pseudo medical systems we outlawed years ago. Homeopathy and acupuncture and Reiki... everything we considered faith healing with no scientific basis."

Gwen shook her head. "We rely on the techniques Constance described to me, as well as ordinary medicines such as can be made from plants."

"And it works," Constance said. "I feel almost human again. This Aura's some kind of energy that confers special powers on a select few, called Weavers. Most Weavers are Healers, but there are others. Bards, who seem to be a weird medieval throwback, and another group called Scribes whose function is murky. At least Gwen couldn't explain it to me." Constance recited like a schoolgirl excited by her lesson.

"Oh great," Harry groaned. "We're dealing with a primitive nature religion."

Elspeth shot him an annoyed glance

Gwen's stance tightened. "I suggest you live on our planet awhile before you cast judgment."

Abashed, Harry said, "I beg your pardon. Of course you're right."

"Elaborate, please," Elspeth said.

Constance took a breath. "Gwen demonstrated how she uses the Aura to re-align energies. I could *feel* it, Elspeth. Moving in my body. Most of the healing is plant based, provided by local healers, because there aren't enough of these traveling Healers to go around. But this wasn't just herbalism, in fact she didn't give me anything herbal. She used her hands. I can't explain it medically, but it's real."

Harry remained unconvinced. "And why just you and Richard? Why not everyone else?"

A pause. Finally, Constance whispered, "We're like them. Or I am anyway. Gwen says I can access this energy once I know how. But I didn't grow up with it, so its strength knocked me flat. At least that's the theory."

Because Constance was clearly impressed, and because they had two years of trusting her abilities and instincts, Harry and Elspeth didn't laugh. Instead, Elspeth said, "What happens next? We need you functioning."

"I will send word that we need another Weaver here, a Scribe," Gwen said, "This isn't a matter of Healing, exactly." She nodded at Constance. "You need training. but it's obvious you can't journey to the Motherhouse, and I haven't the skill to shield you. Beyond that... stay on your ship, I guess. I'm sorry. I wish I could do more."

Later, Harry sat with Constance in the mess hall, watching as she downed a bowl of chicken broth and a handful of crackers. "You believe this rigmarole?" he asked.

She nodded. "Look at me. I'm up and eating. And... it was never part of our training, but Gwen taught me something about listening to the wisdom of the body. Right now mine says crackers are fine, but that cheesecake you're devouring isn't. Think of it as a form of technology, with specifications for different needs. They train for years."

"And what? Wave their hands around and chant incantations?"

Constance kicked him under the table. "We can't discount this, Harry. And it's imperative I find a way to get to this Motherhouse place, so I can learn how to do it. Because our medicines are almost exhausted, and herbs won't be enough."

"If you say so." Harry leaned back and mentally turned more reins over to Elspeth. Transition to life on their new planet, Newfoundland, wasn't going to be as straightforward as he'd hoped. But at least they had their medic back.

Chapter 32

Three nine-days after leaving the Motherhouse, Bryar admitted to Tai that he enjoyed having Kiril accompany them. He'd wanted this expedition to be just the two of them, cementing their relationship – as she well knew – but had come to accept that Kiril was a part of their little traveling show, handling negotiations, setup, food procurement, and whatever else needed doing while Tai accompanied his singing, oration, and flute.

As he'd grown stronger, Kiril had slipped seamlessly and without comment into a support role. From somewhere he'd obtained a bluish sash, which he wore whenever Bryar and Tai wore theirs, proclaiming his membership in what had evolved into a troop.

It was a new way to travel and perform. Bryar found, to his mild astonishment, that he liked it.

Kiril walked beside him now, his health largely restored although he seldom spoke, taking in the scenery as they pushed west along a northern route. Tai as usual had shot ahead, scouting the nearby fields for... well, whatever caught her fancy. She might be his partner, but their relationship did nothing to constrain her natural wildness.

Bryar originally planned to reach the mountains that separated them from the coastal lands, still thirty days or more away, then head south before winter trapped them, but it was already within a day or two of the equinox. They had sixty days of weather decent for traveling, he calculated, before winter roared down from the Northlands, and a long way to go if they were to return to the motherhouse before Solstice. For the moment, though, heat baked the land, drawing a spicy scent from the trees' needles.

The coniferous forest was giving way to fields, suggesting they'd be in a town of some size that evening. The prospect of shelter and food not cooked over a wayfire pleased them all after four days of brushing dust from their sandals under the incessant sun.

By late afternoon they could see the hamlet. Twenty houses, he estimated, several small lodges, outbuildings and barn, and a slightly larger building that most likely held the dining hall, all grouped around a compact central plaza. Enough for an audience, not large enough to stay more than two nights at the most; under the acknowledged obligations to Weavers, they would be offered food and shelter, but the idea wasn't to tax the community's resources.

Bryar was mentally running through his repertoire, planning a performance for that evening, when he spotted two large men coming along the track toward them, one of them carrying a thick staff. Between them—

Diou help them, it was Tai. A beefy hand held each arm, and even from a distance Bryar could see her resisting them, trying to break free. And arguing; a hint of her voice carried through the still air.

He and Kiril both quickened their pace. Wearing her Scribe's sash, Tai should be inviolate. Bryar's hand rested on his knife; he suspected that Kiril's did as well.

"Hello, the village!" Bryar called when they got within shouting distance.

The men stopped. They released Tai, giving her a shove toward Bryar, then stood, hip to hip, arms folded, blocking the trail. Tai stumbled when they pushed her, caught her balance, and scooted down the trail to them.

When they were close enough, the man on the left, his eyes fixed on Bryar's face, said, "Strangers aren't welcome here. Best you turn back to where you come from."

Tai turned to face them, glowering. "Are you saying you refuse to honor the sash of a Weaver?" she demanded.

"Not those as we know," the second man said. "But sashes can be had, and that one..." He gestured at Bryar. "His face is like nothing seen in these parts. What proof you got you ain't some invader, some extra ter... terr..."

Bryar felt himself redden. He rarely remembered the birthmark's existence anymore; Tai's easy acceptance had erased the lingering emotional scars.

"Terrestrial," the first man finished. "Word's out, how you plan to defeat the Midland and take what we have. We're making a stand. Here and now."

A knife appeared in his hand. The other man swung the staff into a ready position. Bryar instinctively closed his hand around his own knife, worn in a loose sling at his waist, pausing when he felt Kiril's hand on his arm. *Wait.*

Good advice.

The day darkened around him as his focus narrowed to the threat posed by the men. He swallowed the toxic mix of embarrassment and anger. Reaching out to position Tai behind him, he said, "I am Bryar of Newcastle, Weaver and Bard. We hoped to perform for your village tonight, like Bards throughout history."

"And that's why you sent your lad ahead, to scout the town and report our weaknesses. We ain't the fools you believe us to be."

Lad. She could still pass as a boy.

"No one believes you're fools," Kiril said coolly, mimicking Bryar's accent. "We too have heard of the arrival of the Terrans. But we haven't seen them, nor have the villages on our route. We have no reason to suspect they are close by."

The two parties glared at each other. Eventually, Bryar said, "If you don't want a performance, of course that is fine. But we are within our rights to request safe passage through your village. At the next town we may fare better."

"We gonna let 'em through?" the second man asked.

"Damn Terrans? Wi' no proof as to their being legit Weavers? What do you think?"

Whatever the second man thought, it took a while to extricate it from his head. They all stood awkwardly, waiting for a resolution.

Finally, the first man said, "We'll round up the men. Long's we keep 'em under guard, we can pass 'em through and send 'em on their way."

Despite Bryar's hand on her arm, Tai managed to step forward. "It is time-honored tradition that Weavers are fed and offered a bed for the night."

"Might be, laddie, but times have changed. We've no proof—"

The proof flashed into Bryar's mind in an instant. Only a Bard could corral magic to bring a performance alive. He wrested himself from the swirling emotions and forced his focus into the Aura. From there he dove into the simplest, most accessible piece he could muster, the Lay of Tommy Thompson, a recitative song known throughout the Midland. Tai caught his intention and pulled his flute from a pocket in his tunic, sorting out the key and joining in at the first chorus. Kiril stepped a little away, then began clapping his hands, keeping the rhythm.

The men stood stock still, eyes wide, listening. Bryar performed two verses, then broke off and stated, in his best declamatory voice, "We are not from the Terran ship. We don't even know where it is. We are Weavers. Invite us to perform, or escort us through the village, as you choose. You have nothing to fear from us."

Although we might have something to fear from you.

The men looked at each other, then turned and led the way to the village.

Alone in the tiny guest lodge – Kiril had wandered off – Tai took Bryar's hands and gave them a shake. "I'm sorry that happened."

"I wish you were talking about their fears and not the damned mark on my face."

Her hand wasn't large enough against his cheek to cover the birthmark. He tipped his head into her palm.

"It doesn't matter, Bry. It doesn't change who you are."

He scowled, turning from her. "A marked man."

"A stubborn one, for sure. That was a brilliant strategem, even though I'm heartily sick of good old Tommy. You can be very persuasive, can't you?"

He shrugged. "Showing the credentials seemed the least risky of the options. But if our sashes mean nothing... that's worrisome. Another time they might not ask questions first."

She nodded. "They didn't hurt me, but they didn't want me around, either. I don't like this."

Bryar held her close, his big hands covering her lithe back. The idea was comfort, but with Tai pressed up against him that way, chest to knees, neither of them wearing more than a light-weight summer tunic...

"Kiril could come back any time," Tai whispered.

"Maybe not." Bryar set her aside, pulled his sash over his head, and draped it on the outer door latch. "He told me about this custom. When you see this token, stay away."

Tai giggled. "You made that up."

"No, I didn't. It's not a bad tradition. Useful."

She never got a chance to reply. His mouth covered hers, her hands explored his soon-to-be overheated body, and for a while they spared no thought for Kiril, or the red mark disfiguring Bryar's face, or the unexpected hostility of their arrival in the small northern village.

Chapter 33

Crossing the Midland, even riding Butter, presented unexpected challenges. Her mount alone excited a mix of curiosity and fear, and it required fast talking in some hamlets to convince the residents she was, in fact, a Weaver, not an intruder from space, and that Butter, far from being a risk, represented a possible resource as horses gradually became available through the land. Butter's placid disposition helped; the younger people, especially, were drawn to the beast, and a few clamored for rides.

She'd never thought she'd have to prove her status, though. Usually a light globe did the trick. Had Bryar and Tai encountered similar challenges? And where might Kiril be by now? It had been almost seven nine-days since he'd left with Bryar, half dead from the catastrophe in the hills. She couldn't swear he was still alive.

Despite it all, she came to Cann, Gwen's village, a mere two nine-days' ride from the Motherhouse. Horses certainly had potential for improving communications, although her thighs and butt never stopped aching, and she dreaded the moment each morning when she had to remount. In Cann, at least, there was no prolonged debate over whether she was Weaver or alien. Gwen hugged her like a long lost daughter.

Green skin. She snorted.

Over dinner, a tasty mutton stew, they caught up with gossip and compared notes.

"Just like us. With different customs, of course, and the accent can be hard to decipher. But they probably say the same about us. Ordinary people, Quinn."

"I'm not surprised. I've spent a fair amount of time with both Joss and Kiril. Neither of them is exactly ordinary, but Joss at least fits in here well. Did you know he's an animal whisperer?"

Gwen nodded. "Rumor carried this far. And the other... changes into a monster? That doesn't sound like us to me."

"That wasn't Kiril's fault. The hills did it to him. Where the hills are concerned, we've been dabbling in things we don't understand. People have died. And Kiril..." She made a helpless gesture with the hand not holding her spoon. "We sent him west, as far away from the hills as possible. But I can't predict if that's good enough, or even if he's survived. He looked pretty rough when I last saw him. Even Dal and Daren couldn't do much."

"Two of our strongest Healers. I miss Dal. We were close."

"Perhaps, if horses become common, you'll be able to get to the Motherhouse more easily."

"How long are you staying, Quinn? I assume you're here to check out the Terrans."

Quinn rested her spoon in the bowl and leaned forward. "And learn from them, yes. There's so much we don't know about our own history, but we've worked out through the others that we must have come from Terra originally. The language similarity couldn't be a coincidence."

"Then you'll love this. Elspeth told me their history speaks of some mysterious ships, kind of like theirs, that left hundreds of years ago and were never heard of again. They figure one of them landed here. Funny to think we arrived the same way they did. And now we have the Midland, the Northlands and Southlands, that place the other side of the hills—"

"Borgonne. That's what they call it."

"Borgonne." Gwen turned it over on her tongue. "It sounds nice."

"It isn't. They're just coming out of a drought, and they've been aggressive about getting aid from us. Cooperation isn't their way. Take care of yourself, and if others starve, too bad."

Gwen shuddered. "At times it's work, living cooperatively, not falling into those same habits. But it's worth it. I've always believed that's part of what we do as Weavers."

"I agree. So, who's... Elspeth?" Quinn's turn to try out an unfamiliar name.

"She's their leader, now that they've landed. Before that, it was a man named Harry. We didn't see them land the first time. It was at night and woke us all up, gave us the scare of a lifetime." Gwen chuckled. "They moved their ship to a place not so close to Cann. I wish you'd been here to see it. It just... lifted up and floated. And it's massive, the size of the village. There are about four hundred people living on it. But Elspeth said the move exhausted their fuel. For good or ill, they'll stay where they are."

"And where they are is...?"

"A good place. South of here, near the river, plenty of arable land. They actually grow food on that ship of theirs, Quinn." Gwen's information bubbled out, now that she had an audience to share with. "We'll help them with seed stock, but they've got vegetables I've never seen before. Animals, too. They're building fencing so the beasts can leave the ship."

A child approached carrying two bowls. "Treacle tart, Sisters?"

"We'd love some, Suann," Gwen said. "Thanks for bringing them over."

"Happy to, Sister." The child put the bowls on the table and fled toward the kitchen.

"Cute kid," Quinn said.

"It's a good life here. I don't often feel a need to leave."

The tarts were swimming in fresh cream. Quinn's first bite lived up to every bit of her anticipation. "This recipe needs to get back to the Motherhouse."

"You take it, or transmit it. We trade for beets to refine sugar – not much, but enough for the occasional treat. The abricoe pastries here use different seasonings, though. I miss the ones at the Motherhouse."

After finishing the tarts and exchanging further information about common acquaintances and varying ways of life, Quinn got down to business. "Tell me about them. Elspeth first, I guess. Anyone else I should know."

"Can you walk? I'll have a look at that foot later."

The night crashed down around them, the sun setting behind the jagged mountains to the west, but Gwen knew the lay of the flat land. After one circuit of the village, they retired to Gwen's quarters in deference to Quinn's foot, as she filled Quinn in on everything she'd gleaned about the Terrans. She ended with the mystery of Constance and Richard and what she concluded must be a reaction to the Aura, although she had never heard of such a thing before.

"I have. Joss experienced it mildly, and Bryar – he's a Bard, my age, you may not remember him – got walloped by it when he tried to go to Borgonne. It's much stronger there."

"I never dreamed the Aura could do harm."

"Neither did anyone. Like with the hills, we're working with something far more powerful than we ever dreamed – and more dangerous. I'll look forward to meeting Constance."

"And screening her, if you can. We need to get her to the Motherhouse for training. But Weavers don't come through this village that often, so I'll ask you to stay here for a couple of days. Our people deserve a taste of you."

Quinn laughed. "Fair enough. I'm worn out from the travel, anyway. I'd like time to sort myself out before I meet our mysterious three-eyed, green-skinned visitors."

Gwen matched her laugh. "That's the rumor? Sustainer help us. You'll like them, you'll see. As I said, ordinary people."

They left Butter in the capable care of the agriculturists and took a donkey cart across the plain in deference to Quinn's mangled foot. Barely visible from the village, the ship was by far the largest structure Quinn had ever seen, dwarfing Gauvain's tower. Its metallic outer coating gleamed in the sunlight. She felt her stomach twist in excited knots, much the way she reacted as a child when a Bard came to Colgate.

A tall woman with a blonde braid and an air of authority, who looked as if she had muscle to spare, met them and signaled one of their agriculturists to take the cart. Gwen introduced her to Elspeth, then left her there to figure it out on her own. It was a short half day's walk between the village and the ship, and Gwen had responsibilities at home.

Below her, as Quinn stood in the entrance to their ship – Elspeth called it a hatch – almost quivering with the need to see inside, lay a busy, well organized community. Near the base of the ship were the beginnings of a settlement, more foundations than buildings but evolving to a plan. Incipient fields filled the plain between the ship and the river, which she identified by the line of forest following its meandering path. Children ran everywhere, shrieking. Their clothing was far from the tunics ubiquitous in the Midland, but nothing like Gauvain's finery either. Not suited for farm labor in the late summer heat, she concluded as she noted that several of the men had removed their shirts. None of the women, though.

Will they strip when they jump in the river? She doubted it, given Kiril and Joss's aversion to being naked.

"The large building will be a barn for sheep, goats, and chickens. We wanted to bring oxen, but there just wasn't time to find a pair. Plowing was a bitch, but we've planted winter crops, favas, rutabagas, kale, and garlic," Elspeth said. "It's too late for anything else. Fortunately, we have food on board to barter. We're all sick of fava beans."

"I heard you have a farm in here. Hard to believe."

"This whole adventure's hard to believe. Making it to this place..." Elspeth shrugged. "Somehow your ancestors found a paradise, and somehow we followed you."

Quinn laughed. "Wait till winter. You might change your mind about paradise. Can this thing keep you warm?"

Elspeth patted the outer skin of the Adventurer. "Yes. We can't move her anymore, but the internal power supply's nearly inexhaustible."

"I'd like to know more about that power supply." So far it hadn't affected the Aura. Perhaps it was different from the power cell. She hoped so. The complications – no, nightmares – the idea conjured...

"I'd like to know more about Weavers and the Aura. We're getting a picture of the culture from Gwen and the others who come to help or trade or just talk, but the rest of it... it sounds strange to me. Makes me uncomfortable."

Quinn shook her head and turned to follow her hostess into the ship. "It needn't."

"Mysterious hills and men turning into dragons?"

Did she know the man in question was Kiril? "More like an overgrown lizard." Quinn paused and swallowed. "I was there, and it was bad. But it happened in the hills and was directly tied to them, and you're a long way from there. In four hundred years, nothing prepared us."

"I assume you've taken steps so it won't happen again?"

The question made Quinn uneasy. "As much as possible. The Aura is a massive topic. We're only just realizing the extent of it."

Elspeth must have noticed her discomfort; she changed the subject. "You'll want to stay here for a while, I expect?" At Quinn's nod she said, "I'll arrange a berth for you. In the meantime, I suggest we begin our shared explorations in the mess hall – sorry, dining hall to you. I think we'll be talking for a long time."

Years. They wove their way through rounded metal corridors, into a box that moved them upwards, and out into a large, efficient-looking room that smelled of very good food.

They'd no sooner sat down over cups of what Elspeth called tea, similar to a popular tisane from the Southlands, when she stood and waved to a man just entering the hall. "Harry! Over here."

The man named Harry smiled and crossed the room to their table. Their eyes met.

Quinn swallowed. He was... well. She hadn't experienced that instant draw to anyone in a while now. Not since Kiril... but no. She refused to honor whatever it was between Kiril and her with the term attraction. That was something primal. Harry showed every sign of being civilized.

Short brown hair dusted with gray. Those blue eyes again. Elspeth had blue eyes, too, as did many of the people milling around the dining – mess – hall. However unusual they were in the Midland, clearly on Terra they weren't anomalous.

Elspeth made the introductions. Harry didn't break the connection as he reached out a hand to shake. "Welcome aboard."

"Thanks."

"Quinn's what they call a Scribe, according to Gwen. A researcher of some sort."

"And you're curious about us." He pulled out a chair and swung into it. A well-worn body, Quinn thought, not too slender, but not heavy. A man comfortable in his skin.

"Very," she said. "And you were the one responsible for getting this..." She gestured with a hand. "All this from Terra to here? The Commander, like Kiril?"

"We heard a couple of them made it," Harry answered. "Kiril would be Colonel McKettrick. As a guess, Joss is Sergeant Worthing."

"Josiah," Quinn confirmed, remembering that first meeting over a year ago.

"So you already know something about us."

"Not enough."

"Tea, Harry?"

He looked at Elspeth and grinned.

"Okay then. One coffee coming up." Elspeth left them, heading for the serving line.

"We're determined to grow coffee trees here, if not in the settlement, then further south," Harry said. "For those of us who are virtually addicted, it's a staple of life."

"We have a drink called caff. It's from a root, not a tree. You're right about addiction."

"Bring two," Harry shouted across the hall. Then he nailed Quinn with that infectious grin again. "Might as well begin your education."

Chapter 34

Bryar scowled at the sight before them. As they'd worked their way south along the western mountains, the rumors of invasion became more rather than fewer, embellished with tales of kidnapping, torture and rape, fearsome weapons. By now the stories didn't include green skin; the Terrans had evolved into giants, destroying everything in their path.

They'd seen no evidence of any of it. The rumors sprang from fear, pure and simple. But few Weavers made it this far west, so even their appearance caused concern.

The route south amounted to little more than an animal track. They were standing beside an east-west gully containing a small, fast-flowing river coming down from the mountains, puzzling how best to cross, when two teenage boys, armed with slings and an arsenal of rocks, appeared on the other side.

The boys chose to fight first and ask questions later. One of them let go with a rock the size of Tai's fist. Bryar shoved Tai behind him, but took the rock on his bicep.

"We're Weavers," Kiril shouted across the river.

"You ain't wanted here. Go back where you came from." The second boy let loose another rock, which landed harmlessly at Kiril's feet.

The first boy emitted a piercing whistle. Bryar looked at the others, rubbing his bruised arm. "Calling for reinforcements?"

"This is getting tedious," Tai said.

"Dangerous." Bryar started them backing away from the bank.

A group of men arrived from the west, not, as he'd expected, to team up with the boys, but on their side of the river. More stones flew – many more.

Bryar exchanged nods with Tai and Kiril. They wheeled and took off the way they had come, only to find themselves outflanked by another posse of stone-wielding villagers yelling at the top of their lungs.

He'd sung about war cries, but never actually heard one. He devoutly hoped the first time would also be the last.

"We're Weavers!"

Bryar doubted Kiril's shout carried above the melee. Before they could defend themselves, they were in the center of a barrage of rocks. Tai was the first to go down, with a shriek and then silence. Bryar skidded to a halt and fell on top of her. The stones pounded his back; he cupped his hands around his head and hoped Kiril fared better.

The assault ended with a dozen large, angry men standing over their huddled figures. Hard hands yanked Bryar to his feet. Kiril received the same treatment, while a man with muscles like hams scooped up Tai. She was conscious; she fought like a demon. The man casually pinned her arms, then tossed her over a shoulder and walked off. Bryar jerked forward and was wrenched back, the hands on his arms tightening painfully.

They'd taken his love, and he was helpless.

Bryar shifted on the dirt floor of their prison which, although windowless, permitted the entry of minimal light through cracks between the boards. They'd spent the late afternoon and evening side by side on a rough bench where Kiril, arguably in worse shape, now lay curled. The room was smaller than Bryar was tall, and he wasn't a tall man. He had no idea where Tai was, or how they were treating her, or how severely she had been hurt.

Tai could take care of herself. He hoped.

His back and legs ached from countless bruises; the uneven dirt floor didn't help. So Bryar wasn't fully asleep when he detected a scratching from the vicinity of the door. He sat up carefully, silently. Kiril groaned in the darkness.

He and Kiril had already spent part of the dark hours attempting to pry free enough boards to allow them to escape, but the effort had been futile, yielding only a torn fingernail that worried him more than the bruises. An open wound, and no way to clean it, never mind use that finger to prove his prowess at music.

His stomach rumbled. It had been nearing time for the evening meal when they were attacked, and they'd been given only a dish of tepid water between them.

The scratching came again, then a click, accompanied by a burning smell and a whispered curse. The door opened very slowly.

"Are you here?" Tai's voice, barely there.

"Don't open too far," he whispered back. "There's no room." From movement behind him, he concluded that Kiril had sat up.

Tai slipped into the tiny space, quietly pulling the door to. "Your packs are outside. Can you travel?"

Instead of answering, Bryar reached out, felt her legs, her slender torso. He shuddered out a sigh and pulled her closer.

"We can travel," Kiril confirmed, his voice a thread.

Tai stooped and landed a kiss on the top of Bryar's head. "Let's go. There's not much time."

She eased the door open again, looked and listened – Bryar had no doubt she was tapping into her refined Scribe's senses to detect movement in the village – then slipped out, her hand finding his as she led them from their prison.

They each snatched up a pack without regard for which was whose, then followed Tai, using only starlight to work their way. Once they flattened themselves against a building, and another time dived for a ditch, but before daybreak they'd stumbled on a trail leading south.

"Stop?" Kiril asked. "We need rest."

"I think we need distance more," Bryar said. Tai nodded agreement. "Is there anything to eat?"

"Only what we came with, assuming they didn't scavenge our packs," Tai said. "They smashed the chitarre, Bry. I'm sorry."

"Don't be. It's replaceable." Tai was whole, if hurting, and freedom stretched before them. He'd possessed that chitarre for years, but it was the least of his priorities now.

In the packs they found waybread and a small store of dried meat, and by common agreement downed the food while they walked. Hunting had been good, and enough streams cut down from the western mountains for water to be plentiful. Keeping their strength up to put distance between them and the hostile village was the highest priority.

"How'd you get free?" Bryar asked around a bite of the tough bread. He had scarcely removed his hand from Tai, touching her back, her face, her arm, since their escape. In the light of daybreak she looked battered, with scrapes and bruises and a tear in her tunic, but she was upright, walking, keeping up with the men. She would be all right.

"I've never used Auric energy this way before," she said. "We're learning things I wish we didn't need to know, from sealing the power cell to the dangers in the hills, and now this. I tried a confusion spell, then a binding, without any luck. So I sort of wove a template into a hard ball and threw it at my guard. Knocked him cold. We never called the templates spells before. I don't like it."

"I don't either." Bryar's mind involuntarily brought up Ezra's prediction, so long ago, that their way of life was vanishing, and his carefree wandering of the byways, carrying music with him, inevitably would come to an end. This trip had proved the wisdom of Ezra's words. Heartbreaking – but not something to share with his companions. Not yet. Right now they needed all the conviction they could muster to get to a safe refuge and heal.

"You've got that quiet thing going that tells me you're thinking." Tai stuffed another bite of waybread into her mouth, then squeezed his hand, hard.

"Yeah."

She leaned closer and whispered, "Don't."

Beyond that, neither of his companions seemed inclined to pick up their conversation, so they walked along in silence. Under a bright, clear sky, with the crispness of autumn in the air, Bryar breathed deeply and wondered what the fate of the Midland would be.

Bryar leaned against the waypost, the first tangible sign of progress they'd had in days. They and the land endured a blast of unexpected late-summer heat, more than three nine-days past the beginning of autumn. He longed to throw off his clothes, but respected Kiril's sensitivities. The man still wore long pants under his tunic.

Besides, if Tai should do the same...

Sometimes having Kiril along proved a nuisance, although he did his best to subtly disappear when it was obvious they wanted privacy, a sensitivity Bryar hadn't expected in the acerbic Terran.

They had two choices, assuming no one planned to take the pass over the western mountains. Bryar had never been to the western lands, but if they crossed, they couldn't get back before winter closed in. And he was growing homesick for the rolling green hills and fields of the east.

Tai sat cross-legged at his feet, idly piping notes on her flute, one he'd been crafting by firelight for much of the trip. He frowned. The F above C still rang slightly flat.

"Decision time," he said. "South or east?" He'd already put his arguments against going west, and his companions were equally weary of nights on the road and waybread, when they could get it.

Kiril, restless as always since regaining his health, paced. "Which way do you reckon the ship is?"

"More or less southeast," Tai said. "Impossible to tell which route is more efficient."

"You really want to see this thing?" Bryar asked her.

"Sure. I'm a Scribe, remember? Besides, Quinn's there."

Beside them, Kiril stiffened, so briefly he might have imagined it. Except he didn't. Kiril and Quinn had never been able to get along; he couldn't blame the man for being reluctant to run into her again.

Tai had mentioned Quinn a few days back, he recollected. It hadn't sunk in at the time; he'd been skinning a rabbit for their supper, hoping to save the hide toward making a warm vest. Winter would overtake them before they reached the Motherhouse.

It would be good to spend time with Quinn again. It could be a long time before she returned to the Motherhouse, especially now that she had found the Terrans.

"South?" he asked. "It seems to me the hostility's less, the further south we go."

"Whatever." Kiril sounded irritable.

"Come on," Tai teased. "You can't expect a signpost saying 'Terran ship'. Though it would be nice if one turned up."

Kiril leaned over Tai and ruffled her hair, grinning. "Brat."

"Hey." She jerked her head away, landing it conveniently on Bryar's thigh.

Bryar laughed. These mock tiffs between them had become part of their routine. Tai didn't really mind, and it showed him an unexpected side of Kiril, one capable of laughing and teasing.

"East," Tai said, hooking an arm around Bryar's leg. "Because there's no telling when we'll find another track east, given how sparse the settlements are."

"East it is."

"Do you want to smoke the meat before we leave here?" She stood, pocketing the flute, and gestured at the day's catch.

"Probably a smart idea, given the heat. You do the fire, Kiril and I'll find wood."

He looked back over his shoulder as he walked away with his companion... friend, he decided, Kiril had become a friend. A man he trusted.

Tai had gathered up what little kindling was to be found near the crossroads and conjured a small fire from it. Through bugs, sore feet, assault, and exhaustion, never once had she complained. Already she was weaving sticks together, making a smoking frame.

To think that despite his penchant for ballads of love, he'd never known.

Chapter 35

This, Quinn thought, was heaven. As good as it gets.

She'd been on board the Adventurer for a nine-day and planned to stay for a year. Or more. The rest of her life wouldn't be adequate for her to document all she was learning.

Butter had stayed in Cann, Gwen's village. As soon as the settlers finished the barn, she planned to bring her horse to the new settlement. To her disappointment, the Terrans hadn't brought horses. Too big, needing too much exercise.

She'd used the nine-day to develop a working map of their way of life. The other questions, questions that might yield answers about their origin, and the origin of the Aura, she was saving. Soon, though. She couldn't deny her anticipation at the prospect of uncovering the truths behind their history.

Harry and the medic named Constance sat with her around the library table. The closest she'd ever been to a library was the biblios in most villages, holding the records of major events. The room held physical books – she idly traced the words in the one open before her with a finger – but also banks of something called electronics. She was no more clear about these electronics than they were about the Aura, but she'd learned to access the files on lit-up screens, and struggled to read the contents. Their printed word was nothing like the carefully scribed script she'd grown up with, not to mention the vagaries of the Eurocorp Standard language, which wasn't the same as theirs, however close it seemed to be.

"I am coping, you know," she'd said to Harry earlier. "I'm getting the hang of it."

"Are you chasing me off?"

She loved how Harry's blue eyes danced, as if instructing her in the oddities of Eurocorp Standard was the greatest happiness imaginable. He was becoming a good friend, but he was a distraction. As often as not they would end up walking the corridors, he laughing as she struggled to memorize the layout of the Adventurer, or exit through the hatch to explore the surrounding land. Outside, Elspeth had the full complement of settlers organized into teams. Before winter set in, they intended to have a barn, shelters for farm implements, and fields ready to yield crops in the spring. Within a year, they'd construct a village; she could understand their urgency to return to the land. Life on the ship was comfortable, if cramped, but even Quinn, accustomed to long days spent indoors over her charts, felt the pull of the natural world.

Although the book still lay open in front of her, she wasn't reading. She was listening to Constance give a methodical, detailed accounting of the symptoms she and one other crew member, a roustabout named Richard, experienced whenever they left the ship.

Roustabout, another new word in a long list of new words.

Richard was, if not replaceable, at least not critical to the success of their settlement. Constance was.

"I'd like to do some simple tests," Quinn said. "Probably Gwen's right and you have Auric sensitivity. Joss does, so why not? But I'd rather be sure before we begin anything more in-depth."

"Is it really that complicated?" Constance asked. "There's no way to just... I don't know, create a magic blanket to wrap around me? I'm going mad cooped up in here."

"Even more complex than you think, if you're truly meant to be a Weaver. We train for about eight years. But no, sorry, no magic blanket. Or not exactly. Right now, investigation, perhaps a temporary weave to allow you to go outside. Later, a more powerful template that will ensure your safe passage to the Motherhouse. If you do have Entrée, you can't risk skipping the training."

Nor can we risk you running around untrained. She didn't need to say the words. Constance had spent time with Gwen, and Harry, through regular visits with the villagers, had a good grasp on life in the Midland.

"I remember seeing it on the video, before we landed. Stone buildings near the eastern mountains."

Quinn nodded, deferring discussion of the hills for another time. "We'd never let you go on your own, plus we'll enter the winter season before you could get there, so you'd have to expect hardships. Possibly hostility, from what I saw."

And what she'd heard. Another Healer passing through Cann had reported unrest, even danger, to Weavers and ordinary folk alike as suspicion swept the Midland.

But before any of that, she had to enable Constance to leave the ship.

"When do you want to start? I'm ready." Constance's lips had pinched together into a grim line.

Quinn smiled and placed a hand on the other woman's. "Don't worry. It's painless. From your perspective, it'll look like I'm in a trance, waving my hands in the air."

"Like Gwen did, when she treated me for... what should we call it? Aura sickness?"

"I've heard others use that term. But no, she would have been sensing for illness and aligning your energies so they flow smoothly. This is more about the brain. Is now a good time?"

Harry stood. He'd followed the conversation closely, but she'd detected his discomfort with their Auric work, no matter how he strove to accept it. "I guess I'll see you ladies around," he said. "I'm supposed to be raising a barn."

Quinn watched him go. She liked Harry. Really liked him. But that spark...

Damn Kiril anyway, she grumbled to herself. Bad enough he was so obnoxious. Did he have to ruin her for any other man? Harry should be everything she wanted. But the spark just wasn't there.

"Can we use your berth, or sick bay?" she asked, proud to be wielding the new terms so comfortably. "We'll need an hour or so."

"Let's do this."

Quinn admired Constance's calm command, very much like Willow's. Where illness and injury were concerned, she took charge. Quinn couldn't wait to see how she responded to the manipulation of the Aura, which made Healing possible.

262

"No doubt about it," Quinn said. "Your connection's strong. Stronger than many trained Weavers. It's no wonder you can't handle the atmosphere outside. I'm amazed it doesn't get to you in here."

"The ship's well shielded. Gwen says some gets through, or she wouldn't have been able to help me the way she did." Constance lay on the bed – bunk – in her cabin, limp. "Honestly, Quinn, that was better than a massage. What magic did you work, anyway, besides putting me to sleep?"

"Didn't mean to." Quinn dragged a chair over and sat, stretching her legs out in front of her, the wounded ankle crossing the whole one. It throbbed, the result of standing and ignoring it for almost an hour. "Very basic manipulation before I began probing. Relaxing your mind makes it easier. Gwen could do it more smoothly, though. It's not my strength."

"I wish I understood what your strength is," Constance said. "It's all very mysterious. In the library, you get on the scent of something and you're damned near indefatigable. But all this about the Aura, weaves and templates and stuff – I don't get it."

"And I can't really explain it in any depth. Once you start training, you'll understand more. I expect you'll prove to be a Healer, but with your strength... time will tell."

Constance raised up at that, leaning back on her elbows. "Isn't that a given? You mean they might turn me into something else?"

Quinn laughed. "Well, you won't be a Bard, that's for sure." She'd heard Constance sing quietly under her breath. "But you're strong enough for a Scribe."

Constance shook her head, adamantly. "I'm a medic. For me, it's that or nothing. Your unusual methods intrigue me academically, but I have no interest in pursuing them for myself."

"Like my friend Willow. She was a Healer from when she was tiny. Bryar too, destined to be a Bard. I didn't have any particular calling when I went to the Motherhouse. I knew I was different, but no more. That's one of the benefits of training. You're forced face to face with what you are. The deepest self."

"I'm forty-five years old. I think I know my deepest self, thanks." Constance dropped back onto her bunk. "Funny. For almost everybody here, life goes on as usual. New roles, perhaps, but it's basically the same. Doing what has to be done, eating and sleeping and raising children. For me, the whole paradigm of my life is changing. Being here at all is hard enough to wrap my head around. Becoming a Weaver... that's beyond my ability to imagine."

"Then you have an idea of how we felt when Joss and Kiril dropped into our world."

"You always mention Sergeant Worthing first. Why's that?" Constance sat up again, this time swinging her legs off the bunk. "Let's go find tea."

"Coffee?" Quinn asked hopefully.

"The stuff's rationed, you know." Constance grinned. "Never mind. Take my ration. I'm not that keen on it."

"I accept." She'd thought she loved caff. But this coffee... she could drink it all day and night.

As they walked down the corridor toward the elevator that took them to the mess hall – so many new words, new concepts – she said, "About Joss, he's integrated into our way of life. He discovered his power, and it freaked him out for a while, but then he got training and found Willow...

"Your close friend."

"Weavers rarely form lasting relationships, mainly because we aren't in one place for any length of time, but also because it's hard for people to understand us. Joss and Willow... I can't be certain, but I think she's pregnant. They belong together."

"Whereas Colonel McKettrick..."

"A rockier road. Their first contact was with Weavers, and without Entrée he's had a harder time finding where he fits. I don't know where he is or even if he's still alive, but he left the Motherhouse traveling with Bryar, and Bryar's getting closer to us. Another nine-day or so."

"I've heard stories of what happened in the hills. You aren't willing to talk about it, are you?"

No, she wasn't. It felt private, a memory too personal to crack open. Or perhaps it was for Kiril's sake. The demon inhabiting him, what he'd done... These were his people. She wouldn't say anything that might threaten his reputation with them. Had he come to terms with himself yet? She hoped so.

"Stop daydreaming, woman," Constance said, pulling on her arm. "I hope he turns up soon. You need to get yourself grounded."

Quinn froze, then gave a helpless shrug. Constance had seen right through her. But maybe, if Kiril did make it to the Adventurer, she'd be able to shake him out of her system once and for all.

So many maybes where he was concerned.

"Coffee calls," she answered. "And then I'll try to figure out a weave to let you spend time off your ship, and that will be easy to renew. Later we'll worry about getting you safely to the Motherhouse."

As the two women stepped into the elevator, Quinn reflected on how much she enjoyed her time with Constance, not a Weaver – so far – but potentially a friend.

Chapter 36

Quinn happened to be outside, leading Butter into her stable in the newly constructed barn, when a bedraggled man appeared on the trail from Cann.

She recognized him instantly.

She'd been aware of Bryar and Tai's approach and looked forward to their arrival but with no confidence that Kiril was still with them. Actually seeing him again...

Quinn kept her distance and watched, her arm around Butter's neck for stability, as Kiril approached, spoke briefly to a man passing him, and strode toward Harry, who had been forking straw into the lift they'd devised to raise it to the barn's loft.

He moved like a healthy man, thank goodness. Healthy and confident.

As to be expected for halfway to Winter Solstice, the weather had turned cold and blustery. The crew from the Adventurer worked with focused dedication, in full expectation of heavy frost if not snow within the foreseeable future.

He didn't see her and had never seen Butter. She stood still, hidden by her horse, as Harry straightened and swiped at his wind-reddened face with a sleeve. Chaff dusted his hair, and he was dressed no better than Kiril in trousers and a woolen shirt over a linen tunic, standard garb for the Midland as winter encroached.

The two men eyed each other. Then Kiril said, "Colonel Kiril McKettrick, Commander, Exploration Pod Three, Amalgamated Expeditionary Force."

Harry didn't smile. "Major Harold Belfontaine, former Commander, Eurocorp Adventurer. Everyone calls me Harry. I'm pleased to meet you at last, Colonel McKettrick." He stuck out a hand.

Kiril looked nonplussed for a moment, then accepted the hand. "You're from Eurocorp."

Surprised, Harry nodded. "Based in Allemane province."

"I thought it would be people from Northam. After we lost touch, we couldn't decide if they'd send another exploration pod or a full complement of settlers. But I never expected a different corporation."

Quinn listened. Now that the two men were talking together, she could detect the differences in their accents. These weren't Kiril's people after all, any more than Borgonnians and inhabitants of the Midland were the same people.

"Northam's administration was in too much disarray to plan another voyage, much less pull it off. We almost didn't make it ourselves. I'll tell you about it later."

"Eurocorp," Kiril repeated. "We weren't at war, were we?"

Harry laughed. "It did get hard to keep track, but I don't think so."

Kiril looked around, taking in the vast bowl of the plain, the distant mountains. "I never fully believed anyone would make it here. I suppose they'd consider me either decommissioned or AWOL by now."

"Or lost. We knew you'd launched and we had your flight plan, thanks to Eurocorp's espionage machine, but we didn't know you were safe until after we landed. We didn't have any plans ourselves, so following you seemed like the best bet. Frankly, I doubt they're considering either of us anything."

Kiril chuckled. "Glad to be of service."

"Let's go in and wash up. Damn straw. We need it for the livestock, though. I'll arrange a berth for you. And a change of clothes?"

"Yes, thanks. You're not in uniform."

Harry barked a laugh. "Sure, I am. Terran uniforms proved to be completely unsuitable to the work we're doing now, and most of us weren't military anyway. I look forward to hearing your story, Colonel."

"And I, yours. And about Terra. What your future plans are..."

Harry was shaking his head and gesturing at the barn as the men walked toward the ship, their voices blowing away with the wind.

Quinn returned her attention to Butter, leading her into her new stable and seeing to her needs.

She received an invitation to join the commanders' table that evening. She and Harry almost always ate together, but this was a formal event, welcoming the hero to the fold. Kiril would love that, she thought – or would he? He had changed in the year and a half he'd been on their planet.

How much would he tell them? What new mysteries would be revealed? How would he react when he saw her again?

Virtually the entire crew of the Adventurer had crammed into the mess hall, many standing around the sides. Constance was among the few not present; she'd drawn a shift in the clinic. When Elspeth called things to order and introduced Kiril, the ship must have shaken on its moorings from the applause and cheering.

Harry said a few laudatory words. Kiril, freshly barbered and wearing Terran clothing, said little. Once the formalities were over and they were seated, he gave her a polite nod. From her place across the table from him, she had plenty of opportunity to observe his first encounter with fellow Terrans. And to develop a fresh perspective. No longer the sarcastic, defensive thorn in her side, she saw a confident man used to command, well respected by his peers for the job he'd done, the responsibility he'd borne.

After the hubbub died down and fully two thirds of those in attendance returned to their shifts, he addressed those at the commander's table, Harry at one end, Elspeth at the other. "I gather you can't go home."

She might be the only one to detect the trace of longing in his voice.

"Why on earth would we want to?" Ben asked. "After Terra, this is heaven."

Quinn had done some research on that mysterious place called heaven and concluded that the word was now used entirely symbolically.

"Besides not having the fuel..." Harry began. His eyes met hers briefly. "I suppose it's a good time to fill you in on what's happened, or at least what was happening when we launched."

"Problems?"

"It started with a major riot in Northam's southwest, about six months after you left. At first it didn't seem to be escalating, but then trouble spots flared up everywhere. Revolts, riots, insurrections. Cities burning, especially the men's. You guys enforced that crazy male-female separation—"

"Which was more humane than your approach," Kiril said.

Harry looked an apology to Quinn. "In Eurocorp, if a couple had more than one baby, not counting multiple births, they were given a choice. Sacrifice the baby or one of the parents. It was brutal, but everyone knew the rules."

"Inhumane, and with no quality control," Kiril muttered.

Harry quickly returned to the riots. "In Eurocorp we figured we were okay. But we were fools. The mood spread. Before anyone bothered to take steps, the Corporation was in crisis, shields were down, government buildings destroyed..."

"Eurocorp had planned this voyage," Elspeth said, "then canceled it. Harry and I met and agreed to continue with the plans if possible. We rounded up as many of the prospective settlers as we could find, but by then travel was almost impossible. Most left with the clothes on their backs."

"They were destroying the command bases," Ben said, "and that included our main missile launch site in western Alleman."

"Basically," Elspeth said, "we made a run for it. Without a full fuel load – there was a shortage – which is why this baby isn't moving anywhere ever again. They torched the launch site a couple of days later."

"We kept in touch for a month or so," Ben concluded. "Then communications died at their end. From what we could piece together from the occasional, random transmission, usually from China Pacific Corporation, there's nothing much left to go back to.

The shields are destroyed, except a few in China Pacific, as are many reservoirs. Cities are unlivable without a distribution network for food." He made a helpless gesture. "A lot of us suspected Terra was dying, but I didn't foresee civil unrest striking the final blow."

"Nor did I," Kiril said. Watching him, as she'd watched him since he'd arrived, she could tell he was shaken, as his last hope of returning to the world he understood vanished before him. "Joss – that's Sergeant Worthing – predicted it. He believed that when you're enmeshed in the upper echelons of management, you lose the focus to see what's in front of you."

"I reckon most of the commoners – what you'd call the lower castes in Northam, Kiril – were too afraid to speak up," Harry said. "But whatever the case, it's up to us now to build a life here. We're strong and healthy. The whole of deck one is agricultural, so we've fed ourselves and will continue to do so while we prepare the land. We've established good relations with the nearest village, and there's a high level of commitment throughout the ship. We're going to make it."

Kiril nodded. "You'll find a lot that simply doesn't exist here," he said. "Speedy transport and communications, paper – most of the population's illiterate. Metal and glass implements are available, but rare and primitive. Plumbing, coffee, insulation..."

"We plan to solve the coffee problem," Harry interjected with a grin. "Quinn's becoming an addict, so we'd better hope the bushes survive."

Kiril looked at her. His expression was unreadable. He looked away.

"In short," Elspeth said, "we intend to live here without seriously impacting the existing civilization. On the whole, it's amazing what they've accomplished. Those early ships didn't carry anywhere near the resources we brought, but they not only survived, they weathered hardships and prospered."

"The lost ships?" Kiril rested his knife and fork on his plate. He had eaten only half of his meal. From his body's lack of tolerance for the richer food the Terrans served or the shock of the news from his home planet?

"We've worked that much out," Quinn said, speaking for the first time. "Right down to isolating which ship. The time's right, not quite five hundred years ago. And the language."

"From what Quinn says, it hasn't all been sweetness and light," Harry added. "The Borgonnians, and her vision—"

"Told you about that, did she?" Kiril actually glared at her, as if her terrible trip into the depths of the Aura should be held only between the two of them.

"Of course," she said. "Harry and I have been piecing together our early history. My vision is the primary concrete evidence, but it explains a lot."

"I bet it does," he muttered, then turned to Elspeth. "So now it falls to you. Integrating into this land and way of life isn't as straightforward as you might think."

"We're learning that. We've already acquired... What should we call them? Auric issues?"

Elspeth looked at Quinn, who said, "We're working it out."

Conversation moved to Quinn and Gwen's work with Constance and Richard, then to the food and livestock they'd transported, the possibility of trading for cows, disease and contamination prevention, something called dry goods, onboard administration, and a hundred other things that Quinn hadn't known until now. She listened avidly, for the moment putting thoughts of Kiril aside.

"Well, well, well," Kiril said.

He had positioned himself against a wall outside the mess hall. Hardly the most welcoming pitch he could have made, but what did she expect? Harry seemed to be an okay guy, and he assumed something was going on there, but Harry was too mild for Quinn. She needed the combustion they struck between them.

And so did he.

"Nice to see you again," she said.

"You're looking good, Quinn. Sleek. Terran life agrees with you."

"Spending so much time without windows is odd, and the food's different." Her words were neutral but guarded.

"The company's good?"

"Yes. Very good. Bryar?"

"They're in Cann. They'll come over in a couple of days."

People flowed around them; a few greeted Quinn or offered him a hand to shake. They kept their voices low and pleasant, like old friends meeting.

"Your foot?"

"Better, thanks. I'll never walk properly. Your health?"

"Fine. You're staying for a while? A cog in the machine of the new colony?"

"For the winter. Did you enjoy your travels?"

"Bryar and Tai are good company. Unlike some people I could name."

Quinn smiled. "Same old Kiril. See you at breakfast."

"After so long a separation?" His voice, as he intended, flowed like an icy river over her, and like an icy river, froze her in place. "I don't think so. I suggest we... renew our acquaintance?"

He took her arm and led her to the aft bank of elevators, in no mood now to be stopped with questions or to let anyone else gain access to his quarry. They both greeted the people they encountered pleasantly, and Quinn made no effort to free herself.

But once he'd closed the door to his cabin, she faced him, laying down the rules. "So you understand, this is to get it out of our systems. It means nothing. It's purely physical. Are we clear?"

No warmth there. And that's how he'd play it. He'd waited a year and a half to control this woman. He intended to enjoy it on his terms.

Without speaking he reached for the bottom of her tunic and yanked it over her head. He followed with his trousers, and hoped she didn't catch the momentary hesitation before he peeled out of his own, Terran issue, shirt. Then he pushed her onto his narrow bed and fell on her, one leg already settled between her thighs. They stared at each other.

Oh yes, they understood each other very well.

Her strong fingers circled his head and pulled his mouth down to hers.

Much later, Kiril leaned on an elbow and looked at the woman sleeping next to him, marveling at how quickly the hostility crackling between them had dissipated. He'd never expected her to fall asleep. She'd wrapped his sheet – a real sheet, not the coarse-woven version common in the Midland – around her, when they'd finished tearing each other apart, but he'd removed it again. He wanted to see her, even if it meant seeing every mark, every suggestion of a bruise against her dark skin.

He'd draped himself to his armpits in the sheet he'd lifted from her. His experience of women was limited, but had never – *never* – involved nudity. He knew the mores of this land, and knew he had to get over his aversion to being naked, but so far hadn't managed it.

Except for now, this evening. Because all rules were off, all proscriptions thrown aside. They'd gone at each other like animals. The tracks of her claws on his back stung. She'd given as good as she'd taken.

The satin of her...

His bunk barely held them both; the length of Quinn's body lay touching his. Kiril carefully shifted onto his back, working an arm under the pillow supporting her head. She murmured in her sleep, but didn't waken. In the dimmed lighting, her skin glowed like the castanya nuts in the villages, waiting to be roasted. He disentangled the sheet and draped it over them both, in the process nudging her closer to him.

He should be sleeping, too, but he wanted this moment to study her, admire the sharp distinction of her skin against his. Only by contrast did he recognize the tension she usually carried with her. No one had ever provoked such out-of-control reactions in him. It was laughable, now, his idea of subduing her. She was indomitable; he'd more than met his match. And yet, in sleep the hard edges that defined Quinn and made him want to control her disappeared. She looked peaceful as a child, her face relaxed, freed from the lines that normally bracketed her mouth and formed a crease between her brows.

Quinn slept the sleep of the exhausted, but not, he thought, of satiety. Their violent union hadn't served to quench his appetite, or hers, although he recognized the lingering effects of his illness and the long, hungry walk from the trail skirting the western mountains, and so was in no hurry to waken her for a rematch.

Watching her sleep, he experienced an unexpected yearning to cradle her against him and comfort her, as he had without thinking after her damn fool venture into the Aura. It occurred to him that their next lovemaking would be the opposite of the first, gentle and lingering. To his own surprise, he didn't want her to go far from him, and it had nothing to do with the monster she kept bound in him. He had no idea what it meant in the long term, but realized, to his amazement, that transforming their confrontational relationship into one involving trust was a goal worth pursuing.

He chuckled to himself, wondering what Quinn would think of that, and let his eyes close, unconsciously drawing her closer.

Epilogue

Quinn received the message in the middle of a brilliant autumn afternoon, one she had already planned to use for a walk, further research into Terran political systems, and her regular shift in the kitchen. For once completely at a loss, she threw the entire plan away and sought Kiril.

She took the path leading downstream along the river, past the mill. In three short years the grassland had been transformed into a hamlet, market garden, and fields of wheat, corn, beans, and lentils to be dried for the winter. Kiril would be in the one-room building near the chanver field. Chanver, which Kiril called hemp, hadn't been imported to the Midland before now, but some wise settler had included it on the Adventurer. Kiril had commandeered the small stockpile of seed, and under his tending it had prospered. It seemed as if every day another use for it turned up, most importantly rope, but it bade fair to be an alternative to linen for fabric as well.

These days his focus was on using the pulverized fibers to make paper, a commodity whose scarcity had always frustrated him.

Positive changes. Because of Kiril.

She paused in the door for a moment and studied the scene in the small room. His back was to her, hunched over his work. A table off to the side held the apparatus he'd devised to make sheets of rough paper. A black and white cat dozed in the shaft of light from the window above his work table; small animals adored him.

His face was all angles and planes now, and his fingers were usually stained from the ash and mure berries he used to make his ink. After first gaining weight with the Terrans' cooking, his body had thinned over the three years they'd been at the settlement, now officially named New Bonn.

His leanness worried her, as did other signs... but she pushed them from her mind as he sensed her presence behind him and turned. He was on his feet in an instant, walking toward her, arms extended.

Trust Kiril to sense when something distressed her. But the last thing she needed was his sympathy. A little acerbity might keep her from falling to pieces.

Not to be. With his arms locking her to him, he rocked them both and said, "Better tell me quickly."

"No, let's go outdoors. I need air."

He'd brought a lunch with him. Using the hand not supporting her, he scooped the bag up and gestured toward a bench along the side wall. "Grab that, will you?"

She seized the blanket as they left the shadowy office for the mellow autumn sun. The Terrans planned a harvest party soon, in honor of good crops and another year survived.

She shook herself free and spread the blanket. "Should you even be here?"

"Where else to be?"

"The clinic, perhaps? You don't look so well."

He shrugged and settled them both on the blanket, looking over the river, close enough to touch when they needed to. "There's a limit to what even Terran medicine can do anymore. You know that. Talk to me."

"I'm not sure I can."

Really, this was ridiculous. She needed to get herself together. She'd suspected this day would come, had anticipated it like a threat hovering over her head – or a promise, historically speaking, confirming the inevitable and handing her everything she'd ever imagined wanting.

Pity she'd never imagined the man beside her. Or the research-rich ship that had carried the settlement of Terrans here to the Midland. Or that she might find a home anywhere other than the Motherhouse.

"Arwen's had a stroke," she said. "They've sent for me."

Kiril reacted with a moment of total stillness before his hand moved to her head and began to play with the tight curls there. "When do you leave?" he asked.

"I don't know. Maybe I won't go."

"Quinn." His voice had lost none of its resonance. Once, that tone of command sent her into a multi-day fury, that he should dare to speak to her so. Now, she recognized it for what it was: a capable man in charge of his world and accustomed to lead, and at the moment trying to get her attention.

She focused her gaze on the distant mountains to the west rather than on him. "They expect me to. But..."

But what, Quinn?

"I'd miss this. Our life here." It sounded weak, even to her own ears.

"I'll miss you. There's no choice, though, is there?"

"It could be a long time before I come back."

"They're calling you to take over the council, aren't they?"

She nodded.

"Then you aren't coming back."

How could she feel so cold on such a perfect day? How could the ambition of a lifetime come to mean nothing?

How could she have found herself in a situation in which what she wanted mattered not at all? She was among the most powerful Scribes currently alive, groomed for years to assume leadership of the Weavers. And there was no one else.

"There are upsides," Kiril said. "You can check on Constance. See Joss's kid."

"Constance is fine. I expect her back here next spring."

But it wasn't about Constance.

"Did you think we'd have this forever?" Kiril asked her, his fingers still playing with her hair. "I never did. From the time this thing infected me, I've counted life in days and seasons, not years."

Quinn twisted around to look at him, dislodging his hand. "But you're doing okay. We've contained—"

"The demon, but not the infection."

In the distance, she could hear a group of kids shrieking over a game. Men called to each other in the fields, joking among themselves. Their voices drifted over the plain.

"Listen to me," he said, claiming both of her restless hands in his. "It's time we faced the truth. I'm dying. We both know it. I might have a year, no more. Less, probably."

"Kiril, I—"

"No, wait." He dropped one of her hands to run a finger around her lips, sealing them. "There's no point pretending it isn't true. And it's okay."

"It's not." Quinn exploded, jerking her remaining hand free, then perversely finding nothing to do with it so letting it drop into her lap. "How can you say that? You could come with me. Or we could recruit another Scribe, devise a more secure binding. We can figure this thing out—"

"No."

She stopped. *No?*

"But you can't just give up."

"You don't get it. I guess there's no reason you should. Thing is…" He turned away from her, reached down to pluck a blade of grass, stared at it, then let it fall. "Quinn, I've done all I ever expected to in life, and more. There's nothing I want now, except you and days like this. But I always knew I'd lose you to the greater good." He snorted. "Greater good, that sounds so pompous. But it's not. We've fought to maintain the integrity of the Midland, you and I in our different ways. We can't give up now. You see that, don't you? "

He stopped and took a breath, shifting his gaze from her to the river. "And as for my going back to the Motherhouse, you know better. If I got anywhere near those hills, I'd be ripped inside out. I'm not afraid of dying here, surrounded by my own people, but the hills… they terrify me. I can't go through that again. I'd rather you didn't ask me to."

Her voice faint, Quinn said, "You're saying to sacrifice us, you and me, for the Midland."

"And for the community of Weavers. And for a way of life. We need you, Quinn, especially with so much unrest. But I'm also saying that there's no option. Your power and skill will be the glue to hold the Midland together. You can't throw that away. I don't want you to. As long as I'm here, I'll be watching and cheering you on."

The sob she'd almost succeeded in suppressing forced its way out, and she threw herself at him, knocking them off balance so they rolled onto the ground. Locked together, she felt him shudder; when she moved a little away and looked, his remarkable blue eyes were wet.

"Please don't think I want this," he whispered.

They stayed there undisturbed until the sun began its descent behind the mountains.

"When will you leave?" Kiril asked again as they walked back to the Adventurer.

She swallowed, hard, but got the words out. "Day after tomorrow, if all goes well. I'll need a day to tie things up here."

"Quinn…"

They stopped; she looked at him.

"I won't be there to see you off. I can't."

"That's okay," she whispered. "I can't, either."

Her mind, so seldom idle, had formed its plans. She would travel by donkey cart, since her foot wouldn't allow her to walk such a distance. Regular caravans passed through Cann; she would join one for safety, and stay on the southern routes where dissent was less fervent. While she loved Butter and dreaded the sixty-day journey ahead of her, her horse served a higher purpose here, plowing, pulling carts and machinery, providing fast communication between New Bonn and Cann when it was needed.

"I hate this."

"So do I."

We all had our love stories, Willow and Bryar and me, she thought. For some reason, she'd believed that meant they would all have their happy endings.

She swallowed again and fought back renewed tears as they entered the hatch and walked to their cabin.

Two days later Kiril did watch her go, from a distance, a solitary woman carrying a pack, riding Butter to Cann. But he turned away before she was out of sight, unable to bear any more.

Surely goodness and mercy shall come to thee, all the days of your life.

He'd never been able to rid himself of the old chant. He'd believed, at one time, that it referred to the woman who had saved him after the crash, whom he later knew as Willow, but he had known for years that wasn't the case. All the goodness and mercy in the universe had been handed to him, right here, and so much of it had been packaged in one angular, irritating woman.

She hadn't wanted to leave him. She'd cried again and clung to him, as they lay sleepless last night.

Kiril's reflections held a tinge of irony as he walked through the Adventurer to their – now his – cabin. He'd done what he'd set out to do, but the end result hadn't been accolades and status on Terra. He'd saved Bryar, and saved the Midland from Gauvain's control of the power cell. Before the incident in the hills he'd been hailed as a hero, although he himself never saw it that way. He'd brought rope, and in the near future would bring paper, and therefore literacy, to the Midland, perhaps playing a role in preserving their history. He'd become a part of the Terran colony, and in the process a part of the future of the Midland.

And he'd found the one thing he never in his life dreamed he'd find, never believed existed, in the form of Quinn.

Quinn.

In all probability, she would never yell at him again. Never storm off in a rage at his words. Never come to him, or he to her, in fury or in tenderness. She had her own destiny to fulfill, and she would fulfill it magnificently. He'd communicate when he could, although until horses and paper became common, the distances still stymied him. But she, the fact and reality of her, was gone.

He entered the cabin and frowned. A scrap of paper lay on his pillow. He picked it up and unfolded it, recognizing it immediately. It was the weave she'd drawn, the day he fled the Motherhouse, which Dal had passed on to him in Stanstead. The one that kept him alive. He hadn't seen it since their reunion here at the Adventurer.

On the bottom she'd written, 'See Gwen'.

Smiling, he pocketed it. Only Quinn. She'd probably been coaching Gwen on working this weave since he arrived.

Her gift of his life – and a subtle reminder to take care of himself.

Experiments with hemp pulp and paper could wait. He readied himself for a day in the archives, continuing her work, exploring their history. That's where her spirit would be; that was the best place to find her.

To My Readers

Hello, and thanks for choosing *The Scribe*.

If you enjoyed this book, well, I don't need to tell you how much reviews mean to writers.

To keep up with my writing, whether fantasy or romance, visit my website, http://lizanncarson.com.

Happy reading,
LizAnn

About LizAnn Carson

It's interesting, trying to condense who you are into a paragraph or two. For openers, I live with one husband and two cats, on the west coast of British Columbia, in a city that's large enough to have all modern conveniences, but not so large as to have hours-long traffic jams or heavy duty pollution. I can follow a trail to my local supermarket, or I can be downtown in twenty minutes.

Yes, I spend most of my time writing (and editing, formatting, critiquing for other writers, battling computer problems, and occasionally tearing my hair out). But beyond that, I enjoy a variety of crafts. I love the new craze of coloring books for adults. Recently I have been learning to play early music (Baroque and earlier) on my baritone ukulele – it works! I walk a lot and enjoy weight training. Once, a long time ago, I owned a yarn shop, and for a while I taught English as a Second Language. My career, on the other hand, was in the world of computer systems development.

You'd be very welcome to drop in at my website: http://lizanncarson.com.